Not Your Ex's Hexes

Not Your Ex's Hexes

A SUPERNATURAL SINGLES Novel

APRIL ASHER

ST. MARTIN'S GRIFFIN

NEW YORK

First published in the United States by St. Martin's Griffin, an imprint of St. Martin's Publishing Group

NOT YOUR EX'S HEXES. Copyright © 2023 by April Schwartz. All rights reserved. Printed in the United States of America. For information, address St. Martin's Publishing Group, 120 Broadway, New York, NY 10271.

www.stmartins.com

Library of Congress Cataloging-in-Publication Data

Names: Asher, April, author.
Title: Not your ex's hexes / April Asher.
Description: First edition. | New York : St. Martin's Griffin, 2023. |
    Series: A Supernatural Singles Novel ; 2
Identifiers: LCCN 2022039368 | ISBN 9781250808011 (trade
    paperback) | ISBN 9781250808028 (ebook)
Classification: LCC PS3608.U5713 N687 2022 | DDC 813/.6—dc23
LC record available at https://lccn.loc.gov/2022039368

Our books may be purchased in bulk for promotional, educational, or business use. Please contact your local bookseller or the Macmillan Corporate and Premium Sales Department at 1-800-221-7945, extension 5442, or by email at MacmillanSpecialMarkets@macmillan.com.

First Edition: 2023

10 9 8 7 6 5 4 3 2 1

To every princess who
really wanted to be the witch . . .

go for it.

Not Your Ex's Hexes

Prologue

Snatch & Grab

Each close encounter chipped away at Rose Maxwell's luck like a pickax through melted butter. By her rough estimate, she had two more run-ins before her well officially ran dry, and she was not letting that happen.

She swerved through the Potion's Up crowd, more determined than ever before to ditch the tail that was hot on her witchy behind. But Christina Maxwell—aka her mother—must have downed a Rejuvenation Potion, or at the very least, a Red Bull. Because she was atypically fast on her feet for someone wearing three-inch spiked platform heels for most of the day.

Rose had hoped she'd push pause on her matchmaking nonsense at her sister Vi's Bonding Announcement Party, but that dream had been dashed with the introduction of Potential Suitor Number One, and then reaffirmed with the not-so-coincidental arrival of Potential Suitor Number Two.

She wasn't hanging around long enough to find out if there was a third. A relationship—especially one initiated by her mother—was the last thing she needed. During the last matchup, she very nearly ended up Mated and Bonded—for *eternity*—to a narcissistic tiger shifter who'd made it his mission to hijack her sister's happily ever after.

She hadn't dodged the shifter-sized bullet that was Valentin Bisset only to get hit by another.

Heels be damned, Rose hustled across Potion's, the Supernatural-themed bar that served as her and her sisters' very own Central Perk, and headed toward the back room. From there, she'd slip away from the party and send an SOS extraction text to Vi or Olive . . . or at the very least, request a *dis*traction.

She didn't get that far.

Less than ten feet away, her mother's head swiveled, and she zeroed in on Rose's location as if she possessed her shifter husband's tracking abilities. If Rose didn't do something quick, it was only a matter of time before that bullet lodged itself in her left ass cheek.

She cursed, mind whirring, and reached for the nearest large object.

Fingers clenched in a soft fabric, she dragged her unsuspecting hostage with her until her back hit the wall, the other person instantly becoming an unwitting barrier against her mother's line of sight. From *everyone's* view, because the stranger loomed over her five-foot-eight-inch frame by at least six inches, and his broad chest, covered in a soft silver-buttoned black dress shirt, more than hid the rest of her.

She almost felt dainty standing flush against this man, and that did not happen often. Or ever. Where Vi and Olive had inherited their grandma's short stature and curvy physique, Rose had been blessed with her mother's looming height and her father's shifter build. It made disappearing into shadows—or dark corners—damn difficult.

Except for now.

"Sorry about the snatch and grab, but you'd be doing me a huge favor if you just stayed here for about fifteen seconds. Twenty would be preferable." Rose slowly skimmed her gaze up the impressively hard chest, barely refraining from leaning in and basking in the man's woodsy citrus scent. It was like catnip for the sexually deprived—which she currently happened to be.

Having been the Prima in Training for practically her entire life, Rose had met her fair share of stunning Supernaturals. Most knew it. A rare few didn't.

This guy, in all his two-day dark blond scruff and glittering gray-eyed glory, was panty-meltingly gorgeous and in the former category, judging by the slowly curling smirk. "If twenty is preferable then thirty or more must be going above and beyond, right? I've always been an overachiever."

Rose swallowed a chuckle.

While most people at the party had dressed up in their finest party clothes, this guy sported faded jeans, the sleeves of his dress shirt rolled up to his elbows to reveal colorfully tattooed forearms corded with muscle.

The voice in her head screamed, *Danger, Rose Maxwell. Danger.* But her sexually deprived regions cried *yummm.*

She matched his smirk with one of her own, her body obviously taken over by a pod person. "Then I guess you and I have that in common."

"Wonder what else we have in common . . ." His voice dropped to a husky purr. "What do you say we go somewhere and find out?"

Rose melted into a puddle of need.

When was the last time she'd thrown caution into the void? She couldn't remember. At that very moment, all she could recall was Violet and Olive's earlier tag-team effort to convince her she needed to "get her witch on."

In Vi code, that meant let loose.

Have fun.

And what Rose wanted most in that moment was to have fun with the man pressed against all her tingly bits, tingling that, for once, didn't have anything to do with the Magic swirling just below her eczema-prone skin.

Conjuring a dose of bravery, she met his lusty gaze with one of her own and prayed she looked turned on instead of constipated. "It just so happens that this place has a back room that doesn't see a lot of traffic."

Gray Eyes's lips twitched. "Maybe we should go check it out."

"Maybe we should."

Goodbye, Boring and Predictable Rose and hello, Rosie Wanton and Free. Maybe her sucktastic luck had just turned a corner.

1

Mr. Wiggles

From clubbing at popular urban hot spots to in-home versions complete with bottomless margaritas and a fifteen-season binge-watch of *Supernatural*, Girls' Nights were long-standing traditions. Some would say a rite of passage. And they had more variations than Yoplait yogurt . . . or sex toys.

Rose was an expert on both.

Her fondness for dairy rivaled only her adoration for Jensen Ackles, but her familiarity with the latter? Pure survival. Poor Mr. Wiggles's batteries had been replaced twice already this week alone, and she predicted at least one more swap-out in her future before the weekend came.

There'd been that backroom tryst a few months ago with a certain tattooed hottie, but as pleasurable an experience as it had been, one drop of moisture couldn't stop a raging wildfire. It was either take matters into her own hands or be persona non grata on Smokey Bear's hit list.

But tonight's GN theme didn't include clubbing attire, alcohol, or the five-speed waterproof vibrator tucked in her weekend underwear drawer, and instead, required all-black hoodies, the cover of night, and the gigantic horse trailer she'd rented earlier that morning.

Side-seat driving, Rose swung an arm in front of her triplet, nearly crushing Vi's nose as she pointed to the gravel lane they'd nearly missed. "There! On the left! Kill the lights and make the turn! Quick!"

Vi eased the truck to the left but kept the headlights on. "If I can't see, how long do you think it will be until I drive us into a ditch? I'm not exactly on Lady Luck's favorite persons list."

From the backseat, Olive, the youngest Maxwell triplet, snortled. "That's putting it mildly."

Vi aimed a glare into the rearview mirror. "Hey!"

"What? I was just showing my sisterly support. I was agreeing with you!"

"Well, stop."

Rose rolled her eyes even though no one could see the gesture in the truck's dark cab. "If you don't turn off the lights, someone will see us coming and then this mission ends before it even begins."

And the whole point of Operation Equine Freedom was to get in, out, and deliver the two nearly emaciated mares she'd seen on her drive earlier that day to their forever homes where they'd be loved and cared for . . . and not whatever the hell the current owners had done.

Rose had passed the run-down barn on her way into the city after a failed meditation class at Jones Beach, and it had taken everything in her not to liberate the poor horses right then and there—sans plan and backup. But she'd channeled her youngest sister, Professor Olive McBrainy Maxwell, and refrained from any rash decisions.

Until now.

"Who the hell's going to see us? We're in the middle of nowhere." Harper Jacobs, the fourth woman in their quartet of liberators, glanced out the side window into the abyss of darkness. With her green-glowing succubus eyes, she could see better than the three witchy triplets combined. "Even if Vi went supernova again and lit up the sky from here to Connecticut, there's no one within a two-mile distance."

The oldest triplet released a hefty sigh. "Seriously? Is this Pick on Violet Day? That happened one time, and only because Rose told me I shouldn't hold back. The second I realized Sparky was off-roading, I reined it in pretty damn quick if I don't say so myself."

"Not quick enough to stop the news station from reporting that we were about to undergo a real-life Independence Day à la Will Smith . . ."

Rose's laugh ended on a snort and a glare from Vi. "What? She's not wrong . . . but control will come with time. You'll see . . ."

"I should only live so long," Vi muttered grumpily.

Unlike Rose and Olive, who'd exhibited their witchy powers at eight years of age like most in the magical community, Vi's powers hadn't manifested until the spry age of thirty-two. Under normal circumstances, it wouldn't have been a big deal, but as the eldest Maxwell triplet, Supernatural law dictated that Vi would become the next Prima—aka witch leader—a position their grandma Edie now held.

A magicless Prima was a bit like having a swim instructor who'd never swum a day in their life. It didn't happen. As the second oldest in the Magical Triad, Rose had assumed the role and spent every waking moment of her childhood—and hell, adulthood, too—training for it.

Until six months ago when Vi's abilities surfaced and Magic itself announced *her* as the next Prima.

Nearly immediately, Rose could *breathe*. As much as she loved their grandma, standing by her side as the Prima Apparent had never felt *right*, and it was because it had never been *her* path.

It was Violet's.

A baby witch wrapped up in an adult-sized package, Vi nick-named her ever-growing Magic "Sparky" because of its love of lighting things up in displays worthy of a Disney light show. At the rate of escalation, it wouldn't be long before she met—and even surpassed—their grandma, and even though her sister would never express her worries aloud, Rose knew it weighed on Vi like an anvil.

Anyone would feel the pressure. Goddess knows she had when she'd been the Prima Apparent. But what Rose knew that Vi didn't yet see was that she'd be great at it. Not at all like Grandma Edie, no. She'd put her own unique stamp on the Prima title and provide a much-needed stir in the Supernatural community.

"Supernova aside . . ." Rose steered the conversation away from Vi's Magic and received a grateful look from her sister. "We're on Long Island for Goddess's sake. We can still be seen."

Harper cocked an auburn eyebrow. "Are we in Manhattan?"

"No."

"Brooklyn?"

"No."

"Queens?" At Rose's pursed lips, Harper waved an I-told-you-so finger in front of her nose. "Exactly my point. If we're not in one of the boroughs, we're in the middle of nowhere. They probably don't even have a decent pleasure club out here."

All eyes temporarily flickered to the succubus demon.

"What? How much do you want to bet? I'll search it right now."

With a heavy sigh, Vi flicked off the lights. "If Lincoln's Jeep comes out of this night with so much as a scratch, I'm blaming all of you. And not to mention I'll never forgive you all for making me be the voice of reason. I don't like it. I don't like it one bit."

"You're the light of Linc's world," Rose said, reminding her sister about her fiancé. "He wouldn't give a damn about the car . . . just that you're okay."

A smile flirted on her triplet's lips as she thought about her True Mate, the Alpha of the North American Pack. Rose's heart ached with the knowledge that they'd come so damn close to missing their second chance at happily ever after. If anyone deserved to find their soul mate, it was Violet.

And Violet couldn't have asked for a better one than the gorgeous wolf shifter. Seeing their eyes light up when they were together was almost enough to make a witch contemplate giving dating another try.

Almost . . . but not quite. For now, Mr. Wiggles would do. She'd just buy batteries at the nearby wholesale warehouse.

A half-mile down the gravel lane and made to look even more sinister by the glowing moon backdrop, a looming barn came into view.

Vi slowed the Jeep to a tentative stop. "If Freddy, Jason, or Michael Myers pop up from behind a hay bale or something it's every witch—or succubus—for herself."

Olive pushed her glasses higher up on her nose as she peered out the window. "This place has definitely seen better days."

Rose agreed. The building and surrounding structures would make the perfect horror movie backdrop. "All the more reason to get those horses out of here. Who has the sugar cubes?"

"I do." The youngest Maxwell triplet pulled a bag from her hoodie. "Let's hope they're sugar addicts like me."

"Does everyone remember their job?"

Rose received three nods in answer.

"Then let's do this."

They all slid out of the Jeep as quietly as possible, Olive's door closing louder than the others with an audible *thud*. She grimaced. "Sorry."

Vi scanned their surroundings warily. "This triplet personality switch thing we're doing is throwing me off. I'm the Bad Idea triplet, Olive is the Brilliant Brain . . ."

"Thank you." Olive smiled with a proud nod.

"And you"—Vi drilled a look at Rose—"you're the—"

"Boring one?" Rose asked, only half-teasing.

"I was about to say the levelheaded one. Not that I'm not up for a little midnight mayhem—Goddess knows I'm a bit overdue—but this is the kind of thing you're usually talking me out of."

Vi wasn't wrong and Rose didn't have an enlightening reason for the triplet-switch except Vi wasn't the only sister out of sorts. Not that she begrudged her sister for coming into her Magic and taking her rightful place as the next Prima Apparent, but until six months ago that had been Rose's future.

Hell, it had been her entire life.

While Olly and Vi had attended summer camps designed for outdoor fun, Rose had been stuck in a room with their grandma learning how to deescalate feuds between grumpy shifters and volatile vampires, and not tick off the witch covens in the process.

Now that Rose had a little extra time on her hands, she was . . . lost . . . and had evidently taken Vi's former position as the Bad Idea triplet. Except this this wasn't a bad idea. They'd load those two sweet mares into the trailer and get them the help they needed.

Harper got behind the steering wheel and flashed them a thumbs-up. "Go get it done, witches. I'll be right here waiting to make a clean getaway."

Rose and her sisters walked as quietly as possible to the dilapidated barn. The only sound other than their breathing was the distant traffic and the soft huffs of the animals inside.

With Olive shining her phone flashlight on the door's rusted slide-latch, Rose yanked on the lock, unsurprised when it didn't budge. She tried again, giving it a little more oomph. It moved an inch before sticking. "Damn it . . ."

"Remind me why this has to be a magicless operation?" Vi asked.

"Because unless these animals have been around Magic before, they could have a bad reaction to it. Getting a hoof to the head isn't on my list of things to do."

"See, I didn't know that." Vi shot her a pointed look. "Which is why I need a wing-witch with this whole Prima thing. Honestly, how long once I get the title do you think it'll be until I offend someone by calling them by the wrong name? It's not only a huge faux pas in the bedroom, you know?"

Rose sighed. "We've had this discussion."

"Discussion implies back-and-forth communication. We didn't have that. It was me begging, and you flat-out saying no. Adrian is

Lincoln's Second-in-Command. There's no reason why I can't have a wing-witch. We could even get you a little button . . . or a sash. No one wears sashes anymore."

As flattered as Rose was by the offer, it wasn't happening. For the last six months, she'd been content living in Vi's Queens studio apartment while she searched for her own *thing*. That *thing* might be a little elusive, but she was determined to find it.

Maybe it was what brought her to this run-down farm in the middle of the night and about to horse-nap two sick mares. Who knows? *She* wouldn't if she let herself take the easy route.

Harper hung her head out from the Jeep's open window, and hissed, "Less chitchat and more breaking-and-entering, please. My spidey senses are tingling and not in a good way."

Vi grumbled, putting her hands over Rose's on the rusty latch. "Fine . . . but we're not done with this conversation. On the count of three, yank with everything you've got."

As they hit their count, they each threw their weight into the pull. It finally released with a heavy groan. The second Rose opened the barn door, they were hit with the scent of horse and hay . . . and a few more unpleasant smells.

Vi gagged, covering her nose. "I have never been so glad to be a cat owner. Even Mr. Fancy Pants's most volatile poops don't smell anything close to this, and they're pretty damn putrid after he eats turkey breast."

Rose sniffed, failing to hide her smirk. "I don't smell anything."

Vi threw her a glare because it was common Magical Triad knowledge that while Rose had inherited their father's mountain-lion shifter eyesight and Olive called dibs on amplified hearing, Vi, unfortunately, had acquired his augmented sense of smell.

Rose chuckled as she aimed her flashlight into the interior. Four stalls lined each side of the barn for a grand total of eight, and all but the two on the end were empty. When the light beam flickered over their resting spots, a chocolate-colored horse and a vanilla-colored horse poked their heads over their doors, shifting their long-lashed stares their way.

"Hey, girls," Rose purred, glancing at the blond mare's wall nameplate. "Let's get Butternut into the trailer first. We'll come back for the chocolate one when she's settled."

Rose's chest ached as she unlatched the gate and got her first up-close view of the horse's state. Her hips stuck out at sharp angles, and if there'd been better light, they'd be able to count every single rib through what little hair patches remained. Whatever this poor creature had been through, she'd suffered through it for a damn long time.

What Rose wouldn't give for a few minutes alone with the owner.

A rush of anger—and Magic—swelled close to the surface, and as if sensing it, the horse shifted anxiously in her stall.

Violet's hand squeezed hers. "Maybe Olly should lead Butternut to the trailer."

"Why?" Rose asked.

Olive glanced to where Rose's fingers still emitted a soft pink magical glow. "She's obviously been through a lot and you're a bit . . . supercharged at the moment."

Rose took a deep breath, one after another, until her Magic slowly receded. "There. All good. Butternut and I will get along famously."

Rose didn't miss the look her sisters shared as she slipped into the mare's stall.

Showing the horse the soft lead in her hand, she gently rubbed the white diamond on the center of Butternut's nose, letting her fingers glide over the ears until she slid the lead into place. The horse huffed and shifted, burying her nose into Rose's hair and making her giggle.

"I think she's ready to get out of here." Rose handed the rope to Olive and gave the horse a gentle rump push. "Let's get you to Equine Disneyland, Butternut."

The mare didn't move except to swing her head sideways, her

big brown eyes looking at her as if asking her what the hell she was doing.

Rose patted her hindquarter. "Come on, girl. You don't want to stay here, do you? Are you two teasing her with the sugar cubes?"

Vi waved a cube in front of the horse's muzzle. "She couldn't care less. Aren't sugar cubes like dangling Jason Momoa in front of . . . me? And if either of you tell Lincoln I said that, you're dead to me."

Olive frowned. "Maybe it's something to do with her condition. We can try and lure her out with grain. I don't know. When it was time for camp trail rides I usually snuck off to go read."

They couldn't afford to be tapped for ideas. They needed to get the two horses on the trailer, and to get the hell out of Dodge—or Long Island—before their owner realized what was happening.

The barn door opened and slammed closed, Harper's appearance startling them all.

"Hells Spells, Harp," Vi hissed. "You're supposed to stay with the Jeep!"

"We need to get this show on the road, witches." The succubus glanced over her shoulder. "They're on our tails."

"Who?"

"The police! Do you not hear the sirens?"

At first, Rose didn't. Her hearing was only a smidge elevated and only when she concentrated so hard Vi joked she looked constipated.

Rose probably looked severely backed up right then. It took a full ten seconds of hard concentration to hear the sirens over her thundering heart, but then with every beat, the wails got louder.

"We need to move faster." She gently pushed on the horse's rump again. "Please, Butternut. Let us help you."

The horse finally shifted, but instead of following Vi and Olive from the stall, the mare backed up, pinning Rose against the wall with her bony behind.

Everyone coaxed and clicked, begging the horse to move as the sirens got louder.

Rose shook her head. "You three need to get out of here. Now."

Vi's eyes widened. "We're not leaving you! Witches who ride together die together."

"And witches who get caught trespassing also get thrown in jail together," she quipped, locking eyes with her sister. "You're the Prima Apparent. What do you think the Supernatural Council would say if you're tossed in jail?"

Vi visibly paled. "Actually, I'm more afraid of Gran. I don't think she's gotten over the whole insulting the Italian warlock commissioner thing yet."

Edie Maxwell, as the Prima and head of the Supernatural Council, had more power in her little finger than did a dozen covens combined. But she didn't need Magic to deliver a disappointing punch. She got the same effect with a single stone-faced look.

Vi lifted her chin. "It doesn't matter. I'll deal with the fallout. I'm not leaving you."

Olive nodded. "No witch left behind . . ."

Harper shrugged. "I give you all ten seconds and then I'm out of here . . . we succubi are lone creatures for a reason."

Rose chuckled, knowing there was no way the sex demon would leave them.

They worked together to coax the mare out from the stall. What felt like a lifetime later, they took their first few steps to the door only for it to be flung open.

Two cops stormed inside, flashlights zeroing in on their faces. "Do not move another muscle! Hands up! Now!"

Harper being Harper, she tossed her hands into the air and grinned coyly. "Who wants to frisk me first? Fair warning, though . . . I'm ticklish."

Rose couldn't suppress the chuckle that escaped with the absurdity of it all . . . until a flashlight beam hit her square in the eyes.

The offending officer muttered a curse. "Maxwell triplets . . . and a mouthy sidekick."

"You've got to be shitting me." A second light beam had Rose seeing rainbows. "Well, hell. You see, this is why I don't pick up extra shifts. Shit always happens. I call not-it on ringing up the Supernatural Council. The paperwork for this will be ridiculous."

"The hell you say. You're the damn shifter. Besides, I did it last time this one got into trouble, and I *still* see the Prima's glare in my nightmares." The Norm officer flipped his light to Violet. "It's your turn for night terrors."

Rose pushed a hopeful smile to her face as she faced the two cops. "Why does anyone have to ring up anyone else, let alone fill out paperwork? It's late and people are sleeping, and not enough rest has been linked to a whole host of medical problems. You could just let us mosey on our way. Spare someone the co-pay."

Both officers turned back to them, matching blank expressions on their faces.

Any hope she had that they'd look the other way was dashed when the taller of the two clicked on his radio. "We've apprehended the culprits, and are on our way in."

Operation Equine Freedom was officially dead in the water.

2

Non-Boo

Half-demon veterinarian Damian Adams needed a night out more than most people required air to breathe, so when his two old college roommates called him up with the promise of free drinks, pool, and generalized stress-relief, he'd dropped his paperwork and his responsibilities at the Marisol Animal Sanctuary and Clinic and met the shifters at Potion's Up.

So maybe he hadn't dropped the paperwork so much as his mentor and grandfather figure had ripped it from his hands and shoved him out the door with a threat not to return for at least four hours. Even Miguel, the retired Norm veterinarian, had sensed Damian's restlessness the last few days.

Or more accurately, his demon's restlessness.

Despite the night being exactly what the vet ordered, it didn't stop Damian from checking his phone six times in the last hour, and four in the thirty minutes before that.

A heavy hand landed on his shoulder.

Lincoln Thorne, his college buddy and the North American Pack Alpha, flashed a crooked smirk. "Are we not entertaining enough for you? Adrian's had an extra beer or two. I might be able to Alpha order him into doing the chicken dance on the pool table if it keeps you here with us a bit longer."

Adrian Collins, the lion shifter and the third in their college trio, chuckled as he leaned over the billiards table to take his shot. "I told you . . . that was a onetime thing."

"That happened twice." Bax Donovan, Guardian Angel extraordinaire, snorted.

They all laughed.

Damian tucked his phone away. "Nah, I'm good. It's just been so long since I had a night away. I don't know what to do with myself."

"Miguel's watching the animal menagerie, right?"

"Yeah. The clinic will be fine, but you know . . ."

Linc nodded knowingly, and Damian knew he got it. In their college days, it had been Lincoln who'd been the serious, career-focused one of the group. As the Alpha of the North American Pack, he'd had no choice but to walk the straight and narrow while Damian and Adrian had their fun.

Especially Damian . . . because as Linc's Second-in-Command, there was a limit to how much debauchery Adrian could get mixed up in. That left Damian to claim the troublemaker title in their friendship, and it had been a moniker the half–demon spawn of one of the most notorious princes of Hell wore like a badge of honor.

It also helped he'd once been the Underworld's most notorious teenage Hunter, trained by Ezeil himself from the time he could barely walk. Damian and his half-brother both. While some kids played dodgeball on the playground, they sparred. When others visited the local swimming hole, they hung out in dark alleys waiting for their next mark to make an appearance. Considering the only approval Damian got from the demon bastard he called Father was when he embraced his darker side, he'd dove headfirst into the Hunt.

He trained. He Hunted. He trained more, pushing his Norm side further away with each haul-in.

At least until his tunnel vision and desire for his father's approval bought himself a nasty hex from a very pissed teenage witch. *That* was a wake-up call, and incidentally was right around the time

Miguel came into his life, tugging him off the streets and away from Hunting.

The older man had showed him there was a whole other world besides the one filled with bounties and Supernatural nasties. He'd taught him ways to keep his demon in check that didn't involve Hunting. He taught him what it was to have a *real* father's approval.

Sometimes Miguel's meditation tactics worked. Sometimes they didn't. When Damian's demon got extra randy, a quick naked romp usually—though temporarily—put the bastard back to rights. Although, the last time he'd indulged, it hadn't been so easy to get his partner out of his head afterward. Or his dreams. Or during his morning rub-outs.

Rose Maxwell—Linc's almost sister-in-law—haunted Damian's head months after their backroom romp in this very bar.

He'd been minding his damn business, thinking how overdue he was for a little fun, when she'd nearly taken him off his feet and plastered her body against his. And what a body . . .

Used to breaking his neck when he looked down at his female companions, he'd barely had to dip his chin to lock eyes with her gorgeous caramel-hued ones. Add in the full breasts that were more than two palm-sized handfuls and hips that were designed to be gripped, and he hadn't had a chance of denying either of them what they'd both craved in the moment.

Having just gotten into town, he hadn't known who she was at the time, but he wasn't so sure it would've changed anything. There'd been a draw he couldn't resist, and one he still felt months after.

Linc's cell rang at nearly the exact moment Damian's notified him of an incoming text. While the shifter handed his pool cue to Bax to take his call, Damian glanced at Miguel's message:

M: Slight incident at the sanctuary, but all is well.

I can make it back in thirty.

M: Don't even think about it. Minimum 4 hours. You
barely hit 2.

But if there's a problem . . .

M: Problem handled. Four. Hours.

Damian frowned just in time to see Linc's mile-wide grin melt
away as he listened to the person on the end of the line. "I'm sorry,
princess, but you're *where*? Violet! What the hell did you do?"

Linc winced, pulling the phone away from his ear as his soon-to-be
Mate gave him an earful that pinked the Alpha's cheeks. "Yeah. No.
You're right. I don't have the full story. Stay there, okay? I don't want
the four of you walking home on your own. The guys and I are only
a few blocks away from the precinct. We'll be there in ten."

Bax and Adrian threw him expectant looks as he hung up, but it
was Bax who asked, "The *precinct*? What the hell trouble did Violet
get them into now?"

"Attempted horse theft. Horse-napping? Horse thievery? I don't
know what the hell to call it. She said something about Operation
Equine Freedom and I was too damn afraid to ask."

Bax pinched the bridge of his nose. "I should lay off the beers
because I can't tell if you're joking."

"I wish I were." Linc chuckled, hanging his pool cue back on the
wall rack. "It was evidently a misunderstanding . . . one that I can't
wait to hear about in person."

"Alright, let's go." Bax shrugged into his leather jacket.

"You guys don't have to go with me."

Bax and Adrian were already headed for the door, the lion shifter
tossing over his shoulder, "The Maxwell sisters and their sexy succubus sidekick got pinched for something called Operation Equine
Freedom. That isn't a story I want to hear secondhand, man. Besides, didn't Vi take your wheels for their little law-breaking jaunt?
Wonder if it got impounded."

Linc paled. "Fuck me."

They all chuckled . . . except the wolf shifter.

"Sorry your night out was cut short," Linc apologized as they followed the other two. "See if Miguel can watch your critters again another night and we'll give it a second attempt. I'll make sure Violet promises to be on her best behavior."

"Actually . . ." Damian couldn't help envisioning Rose Maxwell dressed all in black and wearing handcuffs. "I think I'll tag along. It'll be like old times except it's not you, me, and Adrian doing the jailbird walk of shame. Besides, I could use an interesting bedtime story."

Linc dropped a hand on his shoulder and chuckled. "If you'll be hanging out with this group for any length of time, one thing you should prepare yourself for is interesting stories at least once a week if not more often."

Four blocks and a ten-minute wait later, and the four women, dressed head to toe in black, stepped out from the buzzed-open door at the Fifth Precinct. All sported varied expressions of relief, disgust, and in Harper's case, amusement, the succubus giving the young officer behind the window a little finger-wave that had Adrian releasing a low growl.

While Linc approached his True Mate, and Adrian and Bax approached Olive and Harper, Damian couldn't tear his eyes away from the fourth woman in their law-breaking quartet.

Dressed in an oversized black hoodie, her hair lifted into one of those sexily messy pony-buns that left the arch of her neck exposed, the sight of Rose Maxwell—aka the star of his every sexual thought for the last six months—had Little D twitching in his pants.

Fuck. She was even more gorgeous than he remembered.

The second her gaze caught his, she froze, sneakered feet rooted to the ground. "You . . ."

He cocked a single eyebrow. "*You* . . ."

"What are you doing here?"

"Guess I couldn't stay away . . ." He made it sound like a taunt, but hell if there wasn't a speck of truth to his words.

Ever since he'd come to the realization that sex sated his inner demon—at least somewhat—his motto had been No Repeats. No Morning Afters. It was sex and move on. Simple and easy . . . but there was nothing simple about the way Rose kept unwittingly interjecting herself into his thoughts.

Behind that evening's cat burglar clothes was a woman, who like his own brother, Julius, exuded sophistication from every pore. Classy confidence ensured she commanded every room she walked into, and upon first meets, immediately put people at ease with her social grace.

Damian wouldn't know class if it bit him on the ass, and he was well-known for clearing a room by making people uneasy. The second he'd first bumped into Rose, he knew she was way out of his league, but he hadn't cared.

Still didn't.

And that had the potential to be a huge problem . . . for him. For his demon. And by extension, Rose herself.

"I have to say, little witch, I usually read people pretty well and I never had you pegged as a rule-breaker, or even a bender."

"I'm not," Rose countered.

Kicking up a lone eyebrow, Damian slowly perused her all-black ensemble. "You're telling me that cat-burglar-chic is all the rage in Supernatural high society?"

"I wouldn't know what's the rage in Supernatural high society as I'm no longer *in* it."

Her defensive tone lifted his gaze to hers, and for the first time since she'd stepped into the lobby, Damian looked beyond her gorgeous outer package. There *was* something different, something far beyond the absence of the sexy designer dress and daggerlike heels she'd sported that night.

It took him a while to find it, and then it glinted back at him from her eyes . . . a feeling he was all too familiar with because he felt it every damn day, and sometimes tenfold when his inner demon wreaked havoc.

Tired determination.

As if the curvy witch didn't take up rent in enough of his thoughts, his curiosity about what put that glint there expanded, taking up even more real estate.

✦ ✦ ✦

Disappointment fueled by her failure to free Butternut and Squash led to Rose's dropping her guard for one split second, and that was all the man in front of her needed before seeing way too much.

Damian Adams. Half-demon veterinarian. Linc and Adrian's college roommate.

And her one and only one-night stand.

She'd thought she'd never lay eyes on him again and yet there he stood, his hair curling a little longer over his collar, but still sexy as ever. She soaked up the sight of him like a dry sponge just like she had the night of the Bonding Announcement Party . . . and just like she did every other night in the most sexually explicit dreams she'd ever had.

Oh, who was she fooling? It was every night, so frequently that Harper was half-convinced she was having a secret affair—or had a membership to a pleasure club. According to the succubus, that's how soaked in pheromones she'd become. Or to quote the sex demon verbatim, "You're extra horny lately, Rose."

She didn't need Harper to point that out . . . especially now as she stood in front of the person who'd gifted her her one and only non-BOO—*battery-orchestrated orgasm*—of the year. Maybe eighteen months.

And they hadn't even fully undressed, removing only the necessary articles of clothing for easy access. It made for a quick release and an even quicker escape . . . except there was no running away this time.

This time he stood not more than six feet away, his chin-length dark blond hair brushing against the few days' stubble that peppered his angular jaw. Her fingers nearly itched with the need to sink into his hair's soft depths again and beg him to kiss her senseless.

Their friends' gazes slowly lasered in on them, Harper's eyes narrowing thoughtfully as the succubus sniffed the air like a pheromone-scenting bloodhound.

Hex me.

Rose folded her arms over her chest and, with a quick call on her Magic, not only hauled in her arousal but rebuilt her walls and then reinforced them with mental titanium for good measure.

What was Captain America's shield made from again? Because she used *that*, and prayed to Goddess that it helped.

She dropped her voice, hoping it was low enough to avoid shifter ears. "I'm actually glad that we ran into each other . . ."

Damian dropped his voice to a sexy purr, making her lady bits practically thrum. *"Are* you now?"

"Vi told me that you were moving back to the area soon . . ."

"I did. A few weeks ago."

"I was hoping we could talk about"—her gaze flicked toward their group of friends—"what happened. Between us."

"You mean the feel-good fucking . . ."

Rose shot a panicked look toward her sisters, who were in deep conversation with Linc and Adrian. "Will you lower your voice in shifter company? And yes, I'm talking about what happened at Potion's."

He opened his mouth to speak . . .

"Do not call it a feel-good fuck again. In fact, don't call it anything." She lifted her chin and looked him straight in the eye. "Because it didn't happen. Right?"

He blinked, closing his mouth. Whatever he'd expected her to say, it obviously wasn't that. "You don't want a repeat?"

"No! I mean . . ." *yes*, another orgasm would be nice, but, "no. Why? Do you?"

"Fuck no."

"Excuse me?" She couldn't help the offense that slipped into her voice.

"Don't get me wrong, little witch. It was great. And I think we both got what we wanted out of that encounter, but I don't do repeats. No matter how enjoyable of a time it was."

It was on the tip of her tongue to tell him that he'd only be so lucky if she agreed to a round two, but she refrained. "Then we're in full agreement. No repeat. And absolutely no telling anyone that it happened."

"Ashamed to have fraternized with a demon?"

"Absolutely not. It's just no one else's business."

He studied her as if searching for any hint of a lie, but he wouldn't find one. There'd been discord between demons and witches generations back, before the Supernatural Reveal when Supernaturals stepped out of the shadows and into the light—some literally—but those animosities had mostly long since died down. Partly because of Grandma Edie's hard work. Partly because of pure situational circumstances. And party due to luck.

Nope. Her wanting to keep their non-relationship a secret had nothing to do with his demon side and everything to do with her sisters and Harper, and their incessant romantic interventions.

With a faint nod, Damian's lips twitched. "Well, you're in luck, because it just so happens that I don't talk about my feel-good fucks with anyone, so your secret is safe with me."

"Good. Great. I'm glad we got that settled."

The secret might be safe with him, but she wasn't so sure the same could be said about her libido. As hard as she tried convincing herself that their sexy backroom interlude was a once-and-done thing, her body—and her Magic—pushed back harder, heating the surface of her skin until goose bumps peppered nearly every inch.

And they were both silently communicating, *I don't freaking think so . . .*

3

All the Shits

Rose couldn't count the number of times she'd stepped into the Supernatural Council chambers, but she'd always done so as the Prima Apparent, sitting by her grandma's side as Edie ran through the Council's agenda and often played babysitter to the other Supernaturals at the table.

The Council chairs themselves could be the start of a joke . . .

What happens when you put a witch, a shifter, an angel, a demon, and a vampire all at the same table?

Chaos happened. At least about 40 percent of the time. The remaining 60 was spent showing the world that the Council—who were basically Supernatural Avengers—were ultimate badasses whose bites were definitely as bad as their barks, if not worse.

Less than a year ago, she'd been one of them. Or she'd *almost* been, and had been training in all things magical kick-assery, and that meant not just Supernatural politics, but actual ass-kicking.

There'd been a reason why Rose always wore heels, and it wasn't because of her keen fashion sense or because they made her calves look incredible. Sometimes diplomacy only went so far, and when a witch hit roadblocks, you summoned a well-executed bolt of Magic . . . or aimed a swift kick.

Heels made a statement. Fuzzy rabbit slippers made for a cozy night in.

As Rose waited in the Council lobby, she pondered over which Council she was about to meet and hoped like hell it was the same one Vi, Olive, and Harper had already faced earlier that day. While the attempted horse-napping charges had been dropped by the animal sanctuary owners and the Norm law enforcement, the Supernatural Council hadn't been as forgiving, issuing community service hours.

For Vi and Harper, who had volunteered a million hours at the Kids' Community Center in Astoria, Queens, it had been time already served. And Olive managed to convince Ramón, the angel representative overseeing their case, that her educational background made tutoring at the KCC a more impactful use of her time.

Rose hoped for the same fate . . . help make snacks, read to the younger kids at story time. Maybe start up a Go Fish tournament.

She should've known, with her recent sucky track record in . . . well . . . *everything,* that it wouldn't be so simple. There had to be a twist, and it came when the chamber doors opened and who stepped into the courtroom but a certain sexy grumpalicious demon.

"You've got to be freakin' kidding me," Rose muttered under her breath.

The five members of the Council—plus an apologetic-looking Vi—turned their attention her way as she followed a guard down the aisle to the front. Once there, the gorgeous man who seemed to pop up everywhere turned to give her an unreadable look.

Gone were the torn jeans and faded leather jacket. Damian's hair, combed off his face, showed the prominent angles of his jawbone. As good as he looked, she almost wished he'd been wearing the chest-hugging T-shirt and flirty, naughty smirk that promised a whole host of wicked things.

Before she could open her mouth to ask him why he seemed to

keep popping up, Angel Ramón cleared his throat, commanding attention.

"Miss Maxwell, it's good to see you again"—Ramón nodded—"although I wish it were for a more jovial reason."

"You and I both, Mr. Councilman."

"I'd like to begin by saying that due to your relationship with our esteemed Council head"—he tipped his chin respectfully toward Edie—"I will be taking the lead in this sentencing. Any communication, questions, issues, or complaints will go directly through myself and my office. Is that understood?"

"Yes, sir."

"Good. Then we'll get right to it. While Dr. Damian Adams and the Marisol Animal Sanctuary and Clinic have dropped all official charges with law enforcement, it's the opinion of this Council that there needs to be some form of remediation. It's been the goal of Supernaturals for decades to blend in among the Norms . . . not grace the headlines of news reports, further sensationalizing our way of life."

Damian Adams . . .

Dropped charges . . .

Rose's brain slowly registered the angel rep's words, and when they did . . .

Her head spun toward her only one-night stand, but Damian stood stiff, gaze focused on the Supernaturals in front of them and looking like he wanted to be there less than she did. His gaze occasionally flicked to Julius Kontos, the demon rep, before his face went back to an impressive mask of indifference.

Ramón cleared his throat, obviously realizing he'd lost her attention. "Miss Maxwell . . . ?"

"Sorry . . . I . . ." Rose lifted her chin. "Continue . . . please."

He waited a beat. "As I was saying, there needs to be some form of repercussion. Under the tutelage of Dr. Adams, the sanctuary's director and resident veterinarian, you will complete eighty hours of community service at the Marisol Animal Sanctuary and Clinic."

"Wait, what?" Damian interjected at the same time Rose asked, "Excuse me?"

"I don't believe I stuttered. Eighty hours of community service, filled in whatever way Dr. Adams sees fit. Should you fail to complete your requirements, something a little more . . . structured will be assigned to you."

There went Damian's jaw muscle, tick-tick-ticking. "Respectfully, Councilman, but I run a busy vet practice and sanctuary for abused and medically fragile animals. I don't have time for witch-sitting someone who doesn't know the difference between a hoof and a trotter."

Rose's head snapped toward him as she shot him a glare. "Excuse me. Who the hell do you think you are?"

Damian's hazel eyes glowed. "I'm the one you thought was evil enough to inflict pain and suffering on the animals in my care."

"I didn't know you ran the place . . . or that it was an animal refuge."

A small commotion rose among the Council, all five members—six including Vi—talking one over the other until Rose's sister slipped her fingers into the corners of her mouth and whistled.

Loud. Their sport-loving father would be so proud.

"Oh, good. Everyone heard me." Vi straightened her shoulders and got a faint nod from Edie next to her before flashing Rose an apologetic look. "It only makes sense to have the community service hours fulfilled at the place where the incident occurred. Duties, hours, and schedule will be determined by Dr. Adams, and will only be considered fulfilled once the appropriate signed paperwork has been returned to Angel Ramón's office."

Vi sent a questioning look to the angel. "Does that sound okay to you, Councilman?"

"I was about to require the same thing."

"Then we're all in agreement. Smack your gavel and let's call it a day."

While the Council filed out, Vi shot Rose a quick wink and a mouthed "sorry" before disappearing into the back room alongside their grandmother. She was still trying to wrap her head around what had happened when Damian approached, crossing his arms over his broad chest.

"Six o'clock," he said, voice gruff, and stalked away.

"What's six o'clock?" she called after him.

"Your report time tomorrow morning. Don't be late . . . and get rid of those ridiculous shoes unless you want a horse-shit pedicure."

She glanced at her peep-toe pumps. "You can't be serious. Six in the *morning*?"

Damian stopped at the courtroom door and turned, shooting her a wicked grin. "Horses don't shovel their own crap out of their stalls, little witch. Don't be late. Squash has been fighting off a stomach bug and needs fresh hay first thing in the morning."

Left alone in the room, Rose swallowed a curse. She'd landed herself in a large pile of witch-shit . . . and quite possibly a load of horse shit, too.

She was seconds away from face-planting in *all the shits*.

✦ ✦ ✦

Damian's demon senses tingled, and not in a good way, or in any way he wanted to take part in. It started when he'd run into Rose Maxwell at the Fifth Precinct, and while it wavered in its intensity, it never truly dissipated.

His inner demon was antsy, made even more restless when he'd returned to the sanctuary the other night to find out Miguel's "resolved issue" involved Rose and the near-abduction of his two healing mares . . . horses for which he'd risked his own damn life to liberate from their former owner.

Him. Harm an animal . . .

Hell, animals were the only living creatures on this earth he liked, which is one of the reasons he'd become a vet in the first place. Animals couldn't disappoint you. Give them your loyalty and they gave theirs right back. People not only let you down, they twisted things for their own looming agendas.

And no one had more agendas than those who sat on the Supernatural Council. Oh, they pretended to work for the betterment of their constituents, and maybe a few even backed their words with actions—like Linc and Vi.

But the others? They did what benefited *them*. It was the curse of power, and it took down more than one of the original Supernatural Council members until the only original left was the Prima herself.

But no seat had to be replaced more than the demon chair . . . because it wasn't a demon's first nature to look out for others. Before his banishment back to Hell, even his father, Ezeil himself, had held the position and he'd been the most self-serving demon on record . . . at least until his successor, Julius Kontos, took over.

While in those chambers, Damian had done his damned best not to look in that bastard's direction, but that didn't mean he didn't sense him. *Feel* him. And if Damian—the man—did, then his inner beast sure as hell did, too.

And that was never a good thing.

4

The Demon Doth Protest Too Much

Even birds weren't up this early. Rose downed another large sip of her trusty travel mug of coffee, wishing she'd spelled it with a little extra caffeine to get her through what was sure to be an interesting day. Being up and on the road before the mad rush of commuters clogged the six lanes of the Belt Parkway was unnerving.

No swerving cabbies. No one laying on their horns. She turned her stereo volume up on Lady Gaga's "Paparazzi" to drown out the silence and murmur-sang along with the lyrics.

Thanks to a lack of traffic, she'd made it to the Marisol Animal Sanctuary and Clinic in record time, turning onto the gravel drive and right past the freshly painted sign that most definitely hadn't been there two nights ago.

Stones kicked up as she steered down the lane, hitting her car doors until she pulled into a patch of grass right next to a well-used F-150 pickup.

Flicking off Lady G, Rose slipped into her phone's contact list and tapped on her most recent call. When Vi didn't answer, she hung up and called again, and then a third time until her triplet's groggy voice picked up.

"This better be a matter of global importance, or life and death,"

Vi grumbled. "Strike that . . . I don't care how important it is, and it better be imminent death."

"What's wrong, sis? Too early for you?" Rose feigned being chipper, chuckling when Vi released a string of colorful curses. "I didn't want you to feel left out of this experience . . . especially since you lobbied for it with the Council."

"You could be a little less thoughtful." Vi groaned.

"And you could've suggested the community center."

"Actually, I did before the meeting, but Ramón was adamant you work at the sanctuary. It could've been worse."

"Yeah? How?"

"Xavier Hastings, the vampire rep, wanted to sentence you to cleaning the public bathrooms in Central Park for three months."

Rose gasped. "That toothy jackass!"

"My sentiments exactly. I don't know who pissed in his pint of O-positive, but he's been in a foul mood even for him. Hey! I have an idea." Vi sounded a bit too awake—and innocent. "Why don't we do a sister swap? You be me for the day, and I can be you."

Rose laughed. "If only we were identical instead of fraternal."

Vi muttered grumpily, "Dad's freakin' super-sperm."

"Yeah, let's not talk about Dad's sperm. *Ever.* I take it you have magical tutoring today."

"You say tutoring, and I call it a slow, methodical torture-session in the guise of magical tutoring. But fine, you're right. It'll never work . . . namely because I'm pretty certain Gran installed some kind of magical DNA detector on her front door. But your day is bound to be better than mine. I mean, *cute, fuzzy animals.*"

It wasn't the animals that had Rose wishing the Council had actually opted to give her public bathroom duty. At least then she'd know what to expect . . . but it wasn't as though she could explain that to Vi without admitting what happened between her and Damian at the Bonding Announcement Party.

Rose stared at the two-story barnlike structure in front of her. It only looked a small fraction better in the daylight than it did at night, its weathered wood showing beneath the gaps of old, chipped paint.

"I should go," Rose admitted reluctantly. "The sooner I start, the sooner I'll be done. And I'll probably be doing office-type work, right?"

"Sure. Maybe . . ." Vi went way too quiet to put Rose at ease.

"Do you know some—"

"Have a good day, sis!"

"Wait! What—?"

The dial tone drilled into her eardrum, and then there was nothing to do but go inside and hope for the best. Clutching her coffee to her chest, she followed the sound of softly playing rock music from the half-open barn door.

Mud already caked her new Converse sneakers in a thick layer by the time she stepped inside. "Hello? Is anyone around?"

The sharp smell of hay and poop overwhelmed her senses, making her eyes water. She knocked on the doorjamb. "Hello?"

No answer.

The barn appeared empty and unlike the exterior, was surprisingly clean and tidy, grooming supplies organized and hung up on the walls like decorations. From two of the stalls on her left, Butternut and Squash poked their heads over their open doors.

"Hey, girls." Rose smiled and after letting them both smell her hands, rubbed the soft patch of white on each horse's forehead. "Guess we'll be seeing a lot of each other, huh?"

Butternut huffed as if answering, her breath moving Rose's hair from her face. The witch laughed, giving her nose another stroke just as a low humming from one of the end stalls reached her ears.

She followed the low, honey-slick voice until it was abruptly cut off with a growling curse.

In the last stall, bent over and revealing a prime view of a jean-clad rear end, a shirtless man worked hard peeling away what looked to be rotten wooden boards from the wall. Sweat coated his tan skin, creating a sleek glow even beneath the barn's dim lighting.

And the tattoos . . .

She didn't know which one to ogle first, deciding on the one that spread the entire width of his back, from shoulder to broad shoulder . . . a winged creature with horns, vivid in a rainbow of colors. With every glide of muscles, it almost looked as if it was dancing, moving with every flex.

Rose's mouth dried as the man used his bare hands to pull away yet another rotten board from the wall. It was the only dry part of her body because desire took her by storm, flooding her nearly as severely as it had the night at Potion's.

"Can I help you, ma'am?" an unexpected voice asked from over her shoulder.

Rose squeaked in surprise, whipping around. An older man, somewhere in his late sixties or seventies, with long graying hair and kind brown eyes, smiled at her warmly as his gaze flickered past her to the muscle-fest she'd been caught ogling.

He held out his hand. "You must be Rose Maxwell."

"That's me." She accepted the greeting and wrapped her fingers around his. An immediate telltale tingle on the back of her neck told her that her visual eye candy had stopped working.

Busted.

"I'm Miguel Sanchez. Resident retired vet. And the half-naked one behind you is our resident grumpy vet-slash-handyman . . . Damian."

No, no, no.

Rose briefly closed her eyes on a soft sigh before shifting to put Damian in her view. "We've actually met a time or two."

She'd known he'd had the body of a Roman god, but she'd come to that conclusion by touch alone since for their one and only time together, they'd remained mostly clothed. She sure as hell hadn't seen the elaborate artwork decorating his skin, or the smooth glide of his firmly packed muscles.

Her gaze automatically dropped to his chest and Goddess help her, the ridged valley of his eight-pack abs and that sexy Adonis belt . . .

She yanked her gaze up, but her ogling didn't go without notice.

Damian cocked a single eyebrow, his mouth twitching. "Long time no see, little witch. Oh, and you're late."

"I'm right on time."

"Right on time *is* late when it comes to handling the animals. That's the first thing you should probably commit to memory."

She forced a smile. "Then consider it memorized."

Miguel's focus bounced between them before the older man smothered a grin. "I'll leave the two of you to go over things. Ian, I'm heading to the supply store to change up our order and see where we can make some tweaks."

"Sounds good." Damian nodded.

They both watched Miguel disappear from view, and when Rose spun around, it was Damian's turn to ogle her. His gaze ran from her no-longer pristine white sneakers to her butter-soft jeans and silky tee . . . but unlike her blatantly sexual appraisal, his was more assessing.

"Who's Ian?" Rose asked in an attempt to break the sudden tense silence.

Damian's eyes flickered up to hers. "What?"

"He called you Ian."

"Miguel has a thing for nicknames." He gave her another once-over. "You did remember you'll be working in an animal sanctuary, right? With actual animals?"

She glanced at her clothes. "Yes, but it's not like I need to wear something fancy to do paperwork."

"Office work?" He chuckled and sauntered closer, stopping only when his body heat warmed her skin. "Did you forget about the horse stalls I mentioned? The horses haven't learned how to shovel their own shit in the last twenty-four hours."

Rose stilled. "You were serious about that . . ."

"I don't usually joke."

He leaned closer, his damp chest nearly brushing hers as he reached out a hand. For a hot second, she pictured him slipping those callused fingers into her hair and pushing her against the wall for a soul-searing kiss.

Instead, he plucked something from the hook behind her shoulder, and gently tucked it into her arms. "You'll want to put these on. And there are rubber boots outside Butternut's stall you'll want to slide those pretty feet into."

Rose glanced at the oversized jeans coveralls in her hands. Paint-splattered and grimy, they'd obviously seen better days . . . and unless her nose deceived her, they smelled as though they hadn't seen the inside of a washing machine in a while.

"You expect me to wear these . . . and boots?"

He skirted past her and shrugged. "It's up to you, but unless you're into horse-shit pedicures, you may want to think about it. Or you could always go back to your Council friends and tell them to reassign you somewhere else. We both know you won't last the day here. You'd have to know the difference between a horse and an ass."

She javelined a glare his way, and the damn man smirked. "Oh, I know the difference. Butternut's a horse, and I'm looking at an ass right now."

Damian crossed his arms over his naked chest, the move bulging out his biceps, one of which had a circle tattoo around its diameter. "Is that right?"

"One hundred percent." Rose took a daring step closer, until it was her that stopped in front of him this time, her dirty shoes touching his boots. "And I'll have you know that not only will I last the whole day, but I'll keep coming back until I fulfill all my community service hours because I am a Maxwell. And Maxwell women don't quit."

Well . . .

Except she'd stepped down as the Prima Apparent.

And then she'd quit her short stint as a telemarketer.

She didn't have high hopes for her current job as a Ryde driver, either, already having two strikes with her supervisor. But *this* would be one job she refused to shirk, and she'd see it through until the very bitter end even if she had to wear a dingy-feathered chicken suit that smelled like warmed-up tuna fish.

"Where can I change?" Rose asked, refusing to break eye contact with the smirking demon jerk.

✦ ✦ ✦

Damian couldn't help watching Rose hightail it to the back office, her rear end swaying deliciously in jeans that probably cost a small fraction of what he'd paid for his motorcycle. Once she'd disappeared into the office to change, he grabbed his T-shirt and shrugged into it before checking on the sanctuary's newest resident.

Occupying the stall across from the mares, the newly postpartum pittie lay in the corner, her cream-and-brown-colored head perched on her white paws. As he crouched in front of her to change out the water in her untouched bowl, her sad golden eyes flickered up to his.

"Hey there, girl. Still not thirsty, huh?" He scratched her head and hoped for a pleased sigh or a tail twitch . . . anything to give him hope his patient was on the upswing. But she glanced away, and rolled slightly, giving him her back.

He'd tried—and failed—multiple times to get the pooch to eat. She'd eventually do it, but barely, and only enough to keep herself from withering away completely. IV hydration would only go so far, and it wouldn't cure the root of the problem.

She missed her pups.

The recently pregnant stray had been brought to the sanctuary by a construction crew who'd found her along a busy stretch of road, in mid-labor and in obvious distress. The delivered pups had been too premature to make it and she'd gone on a hunger strike ever since.

"Alright, I'm heading out now." Miguel propped his arms on the rail as he glanced at the dog. "Bella's still not taking anything?"

Damian frowned. "Not more than a drop at a time, and food is less than that. I can keep the fluids going and restart her TPN drip if I need to, but that's not a long-term solution. If she doesn't turn a corner soon, I'm not sure what will happen."

"You'll figure it out. You both will."

He wasn't so sure, but it was exactly like Miguel to think the best of him. He always had, even when he'd been a trouble-seeking sixteen-year-old Hunter straddling the line between Supernatural prison and an early grave.

"So you and . . ." Miguel nodded to the office. "What's the story there?"

"Don't know what you're talking about," he lied, straight-faced.

Miguel's bushy eyebrows rose. "You know damn well what I'm talking about, kid. I may be an old Norm without any kind of 'super' powers, but my observation skills are top-notch, and they tell me there's history between you and our new hire."

Damian glowered at his mentor. "She's not a new hire. She's serving out community service hours and then she'll be on her way."

"Maybe, but you knew her before she staged a *Free Willy* moment."

He sighed, knowing the man wouldn't give up until he got his answer. "She's the sister of Linc's True Mate."

Miguel's gaze flickered to the occupied office and back. "She's the Maxwell Prima Apparent."

"*Was,*" Damian corrected. "She stepped down when Vi came into her powers. Now she's a thorn in my backside . . ."

And the one-night stand that kept visiting him in his fucking dreams, but Miguel didn't need to know that.

It didn't stop the older man from flashing a wide, toothy smile. "The demon doth protest too much, kid. You may be fooling her with that indifferent grumpy thing you've got going on, but you're forgetting who knows you better than yourself. You can't keep avoiding people, Ian."

"Sure I can. It's called work, and if we keep taking in rescues along with all of our regular patients, that makes it even more possible."

"You need human interaction every once in a while."

"That's what I have you for, isn't it?" Damian joked dryly. "Besides, I like animals better than most Norms and definitely better than all Supernaturals. Less complicated. Feed them, shelter them, give them an occasional scratch or two and you've got their loyalty forever . . . animals, that is."

Rose came out of the office decked out in the paint-splattered overalls and rubber boots, her hair pulled up into a high ponytail. She gave him an eat-shit-and-die glare that had him almost smirking until he heard the rumble of a familiar engine pull up in front of the barn.

"Yo, yo! Is everyone up, or are you sleepyheads still sawing wood?" a familiar voice called from outside.

Damian and Miguel followed the sound of the growing banging to find their one and only employee jumping down from their beat-up horse trailer. Terrance Yoshida had volunteered at the sanctuary to fulfill service hours for school and the kid never left, earning himself a spot as one of the few people Damian could tolerate.

Behind Terrance, the horse trailer shook, its occupant kicking the shit out of the interior and damn near putting a hoof through the wall.

"Did you bring a horse or a rodeo bull?" Damian reached for the latch to release the animal. Some didn't do well in confined spaces.

Terrance stopped him. "I wouldn't do that just yet, boss man."

"Why not?" Damian sensed the teenager's hesitancy.

"Because we have to strategize how to get him out without him decapitating one of us." Terrance rubbed the side of his head where Damian noticed a growing red knot. "Jasper doesn't play around.

One kick from him could send a man into orbit. I know because he tried."

"This is the horse from Fink's place?"

"Yep. One and the same."

"His owner said he had only *slight* behavioral issues."

Terrance snorted. "Yeah, he doesn't have any. Behavior, that is. It took a whole lot of prayer, a ton of luck, and some witchy hocus-pocus to get him into the trailer. And it worked for a while, but it wore off about fifteen minutes ago. Let me tell you, it's not easy staying in your lane on the LIE when your haul is moving around like a jackrabbit."

"Did you say they spelled him?" Rose stepped up, her gaze zeroed in on the black horse muzzle pushed against the trailer's venting. "Was this before or after he was already worked up?"

Terrance's eyes widened as if he recognized her, and he probably did. The Norm kid was all about Supernatural society and probably had a subscription to every Supernatural gossip magazine out there. "After . . . but why does it matter? Fink spelled him to make it easier to load him. I mean, it worked for a while."

"And then when it wears off, you have an animal who's confined, not on solid ground, and even more frightened than they were before. No witch—at least a good one—would ever do that to a poor animal."

Terrance shifted uneasily from foot to foot as Rose slowly stepped closer to the confined animal. Jasper huffed through the vent, his eyes wide and watching her approach.

"Why did you take him if he was this out of control?" Damian asked, more than a little annoyed. "We can't put him with the other animals like this, not to mention have him around the clinic clients as they come and go. He'll knock down the entire building, and that's if he doesn't hurt someone—or himself—first."

Terrance kicked his shoes into the dirt. "I had to, Damian. Fink was selling him to a processing plant if someone didn't take him this morning. A fucking *processing plant*, boss man. No way was I about to let him become glue or some shit. He's not malicious or anything. He's just misunderstood."

The stallion kicked the back door, nearly shattering the latch. The entire trailer creaked and rattled.

Fuck it. Terrance was right. Damian wouldn't have left the horse with that asshole, either. Whether they came from Supernatural owners or Norm, the Marisol Animal Sanctuary and Clinic—named after the literal angel who'd owned Miguel's heart—provided a refuge for sick and abused animals. They'd never once turned an animal away, and he wasn't about to start now.

"I'll go get some leads," Miguel said before disappearing back into the barn and returning with a few sets.

"Do you need me to do anything?" Rose asked, watching.

"Yeah. Stay back and out of the way. You're my responsibility while you're here and the last thing I want is for you to get kicked in the head."

She tossed him a hard glare, but he didn't care.

Damian, Miguel, and Terrance worked in tandem to secure the temperamental horse. While Miguel stood at the rear of the transport, Damian and the kid climbed into the main cab, latching two leads onto the halter the stallion already wore.

"Alright, Miguel. When I tell you, unlatch the gate and get out of the way. Jasper will probably back out like his hooves are on fire, and as he does, Terrance and I will follow him through until we clear him from the rig. On my count. Three. Two. One."

Miguel unlatched the door, and as expected, the horse backed out in a rush, his rump bursting out from the rig to break free. But the stallion's sense of freedom was short-lived as Terrance and Damian held him in place.

Black eyes widening, Jasper reared up and kicked out with his front legs.

A hoof clipped Damian in the shin so hard he saw stars. "Come on, boy. We're sure as hell better than Fink."

The horse didn't seem to think so as he spun, nearly taking out Terrance. This was going downhill fast. Behavioral issues his ass. The horse was a menace.

Damian was about to direct them to switch gears and attempt to lead the stallion into the paddock on their left when movement at his side had him freezing in his spot.

Rose eased closer, her hands held out, palms up toward the horse. "Hey, Jasper . . ."

"You need to get back. Now," Damian warned, voice stern.

"It's okay." She kept her gaze focused on the horse. "Isn't it, boy? You're not quite as scary as you wish you were."

"He seems pretty scary to me," Terrance muttered under his breath.

"Rose, I'm serious," Damian added. "Get the hell back before he kicks you in the head."

The horse's head turned toward Rose and the beast blew out a heavy breath, his nostrils flaring as his leg pawed the ground.

"Rose . . ."

"It's okay, boy . . ."

The horse pawed the ground again, his eyes fastened on the approaching witch . . . and then the damnedest thing happened. He *calmed*. No Magic. No strong-armed tactics. Instead of working against Damian and Terrance to break free, the stallion pulled on the leads to get to Rose.

Terrance's mouth went slack before beaming wide. "See! He's a good boy!"

Rose let the horse sniff her hand before she rubbed his nose. "You *are* a good boy, aren't you, Jasper?"

He huffed out a breath, the air making Rose's hair fly back, and the witch giggled.

Damian had a tough time taking his gaze off them . . . off *her*. He suddenly understood Jasper's enamored actions because he felt the draw, too. He felt it, identified it, and buried that shit down deep because no good would come of it.

Miguel chuckled. "Looks like someone was fated to work with animals, huh?"

His mentor's words broke Damian of his spell, and he tossed the older man a warning look that had him grinning. "Let's get him in a stall before he decides to stop being a good boy. Rose . . . do you mind?"

"Sure. Which one?" She held out a hand for one of the leads, and Terrance eagerly handed his over.

"Far end from Butternut and Squash . . . just in case."

Rose led the horse into the barn. They didn't even need the lead, Jasper practically glued to her side as she walked him into the far stall.

Terrance had already filled up the food and water, and by the time he finished, Jasper damn near looked as docile as a kitten. Damian took Rose's elbow and eased her from the stall, and a split second after they closed the door, the stallion reared, front hooves kicking the wall.

Rose yelped in surprise.

"Are you okay?" Damian scanned her quickly from head to toe to make sure she hadn't been clipped.

"I'm fine. He just startled me." She frowned at the horse, giving Damian a good view of her pulse heartbeat at the base of her throat. "I don't know what happened . . . maybe I can—"

"No." He blocked her way back to the stall where Jasper, although still pissed, was no longer kicking the shit out of the walls. "You don't go near that animal. You hear me?"

"But he was calm—"

"Does he look calm now?" She opened her mouth to argue. "This isn't negotiable. You listen, or I'll let the Council reassign you."

She clamped her mouth shut, folding her arms over her chest. "Fine."

"Good."

"You're the boss."

"Yes, I am." He cursed, blowing out a heavy breath. "Terrance will show you what to do and how things work around here."

Terrance stood nearby, already nodding. "Sure. I can do that. I'm practically a professional shit-shoveler."

Damian shot him a look and the kid blushed.

"Sorry, Damian." He smiled shyly at Rose. "Let's give you the thousand-dollar grand tour. I know this place doesn't look like much, but it's practically Magic."

Rose chuckled. "Magic, huh?"

"Yeah . . . because the only time Damian's not a complete grump is when he's here working." Terrance laughed, laughing harder when Damian grabbed a nearby horse blanket and threw it at his head.

Damian watched Rose walk away, wearing the dingy overalls and those too-big rubber boots as she followed the teen out toward the back paddock. Once that problem was out of sight, it was time to focus on the one made even more dire with their new cantankerous addition.

Money.

He'd already revamped the sanctuary's budget more times than he could count and still came up empty. No solution. No plan. Even if a second job dropped in his lap and he found the time to work it, they were all out of luck.

And funds.

As he performed a visual—and distant—physical assessment of Jasper, Damian couldn't help dwelling on the fact that in all the years he'd Hunted, he'd never had difficulty scraping two nickels together. The money had poured in, especially when he'd made a name for himself by bringing in the difficult cases. The upper-level demons. The high-caste warlocks. Feral shifters. Targets most Hunters wouldn't dare take on unless they had a death wish.

Teenage Damian hadn't only loved the challenge. He'd devoured it until Hunting became his *thing* . . . the only thing he was good at and the only thing that gained him even an ounce of his demon father's approval. Rules didn't stop him. What few relationships Damian had had outside of the Hunting world suffered . . . but none more than the one he'd had with his Norm side.

The more he embraced his inner demon, the less Damian saw of *Damian*. He hadn't been fully aware of precisely how off-track his life had gotten until he faced the wrath of a pissed-off teenage witch and earned himself his very own hex.

That was his wake-up call. And finally, after years of Hunting, he realized he had two choices: give up his humanity to become one of the volatile lowlifes he Hunted, or hold on to it with everything he had. Thanks to Miguel coming into his life, he'd chosen option number two.

"Don't know exactly what's going through that head of yours, but we'll find another way." Miguel's callused hand landed on his shoulder in a supportive squeeze. "We always do."

"I'm not so sure we'll be as lucky this time." Damian scrubbed a hand over his face, so tired he could sleep sitting upright and with his eyes open.

"Something will come our way. You just have to make sure you don't overlook opportunities as they arise."

A soft chuckle sounded behind Miguel.

Rose stood, dressed in her barn-chic overalls, and grabbed the nearby wheelbarrow they used for stall-mucking. "That sounds suspiciously like my grandma's life motto."

"I think I'd like your grandma." Miguel smiled.

"Most people do . . . or they're too scared of her to act otherwise." Rose glanced between them. "But I couldn't help but overhear a little bit, and I think I could help."

Damian bristled. "We don't need the brand of help you're offering."

Spine stiffening, she threw her gloved hands onto her hips. "And exactly what help do you think I'm offering?"

"The kind that comes with strings attached to wealthy people with deep pockets." He shot her a knowing look that had her frown deepening. "That's what you were about to suggest, right? *Begging*."

"It's not begging. It's *fundraising*. And I've done it before for charities all over the city . . . including Vi's children's center. I'm sure I could design a plan to help the sanctuary."

"We'll be fine without peddling our sob story around town. Sorry, little witch, but your friends will have to find someone else to help make themselves feel better about themselves. We don't need charity."

Rose glanced at a too-quiet Miguel. "Is he always this stubborn?"

"I'd like to say no, but I can't." Miguel turned his frown on Damian. "It couldn't hurt to hear her ideas."

"I don't need—or have the time—to hear anything. Animals need tending to." Damian ran his gaze over her from head to toe, and tugged his inner asshole to the surface. "Besides, I doubt you'll be here long enough to see a plan through."

Needing to be anywhere that wasn't right there in the middle of the barn, Damian brushed by Miguel and Rose, and headed out into the open air.

He was a jerk. A big one. And nothing made that more evident than when he felt vulnerable and there was someone around to witness it.

Especially if that someone was Rose Maxwell.

Besides . . . if she hated him, she'd keep her distance. And that was definitely best for them both.

5

Save a Cowboy, Ride a Broomstick

Windows down, music blasting, Rose navigated the Belt Parkway at a speed that would make an Indy racer proud, but so was everyone else on the road. It was keep up or get mowed over on the massive highway that went from Sunset Park in Brooklyn to Cambria Heights.

She glanced at the dashboard clock and cursed, picking it up another five miles per hour and praying the state police had fulfilled their monthly ticket quota.

James, her supervisor at Ryde, was already on her case about taking too long to pick up her last two clients. A third time might send him into an actual tizzy.

Most of her clients since taking the job had been businesspeople, either hopping from meeting to meeting, or heading to or from the airport. The second most common were tourists. She liked them the best, finding them personable and chatty with interesting stories to tell. It kept her from being bored out of her mind and worrying about her leather seats, which would never be the same again after providing a Safe Ryde to a recent group of hardy-partying NYU students.

Rose glanced at the GPS on her phone, clocking her time until she reached the restaurant to pick up her next clients. As she pulled up to the pickup zone, she turned off the music and rolled her windows back up.

Three familiar women stepped out from the posh eatery, and somehow Rose knew . . . "Shit a broomstick."

Of all the people who used Ryde, it had to be the I-Squad: Brandi, Tandi, and Candi. She'd barely tolerated them when she'd had to, and now that she didn't?

She debated pulling away and dealing with her boss's anger when Tandi, who was cloned from every mean girl movie ever made, glanced up from her phone. She gestured to her two minions, and they headed her way.

Before Rose could contemplate the use of a Mirage Spell to warp her features into someone new, Candi and Brandi slid into the backseat with Tandi bringing up the rear.

"I hope you know where you're going." The redhead's high voice and snotty attitude instantly grated on Rose's nerves. "I don't want to play navigator for you all the way back to Manhattan. Can you manage that? Or should I call for another Ryde?"

"I'll manage," Rose pushed out.

Tandi looked at her for the first time, blinked, and then her eyes widened before her pink-glossed lips pulled up in a sly smirk. "Well, well, well. Is *this* where the elusive Rose Maxwell has disappeared to? And here I thought you would've taken the time away to get that little 'issue' of yours fixed."

Minion One's and Two's heads spun toward Rose as if just witnessing a fourteen-car collision.

"Hello, ladies." Jaw clenched, she pulled away from the curb and headed toward the parkway on-ramp. "I'll get you guys back to Fifth Avenue in no time."

Rose prayed they'd leave it be and simply talk among themselves, but the whispered mutters in the backseat didn't stay back there for very long. Tandi leaned forward, catching her eye in the rearview mirror.

"How have you been doing, Rose? Chauffeur any celebrities or anything?" Tandi's snide comment earned her chuckles from her two friends.

"No celebs, and I've been doing just fine. And you?"

"Oh, you know . . . I've been keeping busy. Or maybe you don't know since you're not rotating in the same circle anymore." Tandi paused, slipping a coy glance to her friends and back. "Actually, I think running into you is almost kismet or something because I feel like I owe it to you to reach out."

The other woman's smirk couldn't mean anything good. "Owe me what?"

"To break the news to you personally . . ."

If Tandi was going for dramatic—which was her MO—all she achieved was getting on Rose's nerves, but it was obvious she wouldn't be done until she got it all out. "And what news would that be?"

"I've been seeing Valentin."

Rose swerved, earning herself a car honk from the sedan pacing along in her blind spot. Candi and Brandi screeched until she got herself under control, and Tandi threw her a triumphant smile. She'd gotten her reaction.

Rose gritted her teeth, trying to play it cool. "I'm not sure why you thought I needed to know. Valentin and I ended months ago."

And months before the *official* breakup, she'd done her best to find her way out of the damn Bonding Agreement. There hadn't been any romantic feelings for the French tiger shifter for well over a year, and she'd since concluded those feelings hadn't been real.

Not in the least.

They'd been the result of stress and a mother who was eager to marry her daughter off to someone rich and handsome so as to elevate the Maxwell family name.

"I didn't want things to get awkward in case we ever ran into each other at a big social event or something," Tandi lied through her artificially whitened teeth, "but those aren't your scene any-more, so . . ."

"Not really, no. But from what I hear, they're not Val's, either . . . since he lost his European Alpha seat to his Second-in-Command."

And *zing*. As Tandi bristled, Rose mentally checked off a point in her column and fought not to smirk. A witch could get used to this loose vocal filter thing. No wonder Vi didn't usually bother holding anything back. It was refreshing.

One upon a time, the Alpha title came with a family name, a birthright, and a long history of bloodshed and toxic testosterone. But Linc, Vi's Mate, had volleyed hard for change and with the support of the other continental Alphas, they disbanded the Shifter Elder Board and turned the Alpha-ship into a Shiftocracy.

Alphas were now voted into their position, directly by the people they were to lead, and while Linc's North American Pack had voted for both him and Adrian to remain in their seats, Val's pack hadn't. In fact, they'd all but coerced him and his bloodthirsty belief system out of Europe itself and provided an official escort out of the region.

Tandi waved off her comment with a low snarl. "It's a matter of time before the European Pack comes to their senses. They flour-ished under his rule, and now they're flailing with that traitorous SIC in the position."

"Not if he keeps throwing terms like *rule* around."

The witch's eyes narrowed. "Careful, Rosie. You're sounding a bit jealous . . . which is exactly what I wanted to avoid by telling you about Val and myself."

"Jealous I'm no longer tied to a masochistic sociopath?" Rose snorted. "Yeah, call me the green-eyed monster. Good luck with him, Tandi, and I mean that in all sincerity because you'll need every ounce of luck that comes your way."

"All this bitterness really isn't necessary. Not every relationship is meant to work and from what Val has told me, yours and his had issues from the very beginning."

Rose's hands tightened on the wheel.

"He made sure not to place blame," Tandi added insincerely, "but it's a good thing you're stepping back from Supernatural society. Now you can take the time to look at yourself in the mirror and self-reflect. It couldn't hurt at least."

Her knuckles cracked, turning white.

"If you ask me, it's something your sister should do, too, before she makes a mockery out of the entire magical community. I mean, *Violet* as Prima? Witches will be a laughingstock of the Supernatural world with her as our spokesperson."

Rose snapped, her Magic crackling in the small confines of the car and lifting the hair on her arms.

Make digs at her . . . *fine*. Come at one of her sisters and it's game over, bwitch.

Ignoring both the blaring horns and the three witches in the backseat squealing loud enough to rupture eardrums, Rose swerved through four lanes of traffic and pulled over onto the shoulder of the busy highway.

"Get out."

"Excuse me?" Brandi squealed, her eyes so wide it was comical.

Rose let her Magic come to the surface, its pink-and-gold sparks hovering over her open palm, and opened the rear door with a quick flick of her hand. "I didn't whisper. Get out of my car. All of you. Before I Magic your stuck-up asses out. You have until the count of three. One . . ."

The I-Squad quickly stumbled out of the car, practically climbing over one another.

"Two . . ."

Tandi scowled, flinging her expensive purse over her shoulder, her phone already clutched in her hand. "I'll make sure you get fired for this, Maxwell!"

She wiggled her fingers in a mocking goodbye wave. "Wouldn't be the first time, and what do I care? I'll just have more time to *self-reflect*."

With the bwitches out of her car, Rose pulled back onto the highway, a satisfied grin on her face. Goddess, it felt damn good not to do the *proper* thing for once. Yeah, it might earn her a Gran-Glower, but it would most definitely earn her a high-five from Violet, and even a sly wink of approval from Olive.

Riding that high, she let the traffic guide her around town. It was pointless to look up another client because she already knew she would be turning in her Ryde sticker today, but she couldn't bring herself to care.

By the time rush hour whisked her to the Lincoln Tunnel, her cell chimed with a text. Rose punched a button, and the automated female voice read it to her:

SOS. Gran's place. Be ready to kick warlock ass.
—V

"What the hell . . ." Rose, still in protective mode, stepped on the gas and upon breaching the other end of the tunnel, quickly merged onto the turnpike that would take her toward Athens, New York, the small riverside town her parents and Edie still called home.

She made it to her grandma's cottage in record time, her signature pink-and-gold Magic pulsing around her hands as she leaped from the car and followed her sisters' magical signatures to the back of the house where she finally sensed a third—unfamiliar—one.

Not bothering to ring the bell as she prepared to knock heads together, Rose burst through the door. "Whose ass am I kicking?"

A squirrely man squeaked at the abrupt intrusion, and with a quick look at her sparkling hands, visibly paled. "I . . . I . . . um . . ."

"Finally!" Vi stood from the kitchen table, exasperation written all over her face. "Make it stop, Rose. *Please*. Make. It. Stop."

Rose slowly digested the scene. No bruises. No obvious confrontation or threat. In one piece, Vi even looked well-put-together, dressed in a pair of tan slacks and a silky dress shirt. For her sister, it was practically a ball gown.

Slowly realizing there was no real emergency, she let her Magic fizzle out.

Olive, sitting on the nearby leather chair, a book opened on her lap, rolled her eyes. "I tried taking her cell phone away, but her head-lock game has improved over the last few months. I had to tap out."

"There's no SOS."

If Vi could've executed a hex with a single glare, the pale warlock—who looked like a librarian wearing a tweed jacket—would've been graced with a pig's tail. "There totally is . . . make him disappear. All of him . . . and his little flash cards, too."

Mr. Librarian—because Rose still didn't know who this guy was—heaved out an annoyed sigh. "You're not even trying, Miss Maxwell. Maybe if you put an ounce of effort into the task at hand, we could finish before moving on to the next step."

Vi shot Rose a pleading look. "Do you hear this? Previous step. This step. And now a next step. Rose, I'm officially at my limit. If this keeps up, that supernova incident will be nothing compared to what's about to go down."

Vi's purple-and-gold Magic swirled through the room, lifting everyone's hair and making Olive lose her place in her book.

The youngest triplet let out an annoyed sigh until magically charged crackles popped in the air. She jumped up from the chair, which moved from the wind force now that she wasn't sitting in it. "Son of a witch's tit . . ."

Vi was about to go supernova.

Rose sent an apologetic look to Mr. Librarian. "Sorry, Mr. . . ."

"Rogers." He pulled his tweed jacket closer as it flapped in the magical windstorm.

"Mr. Rogers, I think that'll be all for today."

"But the Prima—"

"Doesn't want her home blown to magical smithereens, which is what will happen once Vi reaches her breaking point. Trust me. You don't want to be in the vicinity when things combust."

He scowled before packing up a laptop and what looked to be a million thick manila files. "Fine. But I'll be sending a notice to Prima Maxwell. She hired me to do a job, and I won't be blamed for not doing it. It's my reputation as a Magical Fixer on the line."

"Or a masochist," Vi muttered.

Rose shot her sister a stern glare before glancing back to the skittish man. "Thank you for understanding. I'll make sure the Prima understands as well."

He hustled away, only looking back to throw a seething glare at Vi. Her sister looked as though it took all her willpower not to stick her tongue out at him.

Once they were alone, the magical windstorm slowly died, but not without making them all look as though they had stood in the middle of a tornado.

Rose smoothed her hair back to rights. "Seriously, Vi?"

Violet grabbed a stack of what looked like baseball trading cards, except instead of uniformed major leaguers, immaculately dressed people smiled from the pictures . . . some alone, others grouped by couples. "Do you see this? Flash cards, Rose! He brought his very own, so excited you'd think this was a mint-condition Yogi Berra or Babe Ruth. This"—she shook the cards—"is what my life has come to . . . and then he has the audacity to tell me I'm not trying!"

"Well, *are* you?" Rose popped up a single eyebrow.

Vi tossed her hands in the air. "Of course I'm not! After all, I oh so enjoy feeling like an epic failure. This is impossible. Magic fucked up. I'm no more a Prima Apparent than that male writer guy who writes sad stories is a romance author."

"Magic doesn't misdiagnose, Vi. You're not paying attention." Rose held up the top flash card of vampire Count Dimitri and his consort, Lady Nishat. "Dapper Dimitri and Nice Nishat. Dimitri has his hands in the New York fashion scene, and Nishat is the host of the morning show *Wake Up with Fangs*. Dapper Dimitri. Nice Nishat. Repeat it after me."

Vi muttered the alliteration trick and dropped onto the couch with a heavy sigh. "Why can't I spell myself a memory charm to help me with this crap? It seems like an easy fix . . . instantly match faces to names. No need for studying. No worry of embarrassment."

"Until you throw a spell and a vampire thinks you're slinging hexes around and gets all fangy. And then at the first sign of fangs, shifters go on the offensive and sprout fur . . . or scales. And immediately after that, witches and warlocks will hurl Magic into the mix and all the Norms will trample each other to death to get away from the scary and out-of-control Supernaturals. Would you like me to continue?"

"When you say it that way it sounds bad," Vi muttered before snapping her fingers excitedly. "I know! We can wear those nifty little ear mic things and you can feed me the names!"

"And when I'm not around? You need to learn the names eventually, which is obviously why Gran hired Mr. Librarian . . . er, Mr. Rogers."

"But I wouldn't need Mr. Librarian if you take me up on my wing-witch offer. You'd forever be standing at my side."

A small part of Rose wanted to say yes, be done with it, and move on. It was the easy answer to the question What Will She Do with Her Life? To have a place and a purpose. To have a job where she made a difference. To have—and feel—meaning.

But what Violet suggested didn't feel like *her* meaning.

"Rose . . ." Vi's sympathetic eyes narrowed as she reached for Rose's hands. "I want you to be happy. Olive and I both do."

"And once I find my thing, I will be. Trust me, I'm not squandering this second chance. And please know I'm not saying this to be mean, but this . . . ?" She held up the flash cards. "This isn't my life anymore. This is all yours, sis."

"Bwitch." Vi heaved a couch pillow at her with a laugh.

Rose caught it and dropped next to her. "You're welcome."

They all chuckled.

"Where were you when I sent off the SOS?" Vi asked. "I didn't get you in trouble, did I?"

"I got myself in trouble." Rose's cell dinged and she read the message from her Ryde supervisor, James. "Strike that . . . I got myself fired."

Her sisters shot her twin looks.

"I know! I know. But this time it couldn't be helped . . . the I-Squad was involved."

Vi held up her hand. "Say no more. I get it. But now you have more time to find your thing . . . and maybe have a little fun while you're looking around for it." The oldest triplet wiggled her eyebrows suggestively.

"What are you doing?" Olive asked, looking confused.

"I'm innuendo-ing." Vi danced her eyebrows around again.

"Stop it. It's freaking me out . . . and *innuendo-ing* isn't a word."

"It is if I use it as one, Ms. Scholar Pants." Vi's grin broadened when Olly rolled her eyes. "And I was innuendo-ing because our dear sister is in serious need of fun while she waits for her life's passion to come around. Maybe *physical* passion . . . with a tall, broad-shouldered man with bedroom eyes and a former bad-boy complex, but who loves animals?"

Rose shot her a glare.

"That seems oddly specific." Olly's brow crinkled, the younger sister in deep thought until she gasped, turning to Rose. "Are you dating again? That's great! It's about damn time!"

"I am not dating again, nor will I be anytime in the near future." Rose shivered. "I dodged that bullet once. I'm not so eager to do it again."

"Come on. When the broomstick comes back around, hop on it and ride."

Rose and Violet glanced at their youngest sister before bursting into laughter.

"You know what I mean, right? Save a cowboy, ride a broomstick . . ."

Tears poured down Vi's and Rose's cheeks.

Olly looked confused. "For the love of Goddess, what did I say?"

Vi giggled. "I'm not sure if you meant that to sound so dirty, Olly, but that was impressive."

"Dirty? I don't know what you . . ." Realization dawned, and her cheeks reddened before she broke into her own giggles. "I hadn't meant it like that, but now I do. You can't let Pepé Le Pee-Yew ruin you on penises."

"I like penises. I'm just not eager to get attached to their owners. Literally and metaphorically." Rose shot Violet a stern look as she opened her mouth to argue. "And especially any owner with bedroom eyes, a bad-boy complex, and who loves animals. *That's* not happening in a million years."

"I think the witch doth protest too much." Vi smirked.

"And I think the witch—*you*—has been sampling the potions in the back of Gran's Magic cabinet. Besides, even if I were thinking about diving back into the dating trenches, Damian Adams would be the last person on earth for whom I'd make that jump."

Olive blinked. "Linc's friend? The vet? But he seems nice."

Rose snorted. "If you have four legs and fur, but if you walk on two legs? Not so much. He's arrogant, rude, and not to mention he has absolutely zero interpersonal skills. Oh, and did I mention he's arrogant with the inability to admit that maybe . . . *just maybe* . . . he could benefit from someone else's help?"

Vi lifted her eyebrows. "Now *that* sounded awfully specific. Did your first day at the sanctuary not go well?"

"Oh, it was fine," Rose admitted truthfully. "I enjoyed working with the animals, and the former vet, Miguel, and Terrance, their employee, were incredibly nice and helpful. Oh! And when I was there, they had another horse come in . . . poor thing was so scared. No, the sanctuary's just fine. It's the caretaker of which I'm not a big fan."

"Arrogant without the ability to accept help . . . and more arrogance," Vi clarified.

"Exactly. Evidently money is a little tight, and when I offered my assistance in raising funds, he practically stormed out in a fit, growling about how he doesn't need charity."

Olly and Vi exchanged looks.

"What?" Rose asked.

Olly smiled supportively. "I'm sure you meant well, and I know your heart was in the right place . . ."

"But . . . ?"

"But sometimes in your desire to help people, you go a little overboard."

Vi nodded. "You take over, and while Damian was an ass to walk out like a half-demon man-baby, I kinda see it from his point of view, too. You probably didn't know this, but Damian's father was *upper*-level demon. And by upper, I mean lower. I think. Whatever, he was pretty powerful, if you know what I mean."

Rose's eyebrows rose into her hairline. "Are you telling me Damian's father is a prince of Hell?"

"It's not something he advertises, but I get the impression Damian and his father didn't have a good relationship growing up. At all. I'm pretty sure Dear Dad's solution to everything was to throw money at it, and when Damian went against the grain, he got cut off. I'm fairly certain there's more to it, but bro-code prevents Linc from telling me too much."

"And there I was offering easy ways to throw money at the problem . . ."

Olive added, "If the sanctuary is hurting right now, he's probably struggling with what he knows they need and what he's willing to take. Use your gift of out-of-the-cauldron thinking. If anyone can find a creative way to bring in cash flow without taking it directly from the fat wallets of high society, it's you."

Rose tapped her finger against her chin, her mind already thinking of different possibilities. "Out-of-the-cauldron, huh? I can do that . . . but what if he won't listen?"

Vi smacked her leg. "Since when do Maxwells let that stop us? Lincoln wasn't exactly the type to listen to suggestions that didn't hop out of his own brain, either. Just make sure it's too good of an idea to refuse."

Olive smirked. "Or at the very least, make it one he *has* to listen to."

Make Damian Adams listen? Was that even possible?

Rose wasn't sure even Edie had the power to bring about that miracle.

But it didn't mean she wouldn't try.

6

Let It All Hang Out

Rose picked up the napkin beneath her wine spritzer and let her fingers fidget, tearing the damp paper into confetti as she continued mentally mapping out her game plan. Since her talk with her sisters, she'd been up the better part of the night figuring out a way to help the sanctuary that even Dr. Broody McGrumpy Pants couldn't turn down.

And it was damn hard.

Each idea that popped into her head, she mentally heard his husky growl shooting it down until all she had by the morning was a mountain of frustration, exhaustion, and a tension headache. But as tired as she was, Olive looked ten times worse as she plopped on the barstool next to her, immediately asking Gage, Potion's Up's vampire bar owner, for plain black coffee.

Rose kicked up a dark eyebrow. "Since when do you drink your coffee black? Or drink coffee at all?"

"Since my roomie decided to run her own business from our living room and boasts about twenty-four-hour service," Olive grumbled, eagerly wrapping her hands around the mug when Gage slipped it in front of her. "Thanks. And keep it coming . . ."

"Anything for my favorite Maxwell sister." The vampire flashed a wink. "No offense, Rose. But she's the more tranquil of the three of you and well, I like my quiet . . ."

"If it isn't two of my three favorite witches!" Harper wrapped her arms around each of their shoulders, giving them both a noisy kiss on the cheek before taking a seat. "What are you two doing in a dump like this?"

Gage, drying a stack of mugs from the other side of the bar, shot his employee a dark look.

Harper barely flinched. "Oh, come on. You can't deny this place needs more than a few upgrades. Eco-friendly light fixtures. Buffing and fresh paint. And we may as well demolish the bathroom and start from scratch."

"Keep it up and I'll start from scratch with my staff."

The succubus rolled her expressive green eyes. "Oh, please. You can't afford to get rid of me . . . especially at the rate at which you scare all the others away."

Rose's ears perked, but it was Olive who asked first, "Didn't you finish training someone last week?"

Gage looked wary. "Finished training and fired two days later when I caught her skimming money off the register. Pretty sure your sister cursed me before she handed in her notice because everyone I've hired since Vi left hasn't worked out."

Harper scoffed. "Meaning the grumpy, broody vampire boss flashed a little too much fang—and not in a good way—and scared them back into the unemployment line . . . with the exception of Miss Sticky Fingers. It takes nerves of steel to deal with this guy. Trust me, I know. It's the only reason I'm still standing."

Gage cocked an eyebrow, which the sex demon copied.

"Go head. Tell me I'm wrong," Harper dared the vampire.

"What do I have to do to get rid of *you*?"

Harper chuckled. "You can't get rid of me. I bring the crowd, baby. Get rid of little ole me and this place would be a vacant hole-in-the-wall rather than a busy hole-in-the-wall."

"I can help out a little bit," Rose heard herself saying.

All eyes transferred to her, Olive's mouth slightly opened.

"I know my way around mixing drinks thanks to our Girls' Nights," Rose continued, "and I'm pretty good at handling people . . . perk of all the Prima training."

"You want to work here?" Gage failed to mask his surprise.

Harper squealed. "Yes! Yes! You're hired! When can you start?"

"You can't hire or fire people, Harper. You're not the owner or the manager."

"Which is something we should sit and have a talk about. I feel like I deserve something for putting up with your grumpy fine ass all these years." She shot him a daring look that had him sighing.

"When can you start?" Gage didn't bother arguing.

"After the Bonding Ceremony next week?" Rose suggested.

"Swing by and we'll set you up with the paperwork and work out some kind of a schedule."

"Sure." Rose smiled. Finally. Something was going right today.

"Oh, my God! It's back on!" Harper squealed. Vaulting over Rose, the succubus gave her a faceful of her cleavage as she yanked something off the community announcement wall. "I was just wondering if they would pull this off again this year and—well, suck me. I have that stupid promo event the radio station is making me do and I've already exhausted my usual excuses to try and get out of it."

Olly clutched her precious coffee to her chest as Harper bounced back into her seat, a flyer gripped in her hand. "Are we supposed to know what you're talking about or are we supposed to guess?"

"Here. You two witches go as my proxies, and I won't take no for an answer." Harper shoved the flyer at Rose before she could reach for it.

She blinked, forcing her tired brain to decipher the pictures and words, and then she laughed. She laughed so hard she had to squeeze her legs together or risk dribblage . . . but she was the only one.

"What?" Harper asked, looking genuinely confused at her reaction.

She slowly sobered. "This is a legit event here in the city? The No-Pants Express?"

"Honestly, you Maxwell sisters need to get out more. Yes! Every year, they pick a different train. Riders doff their pants and ride the subway, all getting on at different stops along the way."

Olive looked stricken. "They take off their pants . . ."

"It's called the No-Pants Express for a reason, Olly."

Rose rubbed her head, trying to make sense of the words she was reading on the flyer. Yep. It definitely said REQUIRED: NO PANTS. Also, no photography allowed. At least they had their priorities straight.

"Who the hell would want to ride the subway naked?"

"Not naked. Pantsless. Huge difference." Harper sighed, glancing at the flyer longingly. "It may be an organized event, but there's something about the idea of shedding my drawers and holding on to one of the pole grips that lights my fire. It's exciting. A rush. It's . . . unexpected."

Unexpected . . .

Rose glanced at the flyer again and noted the date a few weeks from now. On the Q train.

Nibbling her bottom lip, she pondered what everyone would think if she did something like this. Her mother would be hospitalized with palpitations. Vi—and definitely Harper—would cheer her on with pom-poms and a megaphone. Olive would probably try and talk sense into her, spouting about the health risks involved in going pantsless on New York City public transit.

The old Rose would agree. She'd probably even come up with numerous alternatives that involved less risk and significantly more clothes.

But she hadn't been *that* Rose in close to six months . . .

"I'll be your proxy," she heard her voice say.

"You will?" Olly asked at the same time Harper did a double take and said, "Really? You'll do it?"

"I'll do it."

"Can I pick out your underwear?"

Rose was poised with an automatic no, and then a little wave of excitement took over. For the first time in forever, she was excited to jump on the subway.

Pantsless.

"Sure," Rose agreed. "Why the hell not?"

If she was joining the No-Pants Express, she might as well go all out. Or more accurately, let it all hang out, and damn if it didn't light a fire in her like Harper said.

Or maybe that flame was because the bar door opened and in strode Dr. Broody McGrumpy Pants himself . . .

Saliva welled in Rose's mouth as she took in his dark denim jeans, formfitting black T-shirt, and worn leather jacket. She'd never once been tempted by the bad-boy type growing up, not even in her teenage years, and yet drool was two seconds away from dripping off her chin.

And then his eyes locked with hers across the room.

Rose momentarily forgot how to breathe. Oxygen? What the hell was that? Her entire body heated as if suspended over a firepit, her limbs warming first, then her core.

Then everywhere.

How did the man make her feel so hot and bothered without so much as a single touch?

"I can't wait to hear the story behind *those* pheromones." Harper bumped her shoulder, pulling her gaze away from Damian temporarily. The redheaded sex demon waggled her eyebrows suggestively. "Don't bother telling me you don't know what I'm talking about because you two unwittingly gave me a delicious little snack."

Rose narrowed her eyes on her friend. "I thought you don't feed off people's lust without consent?"

"I don't . . . unless the Hoover Dam of Lust cracks open and floods the room, and it's either sink or swim. And just so you're aware, you and our resident sexy veterinarian over there didn't crack it, you pulverized the damn thing. Seriously, I might need to head outside and have a smoke, and I don't smoke."

Rose's cheeks warmed, denial at the tip of her tongue as she glimpsed Vi and Linc, and Bax and Adrian stepping into Potion's right behind Damian. "I think you're sensing the soon-to-be-Mated couple."

"Protesting doesn't make it any less true, babe." Harper wrinkled her nose and, grabbing Rose and Olive by their arms, dragged them off their stools. "And FYI, I fully approve of you and the hot demon vet. Much better choice than the French Baguette Who Shall Remain Nameless."

"That demon vet is a stubborn pain in the ass," Rose muttered.

"Oh, but what an ass . . ."

Harper's and Rose's heads snapped to a blushing Olive.

"Olly!" Rose laughed.

"What?" The youngest triplet shrugged. "I notice things other than books. He has a nice ass. It's a fact. I deal with facts."

"You look like my sister. You sound like my sister, and yet . . ."

Behind her glasses, Olive rolled her eyes and disengaged when they reached their table, taking the chair on the opposite side of Vi.

Harper glanced over her shoulder. "Go get yourself a demon, witch." She gently pushed Rose off-kilter.

Taken off guard, Rose stumbled right into a pair of strong arms.

Callused fingers gripped her hips, gently slipping beneath the hem of her cropped shirt as her own braced on a sturdy chest. Her body instantly reacted, goose bumps erupting over every inch of exposed skin, more developing as she slowly glanced up into Damian's gray eyes.

His lips twitched. "Do I throw you off balance, little witch?"

More than he knew . . .

She cleared her throat. "New shoes . . . and it's *Rose*."

He glanced to her sensible ballet-style flats before flashing her a knowing smirk. "Sure . . ."

She narrowed her gaze on him, annoyed as she pulled away and instantly felt the loss of his body against hers. "You're an ass."

"But what an ass, am I right?"

Her eyes widened as their traitorous friends and family chuckled. "How did you . . ."

He pointed to his ears. "Shifters aren't the only ones with good hearing. Demons can hear pretty well, too."

"Well, good for you, but it still doesn't negate the fact you're an ass with a seemingly decent rear end. When someone wants to help you, the appropriate response is 'thank you.' Or at the very least, 'thank you, but no thank you.' You don't growl like a feral animal and then stalk away like an overgrown man-toddler."

"I'm confused. Am I an ass, a feral animal, or a man-toddler?"

"At the moment? All three . . . and the list grows with every sentence that comes out of your mouth. I mean, what jerk won't even listen to an idea that might help the animals under his care?"

Damian's jaw muscle ticked away. "And now we've added 'jerk' to the list."

"If the shoe fits . . ."

"I'd be more than happy to continue this conversation after we've solidified the last details of the Bonding Ceremony. That is why we're here, isn't it? To go over how things will run on Vi and Linc's big day?"

Vi cleared her throat, barely suppressing a grin. "I'm good with waiting so you guys can straighten this out."

An idea struck, one so brilliant it should've emitted a golden glow over her head. "Let's play a game."

Folding his massive arms across his chest, Damian cocked his head. "Something tells me your idea of a game and my idea of a game are a hell of a lot different, babe."

"Pull your mind out of the gutter, *doc*. I'm talking pool. If you win, I'll keep my nose out of your business. When I win, you listen to my idea for the sanctuary . . . and I mean *listen*. With an open mind and without that scowl on your face. Think you can handle that?"

"*When* you win?"

"Yes or no?"

His gaze slid over the antique billiards table in the back of the room. "And how can I trust you won't use Magic to win?"

She snortled. "I don't need to use Magic to beat you at pool."

"Awfully sure of yourself."

"Of course. Why, aren't you?"

His lips twitched as he held out a hand as a gesture to make their way to the pool table. "After you . . ."

Rose brushed past him with a wink. "Warm up those listening ears, doc, because I'm about to beat the pants off you."

As she reached for the triangle to rack the balls, a wall of heat warmed her back. She sucked in a sharp breath as his mouth brushed against her ear. "That sorta sounds like an incentive for me to lose."

The triangle slipped from her hands. Damian's low chuckle sent a horde of butterflies straight to her lady bits, a distraction she couldn't afford if she planned on winning this bet. And she did.

Her heartbeat thundering, she reminded herself of everything that was at stake. Animals' lives. Mari's Sanctuary.

The taste of victory coated the back of her tongue, and it tasted a hell of a lot like vanilla.

✦ ✦ ✦

Low chuckles dragged Damian's eyes away from Rose to where Bax and Adrian laughed openly while the others got comfortable at the nearby booth, looking like they were preparing to watch a Broadway show.

The Guardian Angel shook his head as he leaned against the wall. "You're such a newb, Adams. You should've just listened to her."

"Is that your way of telling me I made a deal with the devil?"

"The devil? Nah." Bax smirked. "You would've had a small chance of coming out on top if you had."

Well, fuck.

Rose waited expectantly from the other side of the table, her delectable mouth pulled up into a coy, knowing smirk.

Double-fuck. That definitely wasn't the face of a woman concerned about losing.

"Are we doing this, doc? The sooner you accept your fate, the sooner we can finish the plans for this Bonding Ceremony . . . and then the sooner you and I can have our sit-down." Rose sweetly handed him a cue. "You can break."

He took off his leather jacket and tossed it into Bax's laughing face before taking the stick. His fingers wrapped over hers, and as had happened before, an immediate zing traveled from the point of contact up his arm. Judging by the slight widening of Rose's eyes, he hadn't been the only one who'd felt it.

He made sure his palm brushed along her skin as he slowly took the cue. "You should've told me you're a pool shark. I can't help but feel a little defrauded."

Her dark eyebrows lifted. "Fraud implies that I told you I've never played the game a day in my life, but I didn't tell you a thing about my abilities. You assumed—probably because I have breasts—that I wouldn't be familiar with it."

"That wasn't it at all," he said truthfully. "I was just confident of my own prowess."

Keeping an eye on Rose, he leaned over the table and took the breaking shot. Balls scattered in every direction, at least four— three solids and a stripe—sinking into various pockets. "I guess I'll take solids."

He shifted around the table for his next turn, picking off two more balls and feeling pretty damn good about himself until Rose walked behind him, her arm barely brushing his back. That zap returned, and he jolted, the cue ball sinking into a side pocket in a disappointing scratch.

He cursed, while she and their friends chuckled.

"Prowess, you said?" Smirking, Rose flicked her gaze from him to the table as she debated her strategy. "Do you want to know how I got so good at pool, doc?"

Sending him a heated look that had his cock twitching in his jeans, she leaned over and drew back her cue. Without taking her eyes off him, she snapped it forward and three of her stripes dropped into pockets with a fourth hovering an inch away from the corner pocket.

"How?" he heard himself ask.

"My sisters and I played every weekend with our grandfather, from the time we were big enough to hold a stick until he passed. Watching us beat his old Army friends was practically his favorite pastime."

"Hear-hear," Vi cheered from the table. The Prima Apparent and Olive clinked their glasses, each grinning wide. "Nothing withers overinflated egos better than being defeated by a twelve-year-old with braces."

Rose took a page from Damian's own book and leaned close, whispering for his ears only, "If you want your ego to remain intact, we can call this a draw and you can listen to my ideas now. I'm good either way, although part of me was really hoping to beat those pants off you. Are you a boxers or briefs guy?"

He played her coy bluff and stepped close. "If you want my pants off, little witch, all you need to do is ask. And while you're at it, we should probably add commando as a third option."

Her cheeks flushed, and damn if he didn't like it. Playing with fire never felt so damn good. "I think it's your turn . . . Ro."

She gently hip-checked him to the left and lined up a shot, her delectable ass less than an inch away from his hand. He clenched his fingers around his cue to keep himself from reaching out and touching it, and watched as she sunk another two balls.

And these weren't simple shots. They required a healthy dose of skill he'd only seen on the professional circuit. In one such move, she quickly sunk her last striped ball. "And then there was one. . . . In which pocket would you like me to sink the eight ball?"

"Back left corner pocket." Although he didn't think it mattered which he chose. He was totally losing. "One thing before you beat these jeans off me . . ."

She paused, her cue poised to take her final turn. "And that is . . . ?"

"Let's go somewhere private when my pants come off . . . because I may be into a lot of things, but exhibitionism was never one of them."

To the sounds of hoots and hollers at the table behind them, Rose took her shot, and sure enough, she banked it effortlessly into the left corner pocket. With a faint smirk, she leaned into his side, her mouth brushing against his ear as she whispered, "In case inquiring minds want to know, I'm a third option girl myself."

She slowly walked to their table, high-fiving her sisters and Harper.

Game over.

She'd won—both the pool game and the mental warfare.

She'd won it all.

Pants-down.

7

Scrap Metal Jenga

Victory never tasted so sweet. It put a pep in Rose's step as she all but bounced toward the main barn, her laptop tucked under her arm. Not that she'd enjoyed Damian's misery for the rest of the night at Potion's Up, but it hadn't sucked, either. He'd alternated between grumbling and going silent, even once attempting to renegotiate the terms of her win.

Not. A. Chance. She'd been long overdue for a triumph, and was holding on to this one with both hands and a vat of superglue.

"Hello, fellas!" She waved to Miguel and Terrance, who'd stepped outside, Butternut and Squash attached to leads at their sides. "Girls . . ." She gave each of the mares a little muzzle-rub.

"You're here early," Miguel pointed out. "And rather chipper this morning."

"And I have every right to be. Is His Royal Grumpiness here yet?"

The two men chuckled.

"Not yet," Terrance answered. "He had an emergency house call late last night and the clinic's first appointment isn't until later, so he's getting a little extra shut-eye this morning."

"Good. Maybe the extra sleep will improve his mood . . . and it also gives me time to prep."

Miguel handed Butternut's lead to Terrance and followed her

into the office, watching as she made room on the file-ridden desk and opened her computer.

"What do you have there?" Miguel asked, curious.

"*This* is my plan to help Mari's Sanctuary without 'begging for money.'" Rose made herself comfortable on the squeaky office chair and loaded her presentation. "And you may want to record this for posterity because even Damian won't find fault in it. And if he claims to, he's lying."

Miguel grimaced, shifting uncomfortably on his feet. "Rose, I know you mean well, but in case you haven't noticed, Ian's a bit of a stubborn mule when it comes to the sanctuary."

She cocked an eyebrow. "Only about the sanctuary?"

The older man smirked. "With just about everything . . . which is why I know that despite your heart being in the right spot, he won't listen."

"Oh, he'll listen . . . because despite being pigheaded, he also doesn't strike me as the type to renege on a deal, either."

"A deal?"

"Why are you sitting in my chair?" Damian's deep voice rumbled, turning their heads toward the door. "At my desk?"

Rose ignored his heightened level of grump. "This isn't a desk. It's a hazard zone with mounds of unorganized papers, and I'm trying hard not to dwell on how long that half-eaten sandwich has been sitting beneath that stack of manila envelopes. I'm not even certain there's an actual desk beneath this mess."

Damian stepped into the office and pushed said sandwich into a nearby trash can. "There. See. Desk. *My* desk . . . which is organized exactly how I need it to be to help me find things. Now, explain why you're sitting there with a computer."

"Because it's time for you to fulfill your end of our bet."

Terrance's head poked out behind Miguel. "Oooh, a bet! I can't wait to hear this!"

"But you will . . ." Damian drilled the teenager with a hard glare. "Don't you have work to do? Animals to feed and stalls to muck? The shit won't shovel itself, kid."

Leaving, Terrance muttered something about missing the fun. Miguel, on the other hand, stayed, watching them curiously.

"Why don't you pull up a hay bale and let me show you how we can not only pull Mari's Sanctuary out of the red and help the animals already boarding, but possibly take on more." Rose smiled sweetly, her grin widening as Damian's frown deepened.

"I don't have time to listen to fantasy ideas. I have a million things to do this morning." He helped himself to the pot of cold, old coffee from the corner table.

Miguel interrupted, "I already did the well-being checks on all the animals and Terrance put the mares into the pasture for their morning field time."

"Then the clinic's—"

"First appointment isn't until Mrs. Ali brings her Yorkie in for her weekly weight check and that's"—Miguel glanced at his watch—"not for a half hour."

"You lost a bet, *doc*." Rose used her best Prima Apparent voice. "And I know we haven't known each other long, but I never once thought of you as the type to backpedal on a deal made. I'd be very disappointed to find out I was wrong."

She wasn't beyond baiting, and thanks to working alongside her grandmother for years she was practically a professional fisherwoman . . . and Damian Adams was a huge freakin' bass.

A sexy, denim-clad, and T-shirt-wearing bass . . .

And she couldn't lie. It was a good thing she was sitting because the sight of a stethoscope shoved into his jeans' back pocket did funny things to her equilibrium.

She held Damian's probing gaze, unwilling to back down, and she didn't. With a heavy sigh moving his broad shoulders, he dragged a stack of boxes next to her and motioned for Miguel to sit, and then he hovered over her left shoulder, his chest so close it brushed her back when he breathed.

"You've got twenty minutes, little witch," Damian's voice grumbled. "And as a recap, I agreed to listen to your idea, not to implement it."

Wearing a smirk, Rose turned until their mouths were one pucker away from touching. Her gaze bounced from his lips to his gray eyes, catching him doing the same. "I'm not concerned. Once you hear my plan, you'll be kicking yourself for not listening to me sooner . . . and I'm gracious enough to *maybe* not tell you I told you so."

"Clock's ticking, little witch . . ."

With a slight roll of her eyes, she shifted her attention back to the computer and brought up her presentation. "If my understanding was right, your objection to fundraising was—"

"Begging rich people to save us," Damian finished.

"Right . . . and while direct fundraising would be the quickest way to raise funds, it's not the only way. Not by a long shot. I researched for hours, and I admit, I almost threw in the towel, but then I came across *this.*"

She clicked on the Bronx Zoo's website, and more specifically, the live camera feed for the very pregnant Jasmine the Giraffe.

Damian looked as confused as Miguel.

"You came across a laboring giraffe?" Damian's brow furrowed.

"Yes! Well, no. Kinda. *Live-feed cameras.*"

Miguel rubbed his beard, speaking first. "Maybe it's because I haven't had my coffee yet, but I'm not following your direction here."

She tapped on the growing number in the bottom left corner of the zoo's camera images. "You see this? There's currently five hundred and twenty-three people watching Jasmine pace in her stall."

"Five hundred people are watching the giraffe right now?" Miguel asked.

Rose glanced at the number. "No. It's now over seven hundred."

"But all she's doing is standing there."

"Exactly!" She beamed excitedly. "And when Jasmine's more active, or when it's feeding time, or when her keepers give her a pregnancy checkup or set up for her enrichment time, that number easily soars into the *thousands*."

"Why the hell would people want to watch a vet examination?" Damian looked confused.

"Why wouldn't they?" She turned in her chair to observe him watching the live feed. "People *love* animals, many more than they do people."

"They're not the only ones," Damian muttered.

"Adoption agencies do these puppy and kitten cams all the time. Think about the Puppy Bowl around the Super Bowl. People who wouldn't have otherwise seen an animal, see them on the camera, fall in love, and then those animals find their forever home. Not to mention it almost always leads to donations. People love helping animals in need. All we have to do is revamp this idea and apply it to the sanctuary."

Damian was already shaking his head. "You want to litter this place with cameras? I don't think so. This is a vet practice, not a reality TV show. I want to treat the animals that come through here, not worry about someone staring at my ass while I bend over to start an IV."

Miguel looked thoughtful. "People watch these things and send in donations?"

"All the time. *For hours.* They become so invested in the animals' well-being they can't not tune in." Rose turned her attention to her more receptive audience. "Can you imagine someone falling so in love with Butternut or Squash, that when they're healthy, they have a pasture of their very own to call home? Not only does a cam-feed have the potential of bringing in a steady cash flow, but kids watch. People ask questions on the chat feature. It's a great connection— and educational—tool."

Miguel glanced to Damian as if waiting for his response, and so did Rose.

He stared at the giraffe cam, his face devoid of emotion. Being unable to read his thoughts drove her near her breaking point. This could help the sanctuary. She knew it. And she couldn't wait to set it into motion.

Finally, Damian shook his head. "I don't like it."

"What the hell don't you like about it?" she snapped, exasperated. "Solving your financial woes, or matching the animals with their perfect owners?"

He shot her a glare. "I don't like the idea of people memorizing the sanctuary's comings and goings, not to mention monitoring *my* comings and goings."

"What does your work schedule have to do with anything?"

Miguel answered, "Damian lives in the loft apartment upstairs . . . but I'm sure there's a way to put the cameras on timers or something, right? Turn them off and on?"

"Of course." She pulled her mind off the fact Damian lived in the upper level of the barn. "And then we could always manually turn the feed on if something special is happening, like if we receive a new resident."

"I don't have time to babysit cameras. I'm stretched thin as it is," Damian interjected.

"There's no babysitting involved. Ignore them. Do your thing, and the viewers will come. We'll probably even reel in a few people who have things for grumpy demon veterinarians who can nicely fill out a pair of jeans."

Damian cocked a dark blond eyebrow. "Excuse me?"

She rolled her eyes. "Don't be so modest. With as many people as will be watching the animals, I'm sure an equal number will tune in to watch *you*. A sexy man is a dime a dozen. But a sexy man who loves and cares for animals is an entirely different breed."

Miguel chuckled, smacking his knee. "Maybe you'll get your own little fan club out of it, kid."

"Just what I've always wanted," Damian muttered. He shot a look at the cam-feed again. "Let's say I entertain this idea for one hot millisecond. What you're suggesting is putting multiple cameras around this place. Cameras cost money, not to mention, the time, knowledge, and expense of hooking them up and maintaining them. Then you add in these chat questions you mentioned. I don't have time for all that."

"I'll make it part of my duties while I'm here. I don't mind. And while I don't claim to be a techie, I am savvy enough to lay the foundation. What I don't know how to do, I'll figure out with the help of the internet . . . and maybe Olive."

"I have some old computer cams I was about to pitch." Terrance appeared in the doorway. "You can have them."

The adults all looked to the older teen.

"Sorry, I couldn't help but overhear some of it. I have about three. They're not the newest models or anything, but they work."

"Then why were you about to get rid of them?" Damian asked.

Terrance flashed him a *duh* look. "Because they're not the newest models. I could even help you set them up. It shouldn't be too difficult."

Rose clapped her hands excitedly. "Three is a great start, and until we raise funds for more, we can rotate them depending on what's happening that day. Like, we can mount one on the fence when the horses are in the pasture for the day, and keep one in the barn. Maybe the treatment room."

Rose glanced to a too-quiet Damian who still hadn't taken his eyes away from the giraffe feed. "Well? What's the verdict, doc?"

"I'll think about it." Damian's voice sounded resigned. "About as long as I'll think about firing people if they don't get to work. Let's move it. Terrance, with me."

The teen and Damian strutted out of the office, taking her rising excitement with them.

Miguel's hand landed on her shoulder in a supportive squeeze. "This is an amazing idea, Rose."

Her own smile wavered. "I'm not so sure Damian thinks so."

"He does, or at the very least, he will because even he can't deny it's a good idea. He's gotten so used to hiding in the shadows that the idea of stepping out into the sun—or the public—makes him a bit uncomfortable."

"That I definitely understand." But being born into the Maxwell family—and the second sister in a Magical Triad—she hadn't had much choice in being in the public eye. "So you think he'll eventually warm up to the idea?"

"Depends on how warm you're talking about." Miguel's chuckle had her smothering her own slight giggle. "Give him time. There's a reason why he became a doctor of four-legged creatures and not two-legged ones. He loves animals, yes, but he loves avoiding people more."

Being the sister of two of the world's biggest introverts, Rose understood the draw of a life out of the spotlight, but she couldn't help wondering if there was more behind Damian's story than not wanting to deal with people.

Not a complete shut-in, he'd befriended both Linc and Adrian in college, and had quickly found a way into the inner circle of their Supernatural friend squad. And it was obvious he cared about Miguel and Terrance a lot, checking on them both throughout the day.

Damian Adams cared.

He just didn't want anyone knowing it.

✦ ✦ ✦

Blood tests. Physical exams. Avoiding a kick in the head by a temperamental stallion with wickedly accurate aim. Add in a few drop-in patients and a surprise surgery to remove a knotted mess of gift-wrap ribbon from a goldendoodle's stomach, and Damian was more than ready to shower off the day's hay dust and grime and call it a day.

Rose surprised him at every turn, from her work ethic to the way she calmed Jasper without so much as a flicker of Magic. She hadn't muttered a single complaint despite being given the dirtiest jobs at the sanctuary, and once she'd finished her own assigned tasks, she often snuck off to help Miguel or Terrance with theirs.

Damian made his last rounds, turning off lights around the barn before seeing that Rose's car still sat outside. He'd assumed she'd escaped at the same time as the others but realized otherwise as he followed a soft melodic murmur to Bella's birthing stall.

Rose sat in the hay, the pittie's head nestled in her lap as she stroked her fingers around the pooch's ears, humming something that suspiciously sounded like a monster ballad from the early nineties. She lifted the small water dish to the dog's muzzle in a gentle offering of fluids, and surprisingly, Bella's pink tongue flicked out, lapping it once, then twice.

"If she doesn't make a drastic turnaround, I'll have to start another IV on her tomorrow." Damian announced his presence.

Rose barely startled. Still stroking Bella's head, her golden gaze flickered up to meet his. "Was she sick before she delivered her puppies, or after?"

"She had a few minor issues beforehand, but all of *this* started the second she realized her pups were gone."

Rose nodded sadly, her fingers rubbing Bella's ear. "She's grieving . . . and there's no one to take care of her?"

"In her condition, not anyone could. She eats and drinks enough to keep her organs from shutting down, but in the last day or so it's almost like she's given up."

Rose cupped water in her hand and held it up to Bella's muzzle. Big brown eyes looked up at the witch before she flicked her tongue out once and then closed her eyes, her head settling deeper into Rose's lap.

First Jasper, and now Bella seemed to be under Rose's thrall, and he couldn't blame them. Something about her even calmed his inner demon, and that scared the hell out of him. Had him thinking things he had no business thinking.

Like a repeat performance of their backroom interlude wasn't such a bad idea.

Never mind he had his no-repeat rule for a reason. Repeats led to the risk of attachment, or at the very least, expectations. His and Rose's one and only time together had already filled him with both of those, and in addition, wondering how much better it would get if they had time, a horizontal surface, and all their clothes off.

His cell rang, saving him from saying—or doing—something stupid like throwing that suggestion at her with an invite to his apartment upstairs.

"Hey, Amir. What's up?" Damian answered, recognizing the number of his colleague who had a practice in the Rockaways.

"Hope I didn't wake you."

"Nah. Just wrapping things up here at the clinic. What's happening?"

"I got an alert from someone in the neighborhood who swears they heard a young canine crying out by that old dumping ground . . . the one between Beach Boulevard and the Cross Bay Bridge. You know the place I'm talking about?"

"Yeah, I know it. You want me to go check it out?"

"I'd go myself, but I'm out of town for my in-laws' anniversary party, and you know I don't like getting animal control involved unless it's absolutely necessary."

"I get it." And he did. The informal—and illegal—dumping spot wasn't a place city employees often relished—or risked—rifling through. They'd be more apt to shrug off the information, letting whatever poor animal that was out there fend for themselves.

"Guess I should be flattered your first thought was to call me," Damian joked, noting his conversation had caught Rose's attention.

"You're the only one I know who'd wade through that shit-show for a four-legged critter."

"I'll head out now and check it out. Thanks for the heads-up."

"Anytime, man. Anytime."

Damian ended the call, realizing Rose watched him curiously. "I have to check out a tip on possibly abandoned pups."

"Someone dumped puppies in these temperatures?"

"I wish I could say that it wasn't common, but I'd be lying. And if they're too young, there's no way they'll last the night, so I'm heading in to the Rockaways."

He grabbed a carrier from the storage room, some soft blankets, gloves, bottled water, and a couple of flashlights.

By the time he had it all shoved in the large canvas rescue bag, Rose stood by the door, already shrugging into her pink puffer jacket. "Can I help you?"

Her question threw him off guard. "You want to go on a rescue call? It won't be a brisk walk through Central Park."

"I should be offended by your shocked look, but I'll ignore it. Besides, I'm not doing anything right now . . . and it's dark."

Damian let out a low chuckle. "I'm not afraid of the dark, little witch."

"Good for you, but I meant that two eyes—and flashlights—are better than one. Especially if time's an issue."

It was on the tip of his tongue to send her home. He'd done thousands of these rescues alone without any issues, and yet the words refused to form. Instead, he handed her a second flashlight, and as his fingers brushed hers, that zing of awareness shot through his entire body, forcing him to suck in a quick breath.

Rose did, too, their gazes locking. In that moment, time froze and he nearly forgot everything but his damn name. The animals. The rescue. The time crunch. All gone for a few slow seconds until he pulled his hand away, but it hadn't mattered.

Ten minutes later, as he navigated his truck toward Queens, his skin still tingled where they'd touched.

In New York, there was no downtime when it came to traffic. Day. Night. Weekend. It was fucked up twenty-four-seven . . . except during rush hour, and then it was SFU (*Supremely* Fucked Up). Luckily for Damian and Rose, they were dealing with the everyday FU traffic and were crossing the bridge thirty minutes later.

"Does this happen a lot?" Her arms wrapped around the empty pet carrier on her lap, Rose glanced his way.

"Does what happen?"

"Terrance brought Jasper to the sanctuary because his owner was about to dump him somewhere unsavory and now abandoned puppies. You collect strays and animals people have already given up on."

He snuck a look and caught her staring at him unabashedly. "It happens way more than I'd like. And it's why the sanctuary clinic is sinking quicker than a Floridian sinkhole. Any money that comes in via the vet practice is immediately used up by the sanctuary, but I'm not about to turn away animals in need. They didn't ask to be put in the situations they're in. *People* put them into them, and if I can do something to help get them out, I will."

Rose watched him like a silent hawk.

Damian's fingers fidgeted on the steering wheel. "What? Why are you looking at me like that? Do I have something on my face?"

"Under all the sexy grump, you have a very caring heart, Damian Adams." She almost sounded surprised.

"Don't spread that secret around town, okay?"

Her lips twitched. "So people don't realize there's more to you than brooding good looks and an attitude?"

"So people don't think something's there that isn't."

"A heart?"

"Exactly."

She rolled her eyes with a dainty snort. "And I thought Harper was dramatic, but you like playing up the tortured hero shtick, don't you?"

Rose thought he'd been joking, but he hadn't.

Yeah, he had a heart. The thumping mass of blood and muscle resided in the center of his chest as it did with anyone, but unlike the typical human—or Supernatural, for that matter—dietary restrictions couldn't be helped. But his wasn't sodium.

Or cholesterol.

Or caffeine.

Damian's was love. The act of falling *in* love.

"I hex you, Damian Adams. When you find that one person and realize they're your everything, you'll lose not only your heart, but your soul . . . and there will be no amount of Magic that will bring it back."

Etched on a mental MP3 file in his head, his ex's words reminded him that what Rose referred to as "his brooding" was one of many tactics he employed to keep people at arm's length. It was right up there along with his one-night-stand rule and no hanging around for breakfast. Hell, he had at least a dozen more, ironic since it was his lack of rules—and boundaries—that had put him in this predicament.

He'd had tunnel vision at the height of his teenage Hunting career, thinking only about his next haul. He sure as hell hadn't considered how the bounty life would affect his fledgling relationship with the witch down the block from where he trained . . . at least not until she felt slighted enough to start throwing hexes around and hurled a doozy of one right at his head.

Or more accurately, his heart.

Back in the day, he might have played it fast and loose, but suddenly, having a real, tangible threat to his humanity had given him the wake-up call he'd needed to step away from the Hunting life.

No Hunting and no deep-rooted feelings of love meant his heart and soul remained intact, and he'd like to keep it that way.

The truck cab grew silent as they got closer to Antoni's Junk & Salvage. Last year, the owner had relocated to a retirement center where there was sun and surf all year round, and the depot—abandoned by his kids, who couldn't have cared less about the place—had quickly fallen into deep disrepair.

Knowing that no one monitored the site, contractors and big companies saw—and often used—it as a free dumping ground for their leftover crap.

As expected, the front gate stood open, the rusted padlock broken either by kids or by whoever had dumped the animals. Damian nudged the gate open with the hood of the truck and carefully steered around debris on the way to the rear fence where Amir's contact had heard crying.

The second Damian put the car in park, the sky opened up, rain dousing the ground in seconds.

"Shit," Damian cursed, reaching into the backseat for his medical emergency bag. "You can stay in the truck and keep the heat pumping because when I find them, it'll be important we get them warm."

"Why would I stay in the truck?"

"Won't you—?"

"If you're about to ask me if I'll melt in the rain, I swear to Goddess I'll hex you so hard your head will spin."

"Wouldn't be the first one," Damian muttered.

"What?"

Shit. *He hadn't meant to say that aloud.*

"Nothing. Just didn't know if you'd be up for it. It's cold. Now wet. And we have no idea where these critters are, or if they're even still here. It won't be a quick search."

She plucked the second flashlight from the center console. "Then it's a good thing there's two of us."

Not waiting for him, she climbed out of the truck. To keep their supplies dry for as long as possible, they opted to take only themselves and the flashlights, and would come back for everything else if—or when—they found the pups.

Damian flickered his light along the fence. "Amir said the crying came from just inside the fence line, so we'll walk the perimeter and keep our eyes and ears open. I'll go left. You go right. When we hit the end, turn around and retrace your steps until we meet back here. Sound good?"

"Got it." She pushed her wet hair, now plastered to her face, out of her eyes. "And we call out if we hear or see anything."

"Exactly."

"Okay. Let's do this."

"Oh, and little witch?" Damian hated bursting her hopeful bubble with a dose of grim reality. "Rescues like this one don't always end on a happy note. Just . . . prepare yourself."

Her nose wrinkled as she dismissed him. "Sorry, doc. Pessimism may be your go-to emotion, but it's not mine. I'll send out the bat signal when I find the puppies."

She turned, giving him a prime view of her wet jean-clad ass. He gave himself five seconds to enjoy it before returning to the task at hand, navigating around the small mountains of metal and steel.

Rain poured in relentless, thick droplets, occasionally obscuring his vision despite the use of the flashlight. At the end of the fence, he turned around and slowly trekked back, his ears straining to hear beyond the pelting rain.

Rose released a piercing finger-whistle. "Over here! I found something!"

He jogged the line, head whipping around. "Where the hell are you?"

"Here!" Her muffled voice came from a few feet away, well beyond the area he'd directed they'd look. "There's definitely something over here!"

Rose lay prone in the deepening mud, her upper body obscured from the demolished—and precariously stacked—cars that she'd shimmied under. One wrong move—or hell, a gust of wind—and the damn thing could topple over onto her.

Crouching by her fine, curvy ass, he gently touched her exposed ankle so as not to startle her. "You need to get out of there."

She ignored him. "I'm almost positive I heard sad little crying. They're in here somewhere."

"Seriously, Ro. Out now. One wrong move and this metal Jenga mountain will crush you into a witch-sized pancake."

Rose gasped. She'd already shimmied herself a few more inches into Death Mountain. "Damian! There's like six of them! *Puppies!* They're soaked and so, so little. I'm not sure they can even open their eyes yet. I just need to squeeze in a little more . . ."

"Switch places with me." Damian dropped into the mud next to her and shone his light inside . . . and sure enough, two feet from the edge of her fingers wriggled six little squirming bundles of pooch. "Come out here and hold the light. I'll go in and get them."

"Don't be ridiculous. I'm already here." He practically heard her eyes rolling. "And I can barely squeeze *my* shoulders in here and you think yours will fit?"

"I'll get Terrance to—"

There was barely enough room for her head to swing his way. Magical static crackled in the air as she drilled him with an annoyed glare, her golden eyes flashing.

Mud coated her chin and cheek, but it didn't make her any less intimidating. "To what? Take a half hour or more to get here? We'll be lucky if they last another few minutes, Damian. They're cold and shivering, and while I'm not an animal expert, I expect they haven't eaten in a few days. And you, Mr. Broad Shoulders, won't fit in here. If I slide in another inch or two, I can pass them out to you. Now go get the damn carrier."

He growled. "Do *not* move until I get back with the supplies."

She opened her mouth to argue. "But—"

"Not. Another. Inch. Or help me, little witch, I will yank you out from under there by your ankles right the hell now." Damian's demon pushed dangerously close to the surface, surprising him in their joint need to remove her from danger. "Do I make myself clear?"

"Fine," she growled back at him. "It makes you a bit of a bossy jerk, but a clear bossy jerk."

With one final, warning look, he ran back to the truck and grabbed the supplies plus a few blankets he stuffed into the carrier. He'd been gone less than a minute and when he returned, she'd already begun commando-crawling deeper beneath the scrap metal.

"Be careful," Damian warned sternly. "If anything looks unstable, you get the hell out. I mean it," he added when he heard her intake of breath. "*Say* it."

"If anything looks shaky, I'll work quicker to get us all out." With a coy wink, she shimmied deeper into the mud and muck.

He cursed himself for letting her do this. Hell, for bringing her along at all. Time ticked away, and by the time only her sneakered feet were visible beneath the rubble, Damian fought for each breath. A split second before reaching his breaking point, her calves came into view . . .

Then her rear end . . .

And then an arm popped out, a wriggling white lump of fur clutched in her hand.

Damian quickly grabbed the first puppy and after drying him off as best he could, tucked him into the carrier. By the time he turned around, Rose reached out to him with another. Five minutes later, they'd collected all six pups.

"Alright. Out. Now." He touched her ankle, prepared to yank her loose if need be.

She slowly reverse-shimmied her way into view and came out grinning from ear to ear. "We did it!"

Damian's fingers wrapped around the back of her head and with a low growl, he dragged her into a searing hot kiss. She leaned into him, dirty fingers fisted in his shirt as she held him until both their heads went slightly fuzzy from a lack of oxygen.

"That was a huge fucking risk," Damian admonished, dropping his forehead onto hers. Fuck. He hadn't meant to kiss her. And didn't mean to keep touching her, and yet . . .

She glanced to the carrier of puppies. "*That* was fucking awesome, but we need to get them back to the clinic."

"Yeah, we do. And quick."

He took her hand as they hustled back to the truck. Rose climbed into the passenger seat. By the time he took his spot behind the wheel, she already had the heat vents on full blast and tilted toward the carrier sitting on her lap.

They bumped and swerved their way out of the junkyard and onto the main street.

Nibbling her bottom lip, Rose peered worriedly into the carrier to watch the puppies. "They're not moving around as much . . . especially the little one."

"They need more warmth." He racked his brain, contemplating pulling over but that wouldn't help. They needed an incubator and meds and definitely hydration.

Movement from the other side of the truck pulled his attention off the road. Rose tucked the carrier at her feet and grabbed a horse blanket from the back bench seat . . . and then her wet coat and shirt were off, and she sat there in a lacy pink bra.

"What the hell are you doing?"

One by one, she brought out each of the pups, tucking them against her chest. "Body heat . . . skin to fur. It works in the movies, so I figured . . ." She shot him a questioning look. "Will it not work? Between the body heat and the actual heater, I assumed . . ."

"That's a great idea." Damian barely masked a mystified chuckle. The witch was damn incredible. "Get them situated and then angle the vents straight at you."

Rose did exactly that as he drove.

She hadn't thought twice about diving into mud, or stripping in a car, or about burrowing those six little—and filthy—furry creatures right into her cleavage. Once the pups were in position, she turned the heat on high and pulled the horse blanket over them for good measure.

Finally, five minutes out from the clinic, one of the pups whimpered.

And then another.

Damian and Rose shared a look, both of them releasing relieved chuckles.

He always knew Rose Maxwell was one hot witch. Now he had the evidence to prove it.

8

Garbage Day

Rose couldn't remember the last time she'd smiled so large, but it felt good. It felt right. Vi had practically glowed as she glanced up at her perfectly fated other half, and if Vi was happy, Rose was, too—and more than a little relieved that it hadn't been her who'd stepped into that Bonding Circle.

Her sister had practically glided toward her soul mate to the tune of an instrumental Bruno Mars song. If she had been in the same position, Rose would've feet-dragged her way toward the Circle to the tune of Darth Vader's "Imperial March." Thankfully, stepping down as Edie's successor meant voiding the Bonding Agreement between her and her fleabag tiger shifter ex whose name will never again fall from her lips.

Never again would she allow someone to pull the wool over her eyes the way Pepé Le Pee-Yew had done to her. Eyes wide open and heart uninvolved—that was her life's new motto. Not that the jerk had broken it.

Thank Goddess.

But now she could make certain it never would be. From this moment forward, she did what—and who—she wanted, and what she wanted right then was to have fun with her friends and family, eat nachos, and later, sneak back to the sanctuary to check on the puppies.

They'd all been holding strong that morning when she'd left the clinic to prep for the ceremony, but it had been hard leaving them even with Miguel watching them closely.

Excitement and cheers filled the air as Linc and Violet danced their way into Roxy's Glo-Bowl. While Rose first thought Vi had chosen the untraditional bowling alley for the postnuptial party spot to watch Christina—their mother—break into hives, she realized now that Roxy's held special meaning for the couple.

Olive's arm linked through hers as they made their way to the refreshment table and the Leaning Tower of Nachos on which Rose couldn't wait to get her hands *and* her lips.

"Are you okay?" Olive masked a yawn as they waited in the nacho line.

"I should be asking you that. You look like a strong wind could knock you over," Rose pointed out. "You're still having roommate problems?"

"I think we've finally come to an understanding. So are you okay? Or are you also wondering if Mom has been taken over by an alien?"

Rose chuckled, still not sure who'd taken over Christina's body. When they'd all gone to the stylist to get their hair done for the ceremony, she'd not only been tolerable, but dare Rose say it, *pleasant,* even calling Harper by her correct name instead of Heather or Hallie, or some other *H* name.

"Totally wondering," Rose answered with a grin. "And I'm fine. I just keeping thinking about the puppies, hoping *they're* okay."

"Miguel would call Damian if they weren't, right?"

"True . . . but it doesn't stop me from worrying."

She'd told them everything about the rescue and the puppies at the salon, and Vi, especially, had listened raptly. It wouldn't be long before her sister came nosing around the sanctuary looking for a playmate for her Maine coon, Mr. Fancy Pants.

"You sure it's only the puppies you're worried about?" Olive's glasses amplified the worry glinting from her dark blue eyes.

"Of course." Rose's stomach fluttered with the small fib. "What else could I be worried about?"

Olive couldn't sniff out a lie, but her former lawyer's interrogation skills were still top-notch even after changing professions and becoming a Supernatural Studies professor at NYU. The truth was, the late-night puppy rescue wasn't the only thing she couldn't stop thinking about.

The second subject was her co-rescuer.

When they'd reached the clinic, she'd watched in awe as Damian's large hands delicately handled each little puppy, giving them the expert TLC—and treatment—they'd needed. He'd been gentle and yet firm. Assertive yet reassuring.

He'd been a walking, brooding, and too-sexy-for-her-own-good conundrum she couldn't seem to get out of her head no matter how hard she tried. And that kiss that rocked her to her core?

If it hadn't been for the puppies' lives hanging in the balance, she wasn't so sure she wouldn't have asked him for another, and for one after that.

Rose's gaze automatically sought him out where he stood with Bax and Adrian, the three men laughing at something Bax had said. Damian glanced her way. The second his gaze locked on her, her lady bits went on instant high alert.

"Why don't you go for it already?" Olive asked, breaking her ogle-fest.

"Go for what?"

"I'm the youngest by like four minutes, not forty years. You know damn well what—and who—I'm talking about. You're both adults. You're both single. Go for it, and partake of the orgasms."

Rose ran her gaze up and down her sister's black cocktail dress, another ceremony detail that nearly sent their mother's head into a spin. "Evidently Mom isn't the only one who was body-snatched. Who are you? Your voice sounds like Olly, but that advice is something that would come out of our older sister's mouth . . . or Harper's."

"Not all their advice is bad. Some just aren't particularly well thought out."

"Neither is that one."

"Why? Because you're not the one giving it?" Olive challenged with a smirk. "He's friends with both Linc and Adrian, and has been for a long time. That wouldn't be the case if he wasn't a good guy."

"I'm not saying he's not a good guy. I'm saying me going for *it* with *him* isn't a good idea. Are we forgetting the last time I *went for it* with a guy?"

"There's one slight difference. Okay, two huge ones." Olive kicked up her fingers one at a time. "First, Vi and I *hated* Pepé Le Pee-Yew from the moment we laid eyes on him."

"Then why didn't you—?"

"Say something? Because if it's something you don't want to hear, you won't. And you most definitely didn't."

She couldn't argue the point because it was true. Tunnel vision—and hearing—was a known fault of hers.

"And secondly," Olive continued, "Damian's not a power-hungry, opportunistic narcissist with psychopathic tendencies. He made a career around *helping* animals. The only animal Pepé liked was the tiger he shifted into."

"Not wrong . . . but what's your point?"

"My point is that they're night and day."

"Being a vet is what Damian does, not who he is."

Olly blew out an annoyed sigh. "Are you telling me he's a narcissistic psychopath?"

"No," Rose denied, "but he's not exactly a Guardian Angel type."

Olive snorted. "*Bax* isn't a Guardian Angel type and he's an actual Guardian Angel. Damian has a past. Big deal. We all have baggage."

Rose smirked. "What baggage do you have?"

"If you only knew . . ." Olive muttered cryptically.

Before she could ask her sister what she meant, Olly's cell rang. "It's work. I better take it. I'll be back in a sec."

Rose stood in the middle of the bowling alley, nibbling on her recently procured cheese nachos, and watched as people, decked out in their finest gowns, sat on benches or leaned against walls to slide into scuffed rental shoes. The kids from the community center surrounded Vi and Linc, everyone practically bouncing in their skin from all the excitement.

Gran had once suggested Vi give up her time at the KCC to focus on her Prima training and her sister wouldn't hear it, vowing she'd make it work. She loved those kids more than her favorite pair of Converse, and that was a damn lot.

Soon enough, Rose couldn't avoid the guests. She eased into her training, plastering a smile on her face as people approached her, some asking questions about the night while others simply marveled at the gorgeous Bonding Ceremony. The I-Squad snickered unabashedly on her left, mocking the people who enjoyed the laid-back affair.

Rose's Magic hovered on the tips of her fingers, letting her know it had her back, and while the trio definitely deserved a lesson in humility, it would be a lost cause. They wouldn't learn anything except one more way to push her buttons.

She spun around, prepared to pull an Olive and disappear outside to call Miguel and check on the puppies when she nearly bowled over a five-foot-tall granny.

Her five-foot-tall granny.

The Prima witch.

Head Witch in Charge.

And more accurately, the woman who could practically read minds, and not from using hocus-pocus. It was her super-granny powers, and those she'd possessed since before Rose and her sisters could even spell their names.

Edie Maxwell lifted a silver eyebrow. "What lit your rental shoes on fire, sweetheart?"

"Nothing," Rose denied too quickly. "I was about to check on the status of the cake."

"You three girls have no poker face. Come, walk with me." Edie linked their arms and turned them both away from the I-Squad's snickering. She nodded politely at a few people as they passed. "Vi tells me you've turned down her wing-witch proposal . . . multiple times."

Rose groaned. "Seriously, Gran. Not you, too."

"I don't bring it up to try and change your mind . . ."

"You don't?"

"Not at all. I'm simply curious as to why you said no. You're a natural leader. Standing side by side, you'd both be forces of nature in the Supernatural world. Together you'd create a lot of change."

"I know, but Violet's the Prima Apparent," Rose pointed out. Edie looked at her expectantly. "How has her training been progressing?"

It was a needless question because they both already knew the answer.

Edie's mouth pinched slightly. "It could be going better. Your sister is much more headstrong than yourself . . . always wanting to know *why* something is done. She's not particularly fond of the answer *tradition*."

Rose snorted on a chuckle. "And yet you hire people like that witchy etiquette guy who is all about tradition. You can't bring people like that on board and expect Vi to follow their rules. Those are the very people who looked down on her for her entire life."

"They're not rules. They're guidelines. And Rogers is highly regarded in the Supernatural community. He's been known to smooth out even the roughest of edges."

"This isn't *Miss Congeniality*, Gran, and Vi isn't Sandra Bullock. No amount of buffing will smooth Vi's edges unless she wants them smoothed. I know you mean well, but *her* way will never be your way. You need to let her do her thing."

Edie tapped her red-painted finger on her chin. "Perhaps you're right."

"I am . . . which is why I won't agree to be Vi's wing-witch," she admitted. "If I do it, then she has a safety net, and as much as I love my sister, I won't be the backup plan. She'll never pave her own way if I'm there to pick up the pieces. She needs to figure out she can do this on her own."

"So wise beyond your years." Edie smiled, patting her cheek affectionately. "But that's not the entire reason you won't entertain the idea, is it?"

Her grandma gave her one of those all-knowing looks. The one that said she sensed the lie before it had even fully formed in her head.

Rose finally admitted, "I need to figure myself out before I can figure out others."

"And are you figuring things out?"

She snort-laughed. "I figured out I don't possess the organizational skills needed to be an office assistant nor the patience or temperament to be a Ryde driver. I'll give bartending a whirl and see what happens."

"Bartending, huh?"

"I'll be filling Vi's spot at Potion's Up. Why? Disappointed?"

"In you? Never, my dear. Only if it turns out that I missed your mother's reaction to the news." Mischief glinted from her grandmother's eyes.

Rose chuckled. "I haven't told her yet, so no."

"Good. Do me a solid, and if I'm not there to witness it in person, record it for me."

Edie squeezed her arm affectionately and pulled her to a gentle stop. "And sweetheart, you'll figure out your thing. And whether it's bartending or party-planning or if that thing changes from week to week, know that your sisters and I all support you."

Edie's words left Rose with a swarm of sensations swelling in her chest. "I know. Thank you, Gran. That means more than you know."

"Oh, I don't know about that. I know a lot of things"—Edie winked, slowly turning her gaze away—"except where to find that nacho tower that had your mother in a rant earlier tonight."

"That would be on your left." Rose gently steered her grandma's shoulders toward the back display. "Go for the jalapeño cheese dip and you won't be sorry."

"Ah! Goddess bless you, child. Also, you're being summoned."

Rose turned to see Olive and Harper waving from the other end of the bowling alley. She waved back with new determination to enjoy the rest of her night. She wasn't as good at bowling as she was at pool, but she didn't quite need the baby bumpers, either.

She took her first step toward fun when karma bitch-slapped her across the face. But instead of a stinging hit, it came in the form of a well-dressed blast from her not-too-distant past.

A pretentious shifter on whom she'd never wanted to lay eyes again . . .

Mr. Pepé Le Pee-Yew . . .

The self-appointed tiger king . . .

Her *ex*.

Valentin Bisset.

✦ ✦ ✦

Even from a distance, Damian sensed the shift in the air the second the tall, dark-haired Supernatural approached Rose. Her body tensed as if prepped to make a run for it and the abrupt change in her demeanor put both him and his inner demon on instant alert.

Bax bumped his shoulder, oblivious to his diverted attention. "Are we putting a friendly wager on this game, or what?"

"Who's that with Rose?" Damian nudged his chin across the room, not taking his eyes off Rose or the man leaning too damn close to whisper in her ear.

The second Bax laid eyes on the guy, he muttered a string of curses no Guardian Angel should know, let alone verbalize. "Bastard's got some balls on him, I'll give him that. Or maybe he's just got a death wish."

Damian slowly connected the dots, and the slight twinge of familiarity. Terrance would've recognized the guy right away, but it took Damian a few seconds longer.

"That's the former European Alpha?" he asked for clarification. *And Rose's ex . . .*

"Thankfully the one and only." Bax folded his tattooed arms across his chest as he glared across the bowling alley.

"Why the hell would Linc invite the shifter who nearly imploded his and Vi's entire future?"

"He wouldn't."

"What's got you two looking broodier than usual?" Olive followed the direction of their attention. "Oh, crapsticks. This isn't good. We need to get that pussycat away from Rose, and then keep Vi away from the pussycat or the fireworks that happen will make the city's New Year's display look like a handheld sparkler."

Bax waited for more, and when it didn't come, he asked, "Do you have a plan for all of that, angel?"

"I'll find Vi and divert her for as long as I can. One of you do the same with Linc, and the other should get Pepé Le Pee-Yew out of here. Pronto."

Olive hustled away in search of her sister.

With a faint nod, Bax deferred to Damian. "Which detail do you want? Linc diversion or taking out the garbage?"

"I got the garbage . . . and Rose." His feet moved before her name had even left his lips.

Halfway across the room, Rose's gaze caught his. A nearly imperceptible head shake warned him away, but that wasn't happening. Tension—and the heightened weight of Magic—thickened the air the closer he got. The hair on his arms damn near stood straight up by the time he reached her side.

"You're missing all the fun, babe." Damian pushed a smile onto his face as his arm reflexively hooked around her waist.

The bastard across from them glanced at the gesture.

Even if Damian didn't already know the shifter was scum, he would've guessed it with a single glance. One good skill he'd learned from his Hunting background was his ability to spot evil in a lineup from a mile away, and this guy radiated it like a damn sun of immorality. He just hid it behind an expensive suit and a vat of nausea-inducing cologne.

"Making new friends, Rosie?" The tiger shifter slid his oil-like grin back to Rose. "Glad to see it. I had heard you'd become a bit of a recluse, and I have to admit, I was concerned."

"Pretty sure she doesn't need your concern," Damian heard his voice counter.

Valentin Bisset transferred his attention back to him. The shifter's inner beast pushed against Damian's own in a hunt for submission. Too bad for him that Damian's demon was a hell of a lot more Alpha than a furry cat and had no qualms about showing it.

Damian held the former Alpha's gaze and let that inner wall he kept between himself and his demon slide down just low enough to let his eyes flash amber in warning. And then in the ultimate fuck-you, he upped the ante with an unconcerned chin lift.

Bisset's jaw clenched despite his playing it cool. "I don't think I caught your name."

"Because I didn't give it." Damian didn't budge. "But I will give you some unsolicited advice. *Leave.* Now."

"I'm not certain I like your tone."

"And I am certain I don't care."

Bisset feigned shocked offense. "That attitude doesn't match the Maxwell family hospitality with which I'm familiar . . . especially toward a global Supernatural leader."

"Well, there you go . . . I'm not a Maxwell. In my family, we showed hospitality by sliding a scythe through your abdomen instead of up your groin."

And that wasn't much of an exaggeration. While Rose's family threw dinner parties, his threw punches. The Maxwells helped create laws, and when Damian and his family weren't breaking them themselves, they enforced them, sometimes with bloodshed and brutality.

Their families . . . their upbringings . . . were day and night.

And yet . . .

Rose snorted on a laugh before she stifled it, barely. "What do you lead again, Valentin? Because it's not the European Pack."

The shifter's eyes flashed gold, indicating his tiger was close to the surface, and Rose's Magic reacted instantly, the electrical pulse raising the hairs on the back of Damian's neck. Anyone within six feet of their threesome turned their heads toward them, no doubt sensing the rising hostility.

Protective instincts shifted Damian closer to Rose in case Bisset did something stupid, like shift.

Instead, a cold, emotionless smile slithered on the bastard's face. "Jae may be temporarily warming my Alpha seat, but your separation from the Prima-ship isn't as short term. And then Tandi tells me you've been struggling to hold a job? Chin up, Rosie. This is New York. There's never a shortage of people looking to hire witches with your . . . skill set."

"Thankfully there's also no shortage of people who would do anything to make sure you never reclaim your Alpha seat," Rose fired back immediately.

Damian cleared his throat, lips twitching as he addressed Bisset. "I think it's time you leave now."

"I think you should try and make me," Bisset sniffed, "*half-demon.*"

Damian snuck a glance at Rose. "Was that supposed to be an insult, do you think, babe? My people skills are a bit rusty from working with animals all day, but I think that was supposed to be insulting."

Rose nodded, playing along. "I think that's exactly what he meant it to be."

"Huh." He turned back to an even more furious Bisset. "Well, I'd rather be a half-demon than a full-asshole."

A low growl rolled from Bisset's throat before he shot to Rose, "You scraped the bottom of the barrel, didn't you, love? Guess I should be thankful I got a taste before you lowered your standards."

Rose beat Damian into moving first.

Wisps of pink Magic sparked from her hands as she stepped closer to the shifter, her eyes flashing. "Actually, Val, it's the exact opposite. I've finally seen my worth and I won't settle for anything less than the best."

Damian sensed the new presence on his left before the figure joined.

Dressed to the nines in a tux so expensive it could feed the sanctuary animals for an entire year, Julius Kontos looked every inch the demon figurehead on the Supernatural Council. Perfectly coiffed. Completely at ease. And the only person Damian wanted to see less than the asshole tiger shifter in front of him.

"Lucky me. It looks like I found the party within the party." Looking bored, the demon Councilman ran his gaze over Rose's ex, his hands tucked into his pants pockets. "What slimy rock did you climb out from, Bisset? The large one on the east side of Central Park? I thought we had that opening filled."

Bisset hissed. "This has nothing to do with you, Kontos, so move along."

"That's not quite true. Being on the Supernatural Council, it's my duty to oversee that the Bonding Ceremony of our future Council leader and all celebrations related to it go smoothly. Think of me as security . . . with horns."

Julius's inner demon showed himself for a split second, eyes—and skin—flashing red before melting back into his human form. In response to the show-and-tell, Damian's own inner hellion stirred, and it wasn't an itch. Or a brush. And it definitely wasn't a caress as he'd heard other Supernaturals describe their second self.

His beast dragged a talon from the underside of his sternum to his navel, leaving behind a scorching trail of pain and misery. It was literally the reflux from Hell.

Julius's eyes glittered as he charged up his Compulsion, his demonic gift of not-so-sweet-talking others into doing his bidding. "You'll be leaving now, and you'll do so without creating a scene."

The tiger shifter fought the mind control with an angry snarl. "Go to hell, demon."

"I'm actually vacationing there next week to work on my tan. Anyone who claims the Caribbean beaches are the best has never been to Sinful Shore, the nude beach in Hell's Level Six." Julius's playful smirk melted away, his eyes flashing again. "Now, leave before I forget where and who I am, and fall back on old habits from years past. And trust me, I wasn't so nice back then."

Damian snort-muttered, "Understatement of the year."

Julius glanced at Damian for the first time, his mouth twitching . . . and that was all the opportunity Bisset needed to make his move. He leaped, one hand shifting into a clawlike weapon as he aimed to hit both Damian and Julius in a single swipe.

Magic crackled and in a blink, the shifter was suspended motionless in the air, a living statue only capable of moving his eyes. Bisset's lips barely moved as he tried—and failed—to snarl.

"Nicely done, Miss Maxwell." Julius chuckled. "Damian, what do you say we take out the trash? It's smelling the joint up. But I claim feet. That muzzle looks a slight less frozen than the rest of him and I can't afford a nibble on the hands. They're my moneymaker."

Damian glanced to Rose. "You good with that?"

"Goddess, yes. Please. Get him out of here."

The three worked in tandem to remove Bisset from the bowling alley, Damian and Julius hefting his body while Rose walked alongside, keeping him frozen until they'd tossed him onto a pile of black garbage bags stacked on the sidewalk.

Used paper plates and boxes flew up, decorating his expensive tux with trash bag confetti, and all the tiger shifter could do was glare.

"What the hell?" A high-pitched squeal pierced the evening air as a flurry of satin and ruffles burst through the bowling alley doors. A tall blonde shot them all what she probably considered lethal glares as she stood protectively in front of Bisset's still form. "You can't do this!"

Rose snortled. "I think we already did, Tandi. Relax. It'll wear off in a few minutes, and then the two of you can slither on your merry way."

Tandi's mouth opened and closed, her face getting redder by the minute. She snarled, "I will ensure that you're never invited to another social event in the city. Mark my words."

"Oh, will you? I don't know what I did to deserve such a favor, but I wish I would've done it a lot sooner."

This time, Damian couldn't withhold the small chuckle. The blonde, with a shifter-like growl, turned back to the garbage-covered Bisset and plucked a banana peel from his coiffed hair.

Rose turned to Julius. "Thank you for the help, Representative Kontos."

"None of that, Miss Maxwell. It's Julius." He bowed his head, making the witch's cheeks pink.

"Then you have to call me Rose. But again, thank you. He's

honestly the last person I expected to see here tonight considering everything that's happened."

"It's not a problem. I'm afraid my Compulsion is a little rusty from disuse, and his tiger was surprisingly strong. But then again, my Compulsion wasn't always the most robust growing up. That honor went to my brother."

Rose blinked. "I didn't know you have a brother. Have I met him?"

The instant Julius swung his gaze to Damian, he knew exactly what was coming, and that there was no stopping him. "If I were any less of a demon my feelings would be hurt that you haven't mentioned me."

Damian shrugged. "Never had reason to."

Rose's head snapped toward Damian and back, her mouth opening and closing. It would've been comical if Damian wasn't so pissed.

"See. Hurt feelings." His half-brother faux-pouted before turning toward Rose. "If you and your sisters lived apart for years without a single call, text, or Google search, and one of them suddenly moved back to town without telling you, how would you feel, Rose?"

"I . . . don't know." She shot Damian an apologetic look. "We wouldn't go that long without seeing or hearing from one another. If we go an entire day, the others would form a search party."

Julius flashed her the mega-smile that used to get his brother anything he wanted growing up. "That must be nice. Doesn't that sound nice, Damian?"

"Only if I had a sibling other than you."

Rose frowned.

Julius chuckled. "Glad to see you haven't changed much, brother."

"Actually, I've changed a lot. Thanks for the assist with Alpha Asshole, but don't feel like you have to stick around."

"Trying to get rid of me already?"

"Noticed that, did you?" Damian's arm slid around Rose's waist, and surprisingly, she let him guide her back to the bowling alley's entrance.

They didn't get far before Julius's voice followed. "You realize you can't run away from me forever, right? Or *him*."

Damian shot his half-brother a warning glare. "I've done fine for the last few years. I imagine I'll do fine for a few dozen more."

"But are you really doing *fine*?" Julius looked casual, his hands tucked deep into his suit pockets. "From what I hear, that little project of yours is seconds away from shutting its doors due to a lack of funds."

"Then I guess you better get all of that ear wax removed because you're not hearing very well, or accurately," Damian lied.

"If you played nice, I could find you work that's more suitable to your talents. Imagine all the dog biscuits and hay bales you could buy with one of your regular payouts."

Damian didn't want to think about it because when he did, he reluctantly admitted that his brother was right. One Hunting assignment would take care of the most pressing things that needed to be done around the sanctuary, things like making sure the water and heat weren't shut off. A second Hunt would put them very close to breaking even, if not slightly ahead.

But he wasn't sure if he was willing to pay the price. "I'm really not in the mood to sell my soul to the devil—or you, so I'll pass."

"Always so dramatic, little brother," Julius called when Damian reached out to open the door for Rose. "What you're doing isn't natural, Damian. Suppressing him will only lead to more trouble down the line."

Him.

Damian's inner demon.

"Natural or not, I'll deal with it," Damian retorted.

"You know where I'll be when you realize you need help, and I'll even be the bigger brother and reassure you that I won't turn you away."

Damian threw a glare over his shoulder. "I don't need your type of help, Jules."

And he didn't.

Once upon a time, he'd done exactly what his brother had wanted. Hell, he'd striven to be a damn demon carbon copy and all it got him was hit, hammered, and hexed.

Literally.

9

Puppy Power

Eagerly clicking that much-desired item into your online shopping cart only to find it already sold out was almost as horrific as setting up the sanctuary's puppy cam. Rose had been at it for an hour, used three different kinds of tape and a bungee cord, and the damn thing still kept tipping over the second she released her hold.

The next attempt would be with the Gorilla Glue in her back jeans pocket, and if all else failed, she'd magically seal the damn thing to the wood beam and hope for the best.

Eager whines from below had her glancing into Bella's birthing stall. The once-sad rescue rolled playfully in the puffy blanket mounds, licking at the squirming bundles of fur in encouragement to keep searching for the milk they sensed nearby.

When Rose arrived at the sanctuary before sunrise to help Miguel feed the pups, her offhanded comment about Bella helping puppy-sit the new additions had led to Miguel's light bulb moment and the two of them making introductions between the six little critters and the sad pooch. Hearing the puppies' little noises, Bella's head had instantly popped up from where it had rested on her front legs.

And the rest—they say—was history.

Bella instantly took to the puppies, bathing them and bringing them to her bed one by one until they all assumed a feeding position.

Rose cried, and not a stray, single tear. She'd sobbed profusely until she became a snot-producing mess. Miguel, the sweet man he was, didn't say a word as he'd handed her a cloth tissue and supportively patted her back.

Two hours later and not only did the puppies have full tummies, but so did Bella, who'd eagerly gobbled up every drop of food and water in her bowls as if knowing she'd need the extra calories and energy to take care of her new charges.

Today was a day of possibilities . . . and maybe later, of naps.

But lack of sleep and tech issues aside, she was first determined to get the puppy cam running before Doc Grump-A-Lot made an appearance. That way she could prove to him not only that her idea would work but that it had the potential to go above and beyond their expectations.

Thinking about the sexy conundrum that was Damian—her theme for last night's insomnia—Rose teetered on her ladder before once again finding her balance.

She'd tried everything to evict him from her head. Edie's calming tea. Physical exercise. She'd even tried orgasming her way to freedom with the help of Mr. Wiggles . . . but nothing worked. At first, she'd chalked it up to the emotional high of seeing her sister Bond with her soul mate. And when she settled from that, she linked it to the way Damian had not only stood up to Valentin, but challenged him—that was where Mr. Wiggles had come into play because that had been hot.

H.O.T.

But then she narrowed the cause of her restlessness to the scene between Damian and Julius Kontos.

His *brother*.

Once the cat hopped out of the cauldron, she'd found herself comparing them. Their eyes, both framed with thick lashes, had the same symmetrical shape with Damian's coloration leaning more to stormy gray while Julius's tilted heavily into a forest green. But other than both men being tall and broad-shouldered, that's where the similarities ended.

Known as a voracious flirt and consummate socializer, Julius charmed every room he walked into while Damian was too busy walking *out* of the room in hopes of avoiding all social interactions. The demon Council representative was hardly ever seen without a smile on his face, and on the few rare occasions Damian's lips twitched with the threat of one, he usually pulled it back.

It was night and day.

Sunshine and Grump.

And while Rose had always gravitated to the sun's bright rays in the past, she couldn't help being drawn to the broody moon-glow of a certain surly vet.

All. Night. Long.

Olive's "go for it" advice had merit, but for as long as Rose lived, she'd never heard of "getting someone out of your system" working. There was a reason why it was used as plots in so many romance novels. The trope was a treasure trove for conflict, and she wasn't so self-assured to think she'd be the one person to make it to the other side unscathed.

Look where it got Vi.

Witch Bonded. Married. *And* Mated. Albeit with her soul mate, so kismet was on her side, but luck didn't like Rose that much. Especially lately. Plus, her life was so up in the air it nearly collided with a jetliner on the daily. Choosing what to eat for lunch was difficult enough. She couldn't fathom nailing down what she wanted in a relationship.

No, thank you. This witch didn't need romantic entanglements. Until her situation—or her view—changed, she'd give Mr. Wiggles a workout and maybe have a replacement model on hand in case he gave out.

"Sounds like a plan." Temporarily distracted, Rose released her hold on the camera and held her breath for one second, then two.

She opened her mouth to hoot in victory when it toppled over for the one millionth time. "Son of a . . ."

With a frustrated growl, Rose yanked the glue from her pocket and squirted a generous dollop beneath the base before smooshing it down on the beam. "Please stay. Please."

She counted to twenty, and then, one finger at a time, released her hold. She didn't breathe. She didn't look at it sideways.

And it stayed.

"Thank Goddess," Rose muttered.

She admired her handiwork a second before climbing down. Two rungs into her descent, her right boot slipped. Her chin smacked against the step, sending a bolt of pain straight through her jaw and her equilibrium sideways. The ladder's weight shifted. There was no stopping the fall.

This was going to hurt.

Rose threw a panicked look beneath her to make sure neither Bella nor the puppies were anywhere they could be crushed, and then she hoped for the best. Tucking her arms over her head like a makeshift helmet, she braced for impact. A second into the fall and she landed with an *oomph*.

Not on the hard ground.

Not even in a hay pile.

Her body instinctively settled into a warm, firm embrace until her firm, spicy-scented chest-pillow chuckled. "Do I want to know why you're on a ladder before the sun even makes an appearance?"

Rose's gaze connected with Damian's, their faces less than an inch apart as he held her in a princess carry. Gold flecks dotted his gorgeous gray irises with a slight mix of green and blue, the colors turning more vibrant the longer they stared.

As she struggled to form words, Damian's mouth curled into a small smirk. The longer she tried saying something—anything—the more aware she became of Damian's nakedness. Well, half-naked.

Shirtless with his tattoos on full display, he provided her with an early morning visual treat that was even sweeter than her favorite breakfast cereal. Her mouth literally salivated.

Olive was right. Something needed to be done about this dry spell. "Why are you walking around the barn without clothes?"

His lips twitched again. "Because I thought someone was breaking into the clinic to steal meds and throwing on a shirt didn't seem as important as making sure the ketamine didn't go missing."

Rose glanced at her hand, reflexively playing with the hair at the base of his neck. She immediately stopped and mentally scolded herself. "As you can see, I'm not robbing you. If anything, the cameras will make it harder for anyone to do that, so you're welcome."

"You may not be robbing the place, but what would the Supernatural Council say about breaking-and-entering? Maybe extend your time here? Imagine how many more stalls that would be to muck out." Damian's eyes glittered with thinly veiled humor.

Rose shot him a glare. "Funny this morning, aren't we? Figures you'd be a morning person."

"And you're not?"

"I am after I've had about three cups of coffee. Approach me with anything less in my system and I can't be held accountable for my actions."

He smirked. "Now's who's being funny this morning?"

"Funny? It's the Goddess's honest truth." Rose returned his grin, only half-joking.

And her hands were back to playing with his hair.

She forced her hands to still. *Again.* "I think it's safe to put me down now. Concussion averted thanks to your impeccable timing . . . and paranoia about ketamine thieves."

Damian dropped her legs, but the arm banded around her waist stayed put. Friction from the rub of their bodies conjured a low moan from Rose, and she wasn't the only one physically affected by their close proximity.

His erection pushed against her stomach. The devil on her shoulder chanted for her to rub herself against him as if he were a scratching post, and she a cat. For a brief second, she contemplated it.

Okay, maybe for a few prolonged seconds.

He slowly released her, stepping back and taking away the temptation. "I answered all your questions, little witch. It's your turn to answer mine."

"What was the question again?" she asked, dragging her gaze away from his upper body with quite a bit of difficulty. "Oh. Why am I here so early? I hoped to get a few cameras mounted before the start of morning chores and when I got here, Miguel was already working with the pups." They both glanced to where Bella nursed the lively puppies, her tongue lolling out of her mouth in sheer canine happiness. "Their story is the perfect one to showcase first."

Damian crouched, and seeing him, one of the puppies tried ambling closer, tripping over his too-big paws. They both laughed. "Was it your idea to put them together?"

"Maybe I watch too many Animal Planet shows, but I saw something about litter fostering once and ran it by Miguel."

"It was a good idea." Damian rubbed the puppy's head before returning him to his new mom. "I should've thought of it sooner. It's like Bella's not even the same dog from two nights ago."

"Don't sound so surprised. People other than yourself do have the ability to have good ideas," Rose teased coyly. "But you're right. Bella's eyes lit up when she heard the puppies, and then when she saw them, her pupils practically transformed into little hearts."

"Four-legged or two, when someone finds their purpose, magical things happen. I'll keep a close eye on them to make sure there are no issues, but so far so good. All seven of them definitely appear to be on the upswing."

Rose wished like hell she'd be as lucky to find her purpose, but that really would be a magical occurrence. Maybe divine intervention.

Before she got stuck on the woe-is-me carousel, she refocused her attention back to half-naked Damian. "While you put on clothes, I'll make sure the camera's syncing to the system. That way there won't be any hiccups when the sanctuary's social media account announces the puppy cam later today."

Discreetly fanning her too-hot flesh, she brushed past Damian and headed toward the office.

"Wait, Mari's Sanctuary doesn't have a social media account," Damian called after her.

"We do now," Rose threw over her shoulder. "You're welcome!"

He grumbled before she even stepped into the office, and she couldn't help but chuckle. She might not have yet downed her three cups of coffee this morning, but hearing Damian pretending to be annoyed was right up there with a triple-boosted caramel macchiato with extra foam.

And cinnamon.

❖ ❖ ❖

On the way up to his apartment, Damian cursed himself and his infatuation with Rose Maxwell, and then compounded the problem in the shower when he resorted to wrapping his hand around his erection, imagining it was hers, because it wouldn't go the hell away without it.

He'd taken so damn long to get his head—and body—in line that even Miguel gave him a look, pointedly looking at his watch when he appeared downstairs an hour later. And then he dove from patient appointments to handyman work in an attempt to avoid bumping into Rose again, but it proved impossible.

The woman was everywhere, working as hard as everyone else. She didn't do anything half-assed. After she mucked stalls, the damn things practically sparkled, and when she fed the animals, she double- and triple-checked she'd given the exact amount needed.

Eventually, he didn't need to look for her to know where she was at every moment, and he couldn't blame it on his demon because even though the bastard had been closer to the surface since the run-in with Julius, he was also eerily content.

That's why Damian spent a good portion of the day looking over his shoulder, half-expecting Julius to pop in and screw things up. Only when the night finally wound down did he let himself relax.

Rose and Terrance sat in the birthing stall with Bella and the puppies, and the witch's soft giggle as the critters climbed all over her lap nearly sounded like music. She looked his way as he passed to the office and as bad as he wanted to go and join them, it wasn't a good idea. Instead, he headed to the clinic and organized his med cabinet, and when it couldn't get any more organized, his gaze drifted to the open laptop on his desk.

"We're getting low on vitamins for Butternut and Squash." Miguel appeared in the doorway and nodded to the supplements Damian had just inventoried. "I added them to the list for the next supply run."

Damian nodded, his hands still shifting items around.

"You know moving things around like a jigsaw won't make more appear, right? Unless you have magical powers to go along with that stubborn attitude."

"If only this could be solved by Magic," Damian muttered, not a fan of hocus-pocus, but if a spell could make money appear instantly, he'd be first in line to snatch one up.

Miguel watched him like a hawk. "You saw him again, didn't you?"

Damian turned to his mentor and grandfather figure. For a Norm, the man was damn perceptive. It wouldn't surprise him if there was a Supernatural somewhere in his bloodline.

"Don't know who you're talking about." Damian locked up the med cabinet and drifted into the office, Miguel following.

"You may be an adult now, kid, but that doesn't mean I'll listen to lies any more than I did when you were a teen." As Damian took a seat, Miguel propped his hands on the desk. "We both knew that once he figured out you were back in town, it would only be a matter of time before he sought you out. Truthfully, I'm surprised it didn't happen sooner."

Damian was, too. His brother might put on a good show of indifference, but there wasn't much in the Supernatural world of which he wasn't aware . . . and that included when new demons sauntered into town. Even in a city as big as New York.

"And?" Miguel cocked a bushy white eyebrow. "How did it go?"

"About as well as expected. Barely veiled guilt. A dash of threat. Pinch of attempted intimidation. And a heap of implied extortion. The only reason Jules didn't go the full gamut was because Rose was there."

"Please tell me you're not entertaining the idea . . ."

"What idea?"

"Ian . . ."

"I'm not, so you can stop worrying." The older man's pinched expression told him he wasn't about to take his advice.

"This is serious, kid. The last time—"

"I know what happened the last time, Miguel. I was there," Damian snapped, immediately feeling guilty. He sighed, rubbing his palms over his face. "I'm sorry. It's just . . . I don't know how much I'll be able to avoid it. Even you have to admit it would solve a whole lot—if not all—of our problems."

"And create a whole host more," Miguel pointed out. "I say this because I care, but I'm not as spry as I used to be. If you fall under again, I'm not so sure I'll be able to pull you back out."

Damian worried about the same thing, but he wasn't voicing his concern aloud and adding to his mentor's worry.

A soft throat-clearing had them both turning to the door where Rose stood. "Sorry to interrupt, but I was about to head out and I wanted to hop on the puppy cam site and see how we're doing."

Damian exited the seat and held it for her. "Have at it, little witch. Can't wait to hear how you fixed all our problems."

She shot him a look but took the seat before sliding in front of the laptop. Her delicate fingers tapped away, and when they slowed, her posture slowly sank. "That can't be right."

"That good, huh?" Miguel asked, hopeful.

Rose bit her pink bottom lip to the point it blanched. "We did get a few donations, but . . ."

One hand braced on the back of her chair, Damian leaned over her shoulder, her hair touching his cheek. He scanned the screen until he found the donation section, and snorted. "Well, at least we can buy that fancy bridle Butternut has had her eye on."

A whopping fifty bucks.

Fifty.

That would barely cover a new bridle.

Rose stood, purposefully bumping the chair into his legs as she stood, her face a hard mask of determination. "When this works . . . and it will . . . I'll demand a very public apology out of you, Damian Adams. Feet kissing may be required. We'll see how magnanimous I'm feeling in the moment."

"If this works, babe, I'll kiss a lot more than your feet."

With an annoyed roll of her eyes, Rose stalked from the office, and after giving Damian a disappointed shake of his head, so did Miguel. Alone and with disappointment weighting him down, Damian could feel his cell phone practically burning a hole in his pocket.

Animals needed to be fed.

They needed medicine.

Jasper needed . . . everything.

Mari's Sanctuary was dangerously close to being out of options, and if that happened, it wouldn't be only him that suffered.

"Fuck a demon donkey." Damian yanked out his cell, and stared at the screen. He started and stopped the phone call three times before forcing himself to see it all the way though. He'd nearly convinced himself to make it a fourth before the person on the other end picked up.

In lieu of a greeting, Damian growled, "I'm ready to talk."

10

Demon Dominoes

Wiping up yet another of her spills while playing bartender at Potion's Up, Rose glared at her phone sitting on the bar as if the inanimate object had insulted her. In a roundabout way, it had. Every time she pulled up Mari's Sanctuary's donation page and saw the same measly fifty bucks that had been pledged from the previous night, she wanted to hurl the thing across the room.

Why didn't people come to watch? Except for @WitchBitch, @BookMage, and @SexySucc, which she was 99 percent certain were her sisters and Harper, there hadn't been much traffic to the site.

Not much traffic. Not much money. Not much help for the sanctuary animals.

Rose didn't like failure, and that's exactly what she felt like.

An unhelpful dud.

Harper's empty serving tray clattered on the bar top in front of her. "You've been wiping the same ring spot for the last twenty minutes, babe. At this point, you've not only polished away the stain, but the varnish on the table . . . and maybe scared away a few customers with a very un-Rose-like glower."

"I don't glower. I don't even know how to glower," Rose defended herself half-heartedly.

"Hey, Gage!" Harper shouted to their vampire boss at the other end of the bar. He spun around, handsome face guarded as the succubus pointed at him but turned to Rose. "See! Glower, and honey, that's what you've been wearing on your face for your entire shift. Talk to Harper." She kicked up a delicately plucked eyebrow and lowered her voice, leaning close so only Rose could hear. "Or we'll go somewhere private and you can talk to Savannah . . . whoever will help you the most."

Rose chuckled.

A licensed sex therapist, Harper the Sex Demon often doled out sexy-time advice whenever the mood suited her. But her super-secret counterpart, Savannah, not only dished out relationship advice, but did so anonymously on her popular radio show, *Sexy Talk with Savannah.*

"Thanks for the offer, Harp, but there's no need to break out Savannah." Rose smiled wanly. "Sex advice would require the partaking of sex and things have been a little lacking lately."

"Then there's your problem! See! All fixed. Savannah does it again!"

Rose sighed, tossing the rag. "I wish it were that easy. I haven't gotten much of anything right lately. Haven't found any hobbies that felt like me. Haven't held a job longer than a few weeks. And what about the sanctuary? Those animals don't deserve to be on the receiving end of my sucktastic luck. Maybe I should've just kept my big-witch mouth shut."

"Nonsense." Harper squeezed her hand. "The sanctuary cam is a good idea. Not just good. It's practically genius."

She snorted. "Tell that to Damian. He seems pretty sure it'll go down in a burning ball of epic flames."

"Because he doesn't know the Maxwell triplets like I do. Seeing as I'm a bit of a Rose Maxwell expert, I'll let you in on a not-so-little secret. *You'll figure it out.* If the cam-feed doesn't pan out, you'll pivot until you find a way *to* make it work. You three are nothing if not determined—and resourceful, and that whole hobby thing? It'll happen when it happens, and probably when you least expect it. My advice is to have fun while you're waiting."

"Have fun . . ."

"Yeah. That thing people have that makes them all warm and tingly?" Harper looked thoughtful, tapping a freshly manicured finger against her lip. "That could describe an orgasm, too. I'm pro-both. When was the last time you had either?"

An orgasm . . . at least one Mr. Wiggles didn't have a hand in? *The night with Damian. Months ago.*

Warm, tingle-inducing fun? *Also the night with Damian.* Damn it.

At the other end of the bar, a horrendous crash had all heads turning to where a blonde stood, her mouth hanging open as she stared at what used to be Gage's extensive collection of high-end alcohol. The vampire was there in an instant, he and the young woman talking in hushed tones before she burst into tears and ran toward the back room.

Next to her, Harper sighed. "And another one bites the dust . . ."

Gage dragged a broom and dustpan from the far corner, shooting Harper a passing glare. "Keep it up, Harper . . ."

"Or what? This broody grump routine only plays into the vampire stereotype. You should try and mix things up. Wear yellow. Wear an occasional smile. Or at least, don't always wear that tattooed Fuck Off stamp on your forehead."

"Do you want me to stick around and clean that up?" Rose asked him, nudging the mess on the floor. "I can stay a little later."

"Nah. We're good. Things are winding down. Harper and I can handle things until closing."

"Are you sure?"

"Absolutely." His lips twitched as he flickered a glance to Harper. "Besides, it wouldn't hurt Harp to work for her paycheck for once."

The succubus rolled her eyes but took the hint, telling Rose goodbye before returning to the floor to take orders. Rose tidied up behind the bar before waving goodbye, grabbing her things from the back room, and heading out.

It was a nice night, the air crisp but not freezing. She forwent the Ryde and the subway and opted for a walk that would hopefully clear up the million and one thoughts in her head.

As she stepped onto the sidewalk, her phone pinged with a notification and almost immediately after, another chimed. She pulled her phone from her pocket and did a double take.

On the sanctuary's home screen, where there'd been a mere fifty dollars, there was now five hundred and fifty. Rose blinked and the number climbed to seven hundred . . . then a thousand. With every uptick in funds, the camera views rose, too, more and more people checking in on Bella and the puppies.

"Holy halos . . . it's working." It wasn't much, but was a damn good sign.

With a little extra pep in her step, she headed down the block. This late at night, the traffic was no longer too horrible, mostly filled with people like her heading home after long days at work.

A motorcycle rumbled past and quickly hung a right at the end of the block, causing a nearby driver to lay on his horn. The sight wasn't usual by New York standards . . . not the bike, nor the noise, but that leather jacket . . .

Not to mention the rider.

A small flutter of awareness low in her stomach told her it was Damian. She stood there on the sidewalk in the middle of Queens, debating her next move. Her bed practically called her name like a siren, but the sanctuary . . .

With a final glance at the still growing number on her phone, she decided she wasn't waiting until tomorrow to tell Damian Adams *I told you so.*

Abandoned construction equipment hindered Damian's speed-demon pace, but she still moved faster than a mall walker in order not to lose him. One block led to another, and before long, she'd ventured into an unfamiliar area of the city. All her earlier excitement melted away, replaced by the soft gallop of her heart as she glanced around the nearly deserted street.

If it wasn't for the flickering neon light of what looked to be a bar a few buildings down, she would've thought there'd been a blackout. Windows that hadn't been boarded up were blackened abysses of nothing, and trash, moving in the breeze, skittered across the eerily quiet street like urban tumbleweed.

She contemplated turning back, and brought up her GPS app, cursing when her phone showed nothing but black-and-white snow. She smacked it and held it up to the sky, hoping to get even a shoddy signal. Instead, it died completely despite her battery being at 79 percent.

"You've got to be freaking kidding me. What else can happen tonight?"

She shouldn't have asked. A prickling sensation ran up the length of her arms, almost as if she'd poked her finger into an electrical outlet. Magic—and not her own—hovered in the air, and thickened with every step she took.

"A cloaking spell . . ." Rose realized. The minty scent was impossible to miss now, and whoever was responsible wasn't only damn powerful but the reason for the failed technology.

Not only did it deter Norms from entering the area, but Rose's phone wouldn't work within the spell's veil, and she couldn't pick a direction and risk walking deeper into it.

"And my sucky luck returns," Rose muttered.

Two figures stumbled onto the street from a tattoo studio's alley. The taller man laughed at his slightly shorter friend, who'd nearly crashed face-first into a nonworking lamppost. They laughed and stumbled a few more steps before registering her presence.

"Hello there, sweetheart." The shorter guy tripped over his feet before catching himself. "Aren't you a dessert for the eyes."

The stench of alcohol and maliciousness poured off him in thick rolling waves that turned Rose's stomach. Choice made. Going *anywhere* was better than letting these two get any closer.

She headed toward the flickering neon light and the sound of low, pulsing music.

"Hey! I was talking to you, bitch!"

His friend chuckled and they tussled playfully. "She's not any ole bitch, Mike. She's a *witch* bitch. Can't you see the Magic on her? She practically glows . . . and I only know of one witch bitch family that has that amount of power. She's a fucking Maxwell."

Hex me . . .

A warlock. They were the only Supernaturals who could see the mystical glow of a Magic wielder.

"A Maxwell? You sure? What the hell would a Maxwell be doing all the way out here? *So far* away from all their loyal admirers?"

"Why don't we ask her?" the warlock teased, his comment making his friend howl.

"Hey you! Are you really the Maxwell witch bitch?" Mike bellowed. He took an obnoxiously loud sniff. "Damn. She smells like fucking cinnamon. My cougar's practically salivating."

Hexing hell . . .

A warlock *and* a shifter. Her luck just kept plummeting.

Rose picked up her pace, but so did Mike and his friend, the two Supernaturals continuing their disturbing conversation as they followed. Rose stepped off the curb and crossed the street, hoping that walking into the Blood Moon—the bar with the only working neon-lit sign—wouldn't be yet another mistake of the night.

It looked more like a hole-in-the-wall than a thriving business, but decent music leaked out from the slightly ajar door, and considering the now cackling men behind her, it was definitely the lesser of two evils.

Rose stepped inside. The closing door smacked her on the ass, pitching her forward.

Dozens of heads swiveled in her direction as she eyed the one and only empty barstool, and gave an awkward little wave. "Good evening . . ."

One by one, most of the patrons turned back to whatever they'd been doing with only a few watching her step farther into the bar. Her Supernatural senses told her vampires and shifters made up most of the crowd, with an occasional demon thrown into the fold.

Two women, sandwiched between a pair of glowy-eyed vampires, gave her outfit a critical once-over before continuing their flirt-fest. She self-consciously tugged her puffer jacket around her body when a shifter fight broke out on her left. A few people scattered out of the way, but most hung around waiting to see who drew first blood.

Potion's Up this place was not.

"You look lost, hon." The bartender eyed her from head to toe, lifting a pierced eyebrow toward her hairline. "Oh, you're definitely lost and you better get found really quick or this crowd will gobble you up and spit you out . . . and not in the fun way."

"There's a fun way?"

The bartender—a shifter, Rose's Magic warned—grinned wickedly. "So, so lost. If I see so much as a glimmer of fang, I'll yank your canines out with my rusty pliers, Andre. And you know I don't make idle threats."

"I'm sorry, *what*?" Rose's voice squeaked.

The bartender's attention slowly shifted over her left shoulder to the tall, gangly vampire who'd literally been a few inches away from her neck, *sniffing*. Rose pulled her jacket up even higher as if it were Kevlar.

"Oh, come on, Char," the vampire whined. "My left fang has barely grown back in from the last time!"

"Then I'd think you'd want to keep them intact."

"Yeah . . ." He glanced down at his feet, shuffling awkwardly.

"And what could you do that would mean you'd be back to gumming up blood smoothies?"

"Put my fangs on someone who didn't ask for it." The vampire gifted Rose a sheepish look. "Sorry . . . unless you're up for it?"

"That would be a no," Rose stated emphatically.

"Can't blame a vamp for hoping." With a small shrug, he turned away and joined a small group of vampires across the room.

Rose nearly laughed at the absurdity of it all. "Thanks for that," she addressed the bartender.

"So, so lost." Char shook her head, her lips twitching with a small smirk. "I can't tell if you're oblivious, foolish, or just damn brave to come out to a place like the Blood Moon on a super full moon night."

A super moon . . .

Well, crap. Definitely oblivious.

Shifters weren't any more dangerous on full moons than any other nights—ignore the Hollywood tales—but Supernaturals still blamed it on things they considered uncharacteristic behavior. It was basically an excuse to act like an idiot and cry *the full moon made me do it.*

Like following a broody veterinarian into an unfamiliar, Magic-cloaked part of the city, and getting chased into a Supernatural bar.

A few more patrons stopped to stare, and the closest—another vampire—slid a hungry stare over her neck. Her Magic reacted instinctively, humming beneath the surface as it sparked up from her palms.

A familiar warmth settled against her back just as Damian's hand clamped down on her arm. "Magic away, little witch. *Now,* or there will be more blood in the Blood Moon than what's on the sign."

"A friend of yours, D?" The bartender watched them curiously. "I know you've been a little MIA, but I thought even you'd remember not to—"

"Yeah, Charlotte. Sorry. I'll get her out of here."

The female shifter slipped Rose a wink. "Stick super close to

Damian, hon. We don't want anyone snatching you away for a little midnight snack."

"With me. Now." Damian steered her through the bar, his hand wrapped snugly around hers.

The deeper they went, the more glares they received. A few feet from the rear emergency exit, a Quall demon reached for her arm.

Damian whirled on him with a low, threatening growl. "Do it and lose your hand."

Rose blinked, startled at the gold flashing in his eyes . . . and did his face change? Morph? She blinked and whatever she thought she'd seen had disappeared, and the demon backed off, stumbling over himself to get away.

She was equal parts intrigued, turned on, and scared shitless.

"Stay close." Damian entwined their fingers and barreled through the back exit. The second the emergency door closed behind them, he spun toward her. "What the hell were you thinking coming here?"

"I'm allowed to speak now?"

His eyes, flickering between gray and gold, narrowed. "This isn't funny, Rose. The Supes who frequent the Blood Moon aren't big fans of witches . . . and you, little witch, had been seconds away from being the Head Witch in Charge."

When he put it that way her inner steam diminished. "It's not like I sought this place out. I followed you, and then I lost you, and then *I* was lost, and then these two . . . you know what? Never mind. It doesn't matter."

"You followed me? Why?"

"I didn't *follow* you."

"You just said you followed me. In those exact words." Damian shot her a disbelieving look.

She sighed. "So maybe it started with me following you, but only because I wanted to tell you about things picking up on the sanctuary's donation page. Bella and the pups are a hit. Tomorrow, I'll put up pony cams for Butternut and Squash, and maybe even Jasper."

"That's great." Damian's head swung left and right, looking around the dark alley.

He wasn't even paying attention.

"I get it. You're not a particularly excitable person, but could you at least manage a small tonal inflection? If you're up for the challenge, maybe even a softly cooed 'ooh.'"

He finally looked at her. "You want a pat on the back? Fine. Good job. *Ooh*. Now let's get you a ride home."

He tugged her away from where his motorcycle sat parked beneath the only working streetlamp. It was on the tip of her tongue to ask what the rush was when a large shadowy figure dropped in front of them, blocking their path.

Damian cursed, and with a sharp tug, dragged her behind him. "Do *not* move until I tell you."

"Why would I—" The shadow stepped into a streak of moonlight, and Rose's eyes transformed into dinner plates. "Sweet mother Goddess."

Bat-like wings stretched out from the broad-shouldered man's back, the apexes adorned with sharp, curved talons nearly as big and thick as her forearm. Locking his lizard-like gaze on Damian, the demon snarled to reveal ultra-long canines dripping with saliva.

The liquid hit the pavement and instantly sizzled.

Okay, definitely not regular saliva.

"Heard rumors you're searching for me, Hunter." The winged demon's deep voice hissed each *s*. "Well . . . here I am."

Damian shook his head. "Don't know where you heard that. The only thing I'm looking for is the meaning of life, and a maybe a urinal. And the name's not Hunter. You must be looking for someone else. Maybe he's inside."

Behind him, Rose rolled her eyes. He'd get them killed yet.

"It's definitely you." The demon sniffed, his nostrils flaring. "The stench of the Underworld's Scourge is impossible to miss."

You're not exactly bathing in essential body oils, my friend.

Both Damian and the winged demon-man stiffened.

Rose cursed. "Hurl a hex . . . Did I say that aloud?"

Damian sighed. "Yeah, little witch, you did. Run."

"What?"

He didn't have time to repeat himself before another winged demon dropped, and then a third. Unlike the original, they'd shed their humanoid façade and stood there in *all* their gray leather-skinned glory.

Damian whirled around, and gently pushed her. "Run! Now!"

The oh-shit look on his face moved her feet at a pace worthy of an Olympic sprinter. Halfway to the motorcycle, her hair whipped around her face and one of the winged demons dropped in front of them, cutting them off from their only escape.

"I didn't realize the meteorologist called for a heavy downpour of demons tonight," Rose quipped dryly.

Damian shot her a look.

"What?"

"You're joking? Now?"

"Normally, I shred paper and pop bubble wrap when I'm nervous, so unless you happen to have any packing material on your person, you'll have to deal with my nervous joking, doc." Her gaze flicked to the two demons behind them, and back. "Have any bright ideas on how to get out of this?"

"You're the one who seems loaded with them tonight. You tell me."

She narrowed her eyes at him. "Now who's joking . . ."

"Hell, babe. I'm not joking. I'm all for listening to any ideas right now."

✦ ✦ ✦

Magic filled the alley, bringing a not-so-subtle breeze that picked up Rose's hair and whipped it around her head. The witch looked like

a gorgeous force of nature, and the sight of her all badass and determined, with pink Magic swirls engulfing her hands, would've given
Damian an erection if he didn't fear for her life.

Hell, both of their lives . . . because dealing with one Gryndor
demon was bad enough. Three was damn near impossible. Brute
strength, skin nearly impenetrable when in their true forms, and
poison-tipped talons put them in a demon class all of their own.

The Run, Hide, & Hope for the Best Class.

He and Rose had already failed at running. They couldn't hide.
That left one option.

"You gentlemen should go about your evening." Rose sounded deceptively calm. "There's no need for this to get ugly."

"Oh, there's a need, witch." The first demon growled, and his entire body—which at first looked Norm despite the big black wings—
turned a stony gray.

"Please don't say it like that. Yes, I'm a witch. But said in that tone,
it's not exactly friendly sounding."

"Anyone who hangs around with the Scourge isn't a friend." He
shot his lizard-like eyes toward Damian.

Rose followed his gaze to Damian, and shrugged. "He may have
the personality of a soggy potato, but he's honestly not bad once you
get to know him. He grows on you. Like super fungus."

"Hey," Damian said in protest. He wasn't sure whether to be happy
she'd defended him or annoyed she seemed shocked by it. "Super
fungus? Really?"

"Would you have prefer I used super *E. coli*? I assure you, fungus
is the cuddlier of the two."

"It's obvious you're the one who doesn't know him, witch." Gryndor Number One chuckled as he stalked forward. "That hybrid
standing next to you is the Scourge of the Underworld. A vile
abomination. He's a damn *traitor*, no loyalty to his own kind nor to
his own sire."

Damian bristled, his hands balling into fists at his side at the mention of *sire*. "I hope to hell you're not insinuating I'm anything like you and your friends. And you better not be implying that my sperm donor deserves anything more than my complete disdain."

Rose swung her gaze from the demon to Damian, her confusion palpable. "What the hell is he talking about?"

Damian glared at the Gryndor. "If you hadn't torn through an entire wolf pack, injuring dozens of shifters before heading off and doing the same to one of the Maine covens, you wouldn't be on the Council's radar. There's no one to blame here except yourselves."

"Enough talking." The demon growled. "I'll rip both your spines from your bodies and use them as coatracks!"

Rose grimaced. "Can you wear coats with wings? Or do you get them specially tailored?"

Damian swallowed a chuckle just as all three demons lunged at once, two from the back and one from the front. Rose blasted a javelin of Magic at the one closest to them, but it ricocheted off his demon skin without the Supernatural breaking his stride, and nearly slammed into Damian's foot.

"Aim for the poison-tipped talons," Damian shouted. "It's their only vulnerable spot while in this form."

"Nothing like a needle in a haystack," Rose muttered, blasting off another shot, which went a little wide thanks to the demon's surprisingly quick speed.

Damian's own inner beast pushed to the surface, quickening his reflexes and sharpening his senses. If he let his demon completely free, things would get a hell of a lot worse, but his second self didn't seem to agree.

Damian grimaced through the pain of keeping himself in check as he met Demons Number Two and Three in a flurry of fists and wings until Rose's sharp yelp turned him toward her.

Her Gryndor advanced, his wings deflecting each magical bolt she threw his way until he whipped out a winged tip and raked it down her puffer jacket as if it were a heated knife through butter.

"Son of a witch's tit!" Rose cried, eyes glittering in the moonlight. "That was my favorite jacket!"

She unleashed another Magic-spear, this time hitting her mark. With a howl, the Gryndor jumped back, colliding with his friend, who collided with the third one. They collapsed like demon dominoes.

Now with the upper hand, Rose swirled her hands, molding her Magic into an oversized Magic-ball . . . and tossed it into the middle of their entwined bodies. The second the orb hit the three Gryndors it split apart, not only confining their arms and wings but rooting their feet to the asphalt.

The Gryndors growled and lashed out.

"Let us go, bitch." The first spit in Rose's general direction, but she didn't so much as flinch.

"Because you asked so nicely . . . *no*." She glanced at the fluff coming out of her torn jacket. "Damn it. I got this on sale, too. It was the last of its color."

Damian propped his hands on his knees, his chest heaving because damn, he was out of Hunting shape. "You could do that the whole damn time? That magical handcuff thing?"

"Demon wrangling wasn't exactly on the approved Prima-in-Training curriculum. I didn't know I could do it until I tried."

"What do we have here?" Julius stepped out from the alley. His gaze bounced from the demons to Rose, and then to Damian. "All three? I'm impressed. That's quite the haul-in even for a Hunter of your caliber. Especially one that's been out of the game for as long as you."

"You told me one, Jules. One Gryndor." He nodded to the three snarling demons. "Does that look like one?"

His brother didn't look the least bit apologetic. "That's what our reports led us to believe, but it doesn't appear as if it were a problem for you. Or should I say, for the two of you. You're quite the team."

At the glimmer in Julius's eyes, Damian growled. "Not happening. This was a onetime deal. From now on, do your dirty work yourself."

"Come now, brother. You have to admit that it felt good to let *him* out . . . just a little bit."

Slipping his hand around Rose's, Damian pushed his shoulder against Julius's on the way toward the motorcycle. "Make sure the money is in my account by morning . . . three times the original offer since your report was off."

At the bike, he handed Rose his spare helmet, and she paused before accepting it with a wary look.

He smirked. "Tell me you're not afraid to get on a bike after you faced three snarling Gryndor demons."

"All I had to do back there is trust in Magic, which has never once let me down. This requires trusting *you* not to splat us against a building or into another vehicle."

"No splatting involved. I promise." He held out a hand and helped guide her into position behind him. She stayed a few inches back, her ass hanging off the seat. "Scoot closer . . . and hold on."

With a little sigh, she hooked her fingers into the sides of his leather jacket and inched closer until the front of her body pressed intimately against his back, and damn if he didn't like it. He waited for her to tighten her hold, and when she didn't, he gently drew her arms around his waist.

Rose hissed, instantly tensing.

That's when he saw it.

Her pink puffer jacket wasn't the only thing shredded. Fuzzy stuffing stuck out from the tear in her coat, but it wasn't all white. Blood tainted the snow-like fabric.

He spewed off a string of curses. "We have to get back to the clinic and treat that cut."

"I won't grow bat wings, will I?" Rose joked.

He gunned the bike's engine. "Hold on, little witch."

"Damian?" Rose squeezed his waist, her voice raising. *"Will I?"*

"It'll be fine. We just need to get to the sanctuary, and you'll want to hold on a little tighter because we won't be following the speed limit."

Her questions ended on a small squeal as he tore out of the alley. Too worried about what would happen if they didn't treat that Gryndor cut ASAP, Damian no longer basked in the feeling of her body pressed tight against his.

Fucking Gryndors. Fucking Jules. Just . . . fuck.

Damian mentally kicked himself for dropping his guard. He'd only meant to scope out the Blood Moon in case he accepted Julius's offered Hunt job. He never anticipated Rose stumbling into the wrong place at the wrong time, much less the Gryndors crashing the party.

Clenching his jaw so tight his teeth ached, Damian let out a small sigh of relief when the sanctuary came into view. He parked and let Rose slide off the bike, the witch already clutching her arm tight to her chest. There was no way she wasn't in a fuck-ton of pain.

When he'd been twelve, he'd taken a talon to the shoulder during what his father had called "field training," and he'd nearly passed out cold. But Rose didn't let out so much as a whimper as she followed him upstairs to his apartment.

Once through the door, he tossed his keys onto a small side table. The place wasn't much, but it was home. An open loft, the kitchen blended into a cozy entertainment room that had a small couch and a single cushioned chair. His bed sat kitty-corner, angled by the window so that on his sleepless nights—which were most of them—he had a decent view of the moon and stars, something that didn't often happen in the city.

He caught Rose inspecting the area as he led the way to the bath-room. "It's not much, but it serves its purpose."

"I think it's great."

He cocked an eyebrow. "Really?"

"Yes, really. I took over Vi's studio when she moved into the brownstone with Linc, and it's not nearly as spacious as this . . . and I bet you don't have upstairs neighbors clog-dancing at two in the morning. And I'm not being sarcastic. They dance on Broadway."

"Clog-dancing? No. But heat isn't the only thing that rises. When one of the horses has stomach issues, there isn't enough Febreze on the planet to stop the stench from drifting up."

She wrinkled her nose, the gesture emphasizing a slight smattering of freckles over the bridge of her nose. "I don't know if you're joking or not."

"Maybe you should try and steal another horse or two and extend your community service sentence so you're around in the summer to find out." His lips twitched as he nodded toward the bathroom. "Have a seat and we'll make sure you don't sprout bat wings."

She did as he said, shrugging out of her jacket with a small grimace. "Where do you want me?"

Oh, he had a few preferences, but he played nice. "Up here."

Gripping her hips, he hoisted her onto the sink counter before pulling out his emergency med kit from the small wall vanity. He flipped open the latch and it sprung open, showcasing the treasure trove of Hunting essentials.

She watched him with blatant interest. "Done this before, have you?"

"Once upon a time, this was a daily occurrence." He laid out the necessary items. Gauze and antibiotic ointment. But this kit also had vials of antidotes, antivenoms, and even anti-thrall serums, which were necessities when Hunting Supernaturals gifted in Compulsion.

Like Damian's dear old dad. The bastard had thrived on getting his sons to do his every bidding, and even back then, Damian didn't much like being someone's puppet. When it had become obvious that there was no breaking Ezeil's influence by natural means—or talents—Damian resorted to black-market anti-thrall serum.

"This will sting like a bitch, but the cut needs cleaning before applying the salve." Damian extended his hand. "May I?"

"Go for it." She offered her arm.

He gently skated his fingers up the silky softness of her skin, tracing the outer rim of redness already setting. He wet the gauze in saline and held it above the gash. "You ready?"

She sucked in a breath and nodded. "Just do it."

He squeezed the first drop of antiseptic, and Rose flinched. Hell, so did he. But she held still as he continued cleaning her up.

"So"—Rose looked away from the gash—"are you going to explain what happened with your brother back there, or am I expected to act as if it didn't happen?"

"Gryndors happened . . . and yes."

"Yes what?"

He cleaned away the last of the dirt and grime and reached for the antivenom salve, his gaze shooting up to hers. "It would be best for everyone if you forgot anything you heard . . . or think you did."

"You're a Supernatural bounty hunter."

"Former . . . and I thought we agreed you'd forget about hearing that."

She snorted. "No, you directed, but luckily for you, I've never been so great at following orders. That Gryndor called you Scourge. For you to be graced with a nickname, you must have been pretty darn entrenched."

"You're really not grasping the idea of forgetting everything you heard, are you?"

"You're telling me *former* Hunters spend their free nights tracking hell demons into seedy Supernatural bars?" Her gaze flickered to where he worked on her arm. "Growing up as the Prima Apparent, I may have been secluded and deluded to some worldly things, but I'm the best at smelling a load of crap, and right now the stench is impossible to miss, and it's not coming from the horses downstairs."

He made quick work of the salve and gently taped a clean bandage over the wound. "How does that feel?"

She flexed her arm. "Like it didn't even happen . . . and like you're evading my question."

"Good. With the salve in place, it'll feel and look like it didn't even happen in a few hours."

"What would happen if you didn't have the salve?"

He smiled mischievously. "Be thankful I had some on hand."

"In your bounty hunter's first-aid kit."

He chuckled. "You won't let this go, will you?"

"I'm sorry, have we met?" She stuck out her good hand. "I'm Rose Maxwell, the Un-Letting-Goer of Things. At least according to my sisters."

Doing the smart thing meant helping her off the counter and walking away, but he couldn't move. Instead, he braced his hands on either side of her hips and dropped his gaze to her mouth . . . and damn if he didn't catch her doing the same thing.

He sighed. "I *used* to be a Hunter . . . in another lifetime."

She rolled her pretty eyes. "I pretty much figured that out, Captain Obvious. And I'm guessing you were pretty good at your job considering you had a nickname and all."

"I wasn't good."

"You weren't?"

He shook his head. "Nah. I was the best."

Rose smirked. "And oh so modest."

As he gave a faint shrug, his attention wandered back toward her mouth. "It's true."

"If you were so good at it, why don't you do it anymore?"

Any thought of kissing her at that moment was doused with that single question. Desire iced over, frozen so solid an ice pick couldn't chip it to freedom.

He found the strength to pull away and put the kit back in its spot. "Because I found my calling with animals."

Rose hopped off the counter. "If Vi's the Queen of Horrible Liars, you're definitely the King. I saw the smile on your face when those demons made the first move. Hell, until that moment, I didn't think you had the facial muscles to pull that off. You got a thrill from it. I did, too . . . once I was done being scared shitless."

"That's exactly the problem," Damian mumbled.

"What was the problem?" Rose asked.

Ignore her and take her home . . . that was what he *should* do. It was the smart thing, but she followed him into his apartment, and damn if he didn't like seeing her in his space, and that brought on a whole new onslaught of issues he in no way could unpack right then.

"Yeah, I get a thrill out of Hunting," Damian admitted. "But I'm not the only one who does. My inner demon likes it, too. Too damn much. He thrives on it. The chase. The violence that undoubtedly erupts, and not to mention the bloodshed. Every time I went on a Hunt, my demon side strengthened, overshadowing the human side."

Realization slowly dawned on her face, but even though she understood didn't mean she *got* it. He wouldn't expect her to.

Rose opened and closed her mouth.

He'd shocked her with the truth, and he'd stunned himself by telling her. The only other people who knew why he'd left Hunting were Miguel and Julius. It's how he preferred it. It's how he kept things uncomplicated.

"Want to know anything else?" Damian honed his inner jerk. "I'm an Aries. Thirty-four. My favorite color is black. And I'm addicted to anything with mint."

And his demon's sparkling personality was why he'd been cursed with his very first hex at the ripe ole age of sixteen . . . but he wasn't about to tell her that, too. He'd already told her more than he'd ever planned.

More than was smart.

"Doc." Rose looked at him with something akin to empathy . . . almost as if she knew he held back more.

"Don't look at me like that, little witch," Damian warned.

"Like what?"

"Like I'm something you need to fix." Unable to keep his distance, he stalked closer until he had to look down to hold her gaze. "I'm not a failing sanctuary about to go under. I'm a man . . . or at least partly. There's no *fixing* me."

Her eyes narrowed. "Was that supposed to scare me?"

"Only if I was lucky."

"You're not as intimidating as you'd like to think, Damian Adams. Yeah, you may have an inner demon, but we all do in some way."

"Does yours have the ability to coerce people into doing your bidding, too? Does it have a knack for spilling blood? Drink up the taste of fear as if it were cinnamon French toast? Because mine always lingers below the surface, waiting for his chance to do all those things. If you're not careful, he'll take you right along with him. Hell, it wouldn't be the first time he brought an innocent along for the ride."

Her gaze dipped to his mouth, her vivid caramel eyes twinkling with flecks of auburn gold. "Shouldn't that be my decision to make?"

Sexual tension blanketed the room until it was damn near difficult to breathe. Hers. His.

It was suddenly difficult to remember why he didn't do repeats. All he recalled was how he'd been unable to evict her from his mind since their one and only night together. Hell, it wasn't even a night. It was barely an hour in the back room of a bar during her sister's Bonding Announcement Party.

"I should take you home," Damian said, his voice gruff.

Neither of them moved.

"And if I don't want to?" Rose's fingers hooked his belt loops and eased him closer.

That's all it took for his remaining control to deteriorate. One step at a time, he backed her up until her shoulder blades met the wall. She peered at him through her thick lashes, her rosy mouth lifting into a satisfied smirk.

"You *should* want to, little witch," Damian announced, damn near purring. "If you knew what was good for you, you'd run fast and far, and wouldn't once look back."

"Didn't I mention that I'm on a hiatus from doing things I *should* do?" Rose asked, her voice breathless and sexy as hell. "Right now, I'm focusing on things I want to do . . . and right now, Damian Adams, I want to do *you*."

11

O-Donors

Did those words come out of her mouth? Under normal circumstances—and less than a few weeks ago—Rose never thought she'd hear those words uttered from her lips. Harper's? Definitely? But the former Prima Apparent who'd been trained to be prim, proper, and polite except when the need called for it?

Nope.

She wasn't the only one momentarily shocked by the admission. Damian's mouth dropped slightly before twitching into a crooked half-smirk. The sight of it was so rare it nearly set her panties on fire right there.

Lust lightened his eyes, but with it was a heavy dose of wariness. "Rose, I—"

"Let me spare you the monologue and give one of my own." She cut him off. "I'm not looking for a relationship. I'd like to stay far away from one as Supernaturally possible, which means whatever happens here would only be no-strings fun."

His fingers slid around her waist, playing with the band of exposed skin just above her jeans. "Are you making fun of me?"

"No, I'm stating facts. *I* don't want a relationship. Tried that. Failed miserably. And nearly magically shackled myself to a narcissistic psychopath for *eternity*. I clearly can't be trusted to choose an appropriate life partner." Rose sighed. "And as for the no-strings fun? It's been a *really* long time since I've had pleasurable sex that didn't involve rechargeable batteries."

Damian chuckled. "I'll try not to take offense."

She grinned as she abandoned his belt loops to run her palms over the soft cotton of his shirt. "That time with you—while extremely entertaining—only lasted about what? Five minutes?"

"It was a bit longer than that," Damian grumbled, his affront making her chuckle.

"My point is that I need fun in my life, doc. Naked, orgasmic fun with a living, breathing person. And I'd very much like you to be the O-donor if you're up for it."

Cupping her cheek, Damian tilted her face toward his as he leaned in, stopping with their mouths less than an inch apart. "The smart thing to do would be to take you home before anything happens."

"Probably." She brushed her lips over his as she spoke. "But I hope you take me to that comfortable-looking bed instead. Or right here against the wall. Right now, I'm not too particular as long as it involves you taking me. Did I mention it's been a while?"

Damian cursed right before taking Rose's mouth in a scorchingly hot kiss that instantly melted her insides.

Like, *not a high enough SPF factor in the world* type of scorch.

Gently fisting his hand in her hair, he held her mouth to his as if she'd even think about pulling away. Not even. And to let him know, everything he gave to her, she gave right back, shoving his shirt up with her free hand in her quest for skin-on-skin contact.

They pulled apart long enough to rip the offending shirt over his head, and then hers. Next to go were her jeans, leaving her standing there in a lacy thong and a see-through balconette bra.

Thank you, Harper Jacobs . . .

Damian leaned back, drinking in the sight of her, and groaned before taking a cloth-covered nipple into his mouth.

Panting with need, Rose unzipped his pants and instantly came into contact with the hot, hard length of his cock. She stroked him, feeling heady on power when he sucked in a sharp breath. "You go commando, doc? I didn't pin you as the type."

"It's been a while since I've had a laundry day." He gave her a coy smirk. "And now I'm really glad I waited to do it."

She chuckled. "Me, too. But I feel like we're still both pretty overdressed."

"Maybe we should do something about that."

They worked in tandem to push his jeans down and off. The second he chucked them away, he reached up and cupped her breasts.

"Enough foreplay," Rose panted, dropping her voice into what she hoped was a sexy purr. "Let's get on with the main event."

"Don't mind if I do." With a sharp yank, he snapped her bra, her breasts instantly spilling free. Next to go was her thong. And then palming her rear end, Damian guided her legs around his waist. The friction of his erection against her clit pulled groans from both their throats.

"Fuck . . ." Damian sent a longing look to his jeans a few feet away. "Condom."

"Spell." Rose's fingers dug into his shoulders as she arched her body even closer, locking her legs tighter around him. "Magical protection. I'm good for another six months."

He arched an eyebrow. "There's a spell for that?"

"There's a spell for everything." Rose dragged Damian's mouth back to hers. "Now prove to me I don't need something with batteries."

"Definitely don't need batteries . . ." Damian slowly slid his thickness through her dampness. With a slight pause at her entrance, he rubbed the head of his cock against her clit . . . once . . . twice.

"Damian . . . please, fuck me."

"With pleasure." With a low growl and one more glide through her folds, Damian slammed into her with one deliciously hard thrust.

The force pushed her body up the wall, and she cried out, savoring the stretch. Larger than she remembered, he filled every inch of her as their bodies moved in sync, each breath stumbling into another until they couldn't go any harder while standing up.

Rose squirmed closer, practically mewling.

"What do you need, little witch?" Damian slid his mouth against the curve of her neck, kissing and nipping his way along her sensitive flesh as he pounded into her. He cupped a breast and rubbed her pebbled nipple with his thumb, making it even harder. "Tell me what you need and I'd be more than happy to give it to you."

"More." Arching her body closer to his, she speared her fingers into his hair. "I need more . . . of everything."

"Hold on to me," he ordered gruffly.

Her hands dug into his shoulders as he walked them to the bed, dropping them both heavily onto the mattress before slowly transferring her legs from his hips to his shoulders. His callus-roughened touch brought goose bumps to her flesh, and the change in angle had her sucking in an excited breath.

Damian's questioning gaze soaked in the sight of her as he hovered above. "Ready?"

She nodded. "Don't make me wait."

He gently stroked her thighs one more time, gripped her just below her ass, and both lifted and plunged into her in one hard, delicious thrust. The sharp, deeper angle rolled her eyes back into her head from the sheer level of pleasure.

"Holy hell, little witch." He pulled out and sank in again, somehow going even deeper.

She fisted the bedsheets in a vain attempt to keep herself anchored. "Don't stop. Don't you dare . . ."

"Like that's even an option."

One thrust after another, it didn't take them long to set a brutally delicious pace, the bed frame smacking against the wall. *Thump. Thump. Thump.*

Their last time together had been quick and fast, not to mention nearly fully clothed. Seeing Damian's body hovering over her, rippling with muscle as he slammed into her again and again, sweat dripping off their bodies, took her to heights she'd never thought possible.

The man was the epitome of gorgeous, his tattoos moving fluidly like moving artwork.

And his eyes . . .

He never took them off her, their stormy gray depths darkening until they almost twinkled like a starry night's sky alight with golden stars. Rose couldn't look away. Hell, she could barely breathe.

All she saw was Damian. All she heard was the thunderous pounding of her heart, and that little voice in her head questioning her ability to have no-strings sexual fun.

Slipping his hands between her legs, Damian stroked her aching clit with a groan. "Come with me."

One caress.

A second.

Third time's the charm.

Her body erupted in a wave of pleasure, wrapping tightly around Damian's cock. He let out a husky release-filled groan of his own as his pace gradually slowed into gentler, uncoordinated movements. By the time he dropped onto the bed next to her, they were both sweaty and exhausted, and sounded as if they'd just participated in a triathlon.

Heck, her muscles felt as if she had, too, deliciously weak and just a smidge bit sore.

Entwining their legs in a jigsaw formation, he pulled her flush against his side. "See? No batteries required."

Rose giggled breathlessly and sank into his embrace. She couldn't have moved even if she'd wanted, which she didn't.

No-strings sexual fun, she reminded herself.

People did it all the time.

Yet she couldn't help feeling as if she'd become the star attraction in her very own live-action marionette show.

✦ ✦ ✦

For the first time in a damn long time, Damian slept through the night. At least if you considered 3 to 6 A.M. the night . . . because after a very brief nap, he and Rose had woken up recharged and ready for round two.

And three.

He couldn't wipe the smirk off his face as he replayed the night over and over in his head like his own personal porn show, too satisfied to care it shouldn't have happened. Even now, as he glanced at her, asleep in his bed, the sheets entwined around her naked body, he contemplated waking her for a fourth round.

She was the first woman he'd ever brought into his private space. The first to sleep in his bed, and to lure him into sleep right next to her. Never get fully naked. Get out fast. That had always been his usual MO . . . until her. Things with the sexy witch never went according to plan. It should worry the hell out of him, but the man and demon in him felt too damn good to give a crap.

He polished off the last of his coffee before brewing a second pot so Rose had fresh fuel when she woke up, and then headed to the bathroom for a quick shower. Realizing he'd forgotten his clothes, he turned and nearly collided with a gorgeous—and fully dressed—Rose.

His hand shot out, banding around her waist to prevent her from flying back.

"Sneaking out?" he teased. "Just so you know, the third step on the stairs has a squeak loud enough to be heard at Jones Beach."

Her cheeks flushed. "I wasn't sneaking."

He gestured to the shoes clutched tightly in her hand and the guilty look on her face. "Could've fooled me, babe."

"I heard the shower water running and I thought—"

"You'd make a quick break for it and avoid a Walk of Shame moment."

"Yes. I mean, no." She sighed, throwing him a glare. "I'm not ashamed of what happened. We're two consenting adults who had consensual sex and an underlying agreement without any hidden caveats or small print."

He leaned against the wall, smirking. "Are we talking about a prenup or the fantastic sex-fest from last night?"

"The sex-fest."

"If you're not sneaking out then why are you tiptoeing out of here like you're making away with my most prized possessions?"

"Because I wanted to avoid the awkwardness of a morning-after conversation. And that's not the same as a Walk of Shame," she added sternly. "I didn't want you feeling as though you owed me morning coffee or breakfast in bed just because we snuggled."

"Ah. Well, there's fresh coffee brewing for you right now—to make sure you get your three-cup morning quota—and as for breakfast, help yourself to whatever is in the fridge. I had actually planned to make some omelets or something, but for some reason, I woke up late and the animals aren't as forgiving about not having breakfast."

She blinked, studying him with her gorgeous caramel-brown eyes. "You were going to make me breakfast?"

He shrugged, self-consciously running a hand through his hair. "It's not a big deal. I eat, too . . . normally. But not this morning because—"

"Animals. Yeah." She bit the corner of her lip as she reluctantly met his gaze. "So . . . about last night . . ."

He waited. "About that . . ."

She waited.

He waited longer, failing to withhold a knowing grin.

When he made no move to finish his thought, either, she sighed. "You're making me say it, aren't you?"

"Honestly, I don't know what the hell is going through your head, but I'd really like to."

She rolled her eyes, obviously annoyed. "Last night was good."

He cocked a questioning eyebrow.

"Okay, it was great." She altered her sentiment. "Mr. Wiggles has nothing on you . . . the way you moved your mouth when you . . ." She blushed, clearing her throat. "Anyway, I don't see why this can't be a regular, or even a semi-regular thing."

All words flew right out of Damian's head because of everything he'd expected her to say, that was at the bottom of the list. "You already want a repeat performance, little witch?"

"We've both established that relationships aren't in our future, right? It's a logical compromise. You're more than welcome to troll the city for your next conquest if that's what you want to do," she added after his silence, "but I figured I'd offer up a different arrangement."

"A fuck-buddy arrangement." He rolled her proposal around in his head, digesting her words. "That's what you're suggesting, right?"

"That sounds a little crass."

He smirked, unable to hide his interest. "You want a sexual relationship and only a sexual one . . . to call one another in the middle of the night for late-night sex-snacks. That would be a fuck buddy, babe."

He'd never once considered having that kind of arrangement with anyone.

He pushed off the wall and slowly advanced until she bumped against the closed bathroom door, steam from the now-hot water slipping out through the cracks.

Her gaze flickered from his eyes to his mouth to his eyes, her heart beating so fast he could see its flutter at the base of her throat. "Then that's what I'm proposing. What do you say? Are you in?"

He should be *so* out, every one of his internal alarms—the ones that had kept him alive through years of Hunting—blaring like a damn tornado siren in his head.

"I say yes," Damian heard himself answer, "but with one caveat."

"Let me guess . . . no emotions involved? Pretty sure that's the definition of an FBA."

"That, too, but I should warn you that shifters aren't the only Supernaturals who are territorial with their Mates . . . or their toys."

Her eyes narrowed into slits as Magic surged beneath her skin. "Did you call me a *toy*?"

His lips twitched. "I just meant I don't share well. You and me. That's it."

"Doesn't that defeat the purpose of no strings? If there aren't emotions involved, what does it matter if we continue to keep ourselves open to see other people?"

He brushed his nose against the curve of her neck as he spoke. "It matters because when I'm fucking you, I better be the only one you're thinking about."

She swallowed audibly. "Oh. That . . . shouldn't be a problem. I can barely manage one grumpy demon veterinarian in my life. I can't imagine throwing another person into the mix. But if either of us gets into the position where they don't want to follow that caveat anymore, we notify the other person. Sound fair?"

"Makes sense."

"Then we have a deal . . ." She stuck out her hand.

He ignored it and brushed a soft, slow kiss along her lips and across her jaw. "We have a deal."

Her breathing hitched. "So I guess I'll be seeing you around . . ."

He forced himself to take a step back, reminding himself about the cranky animals waiting for him downstairs. "We'll most definitely be seeing each other around."

He saw her downstairs to where the Ryde she'd evidently ordered already sat waiting to take her home despite his protests. Just as she was about to climb into the sedan, Miguel and Terrance showed, the two men watching knowingly.

"Uh . . . hi . . . and bye. See you guys later." Rose's cheeks flushed bright red as she waved and disappeared into the car.

With a humorous grin on his face, Damian watched the Ryde car disappear down the lane, and turned to face two distinctly different expressions.

Terrance waggled his eyebrows like a comic book character, giving him a thumbs-up, while Miguel's neutral expression slowly turned into a frown. The teen snuck a wary look at the older man and quickly disappeared into the barn, muttering about stall-mucking.

Damian tucked his hands into his jeans. "You have something to say, old man?"

"I have plenty to say. Just figuring out which I should say first. Are you sure you know what the hell you're doing, son?"

"I thought you liked Rose."

"I do . . . a whole hell of a lot . . . but you know what I mean, Ian. She's not some faceless woman you picked up at the bar. She's working here—at least temporarily—and she's the sister of your best friend's Mate. If things go bad, it'll not only bring a lot of drama, but hurt feelings and worse."

The hex.

Miguel was one of a select few who knew about it, the path he'd been on to earn it, and the fallout that came afterward. As hard as he'd fought to get the damn thing removed, it did come with a small benefit. It woke his demon ass up, or more accurately, put the bastard into a deep sleep.

Damian hadn't realized what was on the line until he'd pissed off his ex by not performing what she'd called The Big Gesture. To this day, he still didn't understand, and he wasn't so sure that he ever would.

"Ian." Miguel's worried voice pulled him away from his thoughts. "You know you're walking a fine line here, right?"

"I have no intention of hurting Rose. And," Damian added when his mentor's mouth opened to interject, "there also won't be any falling in love. With *anyone*. But especially not with Rose Maxwell."

"Intentions don't mean squat when it comes to matters of the heart. You say that now, and you may even believe it, but when love comes around it doesn't give a damn if you never planned for it to happen. Trust me. I know. Pretty much those exact words left my lips when Marisol and I started things up."

He clapped the older man on the shoulder. "I got it covered, Miguel."

"You're that sure of yourself?"

"So sure I'd bet my soul on it," Damian joked dryly.

Because technically, he was.

12

All's Fair in F*cking & Orgasms

If you know what's good for you, head back to the city.
Do it now. Save yourself.

—Olive

Reading her sister's text, Rose cringed. Any hope she'd had for a
drama-free family dinner went up in smoke with each emoji. It was
too late to run now because she'd just pulled up to her childhood
home, and if the curtain movement was any indication, her mother
already knew she'd arrived.

Half the town probably knew because there wasn't much to do
in Athens if you weren't keeping track of your neighbors' comings
and goings. With a higher-than-average Supernatural population,
the quaint little village nestled alongside the Hudson about an hour
outside of the city was where they'd grown up.

It's where Vi had plotted revenge on a surly teenage Lincoln
and where, thanks to Grandma Edie's extensive library, Olive fell
in love with books. It's also where Rose learned to smile, play nice,
and that there was no higher duty than the one you served to your
family.

It was pretty accurate to say that she had a love-hate relationship with going back home, and Olive's text didn't give her much hope for this visit being one of the lovey ones.

If she were any less of a sister, she'd escape before the front door opened, but that wasn't her. They'd shared a womb for nearly eight months. No way was she letting Olly deal with their mother without backup.

Rose's phone dinged.

If you don't listen, at least come around back. You can thank me later.
—O

With a thumbs-up response sent back, she walked around the wraparound porch to the side gate and followed the stone path toward the rear of the house. Voices murmured from inside the kitchen, and Rose slowly crept up the back steps, silently cursing when the motion detector went off, basking her and the entire backyard in a blinding white light.

The back door flung open, and Olive shook her head, hand propped on her curvy hip. She pulled Rose inside and into a hug. "And here I thought you had more survival instinct than this. Don't say I didn't warn you."

"It can't be that bad, can it?" Rose greeted Edie with a kiss on the cheek, and when her grandma grimaced, she cursed. "It's that bad?"

Olive lifted a dark blond eyebrow. "Have you met our mother?"

"Yeah, but I actually thought she was mellowing a bit. She called the other day, and didn't once sigh, groan, or try and set me up with someone."

Olive looked at her as if she'd sprouted a second head, and she couldn't believe the words left her mouth, either, but they were true. When Rose had been engaged to Valentin, Christina had overseen *every* detail of the Bonding Ceremony. From flowers to linen, to what detergent brand the linen was washed in.

Rose hadn't picked a damn thing. Not even her dress.

But Vi's Bonding to Lincoln? Their mother had taken a surprisingly backseat role. Oh, there'd definitely been a multitude of grimaces and a few eye rolls, but for the most part, the ceremony and the other activities had all been Vi's and Linc's choices.

Progress . . .

But Olive's fervent head-shaking told Rose her triplet didn't think so. "I think she orchestrated this thing during Vi and Linc's escape on purpose because she didn't want us to have extra backup."

Rose swallowed a laugh. "Escape? You mean on their *honeymoon*?"

"Whatever. I'm just glad I don't have to deal with Mom alone." She glanced to Edie. "Not that you're not a great ally, Gran."

Edie chuckled. "Oh, I know very well how it goes, my dear. When my brother, sister, and I were your age, we felt the same way. There's no better backup than Magical Triad backup."

Rose studied her sister. Curiousness gave way to concern as she registered the dimness in Olive's usually sparkling blue eyes, and beneath them, the dark circles.

"Are you okay, Olly?" Rose asked. Her sister looked the degree of tired that sent people to bed for weeks. "Are you good?"

"Define good." Olly gifted her a tired smile. "I'm kidding. Everything's fine. Roommate woes are a little more woeful as of late, but it'll get better. At least that's what Gina assured me. Again."

Rose waited for elaboration, and when it didn't come . . . "I'll need more information than that. You look like you'll be face-planting in your plate by the time dessert comes out."

"If it's a chocolate raspberry tart thing that wouldn't be so horrible."

Rose shot her sister a look, making Olive sigh.

"Fine. Instead of working a normal, real-world job, Gina decided to peddle potions and herbs from our living room. At all hours of the night. The second I convince myself to fall asleep, the damn apartment buzzer goes off."

"I'm sorry."

Olly gave her a skeptical look. "I thought for sure you'd say *I told you so* for going to the *Witch's Cauldron* to find a roommate."

"Did you really think I'd do that?"

Olive shrugged, smirking. "Yeah. Because if the roles were reversed, I know I'd be doing some mega gloating right now."

"No gloating here. Besides, it wouldn't land the same way when you're so sleep deprived you could double as the Crypt Keeper."

"Bwitch!" Olive laughed, smacking her arm.

Rose turned to her quietly smiling grandmother. "So, I know why Olive's back here hiding, but why are you?"

Olive snortled, obviously knowing something she didn't. "Oh, you're going to love this . . ."

Edie frowned. "You'd best watch your tongue, young lady."

"Oh, come on, Gran. Admit it. It's a little bit funny."

"There's not even a speck of humor anywhere in this entire ridiculous situation."

Rose bounced her attention between the two witches. "Someone needs to shed some light on this because the suspense is killing me."

Olive giggled. "Mom invited a couple special friends to join us for dinner."

"Friends? Who?"

Edie bristled, finally snapping. "That damn Lionel the Lion from the bakery."

Rose snuck a glance to an amused Olive. "Mr. Gingham? Why?"

They'd known the shifter for nearly their entire lives, the nice man having baked each of the triplets' birthday cakes since their very first one. Hardworking with an easygoing smile, he had a habit of putting everyone at ease who stepped into his shop, and he'd been their grandpa Jethro's best friend.

But as a local baker, he wasn't Christina Maxwell's usual choice for a dinner guest. That honor normally went to dignitaries and celebrities, or anyone up and coming in Supernatural society.

Rose glanced from Edie to Olive and back, and when Edie clamped her mouth shut, refusing to dish any more details, Olive gave her up. "Mom's setting Gran up with Mr. Gingham. Like a set *up* setup."

Edie grumbled, breaking her silence. "As if I'd ever give that old fool the pleasure of my company much less access to everything under this classic hood."

Rose choked on her own spit while Olly broke out in tear-inducing laughs.

"It's outrageous," Edie continued. "I'd been blessed with my soul mate for sixty-seven glorious years until he passed to the other side, and your mother thinks I'd settle for someone who loves talking about different yeast breeds nearly as much as he does himself?"

Olive was first to rein in her laughter. "But weren't you and Grandpa Jethro friends with Mr. Gingham back in the day?"

"Which is how I know he's nothing but a pompous windbag beneath that charming shifter smile." (

Rose brushed away the laughing tears from her eyes, thankful she used waterproof mascara.

"I don't know what you're laughing about, young lady." Edie shot her a coy grin. "Your mama invited a special someone for you, too."

Rose's laughter died immediately. "Wait, what?"

"Why don't we swap? It's always been on the bucket list to call myself a jaguar."

Olive bit her lip, snorting. "I think you mean cougar, Gran."

"I know what I meant, sweetheart. I'm much more of a jaguar than a cougar."

Rose prayed she'd heard wrong. "Christina invited someone here for *me*?"

Edie gently pushed the swinging door open wide enough to see Mr. Gingham in deep talks—about sourdough bread—with their broad-shouldered mountain lion father, and a very immaculately dressed third man.

A familiar well-dressed man.

Cursing vividly, Rose pulled back into the safety of the kitchen. "*Julius Kontos?!* Why the hell would Christina invite the demon Councilman here?"

"Guess she's hoping to get you as adjacently close to the Supernatural Council as possible," Olive answered. "Mom's never without a brewing plan. You know that."

"That will never happen in a million years . . . not me and Julius, and not me having anything to do with the Council." She slid an apologetic look to her grandmother. "No offense, Gran."

"None taken, sweetheart. But I must ask . . . why not entertain the idea of the handsome demon? He's obviously easy on the eyes, and that smile . . ." Edie flicked her eyes skyward. "Sorry, my love. You'll always be in my heart."

"Are you both forgetting the last time I dated?"

Edie dismissed her. "In the words of your sister Violet, Valentin was an opportunist jerk-turd. I've never known Julius to be anything but fair, and a solid addition to the Council. And you have to admit the man's beautiful. If I were a few years younger, your grandfather would have to forgive me on our afterlife reunion. That boy's definitely on my Free Pass List."

Rose scrunched her nose. "Please don't say things like that. Ever."

Mischief danced in Olive's eyes as she pushed her glasses higher onto her nose. "Unless my triplet sonar is on the fritz, I think Rose's refusal of the handsome Councilman has more to do with her interest in someone else than her lack of interest in Julius Kontos. Tell Christina you're seeing someone who's made your skin glow. It might get her to back down. I doubt it, but it's worth a shot."

Rose glanced at her reflection in the window.

Damn it. Her skin *did* glow, but nothing short of divine intervention—or an industrial-sized spell—would get Christina Maxwell to back down on something she'd already set in motion.

"Let me see what's keeping the others," Rose's mother's voice echoed from the other side of the swinging door.

Christina stepped into the kitchen, her gaze taking in their three guilty expressions. "What in Goddess's name are you all doing in here?"

"Hiding?" Olive joked.

Christina's mouth pressed into a tight line. "And here I thought with Violet on her honeymoon, sarcasm would be on the light side tonight."

"Sorry to disappoint."

Rose smirked. She wasn't sure what had gotten into her younger sister other than not sleeping, but it was damn amusing . . . until her mother's attention fell on her.

She gulped. "I stopped by to say I can't stay. Work emergency. Very important."

Rose cringed at the lameness of her excuse. So did Olive, the youngest triplet turning sideways to stifle a smile.

Her mother didn't buy it in the least. "You drove over an hour to say you couldn't stay because of a work emergency? Leave someone stranded in the Bronx without a ride home?"

"I don't drive for Ryde anymore. There was too much . . . traffic." Rose mentally rolled her eyes at herself. "I took over Vi's old job. At Potion's."

Christina stared, waiting for the punch line that never came.

Rose expected a lecture. Her mother was famous for them, often bragging about the Maxwell name and duty and responsibility. Instead, she pinched the bridge of her nose and sighed. "You girls are the reason I upped my migraine medication dosage. At this rate, I'll never have grandchildren to hold and spoil."

Rose and Olive exchanged looks.

"Didn't you once refer to the kids at Vi's community center as vectors of bacteria and bad manners?" Rose asked.

Christina's crestfallen look turned to exasperation. "That's *other* people's grandchildren. Not mine. Why do you look so surprised? Surely I've mentioned that I'd love to become a grandmother while

I'm young enough to chase after them. Of course, they cannot call me *grandma*. Mimi is a viable option."

Rose shook her head. "Not once."

Olive agreed. "Never mentioned it."

Christina rolled her eyes. "Then you weren't listening."

Rose didn't want to startle the pod person currently inhabiting her mother, so she treaded carefully. "Well, I hate to be the bearer of bad news, but Vi's hands are pretty full with a new Mate and learning to become Prima, and Olly—"

"Kills all plants that come into my possession. Unless they're fake. I can keep those alive at least fifty percent of the time," Olly quickly interjected.

"And I'm barely keeping my own head above water," Rose added.

"That's why I invited Julius Kontos tonight." Christina hooked her arm through Rose's, dragging her through the door into the dining room. "A demon like him would have no problem keeping your head above water for you. I hear he was a lifeguard when he was younger."

. . . and in the blink of an eye, the old Christina returned.

Was it too late to fake appendicitis?

Three heads swiveled their way as her mother made needless introductions around the room before plotting out seating arrangements. Much to her mother's ire, Edie vetoed her seat next to Mr. Gingham and sat, instead, between Olive and Rose. Unfortunately, that put Julius on Rose's other side, the Councilman—aka Damian's brother—pulling her seat out for her.

He chuckled, leaning closer. "I'll try not to take it personally that you're not eager to have my babies, Miss Maxwell."

Rose paled. "Excuse me?"

He tapped his ear.

"Sweet mother Goddess. You demons and your super hearing."

"And smell." He took a discreet sniff, smirking. "How did you find my dear brother this morning? In good spirits, I hope?"

She caught her mouth from dropping to the floor, but barely. "I'm not sure if I should be impressed or disgusted."

"Maybe a bit of both." Julius sipped his water. "But have no fear, Rose. While I'm perfectly aware of your mother's intentions for this evening, it's not why I accepted the invite."

"It's not?"

"No."

"Then why did you? In case you forgot, my sister will be the one with the voting power on the Council. You can try and butter me up for votes, but it won't do you any good. And if you think I can somehow sway Damian into talking to you, you're severely overestimating my influence over him."

"While that's an intriguing idea, that's not why I'm here, either."

"Then why are you here?"

Smirking, he leaned closer. "I'm here to offer you a job, Miss Maxwell."

"I have a job."

"That's right. That kitschy little bar run by the vampire. That's not a job . . . that's an amusement with which to pass the time. I have an offer that's more aligned with your specific talents . . . talents that are wasted working at a magical-themed tourist trap."

"And my talents are more aligned to do what?"

Lines crinkled around his eyes as his grin widened. "Have you ever given a thought to bounty hunting?"

She waited for the punch line, and when it didn't come, she chuckled. "You're not serious."

"And why not?" he challenged.

She glanced around the table, making sure no one was focused on their conversation. Luckily her mother was preoccupied talking to Mr. Gingham about her parents' newest labor of love, Supernatural Spirits Winery, which they were about to open a few miles outside of town.

Rose dropped her voice. "Because I can't even say that I barely made it out of that Gryndor situation without a scratch, because I *was* scratched. The only reason I'm not sporting my very own pair of bat wings is because of Damian's stinky salve."

His gaze flickered to her arm. "You hardly struck me as the type to give up on something after one unfortunate incident. But I suppose my brother's wariness was expected to rub off on you sooner or later. I had hoped to intervene before it did."

Rose's defenses lifted, but not for herself. "I don't think it's fair of you to dismiss Damian for doing what's best for himself. If he doesn't enjoy the Hunt, he shouldn't do it."

Julius's brow rose. "He told you why he gave it up? Maybe there's hope for my little brother after all. I'm not sure he's divulged that to anyone outside of his one-person immediate circle."

The thought that Damian had shared something important with her sent her insides into an unexpected tingle.

"Next, you'll knock me off this chair by informing me you know of the hex."

Rose's gaze lifted to Julius's. "The hex?"

"The one placed on him by a witchy ex-girlfriend."

Rose stared blankly, not knowing what to say.

"The threat of losing his soul—and his humanity—upon finding love only compounded his decision to leave Hunting behind. My badass, bounty-seeking brother gave up something at which he excelled to live a life that's a lie." Julius smiled wanly. "I'd hate for that to happen to you, too, Rose. I've *never* seen anyone incapacitate three upper-level demons as quickly and efficiently as you did the Gryndors, and I've witnessed a lot of takedowns through the years. Tell me you'll at least think about my offer."

Rose didn't know what to think . . . about the unexpected job offer or about Damian.

He'd been hexed? By a witch? And not with a case of shifter-fleas or a pimple that wouldn't give up despite prescription meds. Someone hexed him so hard it put his freaking soul in jeopardy?

That was *The Craft*–type Magic, and it gave witches a bad name.

✦ ✦ ✦

There were a million things to do and a fence to repair and yet Damian couldn't tear his gaze away from the back of the barn, where Rose excitedly groomed Butternut while standing in front of a small tripod setup and talking to the camera that she and Terrance had dragged everywhere during their daily routine.

Mucking out stalls?

Video.

Filling the feed troughs?

Video.

He didn't know what people found so fascinating about deworming puppies, but they'd even watched him do that earlier that morning, asking him a million questions about canine health. When you saw the cruelty people inflicted on animals daily, it was nice to know there were those out there who desired the opposite.

And thanks to accumulating donations, in addition to the money from the Gryndor debacle, Damian had made an early run to the supply store to pick up much-needed meds and fencing supplies, along with other odds and ends necessary to turn the sanctuary into a hazard-free zone. Especially the far barn closer to Miguel's place that lay empty, too run-down to be of much use in the condition it was in now.

It was a single check off on a massive to-do list, but when you'd been unable to check off anything for months due to insufficient funds, that one check was a like a damn badge of victory. Even he couldn't help but think it was turning out to be a pretty good day.

"Oh, my Goddess." Rose's sexy rasp had him looking up from where he pounded a new fence post into the ground. "Did I see a smile? Was Damian Adams smiling, or did I get hay in my eye again?"

"No, but you have it in your hair. Come here." Grinning wider, he tugged off his gloves and plucked the stray hay strand from her ponytail, letting his fingers linger over her cheeks.

"I'm sure that's the least disgusting thing on my body right now." Rose glanced at her dirty jeans and mud-covered boots.

He couldn't help but look her over, too, and hell . . .

Instantly semi-hard, his erection pushed against his zipper. Days had passed since the night at his place, and while he'd had reservations about a sexual relationship before, he couldn't find one now.

Evidently, she couldn't, either.

Her caramel eyes shot him a lusty look. "You shouldn't look at me like that with people around, doc. It's not exactly on the down-low."

He shot a glance to where Miguel and Terrance led the horses back to their stalls, oblivious to them a hundred or more yards away. "They're too far away to see anything."

But he wasn't one to take chances . . . at least not anymore.

Linking their fingers, he dragged her to the front hood of the truck, so the massive machine blocked their view, and pushed her against the cool metal. He swallowed her breathless gasp with a searing kiss, and then she tugged his body closer until the edge of his erection pushed against her stomach.

She smirked. "It can't be easy pounding posts into the ground when you have that happening behind the scenes."

"You have no idea how hard it is." With one hand on her hip, he tugged her leg around his waist with the other, changing the angle until they aligned perfectly.

She giggled, running her hands down his chest until she slipped them beneath his shirt. "Oh, I think I do. As you pointed out once before, I'm a fixer. I like to fix things, and I'd very much like to help you with that little problem."

He tucked his mouth into the curve of her neck, lips brushing over her ear. "Is that so, little witch?"

"I wouldn't have said it if I didn't mean it."

His chuckle turned into a groan as she rolled her hips against his throbbing hard-on.

Miguel's and Terrance's voices echoed from across the court, making Damian all too aware where they were. With a heavy, horny sigh, he very reluctantly disengaged his mouth from her body. "As much as I want to take you right here and now, I'm not in the mood for an audience."

"That means that sometimes you are?" she teased.

He winked, enjoying the way her blush crept from her cheeks and down her neck. "The longer we continue this fuck-buddy program of yours, the more I'm sure we'll learn about each other's little quirks and turn-ons. And I have to admit, I really can't wait to discover yours."

Her eyes darted nervously away from his, breaking contact.

"Hey." Catching her chin, he gently eased her attention back to him. "What did I say that sent you running away just now? I was kidding about the audience thing . . . for the most part."

"I'm not running. I'm standing in the same spot."

He frowned. "Rose . . ."

She sighed, looking pained. "I don't *know* what things turn me on . . . other than a select few."

"What the hell are you talking about?"

"I may have given you the wrong idea about my sexual dance card with my whole *fuck me now* spiel." Rose nibbled her bottom lip before he saved it with a gentle brush of his thumb. "My experiences could be called lackluster at best. Monotonous at worst. Present orgasm-donor excluded, of course."

He considered his words carefully, and not like he wanted details, but . . . "Your ex . . ."

"Was a narcissist in every way and in every context imaginable. Mr. Wiggles has been my best friend ever since I lost my virginity to David Hahn."

Damian's anger dragged his inner demon closer to the surface.

With a firm tug, he pulled her snugly into his raging hard-on. "Well, I can guaran-damn-tee that the only reason you'll be using Mr. Wiggles while you're with me is if we want to bring him out of your drawer for a little experimenting. It's now my personal mission to make you come at least twice before I even think about getting my own rocks off . . . and that'll happen with your third."

Her eyebrows lifted, as did her smirking mouth. "Three times? That's ambitious."

"Three times is nothing, little witch. More than likely, it'll be double that amount by the time we're both unable to keep going. Should I tell Miguel and Terry to take off for the day so I can give you a personal demonstration of my ambition level?"

"While I'm tempted to say yes and take you up on that offer, I have someplace to be and I can't reschedule."

"You're passing up six orgasms for . . . ?"

"Dinner with my sisters, and some long-overdue sister talk . . . and then there are a few other things I need to do." Her gaze drifted away again.

He studied her carefully. She wasn't telling him everything. "You sure that's all it is?"

"Just have a lot of different thoughts occupying my headspace right now. It's what usually happens after surviving one of my mother's dinner parties." She smiled, but this time it didn't quite reach her eyes. "My mom's been taken over by a pod person and that pod decided she wants grandchildren."

Damian chuckled, playing with a strand of her hair. "Grandchildren, huh?"

"She even invited the perfect son-in-law. Handsome. Smart. Connected. And your brother."

His fingers froze on her cheek as a heavy knot swelled in his stomach. "Your mother set you up with Julius?"

"Tried and failed, miserably."

"Did he spend the entire night talking about himself and all his accomplishments?"

"We actually spent most of it talking about you." She nibbled her bottom lip again, looking hesitant. "You didn't tell me about the hex."

He froze.

All thoughts. All movement. It wasn't until Rose spoke again that he remembered he could do either. He released his hold on her and stepped back, creating much-needed physical distance. The hurt on her face when she registered it was impossible to miss, and damn if he didn't want to take it away.

Instead, he stayed put. "I didn't, and for a reason. It has no bearing on anything we're doing."

"No bearing?"

He shook his head. "This FBA means no attachments, right? No attachment means no involved feelings. No feelings means I'm not obligated to talk about what happened a million years ago."

"To talk about the fact that some witch hexed you . . ." She looked at him as if he had two heads. "And you're okay with that? With never experiencing *more*?"

Damian tugged a frustrated hand through his hair before tossing the remaining fencing supplies into the back of the truck in hopes of escaping this conversation. "It's not like I have any other choice. It was a Soul Hex. There's no going back from that even if the witch who performed it wanted to, which I can assure you she doesn't."

He'd asked multiple times before Cal made it clear she wasn't about to make his life easier until he learned his lesson . . . whatever that lesson was. He'd even sought out other witches in the hopes that they'd be able to remove it, but if there was one thing his ex was, besides magically talented, it was thorough.

No one had the power to break it. It was something with which he'd had to come to grips.

Rose followed him to the truck, obviously not giving up. "That doesn't make it right, Damian."

"Nope." He slammed the tailgate closed before turning to see her hands propped on her hips, fury lighting up her eyes. "But it is what it is. There's nothing to do but accept it and move on with my life. If that's something you can't do, then we don't have to go any further here."

She blinked, startled by his suggestion. "You want to end our arrangement?"

"Fuck no." He slowly stalked closer, giving her ample time to back away or warn him off. When she did neither, he eased his arms around her waist and pulled her flush against him. "No, little witch, I don't. I want to tell Miguel and Terrance to make themselves scarce, carry you upstairs, and fuck you until we both drop unconscious . . . but you have other plans."

She slid her palms up his arms and played with the hair at his nape, her touch lighting a fire deep beneath his skin. "You fight dirty, but you already know that, don't you?"

"All's fair in fucking and orgasms, babe."

With a chuckle, she shimmied from his hold. "Maybe, and as much as I want to take you up on your offer, I fear Vi's wrath more if I bail on Girls' Night. And while my head's clear of all your orgasm-talk, I had an idea for an adoption fair, but I'm still working out the plan. I'll let you know when I'm ready to share."

"Sounds good . . . but it would sound even better if you shared it while you were naked and in my bed."

"I'll see what time I'm done with my thing tonight, and maybe I'll give you a call."

Damian chuckled. "You'll be giving me a booty call?"

"Guess you'll wait and see, won't you?"

With a coy wink, she headed toward the barn where she said goodbye to Miguel. All Damian could do was stare, watching her get into her car with a short wave. So preoccupied with watching her go, he didn't see Terrance or the kid's shit-eating smirk.

"It's so freakin' cool, isn't it?" The kid interjected his thoughts. "I know I shouldn't be surprised. Anyone who was trained to be the Prima witch has to be one of the biggest Supernatural badasses around, but still . . . I can't wait to say that I know a real Supernatural bounty hunter."

A bowling ball formed in Damian's stomach. "I have no idea what you're talking about, Terr."

Terrance nodded his chin to where Rose's car bounced down the lane. "Rose. Do you think that when she joins the bounty club or whatever, that she'll be able to get me Dog's autograph?"

"Rose isn't a bounty hunter . . . Supernatural or otherwise."

Terrance's excited smile wilted, leaving him looking like a bundle of nerves. "Oh. Uh. I figured she told you. She didn't tell me, but she talked to Jasper while she was grooming him earlier and I was in the next stall with Butternut and I heard . . . never mind."

Rose had talked to the horse.

Rose had told the horse she was bounty hunting?

Damian clenched his jaw until it nearly cracked. "Did you overhear her tell Jasper anything else?"

"No, at least nothing I understood." Terrance shifted awkwardly on his feet. "Maybe she's doing it for her grandma . . . or her sister. They're the big witch leaders, right?"

Something told him Rose didn't get the idea to Hunt from Edie or her sister. If there were a devil and an angel perched on her shoulders, doling out advice, that demon devil was definitely named Julius.

"Tell Miguel I'll owe him one for closing things tonight. I have to head out." Damian tossed his gloves to the teenager and hightailed it into the office to grab his motorcycle keys, and then he went on a Hunt of his own.

Not for an unruly shifter, or a wayward demon, or voracious vampire.

He went on the prowl for a certain, sexy witch.

13

All Aboard
(The No-Pants Express)

Rose hustled across the street, sidestepping a cab that tried getting a jump-start off the line before the blinking pedestrian light went solid. The driver laid on his horn, but instead of dispersing the sea of commuters, more stepped into his path and he had no choice but to wait, his hands flailing impatiently.

Rose chuckled. She loved New York. She always had, but no longer being the Prima Apparent, she spent more time living *in* it instead of passing through it. There were things about the city that she'd never heard of, or visited, and it was a travesty that she was determined to correct.

The Eagles' "Witchy Woman" blared from her bag, earning her glances from passersby.

Immediately identifying the ringtone she'd picked out for Violet, Rose answered the call. "You better not be bailing on dinner. It's been forever since the three of us have had a chance to sit and talk, and like I texted you, I'm worried about Olly. I think we're getting close to needing a triplet intervention."

"Hello to you, too," Vi greeted, her voice amused. "And no, I'm not bailing. As much as I love Lincoln and all his sexy shifter growling,

I need sister time. And speaking of our youngest womb-mate, I'm swinging by Olly's office to pick her up now."

"At NYU? What's she doing there on the weekend?"

"She didn't say, but I think she's been sleeping there to avoid her roommate."

"I knew it was bad, but I didn't think it was *that* bad." Rose paused, thinking about their sister's cramped college office. "Wait . . . where the hell is she sleeping? With floor-to-ceiling books, there's barely enough room for a desk."

"Knowing her, she made one out of the books," Vi quipped.

Rose's idea-maker was already hard at work, thinking up solutions. "Maybe I can convince her to move in with me . . ."

"In the studio? You'd literally stumble over each other anytime the other moved. I'd have better luck."

"A newly married, newly Mated, and newly Bonded couple?" Rose snortled and hung a right, heading down another block. "We both know she'd never agree to that. She'd sooner move back in with Mom and Dad."

Vi cackled because none of them would subject themselves to *that* for *whatever* reason *ever*. They'd fought broom and cauldron to leave the first time around.

"We have to come up with something," Rose pointed out. "At Mom's 'family' dinner, she could've been mistaken as a *Walking Dead* extra without stepping foot in the makeup trailer."

"Strength in numbers. Smart idea. You sure you don't want me to pick you up, too? I don't mind."

Rose glanced up at the nearest street sign, and grinned. "I have a quick stop to make, but I'll meet you at the restaurant. If you're there before me, you know what I like. Go ahead and order."

"Anything with mushrooms, got it."

Rose rolled her eyes, grinning because Vi knew her aversion to edible fungus.

"Oh hey, before I go," Vi added, "does this stop have anything to do with a certain handsome animal doctor?"

Well, that was a bit random. Her internal alarm system came to life. "No . . . why would you say that?"

"No reason. Love you!" Vi hung up.

Rose tucked her phone back in her bag. A twinge of awareness tickled the back of her neck just as a motorcycle engine roared from a distance, growing louder the closer it approached. A familiar helmet-clad head swiveled in her direction before both the man and the machine swung toward the curb.

Seeing Damian drew her to a stop.

He hadn't changed his clothes, wearing the same dirty jeans and work shirt he'd worn at the sanctuary with his leather jacket thrown over it and the zipper undone despite the chill.

Her heart rate kicked up a notch as she forced her feet into motion. "Why do I think bumping into you isn't coincidental?"

"Because it's not. Your sister was all too willing to use her Find a Friend app when I told her I needed to track you down."

"That's not creepy at all," Rose joked.

Damian's mouth pressed into a tight line. "We need to talk."

Oh hells no. Those four words never led to anything good, and she was in too pleasant a mood to listen to whatever came after.

"Sorry, I have someplace I need to be." *And pants to drop,* she thought giddily. "I'll be late if I don't grab the Q train at the next subway stop."

The No-Pants Express waited for no one. Rain. Shine. Hail. Gloom of night. The event held the same standards as the post office, and quite possibly, more.

Rose kept walking, and Damian sighed, leaving his Harley behind as he easily kept pace with her. "Your sisters will understand if you're a few minutes late. Besides, if you miss the Q, you can just take the next one. They run every few minutes."

"It's not dinner with Vi and Olly I'm worried about being late for." Rose couldn't contain her smile, nor her excitement about what she was about to do.

When she'd first told Harper she'd be her proxy, she hadn't had any real intention of going through with it. It had been more of a *could I, should I, would I* situation. The more she'd thought about it, the more she'd liked the idea . . . especially after dinner at her parents' and dwelling on her conversation with Julius.

In all her thirty-three years, Rose Maxwell had never done anything for herself.

Okay, so that wasn't quite true. Toddlers are well-known to be greedy little things and she'd probably been no different, but once it became clear she'd be the witch following in Edie's footsteps?

Not one thing for herself . . . not even moving into Violet's old studio apartment. Yeah, it had given her space as the world cracked and reshaped itself around her, but it also meant Vi hadn't been charged for breaking her rental agreement months ahead of schedule.

Besides her FBA with Damian, the No-Pants Express was one of a sad few things she was doing because it was what *she* wanted, and both were something last year's coiffed Rose Maxwell would have never considered. Not even in her wildest rebel fantasies, and not because of becoming potential headline fodder.

Because it was *fun.*

Exciting.

Joining hundreds of New Yorkers dropping their pants for an un-forgettable subway ride elicited the same physical response as naked time with Damian—sans orgasms.

Well, maybe not quite . . . but it definitely elicited an exhilarat-ing rush.

Rose cursed at the time and picked up her pace, weaving through the throngs of people all on their commutes home. She only slowed when the fountain came into view.

Damian, obviously irritated, glanced around the growing crowd at Union Square. "What's this?"

Rose grinned. "The starting point."

"What starting point?"

"Hello, fellow subway riders!" A man jumped up onto the rim of the dormant fountain, his megaphone squeaking loudly. Somewhere in his late twenties, he waved his hand for attention, and sure enough, the excited crowd slowly piped down. "Thank you all for coming out on a slightly chillier than expected day to participate in the annual No-Pants Express! You all are the bravest of the brave!"

The crowd cheered excitedly, faces pink from anticipation—and the cold.

Damian leaned closer. "Did he just say—"

"Shh." Rose clamped her hand over his mouth. "He's about to go over the rules."

"Rule number one," the officiant called out. "Obviously . . . *no pants allowed*! That usually goes without saying, but knowledge is power and all."

Cheers erupted along with another round of chuckles.

"Second! Don't do anything that'll get you arrested."

Boos echoed around the group, and again, laughter.

"Yeah, yeah, a bummer, I know. But we're able to come back year after year because we behave. So please, *behave*! And third . . . have freakin' fun! Everyone should already have their assigned stations, so let's shed those pants and get moving!"

Short of the Polar Bear Plunge, Rose never saw so many people shedding their pants at one time. She chuckled, full-on cackling when Damian's eyes went wide as saucers as the man next to him shucked his sweatpants to stand proudly next to him in a Scooby-Doo Speedo.

Rose unbuttoned her coat.

"What the hell do you think you're doing?" As her bare legs came into view, Damian looked two seconds away from shedding his jacket and wrapping her up like a witchy burrito.

"Rule number one . . . no pants." She pushed her jeans down, and bracing a hand on Damian's arm for balance, she yanked them over her sneakers.

He opened and closed his mouth like a fish out of water, searching for the ability to speak as she shoved her pants in her bag. His complete shock only confirmed that she'd made the right decision to participate.

"Have a great day, doc! I'll ring you up later!" She sent him a little wave and was carried away by the crowd.

The NPE coordinators had divvied up subway assignments a few days ago, and she'd drawn the Union Square stop on Fourteenth Street. Lucky for her, it was the nearest station, which meant she wouldn't freeze her rump cheeks off while waiting for the train.

She'd crossed the street at the corner when she realized Damian followed behind, his face the definition of grumpy brood. His eyes flickered down to her panty-clad behind.

"Explain to me why you're riding the subway without pants . . . with a lot of other people who also aren't?" he asked.

She shrugged. "Why not?"

His brow furrowed. "I'll give you a million reasons, and they're the different strands of bacteria—and God knows what else—that will be introduced to your gorgeous—and practically bare—backside."

Smirking, she shot him a coy wink. "Are you worried about catching something from me, doc?"

"I'm concerned you'll develop a case of flesh-eating bacteria."

"There's nothing in the No-Pants rulebook that says sitting on the train is required. I'm perfectly capable of standing."

Regular commuters did double takes as the crowd of pantsless individuals all descended onto the platform. Some laughed. Some scowled. Others pulled out phones to document the moment. Damian stepped in front of her and shot a low, lethal growl at a frat boy who'd dared point his cell phone her way. The kid visibly paled before shoving his phone back into his pants pocket and stared anywhere but at them.

"Did you just growl at him?" Rose asked, blinking. "And I swear your eyes did a little glowy thing?"

And it wasn't the first time she'd seen it. She swore the same thing had happened briefly at the bowling alley with Val, and again at the Blood Moon.

Damian sighed. "Can we please go somewhere and talk . . . with pants on?"

"What conversation is so important you expect me to abandon my plans to have it?"

He folded his arms over his chest, the move stretching the softness of his worn leather jacket. "New intel has led me to believe my brother offered up a hell of a lot more than the history of my sorry excuse for a love life . . . something about a job offer? Care to fill in the blanks?"

"*Intel?* Did you give up your vet practice to become part of the spy network?" Rose mimicked his stance, crossing her arms as she waited for the next train. "And nope, I do not wish to fill in the blanks. Especially while that sour look is on your face. I've been looking forward to this event all week. I'm not backing out, and I'm not about to ruin the buzzy fun with *that* conversation."

"It's a bad idea, little witch."

Another No-Pants Express rider frowned at Damian's lack of showing skin. "Dude, rule number one. No pants. If you're gonna ride, you gotta drop your drawers with pride."

A low, rolling growl slid from Damian's chest as he turned toward the hipster, his eyes definitely flashing bright gold. "I'm not taking off my pants."

Rose grinned. "It *is* rule number one."

He glared at her. "Not happening."

"Then this is where we say goodbye. I'll call you later, and maybe we can have that talk."

The train squealed to a quick stop and she hiked her bag higher on her shoulder, preparing to make the mad dash into the car.

"No way am I letting you ride the subway in your fucking underwear. Alone."

"I'm not alone. I have all these people." She glanced to the guy waiting next to them. "And I have . . . I'm sorry, what's your name?"

"Greyson." Grinning, the guy held out his hand.

She shook it. "And I have Greyson here, who seems like a great traveling companion."

"I'm the best."

Damian glowered and for a brief, hot second, Rose thought she'd won. Grinning triumphantly, she waited for the train doors to open when Damian's rambling mumbles turned her to watch him reaching for his pants.

"What are you doing?" Rose couldn't believe her eyes.

"Giving thanks I washed my damn underwear last night."

She couldn't tear her eyes away as he pushed his jeans down . . . and then she couldn't contain her laughter. Tears sprang to her eyes as she tried sucking in oxygen—and failed.

Puppy faces, wearing oversized sunglasses, and interspersed with thick, puffy clouds and smiling cartoon suns, decorated Damian's colorful boxers.

"You think this is funny?" Damian demanded.

She nodded, unable to contain her giggles. "Immensely."

"*Now* can we talk?"

"Sure." The train doors opened, and the crowd instantly moved, Rose included. "But you better move fast."

❖ ❖ ❖

Never in a million years would Damian have guessed he'd reach this level of desperation, and yet there he was, following a pantsless woman into a crowded NYC subway car with people who were as equally without clothes on the lower half of their body.

Himself included.

At some point, he'd lost all control of the situation—if he even had it to begin with.

Ignoring the amused glances of the people around them, he followed Rose into the train, happy she did exactly as she'd said, and went to the nearest support pole instead of plopping into a seat.

Damian shifted, blocking the view of her body from as many eyes as possible as he leaned in, dropping his voice for her ears only. "Look, I don't know what Jules was thinking putting the Hunting idea into your head, but I'm here to yank it right back out. You have no idea what you'd be getting yourself into."

Her eyes damn near glowed as she drilled him with a hard glare, and damn if he didn't feel the sharp edge of Magic crackling the air around them. A few of the other commuters must have felt it as well because heads turned their way.

Rose bristled. "Because a woman like me couldn't possibly understand anything other than the proper way to smile and wave without throwing out my wrist?"

"Whoa. No. Don't put words in my mouth. You know what I mean."

"Do I though?" She lifted her chin and turned, facing him from the other side of the pole. "You don't think it's a good idea. And you don't think I'd be any good at it—"

"Again putting words into my mouth," Damian cut her off.

"So you do think it's a good idea . . ."

"I think it's a disaster waiting to happen, but not because I don't think you'd be any good. As a matter of fact, I think you'd be fucking great at it, and *that's* why I'm concerned."

"That makes absolutely no sense."

"It makes the world of sense, but the fact you don't realize it proves my point."

"You don't get it." She ignored the growing number of stares from nearby commuters. "You have no idea what it's like to fail at *everything* you do. To have no clue where your talent lies because you've never had a chance to figure it out. I finally found one of those talents—after thirty-three freakin' years of life—and you're saying I should ignore it. In the wise words of Vi, that's a pretty dickish move, even for you."

She wasn't wrong.

Not to mention he should've known better than to approach her with a growling demand. If anything, he'd reinforced her desire to go through with Julius's asinine plan.

Damian mentally shifted tactics and prayed he hadn't already fucked it up. He met her gaze and cursed, scrubbing his hand over his face.

Prayer wouldn't be enough.

"This isn't about you or your abilities," he admitted truthfully. "This is about Julius. I know you think a lot of him, but you have no idea what it's like to work with him, Rose. *For* him. I do. It'll be fine until you disagree on a case, and then the Mr. Nice Guy gloves come off."

"I trained my entire life to become the next Prima. I can handle Supernaturals like Julius Kontos."

"What happens the first time you're told to bring in a frail grandfather whose only long-term goal is to see his grandchildren get married? Not all cases are like the Gryndors. A lot hover solidly in the gray area."

"Why would the Council want a sweet old man hauled in to stand trial?"

"Maybe because that old man wasn't always so sweet, and it took a long time for his past to catch up with him. Maybe he forgot to tip his waitress. I don't know, and the point is that whether or not you agree with the reasoning for the haul-in, you'll have no choice but to do it."

"I can handle it."

"You're not taking any of this seriously. Let's grab a coffee or something and talk about this more . . . *please*," Damian added.

"Sure . . ."

"Yeah?" *Well, damn . . . that was easy.*

"We can talk about my job offer right after we talk about your little ex hex . . ."

Never mind. This was a train derailment waiting to happen.

Overhead lights blinked as the subway car approached the next station.

Rose gifted him a cocky, expectant look. "Well, this is my stop . . . unless you still want to have those conversations. No? Then we'll talk later."

Damian followed her onto the platform, pushing past an on-slaught of new riders. "Rose . . ."

She turned, her gaze raking over the sight of him standing there in all his puppy-boxer glory.

When he couldn't form any additional words, she winked. "You may want to put your pants back on before you head up to the street. It's a bit chilly."

She gifted him a little wave and disappeared up the steps.

Damian cursed. He'd seen that going so differently in his head. Hell, he'd seen a lot of things with Rose Maxwell going a lot differently, and that had him worrying about what he'd be blindsided with next.

"Hey, dude. I like your boxers. Can I ask where you got them?" A man, sporting a pair of briefs decorated with bicycle-riding kittens, gave him a slow once-over.

Without answering, Damian turned to hop on the next train back to his bike. He obviously wouldn't get anywhere by talking to Rose. If anything, he'd only made her more determined to go through with it.

That left him only one other option.

14

Naked Parcheesi

Eighteen Years Ago . . .
  Boston, Massachusetts

Damian easily ducked a left jab and spun, landing a hard punch to his victim's kidneys. The sound of a pained *oomph* brought a grin to his face, fueling his need to hear it again. Sweat dripped into his eyes in flowing rivulets, but he didn't once stop moving.

Once you stopped moving you were as good as Gryndor food.

Duck. Dodge. Weave. He followed up each defensive maneuver with a long string of kicks and punches until his inner demon surged to the surface and took the lead. Damian barely had to do a damn thing, letting his other self have his fun . . . and he definitely enjoyed himself more with every curse that slipped from his opponent's mouth.

The occasional blood spray was a bonus.

"And to think you were about to bail out on sparring today." Julius grunted, wincing as he took another punch to the stomach. "Told you that you needed to let loose a little bit. Maybe next time you'll listen to me."

His brother blocked a kick and right-jabbed, finally clipping Damian on the jaw. He leaped back with a growl.

"Watch the face, Julius!" Head snapping up from the sidelines, Damian's girlfriend pulled her head from her book and shot his brother a hard glare, her Magic thickening the air. "I swear to Goddess, Julius Kontos, if you give him a black eye before we get our prom pictures taken, I will hex you so hard you see stars."

Julius rolled his eyes and blocked another attack. "Tell me why the fuck she's here again . . ."

"Because I'm taking her to the dance."

"*Prom* . . ." Julius said the world like it left a foul taste in his mouth.

"If that's the thing where I have to dress up and make a 'big gesture,' then yes."

His brother scoffed. "I don't know why the hell you agreed to that. It's a pointless waste of time. Just think of all the other things you could be doing . . ."

Damian had, and to say he'd tried talking his way out of it would be an understatement, but Cal had been adamant. Her friends were starting to think she'd made him up from the number of times he'd bailed on plans.

Part of him felt guilty, but the other parts felt as Julius did.

Hitting the movies with a bunch of teenagers whose only goal in life was to get high and drunk was a waste of time . . . time he could put to better use. Like training. Or Hunting things that went bump in the night. Sparring with Jules or Hunting in the field, Damian didn't have to hold back. He could be his true, un-human self.

But when he *didn't* choose teenager things, he got put on "boyfriend probation." At least that's what Cal called it.

She also talked about grand gestures, and proving that she—and his pesky humanity—meant more to him than the Hunt . . . which is what this whole prom thing was about. If it got her off his back for a while, he was all for it.

Julius used his temporary distraction to his advantage, and in a quick leg-swipe, plummeted them both to the mats. Chests heaving, they lay side by side, Julius wheezing from the physical effort to breathe.

His older brother had never been able to keep up with him.

"You know"—Jules dropped his voice so only Damian could hear—"I got a tip about a rogue group of Quall demons on the Southside who've been peddling some tainted Supernatural Dust. What do you say? You. Me. Kicking a little Q ass."

Temptation stirred Damian's demon . . .

"Come on, brother. You know you want to . . ."

Damian's gaze flickered over to where Cal sat on the sidelines, her blue eyes narrowed in on the two of them as if she'd heard.

"What the hell are you doing here, man?" Julius whispered. "You know she's not the right person for you. If she had her way, she'd Magic you into a warlock or something . . . or worse. She'd turn you Norm."

Damian shot his brother a glare. "Well, I am half-Norm, aren't I?"

"You're also half-demon, brother. You're not doing either of you any favors by pretending otherwise."

"That sounds dangerously close to something dear old Dad would say."

As if talking about him conjured the demon himself, the demon portal on the other side of the gym flared to life, crackling and sparking until Ezeil himself stepped through.

A full-blooded prince of Hell, their father looked barely fifty years old when in reality he'd been created nearly five hundred years ago. Once a favorite among Lucifer's enforcers and now the demon rep on the Supernatural Council, Ezeil had made sure to train—and raise—his two sons in his image.

He was disappointed almost every damn day.

"Lying down on the job, I see." Ezeil's cool tone showed his displeasure. "Can I not trust the two of you to continue your training while I go on business trips? Perhaps I need to assign you babysitters."

Julius frowned, instantly getting to his feet. Damian was slower to follow, holding his tongue for the time being.

Ezeil's gaze flickered over to the side of the gym where Cal sat. He sighed, drilling Damian with a disappointed glower. "Send the witch away. We have Hunt business to discuss. I've just been informed of a job, and I promised the Council that I'd put my best Hunters on it. It's time sensitive."

"Sure thing." Julius nodded, immediately accepting.

"I can't tonight," Damian admitted grudgingly. "I have plans."

Ezeil's eyebrow lifted. Understanding slowly dawned on him as he flicked a quick look back to Damian's girlfriend. "That's right . . . you *do* have plans . . . and they involve hauling in a horde of Quall demons who've decided that poisoning both Norms and Supernaturals with tainted Supe Dust is an acceptable pastime."

"But—"

His father stepped closer as he began shedding his Norm skin. Yellow eyes with oblong pupils glowered at Damian from less than an inch away, a sign that Ezeil was calling on his power of Compulsion.

Damian instantly pushed against it by raising his own shields. Both practice and the use of the black market anti-thrall serum he'd gotten a few weeks ago kept him from succumbing to the demon's every whim, but it still took a hell of a lot of effort.

As Ezeil realized his attempt to gain control failed, fury darkened his gaze.

"Let me make myself clear, *son*." He dropped his voice to a dangerous growl. "I permit this relationship with the witch only because I know it's a fleeting teenage fancy. But rest assured, when that fancy begins to interfere with my plans for you, I will remove it. One way or another. Do I make myself clear?"

Damian's jaw clenched until it ached. It wasn't the first time his father had used threats to get what he wanted, and it wouldn't be the last.

Ezeil leaned close, hovering just over his ear as he whispered, "Do you need a reminder of who I am . . . and who you are?"

"No . . ."

"No . . . what?"

"No . . . Prince Ezeil."

❖ ❖ ❖

Present Day . . .

New York City

Damian's demon had spent the better part of the last twenty-four hours trying to stage a jailbreak and used his anger toward Julius to do it. Only a few unexpected sanctuary additions kept the bastard at bay, albeit barely, but the second the work was done, the demon got his second wind, scratching his way to the surface until Damian hopped on his bike and headed for Fifth Avenue.

This was one instance when he didn't mind letting his second self get behind the wheel. He made it across town in record time and barreled through the front lobby of Julius's expensive high-rise.

A startled door attendant gave chase as Damian headed toward his brother's private elevator. "Sir! Sir! I'm sorry, but I can't let you go up without resident authorization. If you'll come back to the desk with your ID, I'll—"

"This is my authorization." Damian's amber demon eyes flashed, the beast briefly showing himself through his human skin.

The Norm man visibly paled and stepped back.

"I'm going up there." Damian dusted off his Compulsion and focused it on the man in front of him. "And you won't be announcing my presence."

"I . . . won't."

"No . . . and you'll key me up to the penthouse apartment."

"Of course I will, sir. Here, let me help you."

The older man swiped his badge, and the elevator doors opened, giving Damian access. "Thank you. You've done a great job."

Guilt ate at Damian's stomach as he rode his way up to the penthouse apartment, but it was immediately swallowed by a resurgence of annoyance as the doors opened, hitting him with a wall of music and a large crowd of expensively dressed people.

Colorful artwork decorated the pristine white space, worth more money than Damian would ever see in his lifetime. Everything about his brother's apartment screamed opulence and class. Dressed in faded jeans and his leather jacket, Damian stuck out like a skunk at a perfume stand, and he didn't give a damn.

He had one goal, and upon achieving that, a second.

First, find his brother.

Then, kick his ass.

And only when he'd gotten his point across—and his boot wedged so far up Julius's bum that his toe tickled his tonsils—he'd make sure his brother rescinded Rose's job offer. Would she be pissed if or when she found out?

Absolutely.

Was it worth the risk of her never talking to him again?

Maybe . . . but he couldn't let that stop him from trying.

Damian cased the penthouse, vaguely recognizing Terrance's favorite actors mixed in with a handful of politicians—both Supernatural and Norm. Julius's master plan had always involved making nice with everyone because, according to him, "You never know when you'll need a favor only one person can help you with."

"You look like a man with a mission, and I hope that mission is me." A sultry brunette succubus glided his way, her eyes glowing as if she'd finished one hell of a soul-sucking bender and was looking for another.

"You'll have to find your midnight snack somewhere else because I'm immune." Literally one of the only perks to having a demon side. "I'm looking for Julius."

"Hmm." She tapped her bright red-tipped finger against her full lips. "The last I saw him, he was upstairs in the rooftop solarium, but he was a bit preoccupied with a pretty blonde. They could've long since abandoned this meat market for a more private space. Get me a drink and we can wait for him together? I'm sure I could find a few acceptable ways to pass the time."

"Immune," Damian reminded her. "And also not interested."

She shrugged her slender shoulders and moved on, locking her gaze onto her next target across the room, the poor bastard.

Damian headed toward the balcony, and to the outside stairs that would take him up another level to Julius's little slice of nature.

Despite the cool temps, people loitered in the outdoor space, which included a cobblestoned patio and on the east end, a large, flourishing greenhouse that housed the only demon portal in the city. The DP network could get anyone with demon blood anywhere in less than a wink.

The only problem was that in order to travel, you needed to pull a Darth Vader and embrace your dark side. He'd only used one a handful of times, and after each time, he'd worked like hell to put his demon back in his box because despite being a badass, he was also claustrophobic and always put up one hell of a fight.

Damian found his brother in the largest crowd as he held court on the east patio. Mid-laugh, Julius's gaze locked on his approach. He hid his surprise with a wide smile. "If it isn't my elusive younger brother. What brings you to this part of town?"

Damian ignored the curious looks from Julius's *friends*. "We need to talk, and this isn't a conversation you'll want people hearing . . . *brother*."

Julius's grin melted away as he turned to his fan club. "If you'll excuse me. I better see to this family matter. This way," he said to Damian.

Damian followed Jules through the party to his main-level office.

The second he closed the door, his brother helped himself to a drink at a corner wet bar. "Can I get you anything? Scotch? Bourbon?"

"Answers."

"You don't mind if I have a drink then?" He poured himself a few fingers of scotch, downed it, and helped himself to another before turning around, casually leaning against his desk. "I'll take a wild stab in the dark and say the answers for which you're looking have something to do with a certain gorgeously headstrong witch."

Damian's inner demon growled. "That witch has a name, and she also has no interest in anything you're offering . . . and that includes Hunting."

"Interesting, because it sure as hell seemed like she was interested when I presented the idea to her."

"Was that before or after you told her about Cal?" Damian demanded.

Saying his ex's name after so many years felt unnatural, but he didn't let it stop him because as furious as he was with Julius for putting Rose's life in jeopardy with this asinine job offer, Damian was equally pissed that his brother had opened his mouth at all.

"How was I to know you never brought up your little affliction?" Julius defended himself. "The two of you are involved, are you not? Your scent sure was all over her the other night, and not in a way that meant you spent the time playing Parcheesi. Unless it was naked Parcheesi."

"What Rose Maxwell and I do or don't do together is absolutely none of your business."

"You're right. It's not, but I would've thought that something as importance as a Soul Hex would be brought up at least once with one you've played naked board games with."

"Rose and I have an understanding. There was never a reason to discuss it." Damian's jaw ached from clenching his teeth.

"No strings, huh?" Julius chuckled, swirling his drink before sipping it. "Let me know how that goes for you. As for the job offer I presented to Rose, it still stands . . . especially since she called me thirty minutes ago and accepted."

Damian froze. "She did *what*?"

His brother chuckled. "It's cute you believe you have a say in what a Maxwell witch does or doesn't do, little brother. They're a spirited bunch. They do what they want, and evidently Rose Maxwell wants to try her hand at Hunting."

"*Bounty* hunting," Damian clarified. "Referring to it with a pretty name doesn't make it any different than what it is, Jules, and she has no business doing it. Take the offer back."

"No can do. I may be a lot of things, but I'm not someone who goes back on their word. Her trial period will officially start once she's given her first assignment." A slow smile slithered onto Julius's face. "If I had more fully trained, experienced Hunters on my pay-roll, I wouldn't have to fill my roster with newbie witches . . ."

And there it was.

Julius's real goal.

To put him—and his demon—back into the fold regardless of the outcome.

"You really don't care about anything, or anyone, other than yourself, do you?" Damian asked, already knowing the answer. "So much like Ezeil . . ."

"That couldn't be further from the truth, brother." A myriad of emotions flickered over Julius's face as he stood. "Unlike our sperm donor, everything I do, I do with the people I care about in mind, and you may not believe me, but that includes you."

"You're right . . . I don't believe you. Especially since you're one of the few who knows why I left Hunting in the first place."

"Yeah, something about your humanity . . . but considering you're straddling the edge with your witchy plaything, that excuse falls a little short, don't you think?"

Fisting his brother's tux in one hand, Damian punched with the other, landing a hard right hook to the demon's perfectly sculpted jaw. Julius crashed into his desk, sending everything on it scattering to the floor. "Do not refer to her as a *plaything* . . ."

It took everything Damian had not to land another, and instead, he kept his distance while Julius wiped a trickle of blood away from the corner of his mouth.

The bastard chuckled. "Did growing up under Father's thumb teach you nothing about basic survival, little brother? If I were anything like the sick bastard, you'd have just laid out your weakness in front of anyone eager to take advantage."

Damian hated that he was right as he fought for control. "You don't want to make an enemy out of me, Jules."

Julius sobered slightly. "You're right. I don't."

Damian wouldn't dive too deep into his brother's words, and he also wouldn't waste a second more of time because as different as he and his brother were, like him, Julius wouldn't change his mind.

With his demon lying just beneath the surface, Damian stalked out of the penthouse and down to the street, mentally cursing how off-kilter his life had become since Rose Maxwell walked into it.

Hell, crashed . . .

And he wasn't so sure the resulting flames weren't about to get higher . . . and engulf them both.

15

Liar, Liar, Cauldron on Fire

Fun, family, and friends. That completed the list of approved things occupying Rose's mind at Vi and Linc's official welcome home party.

And flames . . .

Cursing, Rose flung open Linc's high-end oven and nearly took a fire flare to the eyebrows. She doused it quickly with a cool burst of Magic, and reached for what was supposed to be a tray of sugar cookies but sadly looked more like charred hockey pucks. The searingly hot cookie sheet burned her hand.

"Hex me to hell," Rose cursed again.

Olive appeared, holding out a silicone oven mitt. "These usually work wonders to prevent fingerprints from being burned off."

"Hardy-har-har." Using the mitten, she grabbed the sheet and quickly shut the door, praying the smoke alarm didn't go off. "Guess I can cross baker off my list of potential professions. Hockey pucks may have more give than these cookies."

Olive stared at the charred remains, her nose wrinkled in concentration. "Are those penises?"

Rose groaned. It was even worse than she'd thought. "They're wolves wearing witch hats. I thought it would be cute considering Vi and Linc . . . never mind."

She shucked the oven mitt onto the counter and took a good look at her sister and the dark circles beneath her tired eyes. "Olly, you can't keep this up. You have to get out of that apartment."

"And go where?" Olive snagged two carrots from the veggie tray. "Move on top of you in your tiny studio, or in with the newly Mated couple, who at this very moment are upstairs sneaking in a quickie and hoping that no one notices?"

"There's always—"

"If you suggest Mom and Dad, you're dead to me." Olive shot her a warning glare over the rims of her glasses. "This is New York. Good apartments don't magically appear out of nowhere."

Bax strutted into the kitchen. With a quick swipe, he stole one of Olive's carrots. "What's up with the penis cookies? Aren't they supposed to be served at bridal showers? Vi and Linc are already hitched in every way imaginable."

Rose groaned. "They're witchy wolf cookies."

Olive swiped her carrot back and shot the tatted Guardian Angel a stern glare from behind her cat-framed glasses. "Get your own snacks. If you're hungry, there's a whole tray of veggies in front of you."

"But they won't taste as good as yours." He leaned past her, grabbing a replacement carrot, and winked. "What's this about apartments?"

Olive shot Rose a pleading look that said *don't talk*, and under normal circumstances, the Triplet Code of Honor would force her to comply. But this wasn't a normal circumstance.

Don't you dare, Olive mouthed.

Sorry. Not really.

"Olive's been sleeping in her closet of an office at the college because her roommate's been keeping her up all hours of the day and night," Rose divulged. "Vi and I have been on her about moving out before she pulls a Sleeping Beauty and naps for a hundred years."

"Misconception. She only slept until True Love's Kiss," Olive muttered.

Rose rolled her eyes. "You can't keep doing what you're doing.

Something has to give, and if you don't get out of there, I'm afraid what will give will be your health."

Bax's multicolored eyes focused on Olive. "She's not wrong. Lack of sleep is the root cause of a lot of physical ailments."

"I'll take extra vitamins," Olive snapped back. "I'll wait her out and hope she develops a mild case of vitamin B-12 deficiency and needs to catch up on sleep."

"Or you could find yourself another apartment."

"Exactly," Rose agreed.

Olive glowered. "We've already established good apartments don't grow on trees, right?"

"Right," Bax agreed. "But it just so happens I have a lead on one."

"You do?" Rose and Olive asked in unison.

"Yeah. Mine."

"You're moving? Where?" Rose asked.

"Nowhere. I need to pick up a roommate."

Olive narrowed her eyes on the angel. "But you've always said you'd never take a roommate . . . that you value your privacy too much."

He shrugged noncommittally. "I also value paying my rent, which if my landlord keeps raising it, I soon won't be able to do. Contrary to what people think, Guardian Angel salaries aren't on the top-tier list of highest-paying jobs. So if you're game, I am, too."

"For me to move in with you . . . into your apartment."

"Once you moved in, it would be *our* place, but yeah. I call the second room an office, but I don't use it. It wouldn't take much effort to clean it out and throw a bed in there."

"So that I could move in . . ."

Bax slid his attention to Rose. "I see what you mean about her needing to get out of there and get sleep. She's not quite as sharp as she usually is."

"Why is everyone hiding in the kitchen when there's a party to be had?" Vi and Linc stepped into the kitchen, her sister's hair looking a little mussed. "Oh, look! How cute! Little penis cookies!"

Rose and Olive exchanged looks before bursting into laughter, but Rose's was short-lived. Damian brought up the rear looking better than he had any right to in faded jeans and a dark gray Henley, its sleeves rolled up to reveal his corded forearms. If it were possible to spontaneously ovulate, she would've right then and there with everyone's eyes bouncing back and forth between them.

✦ ✦ ✦

Clearing a room was one of Damian's many talents, but this was quick even for him. He'd barely stepped into the kitchen when Vi dragged Linc away, claiming she'd heard someone calling their names. Not long after that, Bax and Olive did the same, and he found himself alone with a flushed-faced Rose.

He didn't mind.

It gave them an opportunity to talk, something he wasn't looking forward to, but which needed to happen, and sooner rather than later.

Even so, knowing they had important things to discuss, his libido ramped up and put him on edge. No woman had ever affected him this way, something—thanks to his chat with Julius—of which he was now all too aware.

He'd come to the party with a game plan in mind, a backup plan just in case, and then a last-ditch proposal should Rose be Rose, and refuse to try something far less dangerous than Hunting . . . like heli-skiing.

Or skydiving without a parachute.

She turned her back on him, effectively acting as though they weren't the only two people in the room. He chuckled. He wasn't that easy to get rid of.

Not bothering to tread lightly, he crossed the distance until a cozy blanket of tingling Magic had the hairs on his arms standing at attention. Giving her ample time and space to move if she wanted, he slid his arms past both sides of her waist and braced his hands against the marble countertop.

The position brought his nose up against the softness of her hair, and he couldn't help but tilt into it, savoring the scent of vanilla and spice. "Found you . . ."

"I didn't realize I was lost." Her hands busied themselves wiping the counter in front of her before switching focus to the burnt cookies.

"Not lost . . . hiding. With your wolf witch cookies."

She turned in his arms, taking him by surprise, and peered up at him through her thick lashes. "You knew they were witchy wolves?"

"It's kinda obvious . . . but let's get back to why you felt the need to hide in Linc's kitchen and make them."

"I wasn't hiding," Rose denied all too quickly.

"Babe, I may not be an expert on a woman's mind, but I am at evasion tactics, and baking when there's already a feast on the other side of those doors is a perfect example." He kicked up his mouth into a grin. "How is this FBA supposed to work if we're never in the same location to act on it?"

"There will be no arranging of anything, nor acting on it while at my sister's house . . . especially if it comes at the price of having to defend my decision to Hunt. *Again.* I'm perfectly satisfied with Mr. Wiggles."

It looked as if it caused her physical pain to say it. He chuckled. "Liar, liar, cauldron on fire, little witch."

He transferred one hand to her waist, dipping his fingers below the hem of her shirt to find her soft, silky skin beneath. "Maybe I don't want to discuss the Hunt, either."

He trailed his hand higher.

She trembled in his arms, her breath picking up. "You don't?"

Damian shook his head, his hand moving a little higher. "I want to remind you there's more pleasurable ways to spend your time than playing Dog the Bounty Hunter."

Rose set her hands on his chest, and for a moment, he thought she'd push him away. Instead, she linked her arms around his neck, her gaze dropping to his mouth.

Sucking in a groan, he palmed her cheek with his spare hand, and tilted her gaze up to his. "What do you say, little witch? Are you prepared to be reminded?"

"You think you can seduce me into changing my mind, Damian Adams?" Rose's breathless voice challenged.

"I don't know, but it'll be a lot of fun finding out, don't you think?"

A sexy smile ghosted over her lips as she leaned closer, diminishing the inch of distance between their mouths. For a split second, Damian thought his plan had worked. Point for him!

Within a millimeter of kissing contact, Rose paused. The lusty little glint in her eye transformed into something else entirely. "I'm not changing my mind about Hunting, and neither is your brother. No matter how many times you threaten him."

Damian muttered a soft curse, his jaw clenching. "The bastard told you . . ."

"To let me know he wouldn't hold me to our agreement if I'd changed my mind, which I didn't. And just so you know, I won't . . . no matter how much you turn on the sexy grumpy veterinarian thing."

All fight drained from Damian's body as he scanned the determination on her face. It was time to rev up the backup plan.

"You realize that in addition to the psychological and emotional demands of the job, there's also the physical," Damian informed her, crossing his mental fingers. "Long hours. Risk of injury. You probably wouldn't have as many Girls' Nights with your sisters and Harper. Your social life will basically be nonexistent."

Rose's lips twitched as if she saw right through him. "Being Prima Apparent got me used to long hours, and with my Magic on board, injury risk is fairly low. And Harper and my sisters understand the need to find my thing. They'll understand."

"And your social life?"

She let out a sexy little snort. "My social life is already nonexistent . . . with the exception of the time I spend with you."

"You're determined to do this, aren't you? There's absolutely nothing I can do to change your mind short of cuffing you to my bed?"

"In all honesty, even cuffs wouldn't work. I can just Magic my way out of them."

Damian mumbled a string of curses, each one making Rose's smirk grow as he mentally receded away from his backup plan and transitioned toward the last-ditch proposal. "Fine, but I have a few requests."

"No way. I—"

He smooshed his thumb over her mouth and silenced her with a pleading look. "Just hear me out, okay? I promise I won't try and change your mind."

"Fine." She nodded her agreement, voice muffled.

"Hunting is dangerous, especially if you go into it with a distorted view about what it's like. Things don't always go as smoothly as they did with the Gryndors."

"And . . ."

Damian couldn't believe the words about to leave his lips. "And I'll do it *with* you. I'll mentor you. Or you can shadow me. Whatever you want to call it."

Filled with distrust, her eyes narrowed. "You want to teach me the Supernatural bounty hunting ropes? Be your . . . *intern*?"

"Do I want that? Fuck no. But as you pointed out once before, I'm the Scourge of the Supernatural Underworld, and if you're hell-bent on doing this, I won't let anyone else teach you but the best. And that's me."

Rose's triumph slowly morphed into one of concern, and it didn't take a genius to tell who it was for. "But you don't do it anymore for a reason, doc."

"And now I have a reason *to* do it."

Catching her bottom lip between her teeth, she shook her head.

"No. I won't let you subject yourself to a way of life you've spent years avoiding just so that I can catch a thrill or two."

He brushed his mouth over hers in a soft kiss, silencing her the only way he knew how, and when she leaned into him, he did it again before reluctantly pulling away. "I meant the sanctuary. The payout from the Gryndor takedown helped a lot, but it was only a drop in the bucket compared to what the sanctuary needs to get in the black again."

"You're doing it for the animals?" Rose asked warily.

"Of course," Damian lied. "I'd already been thinking about taking Julius up on his offer when he went ahead and made you one of his own," he lied again. "But there are rules to this little apprenticeship, which I know you Maxwell women seem allergic to unless you made them yourselves. Still, it's a deal-breaker."

"What rules?"

"We take only jobs *I* agree to. I know you don't think so, but not all assignments are created equal." She opened her mouth to argue, but he kept on going. "In the field, you do *exactly* as I say. If I say run, you run. First lesson: your life isn't worth any payout, regardless of how much it is. Can't enjoy the money if you're dead."

Nibbling her bottom lip, Rose nodded. "That makes sense."

He shot her a disbelieving look.

"What? It does! Contrary to what you believe, I don't have a death wish. I just want to feel useful . . . *alive*. I would actually do this for free, you know. It's not about the money. It's about keeping people safe."

And *that* he believed because it was her, and she was fucking amazing.

His gaze dropped to her lips and back. "There are plenty of ways to feel alive and I'm more than willing to show them to you firsthand."

She ignored his sexual innuendo. "You say jump, I jump. Run, I run. Anything else?"

"You want more rules? I could think up a few more, but they're not for Hunting." Desire doused his body from head to toe as he slid his hand over her backside and brought her closer. "They involve the two of us naked on a bed, or on any other surface conducive to our fuck-buddy arrangement."

Rose rubbed her body against his, a small smirk firmly in place. "I fully support those types of rules, but I think after this party, we should go back to my place so you can go over them again, but in explicit detail. I want to make certain they're ingrained into my memory vault."

"Seems like the responsible thing to do." Damian chuckled. Slower than he ever thought himself capable of, he dropped his mouth onto hers and savored every second of her body wrapped around his.

Rose melted in his arms, and damn if he didn't go a little jelly-kneed, nothing but their desire to be locked together keeping them upright. It was a delicate balance, and it wouldn't take much more than a hearty breeze to steal that fragility away.

16

JBFan4Eva

Inspecting her reflection in the mirror, Rose executed a slow turn.

The black leather pants—albeit snugger than they'd been three years ago when she'd bought them for a Buffy Halloween costume—cupped her butt impressively. Topped with a lacy black-and-blue corset and knee-high boots, the entire ensemble screamed *badass witch*. All Supernatural nasties would immediately give themselves up the second they laid eyes on her.

At least she hoped they did because she wasn't so sure she could run in this getup, and there wasn't enough time to pry herself out of it and pick something different because Damian struck her as a very punctual individual, which meant she only had a few minutes until he showed.

She grabbed her cell phone and made a panicked video call to her most recently called number.

Olive answered on the fifth ring, mid-yawn. "Hey, witch. What's up?"

Rose immediately forgot her own issues. "If you don't accept Bax's proposition, I'll accept it for you. This is ridiculous."

"I had another talk with her, and she swears she'll stick to her promises this time."

On cue, a loud chorus of laughter echoed from Olive's side of the line followed by the dropping of something that sounded suspiciously like a bowling ball.

"Or not . . ." Olive sighed, removing her glasses to rub her eyes. The second she replaced them, she blinked, suddenly wide awake. "Holy hexes, Rose! Did Harper finally wear you down about going with her to one of those clubs?"

Rose glanced at her outfit and cringed. "No. This is my bounty hunting outfit."

"And what are you hunting again?"

"Real funny." She glanced into the mirror for the hundredth time. "I had a momentary lapse of judgment and now I'm stuck with this. Literally. Please tell me it's not that bad."

"Depends . . ."

"On what?" Rose asked carefully, not sure she wanted to know.

"If your plan is to ride the monster-hunting adrenaline high right into Damian's bed. Hey, look on the bright side. If he's as determined as I think he is, he may be the only one to get you out of that getup."

Rose groaned. "I called you because I thought you'd be more supportive than Vi."

Olly shrugged. "Not my fault that you thought wrong, sis."

"Get more sleep. Pronto. Because this snarky, sleep-deprived Olive isn't my favorite person," Rose joked.

Olive chuckled, calling her out on her bullshit response. "Love you, too."

A heavy knock thumped on her front door.

"Tell Damian I said helloooo . . ." Olive waggled her eyebrows suggestively and shut down the call.

The knock landed again.

She couldn't put it off any longer. Even though the rush of Magic to all her hot spots told her who was on the other side of the door, Rose glanced through the peephole out of habit.

Damian was dressed as he had been the night with the Gryndors.

His butter-soft jeans hung off his trim waist, and the black leather jacket—which she'd come to realize was his favorite—hung open, revealing the powder-blue Henley beneath. The only difference was that his hair, usually hanging loose by his jaw, had been pulled into a low nubbin of a tail, away from his eyes and emphasizing his sculpted cheekbones.

"You opening the door, little witch, or do you plan on staring at me all night in admiration from the other side?" Damian joked, his gorgeous lips twitching.

She yanked the door open with a flourish, and then it was his turn to ogle. Lust darkened his gaze as he ran it from tip to toe, and when he met her back in the middle, her Magic—not to mention her body—really liked what she saw.

"You were saying something about admiration, doc?" Rose teased.

"Hunting rule number two: blend in until it becomes impossible, or unnecessary."

"Are you saying I'll stick out in a crowd or blend in too well? I can go change, but it might take a while . . ."

Damian snorted. "Who the fuck am I kidding? It doesn't matter what you wear or where you go. You'll always stand out from others."

She smiled. "That's actually sweet."

"It's not sweet. It's exhibit A of why bounty hunting isn't for you." He grumbled, almost sullen.

Smirking, she grabbed her keys and stepped into the hall before giving his chest an affectionate pat. "Sorry to disappoint you, but I'm not that easily swayed."

"Can't blame a guy for trying."

They headed downstairs where Rose wasn't surprised to find Damian's motorcycle parked along the curb. This time, two helmets hung from the bars, and she picked one just as she heard her name.

Her neighbor, Mrs. Powers, rolled her wired grocery cart, her feisty Chihuahua, Coco, sitting in the basket. As she approached, the older woman gave Damian an assessing once-over. "I wasn't so sure that was you at first, dear."

Rose's cheeks flushed. "It's me. Do you need help getting your groceries upstairs?"

"No, no, but thanks for the offer. I was hoping I'd run into you though, to remind you about that night out we talked about. It's this Friday if you're still interested." The older woman's gaze flickered to Damian patiently waiting astride his bike. "But you might have other plans on a weekend night, and I can't say that I'd blame you for keeping them."

"I wouldn't miss a night out with you for the world, Mrs. P. Count me in."

Mrs. Powers beamed. "You're sure?"

"Absolutely."

"Great! Guess I'll see you there. You remember how to get there, right?"

"Sure do."

With a smile on her face, her neighbor shuffled her way toward their building, shooting a final look back toward her—and flashing a sly wink—before the door shut behind her.

Rose turned toward Damian, and found him with a near-matching smirk, his eyebrows raised. "What?"

"Night out with the neighbor lady?" Damian chuckled as she climbed onto the motorcycle behind him. "Seems like it could be too much fun for a witch to handle. Can you afford to be brought in by the police again?"

"Go ahead and joke, but I have a lot of fun when I hang out with Mrs. Powers. Don't let that sweet old lady exterior fool you. She aided and abetted Vi's Great Fire Escape escape. The lady has moves."

"Do I even want to know?"

"If you're a good bounty hunter mentor, maybe I'll tell you about it."

With a humorous chuckle, he revved the engine, and waited until she wrapped her arms around his waist. The second her fingers locked over his abdomen, he took off like a demon out of hell.

Julius had sent over the file on Virginia Cummings earlier that day, and she'd read the thing nearly four times since, memorizing every detail from her crimes—including, but not limited to, racketeering and the import of rare, dangerous, and *stolen* magical artifacts—to all her favorite local hangouts.

Even her undying love for the Jonas Brothers made it onto the dossier. And it just so happened that the Jonases were performing their last show of their current tour at Madison Square Garden, and all intel pointed to the upper-level demon enjoying the concert from her private box seat. If habits held true, she'd duck out of the venue a few minutes before the end of the concert to avoid the mass exit.

But now after hours of waiting, Rose wondered if Virginia had decided to shirk her old habits, because the show was about to let out and there was still no sign of the demon.

Slowly rolling her neck to work out the building tension, she paced as Damian watched from his leaning perch against the building, his astuteness fueling her nerves even more.

"Keep up the back and forth and you'll wear a hole in the cement," Damian warned.

From an unusually empty Betz Pavilion, she glanced across Thirty-Third Street where music thumped from the event center. "What if she slipped out another exit? Maybe we should split up and walk the block."

"We're not splitting up. All our resources—and the fact Faroi demons are creatures of habit—say she'll exit through these doors and cut across the pavilion. It's just a matter of time."

"And what time is that? Before or after I start collecting social security?" At his amused silence, she threw him an accusing glare. "You're doing this on purpose, aren't you? Killing me with boredom so I'll decide this isn't for me and I'll move on to the next thing?"

He arched an eyebrow. "Now that's a good idea . . . if only I'd thought of it sooner."

Rose rolled her eyes. "Sarcasm doesn't suit you, doc."

"And yet." He chuckled. "*And*, if you remember, *Julius* gave us this assignment. We both know he's not about to do me any favors by giving us a dud target."

He had a point.

When the brothers had picked up their Hunt task, the palpable friction between them had been unmistakable. She couldn't fathom having a tense relationship with either of her sisters, and even with Christina, despite how much her mother grated on her nerves. Add in her dad, and Edie and her grandfather Jethro before he'd passed, and she'd never lacked for close, supportive relationships.

That hadn't been the case for Damian.

She leaned her rear against the railing across from him so their shoes nearly bumped. "What happened between you and Julius . . . if you don't mind me asking."

"Shouldn't you ask if I mind you asking before you go ahead and ask?" Damian teased.

"Just passing the time since Virginia is obviously never leaving the concert. You don't have to answer."

He slowly crossed his arms, the move highlighting his broad shoulders. "Why does there have to be an inciting incident? We could simply not get along."

"Because until recently, you haven't talked or seen each other in years. That's more than not getting along."

Damian's lips remained willfully closed.

"Did it have something to do with a woman?" She bit her bottom lip, debating her next question. "Did it have something to do with the ex who hexed you?"

"That would've been easier to deal with, but no. At least not directly." He studied her carefully, as if assessing her. "I'm not sure you're ready to hear this story."

"Don't think I can handle it?"

"I know you can. I'm not sure I'm ready to face how you'll look at me afterward," Damian admitted, shifting his gaze off her and onto his feet. "It's far from a fairy tale."

"Fairy tales have always been more Olly's thing. It always annoyed me that the princess constantly needed saving by the prince. If you don't want to talk about it, that's fine. But don't use *that* as an excuse."

His gaze latched on to hers, and held. "Julius and I had different mothers, but share the same father. Ezeil. To say he wasn't a father figure is putting it lightly. He had two goals in life. The first, to create good little spawns to boost Lucy's army. And the second was to do the first to secure his position as his father's favorite prince of Hell. That second one is finally what got him kicked off the Supernatural Council and exiled back to Hell because he didn't have anyone's best interests at heart except for his own."

Rose tried hiding the knowledge of what Vi had already told her behind a mask of surprise.

Damian didn't miss a second of it. "You already knew all of that, didn't you?"

"No," she said almost too quickly, before adding, "well, I knew about the prince of Hell part, but I didn't know your father was Ezeil."

She fought not to cringe. Damian couldn't help who is father was any more than she could deter her mother's matchmaking attempts. But Ezeil, the former demon representative of the Supernatural Council, definitely had a reputation—and not a good one. If memory served her right, she'd met him at one of the first Supernatural summits that she'd attended with her gran, and that fleeting introduction had been more than enough for her.

But to be raised by the demon? Rose nearly shivered at the thought.

Damian chuckled dryly, almost as if reading her mind. "Yeah. Safe to say he wasn't the playing catch type of father."

Rose was struck with a thought. "So if Lucifer was your father's father, does that make you a prince or duke or earl or something?"

This time Damian's chuckle was real. "Not even close. To Ezeil's annoyance, he wasn't conceived. He was created. It was enough to award him a prince title and to put him in charge of building up Lucy's elite forces for about five hundred years, but that was about it. So in a second attempt to win his boss's favor, the bastard put extra focus on Julius and myself and hoped we'd be able to achieve what he didn't. Becoming Lucifer's right hand."

"And Julius liked the idea and you didn't?" Rose guessed, slowly digesting everything.

Damian hesitated, looking slightly less sure of himself. "For a long time, it was the other way around."

"Really?"

"My mother had been a Norm, which in Ezeil's eyes was my largest weakness. So I overcompensated. I trained harder. Worked smarter. The more I embraced my demon side, the more approval I saw in his eyes. The more approval I received, the more I sought. It was a never-ending, escalating cycle."

"And Julius?"

"Julius was always more of a lover than a fighter, and was pretty content letting me do the dirty work and taking most of the credit for it. He didn't Hunt because he loved it. He Hunted because of the money it could give him. Me on the other hand? It almost became the air I breathed. By the time I realized I didn't like what I saw in the mirror after a Hunt, it was too late."

Realization had her studying Damian in a different light. "The hex . . ."

He nodded. "Talk about a wake-up call. But during every attempt to distance myself from the Hunter life, Julius shoved me right back into the fray, chanting about embracing my inner demon. The more I did, and the more targets I hauled in, the more perks he enjoyed— including the old man's approval."

"But you stopped . . ."

"I did . . . eventually . . . and all thanks to Miguel. But the second I cut myself off from that life, Julius was cut off too."

"Your father—"

"Denounced us. Disinherited. Whatever you want to call it. We were no longer his problem."

"But you've both done well for yourself. Julius is now on the Supernatural Council, and you went to college, became a vet, and run a sanctuary for sick and abused animals. That's not exactly a shabby life, Damian."

"None of that would've happened without Miguel, and didn't happen before I pissed off the wrong witch. So don't let Julius's 'I'm a Councilman for the betterment of Norm- and Supernatural-kind' fool you. He did it because I wasn't the only one Ezeil cut off, and he'd become so accustomed to living the cushy high life, the Supernatural Council was the only way he could maintain it."

The story seemed so far-fetched and yet not. No sense, and yet *all* the sense. Still, it baffled her mind and stole her concentration until Damian's attention drifted beyond her shoulder. "Looks like Virginia's ducking out."

Rose turned, expecting an eight-foot giant with horns and a spiked tail. Something ferocious and hell-like, much like the Gryndors. Instead, the person headed their way pushed a rolling walker and wore a JBFan4Eva concert T-shirt.

She spun on Damian, who still perched against the brick wall and sported a shit-eating grin. "You find this funny? She's not a day younger than ninety!"

He shrugged. "This is who we've been told to bring in. Have at it, Miss Bounty Hunter. Clock's tickin'."

❖ ❖ ❖

Was it mean of Damian to serve Rose up to the demon? *Yep.* Was it necessary? *Absolutely.*

It was the quickest way to nip this latest fascination in the bud, but in case things went sideways with Virginia Cummings, he was there. Virginia's outer, fragile Norm exterior was a ruse to blend seamlessly into the background, one that allowed the demon to get away with a whole lot of nefarious deeds.

Sometimes Faroi took the shape of kids, or gangly-limbed teens. Others—like Virginia—picked the elderly population as their muse. No matter the size or shape, they weren't any less conniving, or dangerous. In fact, it made them more so, because when they took unthreatening guises, people's defenses dropped, and when guards went down, the demons feasted.

Staying against the building, Damian let Rose take the lead.

She eyed the older woman's approach. "Um . . . are you Virginia Cummings?"

The demon glanced up, gray eyes blinking innocently behind her thick-lensed bottle-cap glasses. "Yes, dear. That's me."

"You're the Virginia Cummings who used to live in Los Angeles? In Pasadena?"

The older woman nodded. "I've been blessed to live all over the world throughout my many, many years. You look familiar, dear. Do I know you? Are you Audrey's great-granddaughter? You look a little like her across the eyes."

Muttering a soft curse, Rose glanced at him over her shoulder. "What do I do?"

"This is the job, babe. Locate the target. Subdue the target. Bring in the target." He nudged his chin toward the elderly woman. "We located, and now you subdue. Break out those nifty magical cuffs and let's get moving so we can move along to the third step."

"I'm not putting an octogenarian in freakin' handcuffs—magical or steel," Rose hissed.

"Eighties?" Virginia chuckled. "If only I were in my eighties again. I'm actually quite a bit older."

Rose whipped her head back toward him, finger pointing. "Did you hear that? She's even older! Julius must've been smoking whatever Olive's roommate is selling from their apartment, because there is no way this little granny is the person we're supposed to bring in. Look at her!"

He did . . . right over Rose's shoulder. All his reflexes went on instant alert, preparing to move if needed. But he kept his voice even. "You may want to get those cuffs on her before things get tricky."

Rose propped her hands on her hips and glared at him. "I'm not hauling in an old woman and her walker to stand before your brother . . . *or* the Council."

The air around the Faroi demon rippled as Virginia's Norm outer layer melted away with every inch she grew. A few distracted moments later and standing in the exact place of the once-eighty-year-old woman was a red-scaled creature with Medusa-like horns and an odoriferous ooze that most definitely didn't smell like butterscotch candies.

Rose sniffed the air, her nose immediately wrinkling with distaste. "What's the smell?"

Damian pushed off the wall. "Turn around and find out."

"Why would I . . . ?" She turned, her eyes widening to saucerlike discs as they roamed up and up, her head tilting back to take in the entire length of the Faroi, which stood nearly three feet above her own five-foot-eight. "What the hell did you do with Virginia?"

With a bellowing laugh, the she-demon tossed the walker aside. "Oh, sweetheart. I ate Virginia Cummings for breakfast nearly four and a half centuries ago."

"Ate?"

"I am *Cumitox*. Entrepreneur. Philanthropist. Acquirer of Magical Antiquities." Cumitox flicked her forked tongue over her lips. "And I would very much like to make you my next vessel. You look absolutely edible . . . and sturdy."

Rose stepped back, shaking her head. "I'm not. Really, I'm not.

I've been told I give people indigestion, and not the kind cured by a roll of Tums."

Damian chuckled. "I think you taste pretty damn good."

Her head swiveled toward him, "Not helpful, doc. Not helpful in the least."

"Oh, you want me to be helpful? Like suggesting you put her in magical cuffs? Oh wait . . . I did do that. Huh. Guess I'm pretty helpful after all."

"Can we save the *I told you so* for when a demon isn't announcing they'd like to make me their next skin suit?"

"Seems a little boring, doesn't it?" Damian asked, using her own words against her.

The she-demon's gaze bounced between them. "Are you married or something?"

"No way!" Rose exclaimed at the same time Damian snorted, "Not even close."

The witch's head snapped to him. "Why do you say it like *that*?"

"Like what?"

She dropped her voice and mimicked him. "Not. Even. Close. *If I ever decide to marry, that person would be the luckiest person on Earth.*"

"Then we definitely know it's not me because the only luck I have is the bad kind," Damian quipped.

"Yoo-hoo!" Cumitox waved her taloned hands. "I hate to break up this lover's quarrel, but can we get this moving? I'd very much love to get to bed and have sweet, sweet dreams of my dear Nicky."

Damian came up next to the Faroi. "Sorry, Tox, but nap time will have to wait. You need to come with us."

"But I don't want to!" The she-demon stomped her foot.

Rose folded her arms over her chest, the move plumping her corset-covered breasts. "Sometimes we have to do things we don't want. It's a fact of life."

"Not in *my* life, witch." Cumitox leaped, taloned fingers spread out as she reached for Rose.

Damian pulled her away from the claws' trajectory with a split second to spare, and the demon howled, swinging around to catch him, too. Damian ducked and the strike hit nothing but air.

Drawing on his inner hellion, he weaved around each punch and kick, his reflexes and increased speed making contact practically impossible. Rose stood off to the side, her mouth slightly agape as she watched.

"This isn't a spectator sport, little witch," Damian jested, ducking yet another swinging fist. That time the *whoosh* of air brushed across his cheek.

Too damn close.

"You want to do that little hocus-pocus thing?" Damian breathed a little heavier as he dance-battled with a now-raging Faroi. "Magical cuffs like you did with the Gryndors would be pretty good right about now."

Cumitox looked more hesitant before taking her next lazy swing. "The Gryndors? You're the two Hunters that took down the Gryndor brothers?"

Damian nodded his head toward Rose. "Technically, she did all the heavy lifting on that one."

The demon stopped, not looking the least bit winded, and stared at Rose. "It takes powerful Magic to incapacitate a Gryndor demon . . . especially the brothers. What's your familial line?"

"That's an awfully personal question for having just met, isn't it?" Rose quipped. "But I'm a Maxwell."

Cumitox's red-scaled face went petal pink. "You're the descendent of Edie Maxwell?"

"That would be my grandmother."

The Faroi slowly returned to the demure form of Virginia Cummings, her face lit up with something akin to awe. "I can't believe the Prima's granddaughter was sent to pick up little ole me! This is almost better than seeing my sweet Nick in concert! I'll go with you, witch. No fuss."

Rose slid a coy, smug look Damian's way. "So you're not going to eat me for a midnight snack and wear me as a skin suit?"

"Oh, no. Absolutely not. This is a much better story to tell my quilting circle. They'll die with jealousy, and that's more priceless than whatever delicious meat is on your bones."

He silently cursed at the wicked gleam in Rose's eye.

He'd brought her along with the hope she'd either be bored to tears or terrified into screams, but she'd experienced neither. Nothing except a healthy dose of determination. As much as that should bother him, he also couldn't help but be a smidge bit proud they'd done it together . . . and his inner demon, pushing against his flesh, agreed.

That was more dangerous than any Hunting target.

17

Third Time's the Charm

Dirty, tired, and more than ready to shower off abandoned subway grime, Rose still would've thought she walked on cloud nine if her boots weren't pinching her toes. As promised, Virginia Cummings—aka Cumitox—didn't cause an ounce of trouble while Rose and Damian delivered her to the Supernatural authorities, and since the assignment didn't take as long as they'd thought, she'd convinced Damian to snag another.

She still rode a Magic high from bringing in the "renegade vampire"—*Drac*—who turned out to be a Norm dressed in vampire cosplay attire with a horribly fake Transylvanian accent. The Supernatural groupie had spent the last couple months living in abandoned subway tunnels, hoping to stumble onto a vampire nest to call his own. He hadn't believed Damian when he'd told him he'd be more likely to find one in a penthouse along Central Park West than the tunnels.

Rose hummed, unable to yank the smile off her face as she worked her keys into her front door.

Damian chuckled right behind her. "You look and sound awfully happy for someone slathered in substances of questionable origins."

She gave him a slow once-over, and bit her bottom lip. Even with dirty jeans and disheveled hair, he still looked edible.

Rose shrugged. "You're not exactly clean, either . . . or grumpy."

Her front door clicked open and she turned. They faced each other in the hallway of her apartment building, Rose all too aware of the adrenaline still coursing through her system, and with it was a healthy dose of raging libido.

Her gaze dropped to Damian's mouth and back, only to catch him doing the same. Lust quickly hijacked all her good sense.

She eased closer, running her hands up his chest, and gently pulled him closer. "Wash my back and I'll wash yours, doc? Fair warning though . . . we are really dirty. It'll probably take a few rinses before we can consider ourselves clean."

His mouth kicked up into a sexy grin. "Good thing I'm up for the challenge."

The telltale firmness pushing against Rose's stomach told her that wasn't the only thing up. They moved simultaneously.

In a mass collision, they stumbled through the door, Rose flicking her fingers to magically close and lock it behind them. They walked, kissed, and stripped their way toward her small bathroom. By the time she turned on the shower, they were a tangle of naked limbs and greedy mouths.

Studio apartments aren't known for spaciousness. The second they stepped beneath the hot spray, Rose got a soap dish to the ass. Damian leaned back to give her room to maneuver around and took a loofa stick to the left ear.

A husky chuckle rolled from his chest, vibrating through them both. "Pretty sure this is more dangerous than bounty hunting. Maybe we should skip the shower."

She grinned and reached out, pulling something slimy from his hair that might or might not have been part of someone's dinner a few months back. "Or not . . ."

Showers had never been this much fun. While Rose lathered her hair, Damian washed his with her shampoo, every move brushing his arms against her slick body. By the time she'd lathered her shower pouf, he'd wrapped his arms around her waist from behind and slowly glided his soapy palms up her torso.

Her breath quickened as he cupped her breasts, his thumbs gently rubbing her already hard nipples. With a small sigh, Rose tipped her head back onto his chest and savored each and every caress.

"Like that, huh?" Damian brushed his mouth against her ear before giving it a gentle tug with his teeth.

She released a small moan. "So far I've liked everything you've done."

"Don't think I've forgotten about my promise, little witch."

The pleasure heating up between her legs made it nearly impossible to think much less talk. "What promise . . . ?"

"Reaching your orgasm quota before things really take off . . ."

Damian's left hand slid between her legs, through her folds, and over her clit while his mouth feasted on the sensitive column of her neck. The double sensations pulled a pleasured whimper from her lips. She wasn't so sure she'd survive to hit that promised orgasm quota.

Before long, she rolled her hips, alternating between lifting herself toward his talented fingers and pushing back against the ragingly hard erection nestled against her lower back. Her body had a mind of its own and Damian was its mind reader.

Pleasure rose, quaking her knees until she thought they'd give out. "Damian . . ."

With the hand still cupping her breast, he gently applied pressure to her nipple. "Let go. Let it all go, little witch . . ."

A gentle nibble on the neck.

A slow circular rub of her clit.

A little pinch.

Rose let go, pleasure swallowing her whole. Her knees buckled and Damian caught her, never once stopping the slow rub of his fingers as he demanded every last drop of orgasm her body had in it to give.

Damian smiled against her neck. "That was one . . ."

She stretched her arm behind him, running her palm over his thigh and the lower half of his rear end. "I want to touch you, too."

"Gotta reach three before that happens."

She groaned. "You were serious about that? That's practically impossible."

He turned her toward him, and backed her against the cool tiles before blanketing her front with his heated body.

He hooked her chin and tilted her gaze up toward his. "I *am* serious. Your streak of lazy, selfish partners ends right the hell now, little witch. If I say you're getting three orgasms before I let you touch me, then you'll be having three. Is that okay with you?"

Rose's throat dried as she studied him and nodded, not trusting herself to speak. They hadn't known each other long, and they'd had their FBA even less than that, but somehow she knew he wouldn't steer her wrong.

Damian's attention flickered to the corner of the tub. "What do we have here?" His lips twitched as he bent over to pick up her purple vibrating dildo, Mr. Wiggles.

She reached for it, but he pulled it away.

"Uh-uh. I'm guessing this is the talented Mr. Wiggles?" Damian smirked.

She made another half-hearted grab for it. "Seriously, doc. We don't have to—"

"Do you enjoy it?" With one push of the button, the vibrator came to life. Its buzzing echoed in the small bathroom. He cocked an eyebrow. "Well? Do you?"

"I wouldn't keep it around if I didn't. And it's waterproof so I can use it anywhere . . ."

"Good to know." With a faint smirk, he dropped to his knees.

Wiggles in one hand, Damian trailed his other from her ankle to her thigh, guiding her leg over his shoulder until she was completely open to him and leaning against the wall for support. He looked up at her from over her mound, a lusty promise on his face. Rose barely remembered to lock her other leg before he leaned closer, using the vibrator in tandem with his tongue and fingers.

Her Magic shifted beneath her skin, warming areas of her body that weren't already scorching hot. With a long, low groan, she fisted her fingers through Damian's hair and leaned her head back against the tiles with a faint thud.

She didn't know what she enjoyed more, the warm caress of his tongue, or the fast vibration traveling through her entire body. Damian's eyes fastened on hers as he pleasured her, and it was hottest thing she'd ever experienced.

She couldn't look away as she bucked her hips closer to his eager mouth, wanting more. Needing more.

She whimpered, and as if reading her mind—and her body—Damian flicked the vibrator up another notch and quickly coaxed her toward orgasm number two with Mr. Wiggles around for the assist.

✦ ✦ ✦

Third time was the charm . . . and also the moment Rose's knees gave out.

With a satisfied grin, Damian slid back up her body, the taste of her on his lips, the most delicious thing he'd ever devoured. He already couldn't wait to do it again.

"And I do believe that was number three." Holding her trembling body against his, he slid his damp hands around her waist and over the swell of her ass.

Rose's eyes damn near sparkled as she dropped her gaze to where his cock stood at painful attention. "That means I get to touch you now, right?"

As if the damn thing heard her eagerness to touch him, his dick twitched. "You sure as hell do, little witch."

Damian shut off the water as Rose stepped out from the shower and reached for a nearby towel. He caught her in a princess carry before she could hide behind it, and she squealed, hands latching onto his arms.

"Please tell me you're okay if we skip drying off," Damian pleaded, his voice husky with need. There was no way she didn't feel his cock brushing against her backside, and just in case she didn't, he purposefully rolled his hips.

She gasped, her body shimmying closer. "But we'll get the sheets all wet and—"

"And . . . ?" He brought his mouth to the sensitive spot just below her ear, and her body practically melted against his on contact.

"On second thought, air drying is the eco-friendly thing to do, and we've already conserved water by showering together. It would be a shame to break the streak now." Wearing nothing but a mischievous smirk, she traced the outline of his tattoo before leaning forward, pink tongue flicking out to taste it. "And I don't know about you, but I'd really like for you to be inside me."

"You're definitely not the only one who wants that. We're still good on the protection?"

"All good, doc."

"Thank fuck." Their gazes locked as he laid her down on the bed and climbed onto the mattress. The second he slipped onto his back, he gently yanked her on top of him.

She sat astride him, her legs on either side of his hips as she glanced down at his already throbbing cock. The sight of her biting her lower lip as she watched it drove him mad with lust.

He resisted the urge to take control, and glanced down to where his erection bobbed eagerly for attention. "You said you wanted to touch. It's all yours, little witch."

Her alert gaze skirted his eyes to his mouth and down his chest and back, but it wasn't the deer-in-headlights look that put him on instant alert. It was her abrupt silence and the sudden nervous tic of her heartbeat fluttering at the base of her throat.

"Rose . . ." Sitting up, he cupped her cheek, gently redirecting her focus to him. "Do you still want this? It's okay if you don't. We don't have to do anything. You know that, right? We can take a nap. Watch a movie. Hell, if you want me gone, I'll grab my things and get out of your hair right now."

"No . . ." She shook her head, palms resting on his shoulders. "I mean, yes. I still want this. I just . . ."

"Just what?"

And she was back to nibbling that sexy lower lip. He resisted the urge to free it and instead, put all his attention on her.

"You can tell me." Damian tried putting her mind at ease.

"Taking what I want—like *this*—isn't something I'm used to doing." Pink rose high on her cheeks as she finally confided in him.

He absorbed her words, rolled them around in his head, and cursed her bastard exes. *All of them.* "Those asshats don't deserve to breathe the same air as you."

Hell, neither did he, but he'd do his damned best to at least try.

Slipping his fingers into her hair, he slowly guided her mouth to his for a feather-soft kiss before gently nibbling her lower lip. "Consider this a turning point. What do you want, Rose? Tell me. If it's within my power to make happen, I'll do it."

She glanced at his still straining cock, already beaded with precum, and admitted softly, "I want you inside me."

"Then take me." Damian dropped his hands to her waist and supported her as she braced her hands on his chest, tentatively lifting her hips.

She rocked on top of him, experimentally sliding her wetness over his aching cock. It was a delicious torture as he lay back and let her set the pace, and as if finally realizing he meant his word, her body moved faster. Her breasts danced in front of him as she moved up and down, and he leaned up, capturing one in his mouth.

Above him, Rose sighed, holding his head to her as he feasted. First her left breast, then her right. With each suck, his cock throbbed, aching to be inside her. And then with another roll of her hips, he was, Rose taking his entire length in one slow drop of her body.

They groaned in unison as her tightness sheathed him like a snug glove. Damian dropped back to the mattress, and running his hands over every inch of skin that he could, he let her set the rhythm and pace.

"Damian." Her lusty gaze met his as she leaned forward, her fingers digging into his chest for extra support as she rode him.

They were both breathless and sweaty in seconds, the only sound in the room the rise and fall of their bodies.

His hands slid around to her ass, and as she dropped her hips, he lifted his, deepening each and every thrust. "That's it, little witch. Take it. Take what you need."

"Oh Goddess . . ." Rose panted, her body quaking above him.

The first signs of release swelled heavy between his legs. He wouldn't last much longer. Not at this pace, and definitely not with her gorgeous eyes staring at him as if looking straight into his soul.

"Touch me," she begged as if reading his mind. "Touch me. Now."

"Like this?" He slid a hand between them and rubbed her clit in a slow, soft circle. The touch elicited a soft gasp and a plea for more, and that's exactly what he gave her.

That was all it took for either of them. Her body tightened around his in an epic release that primed his own and they came together, their bodies losing their synchronous movements as they strived to make it last as long as possible.

They kissed and touched, their lips swollen from the tenacity of their embrace, until the very last wave of pleasure ebbed slowly away.

Rose dropped next to him on the mattress, a satisfied smile plastered on her face. "Holy hexes in a hailstorm . . ."

Damian chuckled. "Now who's wearing the smug grin?"

"Not even sorry."

Neither was he, and the sight of her breathless smile only made him that much more determined to keep it in place as long as possible, and by whatever means necessary.

And that spelled trouble.

For both of them.

18

Panty-Chic

Rose's body ached in all the right ways, for all the right reasons, and she was pretty certain the smirk on her face was permanent despite not yet having had her morning caffeine jolt. If this was post-sex bliss, she could definitely get used to it.

It wasn't just the pleasure—although that had been top-tier epic.

It was everything else that came with it—before, during, and after. Damian made certain she was with him every step of the way, even coaxing her to take the lead. Before him, not one sexual partner had made her pleasure and comfort a top priority. And yes, that spoke volumes about her taste in men.

But it also said heaps about Damian. Despite calling himself a bad influence, the man wasn't nearly as bad as he believed himself to be and something about that was more than a little sad.

Expelling a small sigh, she'd brought her first mug of coffee toward her lips when two thickly corded arms slipped around her waist.

"You made coffee?" Damian's naked chest warmed her back as he pulled her close, his mouth brushing the back of her neck. "You shouldn't have . . ."

He reached for the mug in her hand, which was appropriately etched with WITCH'S BREW.

She pulled it away with a snort. "I didn't. Touch a witch's morning coffee and sparks will fly . . . probably literally."

"Good to know." Chuckling, he alternated between kissing and nipping the curve of her neck. "Maybe we can create sparks for some other reason."

An agreement hovered on the tip of her tongue when the front door jiggled. A second later, Rose's head turned as her sisters' voices echoed through the small foyer, and then Vi and Olive appeared in the flesh.

Rose blinked, both mind and body frozen. They all had keys to each other's places and used them at will. She'd never had a reason to be wary of unexpected drop-ins . . . until now.

Olive noticed her first, and when the youngest triplet's eyes widened behind her glasses, Vi glanced their way.

"Well, well, well." Vi chuckled, giving her T-shirt and panty-clad attire a slow, calculating perusal. "I daresay you have that just-fucked glow to your skin. Almost literally. And about damn time. Where is the lucky bastard so I can thank him personally?"

Rose glanced toward the mirror on the other wall, and immediately realized two things. The first, that there definitely was a magically luminescent glow coating her skin. And the second, that at some point between the front door opening and her sisters spotting her, she stood alone, Damian nowhere in sight until two seconds later when he strode out from her bathroom fully dressed.

Vi's smirk stretched from ear to ear. "And the source of the glow appears. Hello, Damian. I'd usually ask how your morning is going but I already have a pretty good idea."

"Violet!" Rose's cheeks reddened.

Damian didn't even bat an eye, chuckling in response. "Vi . . . Olive. The two of you look lovely as always."

"Then you haven't seen me after spin class." Vi wrinkled her nose and glanced at her stylish purple pantsuit. "And this Barney costume is being exchanged for joggers the second we're done with this grand opening. And while I'm being real, I'll probably force Olly to drive home so I can change in the backseat while in transit."

Olive chuckled. "Oh, the good ole days."

Vi took another look at Rose's half-dressed appearance. "Not that I don't love the idea of watching Christina's head spin off her shoulders when you walk into the event wearing your best panty-chic, but it's a bit cold outside. You may want to throw on another layer or two."

Rose blinked. "What event? I don't remember—fuck flying broomsticks. The winery opening is *today*?"

"Guess that's my cue to leave," Damian announced. He turned to her with a wink. "Walk me to the door?"

"I'm sorry," she apologized in the foyer. "I completely forgot about this opening thing for my parents."

"Well, you were a little busy." He smirked.

Her gaze flickered to where her sisters unabashedly watched, neither bothering to look away. "Sorry about them, too. I wish I could say they weren't always so intrusive, but they are. It's our thing."

"I'm just sorry we couldn't have a repeat performance before I headed out, but there's always later, right?" Wrapping an arm around her waist, he eased her closer.

She propped her hands on his chest and sank into his embrace. It wasn't as if Vi and Olly didn't know what they'd been up to. A witch doesn't get a sexified *glow* from playing Uno.

"When can we do it again?" She peered up at him through her lashes, hoping she looked more seductive and less something-in-her-eye.

"Eager, huh? I like it." His gaze flickered to her mouth.

"Are you kidding me? That was the most fun I've had in ages . . . even if Virginia didn't turn out to be the Big Bad we thought she was."

It took a moment for him to register her words, and when he did . . .

Rose giggled. "Oh, did you think I meant something else?"

He chuckled. "Point in your column, little witch, but maybe we can postpone our repeat until tonight?"

So, so tempting. And it was on the tip of her tongue to say yes.

"Actually, I have some pretty lively plans for later." She fought against a grin as an idea formed in her head. "You can come with me if you're up for it, but fair warning, rolling with this group isn't for the faint of heart."

"No?"

She shook her head. "Only the strong survive."

"Good thing I'm pretty good at holding my own. Count me in."

"Tick-tock, lovebirds," Vi chimed, tapping her nonexistent watch.

Rose dropped her head onto Damian's chest with a groan. "But first, I'll have to survive this freaking opening."

Her temporary pillow vibrated as Damian chuckled. "It's just peopling. You did that professionally, didn't you?"

"And it wore me out then, too. But now I'm the *ejected* Prima Apparent. As far as anyone knows, that's never happened before. I may as well be the two-headed snake at the zoo."

"Nah, you're definitely a lot cuter." He casually slid his palm down her waist. "And look, no scales. I would've seen them after last night."

She honest-to-goddess blushed, making Damian chuckle. "Call or text me the time and place, and I'll meet you for these lively plans tonight. Vi? Olive?" He turned to the other two Maxwells, flashing them a wink. "Catch you later."

They all waved to Damian as he left them alone. Rose mourned the loss of his touch immediately and took a private moment to collect herself for the incoming sister interrogation.

Instead, she turned to meet Violet's annoyed huff. "I will never forgive you for this, Rose Marie Maxwell."

"For—"

"Divulging something this juicy involves wine, ice cream, and quite possibly a *Magic Mike* rewatch, and now we'll have to hear it from inside the car." Vi shooed her toward her bathroom. "Get a move on, because if we're late for this grand opening and Mom breaks into one of her rants, that's another thing I'll never forgive you for."

Rose grinned, knowing her sister would do no such thing, and practically skipped into the shower. Not even the threat of earning Christina's ire could dampen her current mood.

"Hey," Olive called out, "what lively plans do you have tonight?"

"Mrs. Powers," Rose answered back. Hearing Vi's chuckles, her mischievous giggle turned into full-blown laughter.

Having been Mrs. Powers's neighbor for years before moving in with Lincoln, the oldest triplet knew exactly what kind of night lay ahead . . . and it made Rose a little happy knowing Damian had absolutely no clue.

✦ ✦ ✦

Wolves and witches and angels, oh my! An eclectic array of Supes and Norms came out to celebrate the grand opening of Supernatural Spirits Winery, a boutique vineyard located on the outskirts of Westchester. The idea had been their father's brainchild, an off-hand comment made while talking with friends, and Christina had latched on and run with it, the winery becoming their mother's latest obsession.

Most Supes had to consume copious amounts of alcohol to feel even the slightest buzz, but the spirits brewed at SSW catered specifically toward Supernaturals and their higher-than-average tolerance.

No one was more surprised than Rose to find the entire winery had an understated, comfy atmosphere. Christina did things to excess, but the entire facility featured a rustic, natural beauty and had the homey feel of Napa Valley wineries, right down to the hardwood floors and creamy walls. Upcycled wine barrels doubled as decoration and provided accent touches to everything from hanging artwork to the doors and handles.

It was adorable and not the least bit ostentatious. Maybe Rose's father had had more say in the design than she'd previously thought.

Sipping a sweet raspberry rosé, Rose eyed Vi and Edie across the room. Edie listened raptly to something Angel Representative Ramón said and her sister pretended to. Olly had retreated to the bathroom fifteen minutes ago and had yet to return, but what concerned Rose most was that she'd lost track of her mother.

In social situations like this one, that was never a good thing because the second you lost sight of her, she'd pop up with a surprise, and not one involving horn-blowers and confetti.

"And there's my elusive daughter now," Christina's songlike voice chimed.

"And let the games begin . . ." Rose conjured every drop of patience before turning toward her approaching mother.

A tall, lithe blonde walked next to her, both wearing near-matching smiles. Rose reflexively pushed one to her face, too.

"Rose, sweetheart." Christina pulled her into an affectionate hug that caught her off guard. "I wanted to introduce you to someone I think you'd get along with fabulously. This is Callie Sanderson, from the Massachusetts coven. Callie, this is my second-oldest pride and joy, Rose."

Callie held her hand out, gifting her a genuine smile. "It's a pleasure to meet you. I've heard so many great things about you."

"Sanderson? From Massachusetts?" Rose accepted her hand with a teasing smile.

Callie laughed. "Oh, and it gets worse. Even though I live in New York now, I was born and raised in Salem, and I have two sisters. Every day we thank Goddess our parents didn't name us Sarah, Winifred, and Mary."

They laughed, and Rose's hesitancy about this woman melted away. "My sister Vi would definitely have a field day with that. She's the biggest *Hocus Pocus* fan on record."

"Don't steal my witch card, but so am I."

They laughed.

"I was excited to get an invite to this opening, because I've been wanting to meet you for quite some time," Callie admitted, almost bashfully. "I hope this doesn't sound too stalkerish, but I've been a huge fan of your charity work for years. It was one of the reasons why I began my own nonprofit organization a few years ago. Sparks of Hope."

Rose's eyebrows lifted. "I've heard of you. Your organization has done a lot of great work all over the globe, especially with medical access and with LGBTQ+ youth."

"We try to do as much as we can, but the need is limitless, so if someone such as yourself has heard of us then we must be doing something right." Callie blushed. "My curiosity is forcing me to ask you this, but what are you working on right now?"

Beaming proudly, Christina laid a hand on Rose's arm affectionately. "Rose is working with a nearby animal sanctuary, and has even taken it upon herself to volunteer her own personal hours to help with the running of the place."

Rose tried clarifying, "Well, it's not like—"

"Oh, if you'll excuse me. I'm being summoned by Rose's father." Christina hustled away, leaving the two of them alone.

"So, an animal sanctuary?" An impressed look twinkled in Callie's eyes.

Rose chuckled. "Yeah, about that . . . you should know that those volunteer hours are part of a community service sentence I received from the Supernatural Council."

Callie's eyebrows lifted as she sipped her wine. "Oh, I do love a good story and I sense a doozy."

"I erroneously assumed that two emaciated horses in a field were being abused by their owner and I staged a jailbreak with my sisters. It turned out the place was an animal sanctuary and the horses had already been saved and were receiving care."

"Oh no."

They both chuckled.

"Oh, yes." Rose nodded. "But luckily the Council saw my heart was in the right place and I'm now fulfilling some community service hours. And while I'm there, I'm trying to help them bring in some funds to take care of the animals."

"It's a labor of love. You can't help yourself."

"Exactly." *Finally, someone who understands . . .*

"That's how I feel about Sparks of Hope. It started with a love for rescuing animals, then for supporting voting rights, and then my passion projects snowballed from there." Callie looked thoughtful for a second. "I hope you don't mind, but I asked your mother what you're doing now that you're no longer the Prima Apparent and she mentioned you're still considering your choices."

That put a glowy spin to the way she'd been floundering . . .

"I love my job," Callie continued, "and I employ some amazing, inventive, and driven people, and I would be absolutely ecstatic to have you come on board."

And that had not been what she expected.

"You're offering me a job?" Rose asked.

"A job? No. I'd love for you to come into Sparks of Hope as my *partner.*"

First, Rose could've been knocked over by her mother's unexpected support and affection, and now again. "Um . . . wow."

"I'm sorry, I'm getting ahead of myself. You see, I love my job. I love making a difference and encouraging the world's youth to do the same. But as my fiancée points out routinely, I can't be married to my job and to her." Callie laughed. "And honestly, she's right. The company is now in a position where I feel comfortable sharing some of the responsibility, and even though I haven't officially met you until now, I knew you'd be the perfect fit. I guess you could say that Magic told me."

"I don't know what to say."

"Then don't say anything. I know this came out of left field. Think about it. And if you're not ready now, I completely understand. The offer is open-ended. I won't fill it with just anyone, so . . ." She handed Rose a card etched with the Sparks of Hope logo. "Call me with any questions, and if you need help with that sanctuary, or you need someone to bounce around some ideas with, I'm your witch."

"Thank you, Callie, that's a generous offer all the way around," Rose said, meaning it. "I'll think about it."

They talked for another minute before Christina returned with a matchmaker twinkle in her eye and a "handsome shifter" Rose just *had* to meet. Seeing the sheer panic on her face, Callie played interference by asking for an introduction herself.

Thank you, Rose mouthed gratefully to her new friend.

All in all, it was a pretty good day and Rose couldn't help but think that maybe karma had finally decided to cut her a little slack . . . and she hoped it kept coming.

19

Bingo!

Nerves weren't something Damian was accustomed to having. As a Hunter, giving in to nerves got you killed. In vet medicine, it killed your most vulnerable patients. In a lively night out with a sexy witch, he wasn't sure what it got him, but as he pulled up in front of the address Rose gave him, he was certain he was about to find out.

Knowing she loved keeping him on his toes, he'd expected a bar, or maybe a pool hall so she could beat his pants off yet again. Maybe even a nightclub where she could literally dance circles around him because his hips had absolutely no damn tempo.

But *this*, he sure as hell didn't expect.

Pulling up the GPS on his phone again, he double-checked the address to make certain he'd gotten it right, and saw Rose step out the main doors.

He momentarily forgot what he'd been about to do. Formfitting blue jeans cupped her ass deliciously, and her hair, pulled up in one of those sexily mussed pony-buns, revealed the delicate slope of her neck and his favorite nibbling spot below her ear. She scanned the sidewalk, pulling a pink zip-up sweatshirt tightly around her body, and stopped when she saw him sitting in his truck.

She waved, standing beneath the lit sign for the Restview Retirement Center & Community Hall, her eyes twinkling as he climbed out from the driver's seat. "You found the place! I was beginning to think I scared you off with the wild night talk."

After locking the truck, he made his way toward the curb. With each step, Rose's smile grew until it reached ear to ear, and it was a gorgeous sight. He'd seen her decked out in a fancy gown at Vi and Linc's Bonding Ceremony. He'd enjoyed the sight of her naked, curvy body undulating above him. But she'd never looked as beautiful as she did now in jeans and a hoodie, and it took a slow minute for him to realize she was waiting for him to say something.

He cocked an eyebrow and couldn't help but chuckle. "A wild night out at the retirement hall? Doing what? Playing chess? Shuffleboard?"

She scoffed and looped her arm through his and led the way inside. "Shuffleboard is for amateurs. You haven't lived through an extreme game until you've bingo'd with the most lethal bingo players this side of the Hudson River. And I'll have you know, there's no one more lethal about bingo than the people through these doors."

He almost asked her to repeat herself when they stepped into a large hall. Rows of tables filled the room, lined up like a bingo hall army, and front and center stood the general, with bushy white hair, speaking loudly into a crackling microphone.

"B-seven," he announced. "B . . . seven."

The senior citizens mumbled at their tables, some as they enthusiastically stamped their colored markers onto the cards in front of them. Others grumbled, not finding the called number. *Bingo*.

"Your lively night involves numbered squares and pretzel bowls?" He shot her a coy look.

"Do not judge this night by the game or the snacks. I'll have you know that this crowd can be seriously cutthroat." She fought against a forming grin, pulling him to a gentle stop. "I need to know that you can handle this, doc. It's not for the faint of heart, and you definitely don't want to divert your attention for longer than a second or else they'll sense your weakness and go in for the kill."

"Are we still talking about bingo, or some show on Animal Planet?" Damian chuckled.

"You jest, but I'll have you know that both are extremely entertaining ways to pass the time."

"You know what else is entertaining?" He leaned close, and dropped his voice to a low rumble. *"Sex."*

Her lips quirked. "Well then, I'm glad I could expand your entertainment activities repertoire by one more."

A familiar older Norm woman glanced up from a nearby table and waved.

Rose grabbed his hand, their fingers reflexively entwining as she led the way to the table and took one of the empty seats. She patted the one next to her. "Sit and stay a while. Be *entertained*. And let's see how lucky you'll get tonight."

The double entendre didn't pass without his notice, and they both broke into soft chuckles, his growing more amused by the second. He'd barely sat his ass down when the woman from outside Rose's building narrowed her gray eyes on him.

"You're him, huh?" She pursed her lips, studying him as if he were a bug under a microscope.

A quick glance to Rose revealed nothing as she pulled unused bingo boards from a stack and laid them out in front of her. Damian shifted awkwardly in his seat. "Depends on *the him* you're talking about, ma'am," he said politely.

Her brows lifted. "Are you sassing me, boy?"

"No, ma'am . . . just not sure who you think I am."

"You're the one with the sweet hog who took our Rose here for a ride the other night."

Damian damn near choked on his own spit. He coughed, and earned himself a pat on the back from the smirking witch in question. "You okay there?"

"Yeah." He wheezed slightly before finally clearing his throat and turning back to the older woman. "I do happen to have a motorcycle that I'm pretty fond of. I've had it for a long time."

"It was parked out front of our apartment building all night the other night . . ."

Damn if his face didn't feel warm. "Yes, I think it was."

He shifted in his seat again until Rose's arm brushed against his, the touch gifting him a little jolt.

"Greta, you're making him uncomfortable." Rose admonished the older woman with a humorous chuckle. "Didn't we have a talk about this before he arrived?"

"I'm just seeing if the boy's got chops. Gotta have chops if he's gonna roll with the Maxwells." Greta glanced to him. "Just so you know, you need to beef up yours a bit, son. They're a bit underdeveloped."

"Duly noted."

Damian would've felt like he'd walked onto the set of *The Twilight Zone* except for the fact that Rose's vanilla scent invaded his senses, escalating to high-def when she leaned closer.

"Damian Adams, this is Greta Powers, my very nosy but well-meaning neighbor whom I inherited from Vi. And these handsome fellas," Rose nodded to the two older men at the table, "are Henry Jansen and his husband, Otis."

Damian nodded. "It's nice to meet all of you."

Henry passed him four empty cards. "So, Damian, what's your game of choice? Old-School, Four-Square, Blackout?"

He leaned toward Rose. "Am I supposed to know what that means?"

She smirked. "They're different versions of bingo."

"Ah." He turned back to Henry. "I guess I'm pretty old-school . . . all in a line, right?"

He also had no fucking clue what was involved with the other ones, but he soon found out, because as the next game started, his tablemates wouldn't hear of him sitting out and watching. Rose alternated between helping him keep up with the called numbers and chuckling as he struggled to keep up by himself.

And as if that wasn't bad enough, his three new retired friends teased him every chance they got. Before long, he'd dished it back and found himself laughing with Rose and her odd group of friends more than he'd laughed in the last year.

He watched Rose as she scanned each of her boards—six of them—for the latest called number, her lip caught between her teeth as she concentrated.

He leaned close and whispered in her ear, "What I wouldn't give to be that lip you're nibbling, little witch."

Her head spun toward him, caramel eyes wide. "What?"

"Bingo . . ." He smirked.

"Huh?"

Taking her hand that held her marker-stamp, he slowly stamped the O-69 on her top right card. "Bingo, little witch. And what a number to win it on."

"Bingo?" Her cheeks flushed as she realized what he meant, both with the innuendo and the bit about the game. "*Oh!* Bingo. Bingo!"

She jumped up, waving her hand.

The announcer and his assistant continued with the next number until Greta slipped her fingers into the corners of her mouth and let out an earsplitting whistle. "Hey, Tooley, you big oaf! Our girl has a bingo here, so stop your yammering!"

Damian chuckled as Rose read off her numbered row before bounding up to the front to collect her prize. When she returned to their table, she showed it to him proudly, displaying it as if she were Vanna White.

"All that work for an ice cream?" Damian eyed the gift card she now clutched to her chest like the ultimate treasure. "Seems like a bit of a letdown if you ask me."

She gasped in mocking outrage. "A *letdown*? For the sake of our friendship, I'll pretend I didn't hear those words come from your mouth. This isn't for just any ice cream. This is for Sabirah's Soft-Serve Shop, and if you don't give it the respect it deserves, I'll be keeping the ice cream all to myself later tonight."

"Later, huh? You mean the lively night doesn't end at bingo?"

"Not if you play your cards right." She winked, and damn if her coy smirk didn't do things to his insides. "But I'm afraid that requires you to get a bingo."

"Then I guess I better up the ante and increase my chances." He grabbed four more bingo cards, and keeping his eyes locked on hers, added them to the two already in front of him.

Greta, Henry, and Otis howled in laughter, Rose's neighbor flashing her a wink and a soft, "I like him, hon. Much better than that pompous kitty cat with the pretentious sports car."

"Yeah, I think I'll keep him around for a bit." As she brought down her stamper on her card, Rose's hand froze. Her gaze snapped to him. "I didn't mean . . . well, I did, but . . . you know . . . right?"

She looked stricken. Panicked.

He couldn't help it. He laughed, sliding his hand over hers and giving her fingers a firm squeeze. "Don't worry, little witch. I was thinking about keeping you around for a bit, too."

While Rose appeared to breathe a little easier, Damian's breath stuck somewhere in his chest, expanding until it damn near throbbed with the building pressure . . . because those words were truer than he had realized.

Until now.

✦ ✦ ✦

Rose started the evening with big plans, the first of which had been to watch Damian squirm when dealing with Mrs. Powers and the Restview Crew. The squirm never came and he'd taken it all in stride, so much so that Greta gave her official stamp of approval before they'd dropped her off at her apartment door a few minutes ago.

Her second plan—if Damian had somehow managed to pass the first—involved him, her, and the freshly laundered sheets she'd put on her bed earlier that morning. But now that she and Damian stepped into her apartment—blessedly alone for the first time that night—it took everything she had to suck down a yawn.

She tried stifling yet another one and her jaw cracked with the effort.

"Sorry," she apologized when Damian shot her a curious look. "I just need some coffee and I'll be good to go for the second half of our lively night."

His lips twitched. "Unless your idea of lively involves your pillow, some shut-eye, and a few sweet dreams, I'm not so sure."

"No, no. I'm good." Coffee was the cure-all fix she needed . . . maybe with a shot of Red Bull. Vi swore by the stuff.

"Rose." He caught her hand and hauled her back, his hands settling gently on her hips.

Her heart did a little flutter, and she couldn't even blame it on a jolt of caffeine. Used to grumpy Damian, and a huge fan of orgasm-donor Damian, she'd been blindsided by this new version. The one that volleyed witty comebacks with her eighty-year-old neighbor and wanted to play one more game of bingo before they threw in the towel.

"I think I should tuck you into bed." Damian's regretful gaze flickered to her mouth.

She ran her hands over his taut chest. "And tuck yourself in right next to me, right?"

"Not sure much sleeping would happen in that scenario, although the offer is damn tempting."

She opened her mouth to ask him to stay anyway, but stopped herself at the last minute.

Ask him to stay and do what? Fuck-buddy arrangements included one activity, and one activity only, and she'd already duped him into bingo night at the senior center. Not to mention her verbal slippage about keeping him around.

Talk about stiletto-in-mouth.

Doing the smart thing meant saying good night and climbing into bed as he suggested before she muddied the waters—and their understanding—even more than it already was. Yet she didn't want him to walk out the door.

Damian looked a bit unsure himself, too, or maybe that was her reading into things.

"The way I see it, we have two options on how the rest of the night plays out," he said, fingers flexing on her hips. "Option one is me leaving so you can get some much-needed sleep."

She wrinkled her nose as if she smelled something foul, making him grin. "What's the second one?"

"We could watch a movie . . . or something."

She blinked, thinking she'd heard wrong. "A *movie*?"

"Maybe the one Greta and you were talking about earlier tonight. What was it? Your favorite?"

"*Say Anything . . .* ? With John Cusack?"

"That was the one."

She lifted her brow. "You realize you're suggesting we watch an eighties rom-com together, right? I'm always up for a night of Cusack and grand gestures, but you need to know what you're getting yourself into before you fully commit."

"Grand gestures?" It was Damian's turn to look like he'd smelled something rotten.

She fought a smile and failed. "Do you have something against grand romantic gestures, Dr. Adams?"

"Only the point of them, why people expect them, and what's so great about them."

Her mouth opened and closed as she tried—and failed—to form words. "So here's how the rest of the night's gonna go, doc."

"I'm listening."

"While I change into my favorite movie-watching yoga pants, you're going to sit your sexy rear end on my less-than-comfortable couch and mentally prepare yourself to have your opinion on the grand gesture changed."

He grimaced. "How about a nice, ear-quaking action flick or maybe a horror movie?"

"Oh no, you opened this can of worms and now it's time for you to go fishing." Chuckling, she disappeared behind her privacy screen.

"Do you want me to make popcorn or something?" Damian asked.

"Sure. I have some microwavable bags in one of the left-side cabinets."

Cabinets opened and closed while she slipped into her favorite fleece-lined yoga pants and double-checked herself in the mirror. Her rosy cheeks could've been from the walk to her building, or maybe it was nerves.

Because she was about to watch one of her most-loved rom-coms with her newly minted FB. Talk about an upside-down world.

By the time she finished making herself somewhat presentable, Damian had commandeered her empty fruit bowl and filled it with popcorn. Sitting side by side made sense to share food, but it also wreaked havoc on her libido, which informed her she wasn't as tired as she'd previously thought.

Every brush of arms and bump of fingers, Rose became more and more aware of Damian and less invested in the movie. At least until his first snort of disbelief and subsequent mumbles.

Pulling her gaze away from the impending iconic boom box scene and resting it on the man next to her, she lifted a single eyebrow. "Do you have an issue?"

"Nah. Just . . . watching the movie." He tossed a handful of popcorn into his mouth.

"And inserting your very own Statler and Waldorf commentary." She nudged her chin to the TV screen where John's character climbed out from his car, trench coat flapping in the breeze. "This is a really sweet part of the movie."

He snorted, and in went another handful of popcorn.

"I don't speak man-snort, so you'll have to tell me exactly what you don't find poignant about this scene."

"How about everything?"

With a loud gasp, she yanked the popcorn bowl away from his outstretched hand. "You did not just say that."

"Pretty sure I did." At her continued not-so-mock outrage, he chuckled. "He thinks standing in front of her house, playing a song in the dead of night, will make her change her mind. She broke up with him for a reason."

"Not a good one."

"Just because it's not one you like, or agree with, doesn't mean it's not valid. They had a good time together. Great. I'm all for the having of fun. That doesn't mean they're good *for* each other. Her father had a point. Give him a pen and let him move on."

Rose turned all her attention to the stranger sitting next to her and contemplated dumping the entire bowl of popcorn over his head. "How can you say that?"

He looked amused at her appalled expression. "I move my lips and the words spill out. It's easy. You try it."

"*That* is a romantic gesture." She pointed to the TV screen where John Cusack still held up a boom box, "In Your Eyes" playing loud.

"*That* is disturbing the peace, and not to mention the girl's trying to sleep. Let her sleep."

"She's not sleeping. She's in turmoil. How can you not see the poignancy of this moment?" She stared at him, aghast. "He knows he'll get in trouble, and he knows it may not even work, that it's a long shot, and yet he still does it. To show her where he stands."

"He's standing in front of her house with a boom box. Sorry, little witch, but I don't see what's so grand about it."

With a low growl, Rose stopped fighting the urge to throw popcorn at him and upended the entire the bowl over his head. The bastard laughed, and Rose laughed, too, dodging a handful of popcorn he'd picked up and tossed back at her.

Soon, they were in a heated popcorn battle with the heart of the eighties rom-com on the line.

Wiggling to her knees, Rose struggled to shove popcorn down his shirt, but the damn man was too fast and too strong, easily holding both her wrists in one hand, and instead, shoved a few pieces up her own.

When he changed tactics from popcorn shoveling to tickling, Rose squirmed to get away, hitting DEFCON-1. It was either play dirty or pee her pants, and her clean underwear drawer was too low on stock for her to accept the latter.

Rose summoned her Magic to the surface, and it came eagerly, instantly raising the hair on the backs of Damian's arms.

"We're playing dirty now are we, little witch?" In a quick move, he wrapped his arms around her waist and, taking the brunt of the fall, rolled them to the floor. He grinned wickedly. "I win."

Magic swirled around her hands, and with a small burst of energy, she flipped their positions. Palms braced on his chest, she sat astride his hips and grinned down at him.

"You were saying, doc?" she teased.

His hands anchored on her upper thighs, holding her close. "You may have won this round, but you'll never convince me that this grand gesture thing is a real, worthwhile thing."

"We'll see, doc." She smirked, his determination sparking her own. "We will see."

20

Buffy Banter

People who believed in the chaos of the full moon either worked in healthcare or in a bar, because there was no other explanation for the pure bizarreness that walked through Potion's Up every time the door opened.

Fights. Feuds. Squabbles over blood donors.

Rose's hair still smoked from the night's earlier dragon shifter altercation. A lesson learned on her end: don't stand between a shifter that can spew fire and a Mate suspected of cheating. As it turned out, the shifter's Mate and the man she met in the corner booth were cousins, a misunderstanding for sure, but it didn't make Rose's singed hair any less real.

Chaos, Thy Name Was Friday Night.

Gage shot her a concerned look, expecting her to quit at any moment. "You good over there, Maxwell? That dragon got a little too close for comfort."

"He singed off an inch or two, but it's okay. I'll use some hair-healing conditioner tonight when I shower off the day and it'll be good as new by morning." *She hoped*. If not, she might be sporting a layered bob, a hairstyle she hadn't rocked since middle school.

"I'm impressed." Gage continued stacking the tower of clean mugs into the lower cabinets.

She passed a customer his beer refill. "At what? My ability to pour drinks?"

"Your restraint. Vi would've threatened to hex at least a dozen people already tonight, or at the very least, stuck pool cues into certain orifices."

Now *that* she could see her sister doing. "I won't deny it. That bachelorette party came pretty damn close to being hexed with Wicked Witch of the West noses when they asked to see my witch's wart."

Gage chuckled, the gesture lightening his eyes. "Now wouldn't *that* have made memorable wedding pics?"

"Stick me with a dildo and turn it on high speed." Harper's tray hit the table as she stared agape at the usually serious vampire. "You *laughed*. I've never heard you laugh. Hell, I didn't think you possessed the proper throat muscles!"

He rolled his eyes. "I laugh."

Harper shook her head. "Grumble? Yes. Mutter? Yep. Scowl disapprovingly? You betcha. But laugh? Nope." She turned to Rose. "Did you spell him? You did, didn't you? Come on, you can tell me. I won't turn you in to the authorities."

Rose lifted her hands in mock surrender. "No spellcasting here. His laugh is Magic-free . . . at least from this witch."

"I call bullshit. It's either a spell or divine intervention."

Gage glowered at the succubus. "Will you ever stop busting my chops?"

"Sure. When someone comes along who can do it better. I put an ad in the *Supernatural Gazette,* so . . . fingers crossed."

Rose's watch beeped, signaling the end of her shift. "Wow. Time flies when you're dodging dragon fire. Gage, do you need me to stay or . . ."

"Nah. Go. Harp and I can deal with the stragglers. It's winding down."

No need to tell her twice.

It had been days since she'd laid eyes on Damian where there wasn't a furry critter either crawling over them or wedging themselves between them. And despite the fact she loved seeing Bella's and the puppies' daily progress, she really needed some one-on-one time with their somewhat cantankerous caretaker.

Her fingers itched to make the long-awaited booty call the second she stepped outside.

Harper stuck her head into the break room just as she'd slid into her coat. "Oh, good. You haven't left yet."

Rose groaned. Damn it. She should've moved faster . . . *freakin' heel blisters*. "Gage changed his mind about me leaving?"

"What? Oh, honey, no. A sexy-as-hell demon is up front asking for you. Whatever he asks of you, do it. He's dripping lust pheromones as if he high-dived into an Olympic swimming pool filled with the stuff. If you don't make an appearance soon, I'm gonna have myself a midshift snack." Harper winked and disappeared back to the main room.

A wave of excitement washed over her as she thought about Damian. Guess she wasn't the only one who'd thought about making that FB call. He'd just decided to do his in person.

She hightailed it out to the front bar, a grin already on her face, but he wasn't the demon waiting for her.

Julius Kontos leaned against the edge of the counter, a woman at each side in heavy flirt mode. Unlike other times she'd seen him, he didn't seem invested. He stood politely and listened to what they said, occasionally giving them a nod or a smile, but the smile didn't reach his eyes.

On anyone else, it might have been cause for alarm.

On Julius, who almost always seemed to find amusement in everything, it was cause for panic.

His gaze met hers, and after saying something to his admirers, he met her by the front door.

"Hey, Julius. Is everything okay?" Rose asked, concerned.

"Have you any idea where my wayward brother may be?"

Not what she'd expected him to ask. "My guess would be at the sanctuary like he is on most nights. Is everything okay?"

"Not in the least . . . and he's not answering. Not at the sanctuary, and not his cell. And before you ask, I also had a third party ring him, knowing the high likelihood of him not answering my call."

Rose tugged her cell from her pocket and dialed. It rang twice before his voice mail picked up. She hung up and tried the sanctuary, getting the same result, and then she tried both a second time.

"I'm sorry," Rose apologized. "If I hear from him, I'll let him know you need to speak with him. Is there something I can do?"

"No. No, this requires a . . ." He looked at her, desperation straining the corners of his eyes. "What the hell. I'm desperate."

"Way to make a witch feel special, Julius."

"I don't have the luxury to guard feelings, Rose. There's not enough time to go through the proper channels to find someone adept to handle the situation."

"I'm still waiting to hear what situation you're talking about."

"Remember the Gryndor brothers you and Damian very efficiently brought in? It turns out their Mate is demanding their release . . . or else."

Okay, so that sounded bad. "Or else what?"

"I'm not certain we want to find out. In fact, I know we don't, and since releasing the captured Gryndors is out of the question, we need to go on the offensive. Quickly. Before things go too far and people get hurt. Damian may be a pain in my ass, but he's the only Hunter equipped to do this job . . . except for you. You managed the first trio pretty well."

Rose nibbled her lip as she weighed her options, which were not good. "Under different circumstances, I'd be first to help you out, but I promised Damian I wouldn't do any Hunt jobs without him. It was one of his conditions."

"Normally, I'd accept that, but I'm at a loss as to what to do. If it makes you feel better, I'll go with you. It's been a day since I've been in the field, but I hear it's like riding a bicycle."

Saying no would be the smart thing. Two letters. One syllable. N-O.

But then she thought about the money, and all the good it would do the sanctuary animals, and yeah, the load it would lighten from Damian's shoulders.

Rose redialed Damian's number once more, and this time, left a message.

"Don't get grouchy, but Julius is in a huge bind and neither of us can reach you, so I'm helping him out. And you don't have to worry because he'll be with me. I'll let you know how it goes, so . . . bye."

She hung up, already knowing Damian would blow a gasket when he listened to it. "So where do we find a Gryndor Mate?"

❖ ❖ ❖

They didn't seek too hard. The second they got into Julius's car, the news blared about the massive winged demon terrorizing Times Square, but hearing about it and seeing it firsthand were two vastly different things.

Mouth gaping as she crouched behind a cement barricade, Rose looked up at the massive female Gryndor sitting on top of the jumbotron TV, her wings stretched out wider than a minivan was long, and cursed.

"She's huge . . . and pissed. Why is she so huge? She's like easily double the size of the Blood Moon Gryndors," she pointed out.

Julius snuck a glance from around the corner, keeping his head low. "Gryndor females are notoriously larger than the males, and quite a bit more volatile."

The demon howled into the skyline, the noise shaking the ground.

She snorted. "Gee, I never would've guessed."

"Their venom is quite a bit more potent, too. It's one of few poisons that can knock another demon on its ass. Even an upper-level one."

She shot Julius a hard glare.

"What?" he asked innocently.

"I feel like there's an awful lot of information that could've been shared on our drive here, Julius."

"Would it have changed your mind about coming?"

Damn it, no. And he knew it, too.

From beneath the red-step bleachers, a group of tourists broke into a run, making a mad dash toward the hotel across the street. With a mighty roar, the massive Gryndor took flight. She swooped through the air like a scary hang glider with scales until midway, a fuzzy Elmo caught her attention. The street character beelined for a tearstained little girl crouched alone by the wheel of the nearby pretzel stand.

The Gryndor roared again, her immense jaws wide open as she targeted her new victims.

"Oh, I don't think so." Priming her Magic, Rose stepped into the open and fired off a warning shot that flew millimeters over the demon's left shoulder. The Gryndor paused her pursuit, her head swiveling until locking on Rose. "Just because you're having a shit day doesn't make snarling at everyone who crosses your path okay."

Behind her, still hiding, Julius cursed. "Fuck. She's looking this way."

"That's the point."

The Gryndor released another eardrum-piercing roar. "I. Want. My. Mates."

Rose shrugged, forcing herself still while every fiber in her body told her to run and hide. "Get in line. Most of us would love to find our special someone, but that doesn't mean we'll terrorize an entire city until we do."

"They've been taken by the Council."

"Then they obviously did something they weren't supposed to do . . . kind of like what you're doing now."

"I. Want. My. Mates."

"You. Can't. Have. Them," Rose enunciated slowly. "For the love of Goddess, partners can be fun to have around, but they shouldn't be your entire being. Find a hobby or something. I hear online book clubs are all the rage right now."

The Gryndor flew at Rose, her long, venom-dripping talons extended as if she'd love to rip her in half. And judging by the gleam in the she-demon's red eyes, that's exactly what she planned. Been there, done that, not risking bat wing growth again.

This one wouldn't be as easy to sway as Virginia.

Julius finally stepped alongside her, looking prepped to dive back into safety at a moment's notice. "And I thought you were the more stable option between you and my brother. I take it back. I take it all back."

Rose flashed him a wink. "Have you never watched an episode of *Buffy*? There needs to be banter before a showdown. Otherwise, it's boring."

"If by boring you mean it ends quickly and without casualties, then I'm all for boring and skipping the *Buffy* banter."

"Says the Supernatural playboy of the year three years running."

"*Four,* and it would've been five if it weren't for the ridiculously roguish Adrian Collins, that damn Second-in-Command. Bastard has more charisma than Charisma Carpenter."

Rose cocked an eyebrow. "Never watched *Buffy,* huh?"

He wrinkled his nose. "Never a fan . . . now *Angel,* on the other hand."

The Gryndor's massive leathery wings flapped, so huge they created a burst of wind that blew Rose's hair from her face. The demon nearly took out a young couple escaping toward Eighth Avenue, but Rose blasted another arc of Magic, veering the Gryndor off-course and to the right.

Julius cursed. "Is pissing her off more a good idea?"

"Making her angry means she'll get here faster." Rose stepped closer to the approaching demon.

The Council rep gave her a baffled look. "And that's a good thing?"

"I'm not a magical sniper. My long-distance Magic blasts aren't as accurate as closer targets, and I can't run the risk of something, or someone, getting caught in the crossfire." Rose lifted both palms in the air as she mentally tallied the distance. "That's right, a little closer."

The she-demon swiped at a cowering group of teens, and Rose sent out another deterring blast. "Keep your eyes on the prize, hon! I'm right here!"

The Gryndor roared, showing off her massive teeth, and picked up the pace. *Finally.*

"Incoming!" Julius pulled an older woman out of the way as she stepped into the line of fire.

The Gryndor extended a hooked talon toward Rose, and she ducked, firing off the first shot of up-close Magic. The she-demon whirled its wings around her massive body, using her thick scales to protect herself from the brunt of the force. She barely flinched, her cloven hooves gripping the asphalt of Seventh Avenue, tearing it apart as she dropped to the ground with a ground-shaking thud.

The red-eyed demon glared at Rose as she took one step forward, and a second . . . and then flickered before blinking out of existence.

"What the hell . . . ?" Rose spun around, looking for her, making herself a little dizzy. "They can teleport? Julius!"

"Camouflage! Behind you!" he shouted in warning, but not before something hard slammed her between her shoulder blades.

Rose pitched forward, airborne until crashing headfirst into a cement traffic barrier. She dropped to the ground with a groan, blinding pain stealing her vision for a panic-filled few seconds.

Calling her Magic back to the surface, Rose pushed herself to her feet. It winked in and out, confused by the slight fuzziness in her head. "Damn it, come on."

She shook her hands, and with another sharp tug, her Magic burst to life with pink-tinged flames. "Now we're talking . . .

"And speaking of talking . . ." She turned back to the still grounded—and fuming mad—demon. "Let's have a conversation about this like two rational women, okay?"

"I. Want. My. Mates!" The demon lunged.

Rose groaned. "Seriously? Have you not listened to my suggestion about the book club?"

A split second before she fired off a stun spell, a little boy darted into the street between them. Rose froze to avoid accidently hitting him, and the brief pause cost her a talon to the torso.

Liquid fire shot through her body, buckling her knees. Somewhere in the distance, Julius shouted and the she-demon roared. Rose went airborne, briefly wondering if Bax had carried her away, but then her body crashed with another flare of pain, this one sinking bone-deep.

Rose fought to open her eyes to the chorus of frightened screams. "Ju-Julius . . . ?"

Through hazy vision, she watched Damian's brother insert himself between the Gryndor and a group of tourists, his human skin melting away. He stood there in his demon form as he shot her a worried glance, but his stroke of bravery wouldn't be enough.

People ran in chaotic swarms. Kids cried. The Gryndor once again shouted for her mates.

Through dimmed, hazy vision and searing hot pain, Rose summoned her last ounce of Magic and fired off the most powerful stunning spell she could conjure before the darkness wrapped itself around her like a weighted blanket.

✦ ✦ ✦

Waiting for paint to dry was more entertaining than staring at his cell phone buried in a large ziplock bag filled with rice, and praying the damn thing dried out.

Jasper and his abrupt-onset skittishness.

The stallion had earned himself field time that morning for good behavior, and even went back to his stall without a problem. But the second Damian let down his guard and turned to hook up his feed bag, the animal reared. He'd narrowly avoided a hoof to the head, but his cell hadn't been quite as lucky, dropping into a filled water bucket without him realizing until he found it hours later.

All he could do now was hope for a miracle.

The sanctuary phone rang, and he glanced at the caller ID, hoping it was the one person who could turn this sucky day around. He'd nearly called her a dozen times since she'd left the sanctuary earlier that morning, and nearly a dozen times, something always got in the way.

But the caller wasn't Rose.

It was the one person who could sink his mood straight into the pits of hell. Almost literally.

The phone ceased ringing only to start up again two seconds later.

"The answer is no, Jules," he growled, finally answering. "Hell. No. Find someone else to clean up your mess tonight because I'm not interested."

"Where the fuck have you been?" Julius's shout pierced his ear.

"Excuse the hell out of me, but you're not my keeper. It's none of your business where I've been or—"

"You know what, you're right. I don't give a demon's scaly ass, but yours better get to the Maxwell house in Athens right the fuck now."

A cold sense of dread flickered up Damian's spine. *Maxwell.*

He was alert in an instant. "What happened?"

"One second Rose was kicking serious demonic ass and then . . ." Julius muttered a curse. "It happened so damn fast. Less than a blink and then . . . shit, Damian."

"What. Happened?" He'd already grabbed his keys from the wall hook and was running to his motorcycle. "Start explaining, and with actual words that make fucking sense!"

"It doesn't look good, man." Julius's voice dropped to a near-whisper. Damian could practically see his brother dragging his hand through his hair, a habit he did whenever nerves bested him. "Rose's sisters and the Prima are working on her right now, but get here, Damian. Quick."

"Fuck." Forgoing his helmet, he turned the ignition, his bike roaring to life. "It'll take me at least an hour to get there."

"Use the demon portal at my place. I'll call the staff ahead of time to make sure they let you up."

Damian cursed. A demon portal . . . which meant that in order to use it, he needed to let his inner beast resurface, and who knew what the bastard would do once he was given the reins.

Skidding on the rocks as he dropped the phone and peeled out from the sanctuary parking lot, Damian already knew he didn't care. He'd do whatever was necessary to get to Rose sooner. Julius had nerves of fucking steel, always the optimist even when facing an apocalypse. Him admitting something wasn't good meant it was a hell of a lot worse.

Damian flew into the city, veering through traffic, blowing lights and disregarding every traffic law. Despite how fast he'd gotten to Julius's building, it had felt like a lifetime passed.

He'd barely shut off the bike's engine before the door attendant had the front door open for him, and another with a key card stood by the elevator that would take him up to his brother's penthouse.

Damian's stride didn't break once as he headed up to the rooftop greenhouse and to the stone archway nestled in the garden's center. Chest heaving, he stood in front of the ancient Hell Stones, their power radiating in waves strong enough to nearly buckle his knees.

The gateway didn't look like much to the naked eye, just a stumble of stacked stones in varying shades of gray and red, but add a dash of demon blood, a picture-perfect mental image, and voilà. Instant portal to anywhere your heart desired.

Damian's desired to lay eyes on a certain mouthy witch.

"Alright, you ornery bastard," her murmured to his inner demon. "Let's do this."

He didn't wait long; even his beast was champing at the bit to get to Rose. His bones shifted, vision becoming crisper. More vivid. All his senses went into HD mode—high demon.

Unlike Julius, whose human skin melted away, replaced by the reddened hide of their Beezus demon father, Damian retained his Norm shell with a few slight structural alternations.

Sharper cheekbones. Slightly more elongated chin. If he looked in a mirror, his eyes would have already transformed from slate gray to a muted amber, glowing not too unlike the vampires in that popular teen series.

A rush of anger and the urge to bash anyone's head who got between him and Rose washed over him, alerting him the change was complete . . . and then he dug his keys out from his pocket and sliced his palm.

"Rose Maxwell." He brought up an image of her in his mind . . . her coy, sexy smirk, and the way she'd sprawled out next to him in bed, satiated and sexified. And then he slapped his hand on the portal archway. "Make it fucking snappy."

It had been years since he'd used a demon portal and his stomach protested the abrupt move, lurching as the greenhouse melted away. The second the feel of the cool stone disappeared from beneath his feet, he took a step, and then another, each one weighted to the nonexistent ground.

Damian fought through the vertigo, and while he stumbled twice, it only took a few more steps before his boot crunched on solid ground.

He took a second to reorient himself before registering the large house on a hill, its windows lit up as if summoning someone from the Hubble.

But Rose wasn't there . . .

His demon turned him to the dimly lit path leading toward the much smaller cottage nestled against the Hudson River a hundred yards away. Edie Maxwell's cabin. Hugged by a broad wraparound porch and adorned with blooming flower boxes despite the frigid temperature, the cozy place could only belong to the current Maxwell Prima.

Damian jogged up to the steps, pausing at the sight of the shadowy figure sitting in one of the rocking chairs.

Julius's torn shirt exposed long, deep scratches on his chest, and his nose looked broken in at least two places. Add in the five o'clock shadow that decorated his usually clean-shaven face and the blood on his expensive suit, and Damian almost didn't recognize him.

But his inner hellion did.

His beast growled, drawing his brother's attention. Julius met his gaze, and then the anger Damian had barely kept at bay soared back to the surface.

Julius immediately stood and backed up, hands raised.

It took all Damian's control not to put a fist through the bastard's face, and that control snapped as he reached for the door and Julius warned, "It's a bit intense in there right now. I don't think you should interrupt them."

He had Julius pinned against the house in less than a second, Damian's arm pushing precariously hard on the other man's throat as he released a low, menacing growl. "If only you would have *thought* sooner, this wouldn't have happened."

He had to give his brother credit for not attempting to break free.

Julius looked him in the eye, his breath whistling as a myriad of emotions came and went across his face. Damian didn't care about any of them. Especially the guilt. The bastard should feel guilty because this had his stench all over it.

"If you have any self-preservation," Damian threatened, his voice deceptively quiet, "you won't talk to me. Or look at me. Or even breathe in my direction. If you do, I won't hesitate to snap your windpipe in half. Do you get me?"

"Thought you didn't want me to talk?"

Damian applied more pressure. "You're always after me to embrace my other side. Well, one more out of you, *brother,* and you'll finally get your wish."

Julius coughed. "Okay. Sorry. Fuck . . . the world's spinning."

"At least you're breathing, although I can't promise for how long."

Guilt flooded into Julius's eyes. "Damian, I'm sorry. I know I fucked up. I never should've asked her to—"

"Damian?" Olive stood at the threshold of a now open front door. Her gaze bounced between them, concern written all over her face, and shimmery green Magic hovering above her palms. "Is everything okay out here?"

"We're good." Damian released his brother, ignoring him as Julius dropped his hands to his knees and sucked in air by the mouthful. "Is Rose okay?"

"We're almost done working on her—"

"Working on her?" Panic seized his throat, making it tight. "Should we be taking her to the hospital, or . . ."

The youngest Maxwell witch gave him a funny look.

"Right. This isn't something Norm medicine can fix. Can I see her?"

Olive glanced at Julius and back, looking unsure. "We can't afford distractions."

"I won't distract anyone. I swear. I just . . . need to see her. Please."

She studied him closely, and it took him a spare moment to realize he was still demon'd out. He dragged that bastard back to his cage, but not without breaking a slight sweat. Once all his parts were back to rights, he gave her another pleading look.

"Please, Olly," he begged.

Fuck, he needed to see Rose more than he required his next breath, and he couldn't let himself dwell on why, too consumed with the need to see her for himself. If Olive told him to go away, he would . . . at least off the porch. But he wouldn't go a step farther.

He couldn't.

"Let the brothers in, dear." Edie Maxwell's voice spilled onto the dimly lit porch. "But any more of that porch nonsense and I'll happily blast them to another continent. One that doesn't have demon portals for easy transportation."

Olive cocked a blond eyebrow, glancing from Julius to Damian. "Well? You heard the lady."

"No more nonsense," Damian promised.

Julius nodded. "Sorry, love."

Olive studied them both a few seconds longer before nodding for them both to follow. "Stay back, stay quiet, and for the love of Goddess, *don't* interfere. Gran isn't the only one with the ability to give cross-continental ass-blasts."

"How is she?" Damian asked, stepping into the house.

"Better than when she got here," Olive answered grimly.

He scanned the cottage until his gaze landed on the barn-style kitchen table and the pale, unconscious Rose lying on top of it. His feet froze to the floor.

Devoid of the blush he loved seeing creep into her cheeks, Rose's pale skin starkly contrasted her dark hair, and her lips, usually a petal pink, nearly matched the rest of her. The only color in the vicinity was the pool of bright red blood beneath the table, and on Violet's and Edie's hands.

Rose's blood.

He shifted close and immediately received a stern look from Olive.

Edie and Violet, their eyes closed, held their hands over Rose's stomach, their purple-and-gold Magic swirling over the gash responsible for so much blood loss. They murmured repeatedly, focused on their task while Olive slipped past them to dip her fingers into the ceramic bowl by Rose's head.

She recited her own gentle chorus as she gently rubbed the bowl's concoction onto Rose's temples, and then walked around her sister and grandmother to place more on the base of her throat, her wrists, and finally, the tops of her feet. Once done, her hands joined the other two witches', her soft green Magic intertwining with theirs.

After his ex hexed him for being a demonic asshole, Damian vowed never to get mixed up in witch affairs again, and he'd kept that vow. Until now. No way was he turning away.

With his gaze locked on Rose's pale face, he missed the fact that the musical chanting had stopped until Violet said his name. All three Maxwell witches watched him with varying expressions.

"Is that it?" Rose still lay unmoving on the table.

The Prima gifted him a small, exhausted smile. "She'll be okay. She's made it through the worst of the healing."

Her words didn't match the worry on her face.

"When?" His voice cracked. "When will she be okay?"

"When her Magic restores enough to finish the healing process. Maybe you two can help relocate her to the back bedroom."

"Of course." Julius stepped forward as if to touch Rose.

Damian growled. "*I* got her."

His brother held up his hands and backed off, the first smart thing he'd done all night.

Damian paused at the table, his palms dry as he contemplated what to do and where he could touch her without hurting her. "Is there any place I should avoid?"

"The Gryndor taloned her left torso, so be careful," Olive answered. "And then be extra gentle when you lay her down on the bed. Vi set the broken ribs without much difficulty, but it'll take a few hours for them to mend. And then there's the concussion. Head injuries take a little longer to resolve."

"I'll brew more healing tea to help speed up the process." Edie plucked at the dried herbs hanging from the exposed beam above her kitchen sink.

With Olive's guidance, Damian gently eased his arms beneath Rose's legs and behind her shoulders, holding his breath as he lifted her from the table. A soft moan escaped her lips, and damn if hearing it didn't feel like he'd taken a knife to the gut.

Olive nodded approvingly and led the way to the back room where she gestured for him to place her in the lone bed. He carefully eased her head—and the rest of her—onto the soft mattress, and then Olive gently tucked her sister beneath the covers.

Satisfied she'd be comfortable enough, she turned to him, tucking a piece of fabric into his hand.

"For the gash on your hand," Olive answered his silent question. "You're dripping life juices, and not even the Goddess herself can help you if you dirty Edie's floors with it. Do you want me to heal it?"

He'd completely forgot about the cut he'd used for the portal. "It'll heal quickly on its own, but thank you."

Rose murmured softly in her sleep, her brow furrowing as she shifted in bed.

"You mentioned she had a run-in with a Gryndor demon?" Damian asked. "I've faced off with a few through the years, and this is a pretty severe reaction, isn't it? I don't know that I've ever seen one like this."

"It was a female. The Mate to the three you two captured a few weeks back. She caused quite the scene in Times Square, and Rose, being Rose, intervened when the she-demon went after a little boy."

That sounded like Rose, alright, but what he knew that Olive didn't was she'd been put in that position by his brother.

"Olive, dear." Edie walked into the room. "Can you help Vi get the kitchen back to rights? I'll get Rose to drink a few drops of tea and then I'll be along in a bit to help."

"Of course, Gran." Olive gave him a small smile and left him alone with the Prima.

"Do you mind if I stay here with Rose?" Damian gestured to the chair next to the window. "I'd like to be here when she wakes up."

"Knock yourself out, my boy. Just not literally. These massive healings take a lot out of these old bones." The Prima smiled warmly, and gently brought the mug to Rose's lips where she sipped it once before falling still again. "But I should warn you not to expect her eyes to open anytime soon. She'll be asleep for the next few hours, if not a day. Ridding the body of Gryndor toxin isn't a quick process."

"Consider me warned, Prima Maxwell."

She winked. "Call me Edie . . . unless I have reason to be cross with you. Then you can call me Your Worst Nightmare."

Damian chuckled softly, and when the Prima left him alone with Rose, he pulled the corner chair next to the bed and reached for her hand. Her skin was cool to the touch. He missed her usual warmth instantly, and tried his best to gently rub heat into her fingers.

His heart still hadn't fully returned to his chest, partly clogging his throat ever since he'd answered Julius's phone call.

He'd lost track of time when he sensed an unwelcome presence hovering outside the door. Damian stiffened but refused to relinquish his hold or his attention on the woman in front of him.

"If you know what's good for you, *brother*, you'll be gone before she wakes up," Damian warned, knowing his brother's scent anywhere.

From the doorway, Julius murmured quietly, "I really am sorry, Damian. I shouldn't have—"

"No, you shouldn't have." Damian growled quietly, his demon once again pushing close to the surface. He took a deep breath before barely turning his head toward his brother. "And we'll be talking about that at another time that's not now."

"I understand." Jules nodded grimly, and turned to leave.

"And Julius?"

His brother glanced back at him warily. "Yes?"

"Find someone else to do your dirty work because both Rose and I are officially done. Push me on it, or go around me, and you'll get a firsthand glimpse of the beast you so desperately want me to embrace."

Julius left without another word.

Damian half-expected Rose to wake up and yell at him for making decisions on her behalf, and it was a lecture he craved hearing like he'd craved nothing before.

Even to retain what remained of his humanity.

21

It's Five O'Clock Somewhere

Rose bolted upright with a sharp gasp, heart lurching in her chest as each breath stumbled over the other in a mad dash to push fresh air into her lungs. The abrupt move sent a searing jolt of pain through her abdomen and she sucked down a hiss.

It took a minute to rein in the double-assault, and while she did, she slowly registered the pale yellow walls and white lacy curtains that looked familiar and yet not. She definitely wasn't at her place because the room was blessedly warm and her building's super still hadn't managed to fix the dilapidated furnace.

Rose kicked the gold-threaded comforter away from her bare legs and peeked beneath the IT'S FIVE O'CLOCK SOMEWHERE T-shirt for the source of the hot, throbbing pain. What she found confused her even more: her braless boobs, and bulky white bandages that wrapped around her torso and covered her from the waist of her panties to the bottom edge of her sternum.

"Definitely didn't go to sleep with this here." She poked it. A searing pulse of pain ripped through her abdomen, stealing her breath. "Found the source. What the hell . . . ?"

A mummified abdomen. A pounding headache. Gran's clothes. How the hell did she get to Athens, and into Edie's bed? *And why?*

Did she get hit by a Mack truck? Or maybe a bicycling tourist finally took her out because let's face it, it was only a matter of time before *that* happened. Throwing together busy, narrow roads and out-of-towners who didn't know how to navigate them was a multi-vehicle accident waiting to happen.

Shifting slowly in bed, Rose worked her way through her fuzzy memories, starting with the last fully formed one and working backward. *The Gryndor.* At Times Square, she'd climbed out of Julius Kontos's Audi and . . .

Loud shouts, two of which were distinctly male tones, erupted from her gran's living room. Something crashed, the sounds drilling a pain-wave right through her temples. Vi's not-so-veiled warning went ig-nored as two freight trains slammed together.

Enough was enough.

Pulling up her big witch panties, Rose sucked down a groan and padded barefoot to the living room. A vase crashed against the wall, a scant few inches shy of hitting her head.

Vi threw her an apologetic look. "Sorry, sis. I tried dousing them with water to cool things down, but it didn't work as planned."

Normally, she'd have a snarky comment at the ready. Instead, she turned to the *them* her sister had mentioned, and shot both Damian and Julius hard glares. Not that they noticed. Locked in a battle of wills and fists, the two men moved around the room as if it were a boxing ring.

"Pretty sure I told you to be gone." Damian swung at his brother and Julius ducked, the hit clipping his shoulder instead of landing on his jaw.

"And I told you I wanted to make sure she was okay first." Julius—in full red-skinned demon mode—returned Damian's punch with one of his own, landing a solid hit to the kidneys.

Damian winced, but didn't stop moving. "Maybe you should have thought about that before dragging Rose to a Hunt involving a fe-male Gryndor, asshole! Do you have any idea what that she-demon's toxins could have done to her?"

"Yes!" The demon representative's flushed face blanched to a pale petal pink. "Why do you think I brought her straight to the Prima?"

"Well, thank fuck you had *some* sense in your damn head."

"Stop . . ." Rose's voice caught in her throat, croaking softly.

The brothers continued their brawl.

"Stop it . . ." Rose demanded, clearing her throat.

Neither so much as acknowledged her presence.

"Guess we'll do this the hard way." Taking a deep breath, she summoned her Magic. Instead of its usual quick blast to the forefront, it slowly filled her empty well, gliding its way through her body and toward her palms like a leaky faucet.

"You've got to be kidding me." Winded and a little light-headed, she leaned on the doorframe for support and kept her right hand trained on the dueling demons. The second she built up enough oomph, she fired.

A hot stream of Magic collided with Julius and Damian, the flickering pink power-surge spilling them onto their asses. It lacked its usual punch, but it did the trick.

They noticed her for the first time, Julius releasing a relieved sigh as he collapsed onto his back. But Damian's emotions flickered over his face too fast for her to pin one down.

His gaze ran over her from toe to head, its intensity conjuring a fresh wave of goose bumps that had nothing to do with the room's temperature and everything to do with the slight rev to her libido.

Rose mentally snorted. At least the Gryndor toxin hadn't squelched her sex drive.

"Should you be out of bed?" Damian asked, looking ready to escort her back down the hall.

"Probably not, but it's difficult to rest when two jackasses are butting heads in the next room. I was afraid if I let it go a second longer, one—or both of you—would come through the wall and land in bed with me."

Julius smirked. "I wouldn't have mi—"

Olive flicked her hand, magically sealing his mouth shut. "Now is *so* not the time."

Rose chuckled. Her shy sis was turning into a badass . . . or was at least badass adjacent. Olive spared the demon rep a warning look before dropping her silencing spell.

Julius surged to his feet with an immediate apology. "Not that this hasn't been a fun night—and morning, but I have Council meetings that I can't cancel."

"Then by all means, leave. *Finally*," Damian muttered under his breath.

Julius ignored him. "I'm glad you're okay, Rose. And I'm sorry I put you in that situation. If you ever need anything, don't hesitate to give me a call."

From across the room, Damian growled.

Olive glanced between the two brothers before pulling out her cell phone from beneath her bra strap. "Oh, look. Gran texted. She wants to see Vi and me up at the main house. Why don't we walk you out on our way?"

Vi blinked, reluctantly pulling her attention from the show in front of her. "Gran doesn't text."

Olly elbowed her. "It looks like she took it up since we last saw her."

"You mean an hour ago?"

Olive's eyes widened pointedly behind her glasses.

"Oh. *Oh!*" Yanking her own phone from her pocket, Vi glanced at the blank screen. "Look at that. She sent me a text, too. We better get up there before her patience goes AWOL. Come on, Julius. Let's order you a Ryde back to the city because we're fresh out of demon portals."

Vi slipped Rose a quick wink before ushering everyone out the door and closing it behind them.

"Sorry about them. They're not exactly subtle." Supporting her stomach, she ambled to the couch.

Damian hustled to her side and guided her slow sink into the cushion. "Can I get you anything? Pain meds? A blanket? If kicking Julius's ass would make you feel better, I'll go after him right now."

She fought to keep her face free of a grimace. "There's no need to go into doctor mode. I'm fine."

Damian frowned. "Says someone who'd been lying in a pool of her own blood less than eight hours ago."

"Well, yeah. I was a little unconscious for that."

Thankfully. Unlike Olive, who possessed a stomach of steel, Rose couldn't handle blood or bodily fluids of any kind. Thinking about what Damian might have seen when she'd been out cold turned her stomach.

"Do you want to tell me why you and your brother turned Edie's living room into a WWE ring?" she asked, changing the subject.

"You seriously need to ask me that?" He pulled a frustrated hand through his hair. "Maybe we should have this conversation when you're feeling better."

"Maybe we should have it now."

He shot her a half-hearted glare. "You're pretty insufferable for someone who came within an inch of dying."

She shrugged her unaffected shoulder. "Ask my sisters, but I'm pretty insufferable most of the time. It's a talent. Now start talking, doc."

"Julius had no business asking you to go on a Hunt by yourself, much less one involving a female Gryndor." She opened her mouth, but he cut her off. "And don't tell me he went with you. He hasn't been in the field since he put on his Council suit. He had no business making you think he had your back."

"Maybe not, but if we hadn't gone, things would've been so much worse. That she-demon didn't care who she hurt. It was the middle of Times Square, doc. Do you have any clue how many people are in that one-block radius at any given moment?"

Damian carefully sat on the cushion next to her. "Don't use common sense on me right now, little witch. This isn't a common sense moment. This is a pissed-off moment and I'd like to be pissed a good while longer."

As the tension in his shoulders slowly drained, Rose chuckled. "Can we have a napping moment? Because mine was cut short and I'd like to get back to it."

It was his turn to chuckle.

"Come here." Damian gently eased her head onto his lap and she curled her legs up, getting into a comfortable position.

His fingers played with her hair, sliding through her scalp, the soft touch making her moan. "That feels *really* good."

"At least I can do *something* right tonight," he muttered.

She stared up at him. "What's that supposed to mean?"

"Nothing." He glanced away.

"Uh-uh." Grabbing his chin, she rerouted his attention back toward her. "What did you mean?"

He went quiet, pulling himself away despite her upper body still lying in his lap. He was there, but not *there*. Something told her if she pushed too hard, he'd disappear completely.

Damian sighed softly. "I can't even explain the thoughts that went through me when Julius called, and then when he told me to use the DP at his place . . . *fuck*. I didn't hesitate."

She waited, gently coaxing him to share more. The pained, frustrated look on his face told her she didn't know what that meant. "And that's a problem, why?"

"Because when I called on my demon to gain portal access, he was right there. Like, *right* there, waiting with bated breath to burst free and take his show on the road. The last time he'd been that close to the surface, I'd stood in front of my ex, covered head to toe in Quall demon sludge, listening to her curse me out. Literally."

He stopped talking, shaking his head as he clammed up.

"Damian . . ." She gently sat upright, and reached for his hand, but he was already standing.

"I wanted to rip Julius's head off his shoulders tonight, Rose, and before you tell me that it's normal for siblings to fight, I should warn you that Julius and I have never been *normal* anything. We'd been trained to fight since the moment we could walk. If we squabbled over the same toy, there was nearly always blood spilled. And with Ezeil being who he was—when he was actually present—he didn't stop it. He encouraged it. That's a damn hard habit to break . . . especially with my demon riding my ass the way he's been lately."

"I'm sorry." It seemed an inadequate thing to say, but she didn't know what else *to* say. Tears gathered in her eyes as she thought about the childhood that Damian must have had, one so different from hers and her sisters'. "Is there anything I can do for you?"

Damian looked shocked at the offer, and then he fidgeted, looking ready to climb out of his skin as he shook his head. "If you're certain you're okay, I need to get back to the sanctuary to check on the animals. I left pretty abruptly."

"Sure. Okay."

Damian placed a gentle kiss on her forehead. "I'll check in on you later, but you should take that nap. I'll let Vi and Olive know you're here alone. Behave, little witch. Let people help you for once, okay?"

He paused at the door and smiled wanly before disappearing outside.

What the hell happened?

One moment they were serious, and the next, joking. And then in another blink of the eye he practically ran out the door as if she'd suggested a stroll down a wedding aisle. She was still attempting to figure it out when Vi and Olive appeared with a cloudy spark of Magic and the use of their gran's short-distance teleportation spell.

"What's going on? Why did Damian leave?" Vi asked, looking as confused as Rose felt. "With the way he was acting all . . . grrrr . . . I thought for sure he'd tuck you in for the night, and then tuck himself right next to you."

"If I knew why I'd explain it to myself first." A severe flash of white-hot pain quickly overshadowed her worry. "Son of a witch's . . . hex me, this hurts."

"Pain med time!" Vi hustled into the kitchen and immediately pulled out the blender, then strawberries. Next up was ice.

"What pain meds involve frozen fruit?"

Violet pulled out three tall hurricane glasses and plunked them on the counter. "The strawberry margarita kind. Best thing about magical healing that Gran has taught me? No need to avoid alcohol. In fact, it's highly encouraged, and I am nothing if not a freakin' cheerleader of encouragement, baby."

It was on the tip of her tongue to decline, but Damian's ominous tone and indecipherable look had brought a fresh wave of worry.

"You know what? Put a bonus shot of tequila in mine. I nearly died less than twenty-four hours ago. I think I deserve a little something extra."

"Now that's what I'm talking about!" Vi grinned. "Midnight Margarita Madness, here we come! Olive! Cue the music!"

✦ ✦ ✦

Damian sat in the Blood Moon's corner booth, alternating between staring at the hole in the wall and staring at his untouched beer. After leaving Rose like the demon shit he was, he hadn't known where to go or what to do, knowing only that he didn't want his funk to touch her in any way.

It was ironic he'd ended up at the Supernatural bar that had whetted her appetite for Hunting.

Within minutes of his arrival, a few regulars tried messing with him, but he quickly shut it down—and had the sore knuckles to prove it. Immediately after, he'd felt lighter. Not *better,* but the intense pressure that came when his demon pushed hard had lessened a minuscule fraction.

Letting him out to play, and then locking him up tight again, made the bastard a bit randy and Damian unfit for human interaction. Hence the Blood Moon.

Someone slipped into the seat across from him.

"How many has he had?" the familiar voice asked.

"You're staring at it," Charlie—the Blood Moon's owner—answered. "The least he could do after scaring away all my customers is to keep ordering bloody drinks."

Damian turned his attention to Julius, and glared. "What the hell are you doing here?"

"I missed your sparkling wit and charming disposition," Julius said dryly before gifting the shifter a mega-watt smile. "And go ahead and bring us two more of whatever's on tap."

"That's it?" Charlie asked. "I mentioned he threatened to decapitate one of my regulars with his bare hands, didn't I?"

"Tack on a couple of your most expensive shots, too." Charlie waited pointedly, and Julius sighed. "What else do you want, Char?"

"Top pick of any Hunt assignments for the next five years."

Julius kicked up a lone eyebrow, inspecting the Hunter from head to toe. His perusal—and Charlie's complete lack of give-a-fuck—*almost* made Damian smile. This would be a fight his brother wouldn't win.

"One month," Julius offered.

"One year," Charlie countered.

"Six months and you agree to take on any special assignments that I feel you may be a good fit for."

Charlie mulled it over, nibbling on her lip ring before giving a faint nod. "Fine. But I'm still charging you for those top-notch shots and the two beers on tap."

With a sway of her hips, she turned, leaving them alone.

Julius grumbled. "Remind me why I thought it was a good idea to put her on the Hunt payroll?"

Damian snorted. "Knowing you it was because you liked the way she filled out her leather pants."

"Ah. That's right."

"What the hell are you doing here, Jules?" Damian asked. "In case my fist in your face didn't clue you in, we're definitely not in a grab-drinks-and-gab phase of our relationship."

"Trust me, I wouldn't be here if it weren't for your pretty little witch asking it of me."

He swallowed down his surprise by taking the first sip of his warm beer. "I don't *have* a witch. Besides, I didn't realize you and Rose were so chummy that she'd feel comfortable asking you for favors."

Damn, is that jealousy?

The more he tried to stanch it, the more it ate away at his stomach, and Julius, ever the bastard, smirked knowingly. Damian's second half lapped up his brewing anger like chocolate-chip cookie dough.

Julius chuckled. "For not having a witch, you knew exactly who I was talking about, didn't you? Relax, brother. She called because she was worried about *you*. The alcohol may have played a small part in the decision, too. Frozen margaritas if the roaring blender in the background was any indication."

Damian wasn't sure which reason was worse. That she'd been worried about him enough to call on Julius, or that she'd been upset enough when he'd left that she dove into all the frozen fruity drinks that led to it.

He stood, eager to get away from both his brother and the unwelcome feelings he didn't know what to do with. "You found me. I'm breathing. If you'd like to continue doing the same, I'd suggest that the next time Rose asks you to check on me, you let your survival instincts kick in and tell her no."

"What are you doing, man?" Julius asked with a sigh as he turned to leave. "You've avoided the Hunt all these years because it means accepting your true self, and yet you're okay with it when it comes to the witch?"

"I wasn't letting her put herself at risk. I wasn't there earlier tonight and look what happened. Besides, you have me right where you wanted me so what are you complaining about?"

"Not complaining, just pointing something out. Don't get me wrong, I understand the lure of a good woman. Hell, if I caught the attention of one of the Maxwell witches, I might take stupid risks, too. But that's what you're doing. At least that pesky hex of yours won't come into play if you keep it a Hunt thing."

"What I'm doing—especially with Rose—is none of your damn business. Stay away from me. Stay away from her. Just . . . stay away."

Damian shot off a few more glares as he passed through to the exit and fought not to dwell on Julius's words. As much as he wished they had no foundation, they did . . . and he'd known it before he'd agreed to their fuck-buddy arrangement.

And he hadn't cared.

22

Dr. Pleasant

Rose tucked one of the puppies beneath her zippered coat and giggled as a little pink tongue flickered out, gifting her a multitude of chin-kisses while the pup that Callie snuggled close to her chest did the same with her.

They'd met at the sanctuary earlier in the morning, well before any civilized human beings should be awake because the other witch had to catch the first flight out of JFK. After being laid up for days at her grandma's, and then confined to her own apartment for a few more, Rose nearly ran through the city when the other witch called to check on her and offered to bounce around ideas for the sanctuary's adoption fair.

Callie rubbed the puppy's forehead. "I can see why you love it here. I may stage a 'rescue' so I can be sentenced to community service hours at a place like this, too."

"It definitely doesn't suck. I mean, I wasn't thrilled with the idea in the beginning, but it turned out to be what I needed. Even the cantankerous owner grew on me." Rose grinned, picturing Damian in his faded jeans and work shirt, his stethoscope tucked into his back pocket.

Yeah, he'd definitely grown on her.

They'd played phone tag the last few days, and he'd popped up at her front door a couple times to check on her in the guise of making sure she was taking Edie's herbal supplements. But he'd only stick around for a few minutes and then he'd make an excuse to leave like he did the night of the Gryndor attack.

Or maybe that was her being self-conscious and seeing things that weren't there. It wouldn't be the first time, at least according to her sisters.

Callie watched her curiously, a smirk pulling on her lips. "Something tells me that cantankerous owner has done a lot more than grow on you."

Rose's cheeks flushed. "Maybe. But I'm only here temporarily so there's no point in getting too attached."

"The thing about temporary is that it doesn't take much for it to transition to permanence. Think about all those failed fostering attempts. A bighearted animal lover takes in a litter of kittens, ends up falling in love, and they never leave the house again. Just saying, it wouldn't be the first time for it to happen and it definitely wouldn't be the last."

Rose shifted awkwardly on her feet and tried pulling the focus back to the fair. While snuggling their puppies, they walked through the grounds and toward the large open space between the two equipment barns.

Callie assessed the area with a critical eye, nodding. "There's definitely more than enough space for you to do what you want. And you said that back barn up on the little hill is empty?"

Rose nodded. "It goes mostly unused now so it's in a bit of disrepair, but with a few nails and some heavy dusting, it could be the perfect meet-'n'-greet spot for the animals and their prospective families. Doc wants to keep the main barn and clinic as free from people as possible, so if we keep most of the activity up this way, that would be best."

"And you wouldn't have a problem relocating the animals up for adoption?"

"Jasper isn't quite ready for the public yet, but Bella and the puppies will be easy-peasy, and definitely Butternut and Squash. Then we have the extra benefit of the training ring right there, so families can interact with the horses one-on-one and see how well they fit together."

"And you're putting vendors along the left side?"

"It'll be a who's who of food trucks, all of whom volunteered to give the sanctuary a huge chunk of any revenue made. And then a few local stores offered their time and supplies. The party store in the next town over offered to hand balloons out to the kids. Sometimes I forget how generous people can be."

Having walked back around to Callie's car, the two witches stopped. "This will be a fantastic event, Rose. There's no way you won't find homes for all these animals."

"And the animals from the nearby shelter. I extended an invite to them, too, so they'll be bringing some of their adoptable animals as well. The more, the merrier. But it's not about finding them homes. It's about finding them the *right* ones."

Squirming, the puppy beneath her jacket—whom she'd dubbed Cusack—licked her cheek as if in agreement.

"You're off to an incredible start." Callie reluctantly handed over her black-and-white puppy. "But if I don't get out of here, I won't only be late for my flight, but I'll get caught smuggling this little one on board with me. Not only would the airline frown at that, but so would my fiancée. We already have four rescues of our own and are fostering a fifth. She told me no more."

"Ah, so that's how you know about failed fostering."

"I'm practically a professional at it." Callie laughed. "So, good luck, and make sure to send me all the event details so Nisha and I can be here for the big day. Maybe I'll even convince her we need one more. It's always more difficult to say no in person."

"Thank you for everything, Callie. Safe travels, and I'll see you at the Kids' Community Center gala?"

"Wouldn't miss it for the world." The witch waved as she started up her car and headed back toward the main road. Rose waited until she lost track of the rear lights. "Let's get you two back to your mama for a little breakfast, huh?"

She settled the pups into the birthing stall and they immediately tripped over their big feet to get to a waiting Bella. They dove in heartily, pushing aside their brothers and sister with their little rumps until they found their favorite spots.

With a smile, Rose turned—and collided into the chest of a very *un*smiling Damian.

He caught her before she tumbled back. "What the hell are you doing here?"

"Good morning to you, too, Dr. Pleasant."

His frown deepened.

"Did you forget I still have a few more service hours to fulfill?" She eased back from his hold because if she didn't, she'd rub herself all over him like a cat in heat. "And what the hell are you doing with that attitude? Wake up on the wrong side of the hay bale this morning?"

"You should be home resting. You have no business coming in today." He headed to the office, but not before she saw that jaw muscle ticking away.

She followed. "Actually, I got a clean bill of health from Edie and my doctor. All healed. No residual Gryndor toxin found. I might have a bit of a scar, but they say scars are sexy, right?"

He threw her a glare from behind the desk. "You're joking about what happened?"

"Yes, and evidently you're not." She rounded the corner and perched her ass against the edge. He shifted away enough for her to notice. "What's going on here?"

"I'm working. Or trying to."

"You know that's not what I'm talking about. After being all weird and cryptic, you leave Edie's house and then I don't hear from you for days. You call when you know I'm not around. You stop by long enough for me to answer the door, and then you turn around and leave with a grunt and a lame excuse about something you need to do."

"I don't—"

She shot him a glare.

"Okay, so maybe I did a few of those things, but only because you need to focus on your recovery and not on any of my issues."

"So something *is* wrong?"

In a retreat, Damian skirted around to the other side of the desk. Rose flicked her wrist, and hooked her Magic—lasso-style—around his belt loops and reeled him in as if he were a fish on a hook. He protested, sighing her name, but he stopped in front of her.

Sitting on the desk with Damian's larger body standing between her open legs, she tilted her head up to meet his gaze.

"It's going to be a busy day, little witch," Damian warned. "The animals—"

"Won't be expecting you until their regular feeding time in an hour. Supplies aren't delivered for another two, and your first clinic appointment isn't until"—she peered at the desk calendar on which she sat—"after lunch. What other excuses do you want to spew to avoid being alone with me?"

"I'm not avoiding you." His eye twitched.

"And yet this is the first time we've been alone for longer than five seconds in over a week." She peered at him through her lashes, hoping she looked sexy instead of constipated as she slowly slid her hands up his gray T-shirt. "You, Dr. Adams, are in breach of our FBA contract and if you don't remedy your actions quickly, you could be in for a whole host of legal problems."

His lips twitched into a small grin. With a low sigh, he eased closer, his palms running up her jean-clad thighs to cup her ass. He yanked her closer, the move eliciting a little yelp.

"Breach of contract, huh?" Desire lightened his eyes to a beautiful glowing amber. "That sounds like a pretty sticky situation."

"The stickiest." Curling her fingers into the soft cotton of his shirt, she drew him closer until their lips were less than an inch apart. "If I were the type, I would've already filed a formal complaint."

"And you're not the type?"

"Nah. I much prefer overseeing the situation myself with a more hands-on approach." She brushed her mouth against his in a soft caress. "And this is me handling it . . . and asking you to handle me."

Rose half-expected Damian to pull away. To put distance between them like he'd done for the past week. The thought of it left an ache in her chest that nearly hurt worse than that stupid Gryndor talon.

She cared for him far beyond their fuck-buddy arrangement.

Callie had been right. Sometimes temporary things develop roots, and suddenly, Rose wasn't sure she wasn't also in breach of the no-attachments clause in their FBA. She'd become a romance cliché, vowing no strings and yet getting caught up in an elaborate Supernatural marionette show.

✦ ✦ ✦

Damian needed to tell Rose their arrangement was null and void. It was the smart thing to do, and he'd practiced the speech to his reflection the previous night, but now that she sat in front of him, his hands on her skin and her sweet vanilla scent in his nose?

He couldn't do it.

Couldn't think of a damn reason why he should, every earlier doubt now a distant memory, replaced by his need to keep her close.

"You want me to handle you, little witch?" Damian dropped his voice, his lusty need to feel her against him making him tug her against his growing erection.

Her gaze dropped to his mouth and back, her own lips curling up. "In the worst way. Like in a really, really bad way. It's been a long, hellish week."

"We have less than an hour before Miguel and Terrance show up for the morning feedings."

"Plenty of time, and just so you know, I meant it when I said I got a clean bill of health. Fully healed. *No* restrictions." She inched her hands beneath his shirt, her soft touch making him suck in a breath. "I don't need foreplay, Damian. I just need you. Well, you and orgasms. At least two, but three is preferable."

"Giving orders now? I like it." Chuckling, he splayed one hand on her chest and eased her flat against the desk before popping open the button on her jeans.

Rose released a gasping *oh* of surprise, and smirked. "And I like where this is going."

Working together, they tugged off both her pants and her panties, and then she did the same with her shirt and bra.

Seeing her spread open for him like a gorgeous—naked—buffet, Damian groaned. "This is how every morning should start."

"Speaking of starting . . . I'm still waiting for my handling, doc."

He hooked his boot through the bottom rung of his office chair and pulled it close, sitting and scooting forward until he sat even with her already wet pussy. "Get ready for your handling, Miss Maxwell."

As he leaned in for his first sweet taste, their gazes locked. Damian took his time, and with each slow swipe of his tongue, Rose's breath shuddered. Her hand landed on top of his head, fingers spearing through his hair as she held him against her.

Damian feasted like a man starving, devouring not just her taste, but every soft sigh and gentle quiver. And especially the sound of his whispered name falling from her lips.

"Damian." Her grip on his hair tightened and he picked up his relentless pace, eager to fulfill her demand of at least three orgasms.

With a gentle suck to her clit, she came apart in his arms, knees bumping against his ears as her body quaked in release. As her breathing slowed, he gentled his touch, and then slipping first one, then two fingers into her tight channel, he brought his mouth to her clit all over again.

Rose's legs trembled. "Oh, my Goddess."

"Let's go for number two." He fucked her with his fingers, curling his digits, and rubbed that sensitive spot that would make her come apart again.

"More." Rose lifted her hips to meet his hand. "I need more, doc."

Fuckin' A. So did he.

With another pump of his fingers, her body erupted into a second orgasm. "In me! Now!"

His hands damn near shook as he fumbled with his jeans, the desire to be inside her riding him hard. Unable to wait any longer, Rose magically unbuttoned his pants, and then her soft hand wrapped around his aching cock and guided him straight to her entrance.

His mouth caught hers the second he plunged inside.

They devoured. They touched. They rocked against each other until the desk moved back and forth across the floor with every thrust. This time when Rose came, she pulled him with her, both climaxing in a peak of pleasure so high he was certain he'd never come down.

And he wasn't so sure he wanted to.

23

Celestial Sexcapades

Rose couldn't contain her laughter as she watched the showdown happening in front of her. More amusing than a night at the movies. More thrilling than a Broadway play. The standoff between Violet and Christina was pure, unfiltered entertainment, and no one could've expected it when Christina crashed their Girl Glam session—along with Edie—prior to the Kids' Community Center gala.

GG sessions were how the triplets—and Harper—mentally and physically prepared themselves for big events. Always with jokes, and usually with a glass or two of wine. But with everyone busy doing their own things the last few months, it had been a hard tradition to keep up. They'd made the extra effort to ensure it happened tonight, and this time, their mother came along for the ride.

And it didn't suck.

Rose had laughed more in the last thirty minutes than she had all week.

Locked in a stare-down to put any two teenagers to shame, neither Vi nor Christina showed signs of backing down. Their mother was a formidable witch, but her determination had nothing on Vi's when her mind was set. And no way was Vi sliding into the four-inch heels Christina thought she *had* to wear.

"My money's on Mom." Olive placed the first bet. "I feel like she's overdue a win. Even with the success of Supernatural Spirits Winery, she's had a backlog of losses."

Edie snorted with a shake of her head. "Maybe, but your sister has that glint in the eye. She won't back down easily."

"Why? Because she's the Prima Apparent?" Harper asked, not taking her eyes off the two witches.

"Because she's my granddaughter." Edie grinned, glancing to Rose. "What's your verdict, dear? Sister or mother?"

Rose exchanged glances with Harper before they both simultaneously chanted, "Sister."

"Fine! Have it your way." Christina backed down and shot a playful look toward Rose and the others. "And you're not in a magical bubble. We can hear you."

"We know." Rose grinned.

Christina rolled her eyes playfully. "I blame this all on you, Mother."

"Me?" Edie failed to suppress a chuckle. "They're *your* daughters."

"But you raised them more than I did." Christina blinked and looked away, but not before hiding the sheen of tears.

This woman in front of them looked like their mom, decked out in her gala finest with her curled hair sitting high on top of her head. But she didn't sound accusatory, and there wasn't an ounce of her usual Southern passive-aggressive haughtiness. Christina looked a bit guilty, and a smidge sad.

Rose exchanged silent looks with her sisters.

"Mom, are you okay?" Rose reached out to squeeze her mother's arm. "You haven't seemed yourself lately."

"I'm fine. I just . . ." She sniffed. "Had a little health scare and—"

"You're sick?" Olive asked.

Vi gasped. "What's wrong?"

Christina held up her hand, silencing everyone's concerned questions. "It was a *scare*. I'm fine. But it was potent enough to wake me up a bit, and I realized I haven't been there for you girls the way I should've been."

Her gaze flickered to Edie. "It wasn't easy growing up under the shadow of the Prima. The expectations people made of me because of it . . . it was stressful to say the least."

Edie frowned. "Oh, sweetheart . . ."

"No, no. I'm not trying to gain sympathy. I know it doesn't excuse my actions through the years, but . . ." Christina took her time looking at each of her daughters. "I knew the pressure each of you would be under as you carry around the Maxwell name, and in my quest to prepare you for it, I unwittingly placed more of it on your shoulders . . . and I'm sorry."

Christina turned to Vi. "If you don't want to wear the heels, then don't. You'll be the only one of us that isn't applying ointment to raging blisters by the end of the night."

She turned to Olive. "And I know I haven't always been supportive in your career shift, but you should know I'm immensely proud of you. You are good at everything you do, and your students are lucky to learn from the best."

Finally, she turned to Rose, whose mouth had already gone dry.

Christina smiled wanly. "And you *will* find your thing, Rose Marie. And when your heart tells you it's the right fit, hold on to it with everything you have."

If she wasn't so shocked at this new, emotionally open mother, she would've laughed at the abrupt, awkward silence filling the room.

"You had me at *I don't have to wear the shoes.*" Vi flung off her heels, the move dropping her three inches closer to the floor and creating a tear-streaked round of laughter.

Five minutes later, they were off to Guastavino's, enough behind schedule to meet up with her father, Linc, Bax, and Adrian, and still arrive fashionably late.

Rose hung back and let the couples walk into the event center first. It gave her a prime view of her parents—who'd never been the PDA type even at these kinds of affairs—holding hands as they walked into the hall. Linc and Vi were Linc and Vi, deeply in love and practically wrapped around one another with cartoon hearts twinkling in their eyes. Harper did her best to avoid Adrian's excessive flirting.

And Olive . . .

Walking next to Bax, her triplet seemed oblivious to the way the Guardian Angel watched her every move. She shifted left, he shifted. She slowed, he slowed. As if knowing he was being studied, the angel glanced over his shoulder.

Rose flashed him a caught-you smirk and he quickly looked away, immediately engaging Adrian in conversation.

She chuckled.

Once upon a time, she'd told her sisters—and Damian—that romantic entanglements weren't in her future, and she'd meant it. But she couldn't deny something felt missing . . .

She had the friends. The dress. In five minutes, she'd have yummy pigs in blankets.

It was Damian.

She missed the grumpy, half-demon veterinarian who never ceased to make her blood—and her body—boil.

She'd almost invited him multiple times, but did FBs attend events like this? She didn't think so, and so she'd kept quiet, not wanting to put additional strain on their already strained relationship. She resigned herself to being the seventh wheel on what she hoped would be a quick, entertaining night.

The second their party stepped into the gorgeously decorated Guastavino's, Edie quickly whisked Vi and Linc away, and Harper beelined it for the bathroom in the hopes of losing Adrian. It wasn't long before it was only Olive and Rose.

The youngest triplet pushed her glasses up her nose. "What do you say to finding drinks, and then a corner we can hide in until it's socially acceptable to go home?"

Rose glanced at the overfilled room. "You had me at hide-and-drink. But do you think there's any such place we won't be found? Pretty sure everyone in the city is here tonight. Too bad you didn't bring a book with you. You could've commandeered a seat and then glared at anyone who dared interrupt your page time."

"People who interrupt someone obviously engrossed in their book has true evil in their heart. I'm just saying. But," Olive added, "it just so happens that I have a reading app on my phone. Words will travel, so let's travel . . ."

"Do you want to ask Bax to join us?" Rose teased wickedly.

Her sister scoffed and linked their arms. "About as much as I want a raging case of witch pox. Anyway, leave the hiding to me. I'm practically a professional."

They each collected a drink, and true to her word, Olive found a quiet spot in the solarium. A stone bench, surrounded on three sides by lush greenery, provided the ultimate place to disappear, and the second they sat, Olive pulled up her phone . . . and her reading app.

"Tell me what's going on with the silent treatment," Rose requested, risking the interrupted reader glare.

"Pure evil. And I don't know what you're talking about," Olive lied.

"Bax looks even more sullen than usual. Did he change his mind about the roommate thing?"

"I wish," Olive muttered.

Rose's curiosity was piqued. She shifted closer to her sister, elbowing her in the side. "Clarify that remark. Pronto."

Olive's shoulders, and her phone, drooped. "He won't let it go. Why can't he take no for an answer? Why?"

"Probably because he sees what we do, and in true Guardian Angel fashion, he wants to do something about it."

"Great. He's acting out of a hero complex and I'm the damsel," Olive muttered grumpily. "That's even worse."

"You can't survive much longer on the amount of sleep you're getting, Olly. Eventually, there will be a breaking point. The people who love you don't want to see that happen."

"He keeps telling me it's a money thing."

"And that very well may be. New York rent isn't cheap."

Olive didn't look convinced. "He's managed fine on his own all this time."

"Circumstances change. Bax doesn't exactly go around spewing about his personal life—especially anything to do with angeling. For all we know it could be crap pay—or no pay. Maybe he's not managing as well as he'd led us to believe."

Olive pushed her glasses up. "You think that's it?"

"Honestly, I don't know. But whether he extended the offer because of a hero complex, or a financial one, what we both know is that he wouldn't have offered unless he meant for you to accept it."

The youngest Maxwell sighed. "I don't want to go from the frying pan into the bubbling cauldron."

"There may be some boxer-clad sports-watching in your future, but Bax won't be dealing magical herbs from the living room sofa."

"That's not what I meant."

Rose waited expectantly for elaboration.

"He's *Bax*. Listening to celestial sexcapades through bedroom walls isn't high on my to-do list. I'd rather deal with stinky herbs."

"Celestial sexcapades?" Rose burst out laughing, tears coming to her eyes.

"You know what I mean!"

"Honestly, I don't, but I really wish I did."

"It looks like someone nabbed my hiding spot before I could get here." A familiar voice had both sisters looking up.

Wearing a gorgeous green silk gown that molded to her curves, Callie stood in front of them, her eyes smiling. "Is there room for one more?"

"Have a seat and join the hideaway party." Rose patted the spot next to her. "We were talking about celestial sexcapades."

The other witch's eyes lit up. "This conversation sounds a hell of a lot more interesting than anything happening out there. But be forewarned, I may use this opportunity to convince you why it would be awesome to work together, too. I haven't forgotten you still owe me an answer about Sparks of Hope."

"Consider me warned." For the first time in a while, Rose let herself enjoy the moment—and the company. And she didn't worry about societal optics.

✦ ✦ ✦

Jasper kicked the stall door, the force quaking the entire barn. A few more hits like that and the damn thing would cave regardless of the reinforcements made.

Miguel, his mouth pulled into a frown, studied the freaked-out creature in front of them. "What the hell has gotten into him? He was perfectly fine this morning. He even let Terrance groom him."

"He's been like this for an hour, and he won't let me get within four feet of him so I can check him out." Demonstrating, Damian reached for the stall latch. The stallion's nostrils flared as he reared, kicking out yet again. "If he keeps this up, he'll hurt himself."

"Rose has a way with him. Maybe she could calm him enough so you can peek under the hood."

Damian shook his head. "She's at some event for the Kids' Community Center. I don't want to bug her for something like this. I'm the vet for hell's sake. I should be able to manage one horse."

Miguel watched him curiously, but he ignored it, studying the frightened animal in front of him. Or struggling to. His thoughts drifted to Rose, which is where they'd been when he'd barely dodged Jasper's first kick to the head.

He'd told himself that he couldn't have gone to the fundraiser even if she'd asked. Not with a new equine resident arriving first thing in the morning. And now with Jasper's freak-out, he was especially glad he hadn't left.

FBs didn't serve as escorts to upscale, high-society events where everyone talked about who was wearing what, and who was wearing who. Especially if that FB was him. Those puff-and-parades were more Julius's thing, a stage where he could flaunt his stuff and his latest side piece.

Yet he couldn't help wondering what it would've been like to have Rose on his arm . . . to hold her close for a dance or two. Without clothes. With clothes. Dressed in a four-layer snowsuit. It didn't matter. He just liked having her nearby.

And fuck . . . that's why he'd tried keeping his distance the last few days. He liked having her around too damn much for it to be good for either of them.

Jasper's tail flicked wildly, and he kicked again, this time the force splintering the edge of the door.

Miguel looked at him expectantly. "Ian . . ."

Damian sighed. "Fine. I'll call her . . . because if I don't, we'll be treating him for a broken leg on top of whatever this is."

He reluctantly pulled out his cell and dialed, and when she didn't answer, he left a message on her voice mail to call him back. But a few minutes later, when he and Miguel floated the idea of giving Jasper a sedative, Damian realized he couldn't wait for her to see his message.

He jumped on his bike, and using the back way, arrived at Guastavino's in record time. In the trees lining the entryway, pristine white lights glittered, basking the historical building in a magical glow that purposefully resembled a wintry city wonderland. The large curved windows displayed the glammed-up partygoers inside as they danced and talked, oblivious to the chaotic world outside.

Pulling over to the curb, Damian slipped off his bike and yanked off his helmet.

A red-jacketed valet gave him a long once-over. "I think you're in the wrong place, dude."

Damian handed him a fifty. "And I think you'll keep this bike right here until I get back, *dude*. I'll be less than ten minutes."

The young guy contemplated it a few seconds before shrugging and shoving the money in his pocket. "Whatever floats your boat, dude."

Damian hustled up to the front door only to be stopped by a tuxedoed guard checking invitations. "Sorry, sir, but I need to see your invitation, which if you had one, you would've also seen that there's a dress code."

Damian wrestled his demon for control, but he glanced at his dirtied jeans and flannel work shirt. Hell, he wouldn't let himself in to an event like this, either. "Trust me, I don't want to be here any longer than necessary. I need to find one of your guests, and then my eyesore self will be out of your hair."

"I suggest you call them to come out here to you."

"Gee, why didn't I think of that? Oh, that's right . . . because I tried."

The guard was Norm. A quick flash of his demon eyes, and Damian could easily force him aside. But he really didn't want to do that, especially with the bastard playing peekaboo all too easily lately.

"Damian?" Julius appeared behind the gatekeeper, and like the valet and the guard, took in his disheveled appearance. "Glad to see you dressed up for the occasion, brother."

"I'm not in the mood for your humor, or anything else from you, Jules. I need Rose."

His brother's smile slowly melted. "Is everything okay?"

Damian gave him withering look.

"Right. You don't owe me answers." He turned to the door guard. "It's okay. He's with me."

The guard shifted awkwardly on his feet. "But I'm under direct orders not to let anyone in who doesn't have an invitation."

"And I'm giving you new orders."

"But—"

"Look." Julius clapped his hand on the other man's shoulder. "You could refuse him entry, saying you were only doing your job, but then I'll be forced to find that gorgeous Prima Apparent, Miss Violet Maxwell, and tell her you're refusing to let in one of her guests."

The Norm's face paled. "The Prima Apparent?"

Julius nodded.

The man gulped nervously. He whispered, "She scares me. I saw that video of what she did to that former European Alpha, and I didn't sleep for a week."

"You're a smart man to be scared because she's a formidable woman, and I don't have to remind you that she's Mated to the North American Alpha, right?"

The guard gulped. "No . . ."

"This man right here"—Julius nodded toward Damian—"happens to be Lincoln Thorne's best friend. Knowing that, if you still want to deny him entry, you are a braver man than myself."

The guard bounced his gaze from Julius to Damian and back. "You'll take full responsibility for him?"

"Total."

"And you won't let him out of your sight?"

"Not for a second."

"If I get reprimanded for letting him inside . . ."

"You won't be, and if someone tries, I'll tell them I used Compulsion on you, okay?"

The Norm stepped aside, allowing Damian into the building.

"Thanks," Damian grudgingly said to his brother.

Julius nodded, his face devoid of his usual snarky smile. "No thanks needed. You wouldn't be at one of these things unless it was an emergency. Is there anything else I can do?"

Damian shot him a glare. "I think you've done enough, don't you? If this is your way of apologizing for what happened, it won't work and I don't accept."

"It wasn't." Julius sighed. "Okay, so maybe I hoped the good deed wouldn't go without a little appreciation. Can't blame a guy for trying.

And I'll do you another. Rose is in the solarium with her sister. I can take you there."

Damian followed his brother through the gala, the two of them receiving more than a couple looks. Hell, he would've looked, too. Dressed in a designer tux that had been tailor made for his tall frame and broad shoulders, Julius looked as if he'd stepped off the pages of a fashion magazine, whereas Damian looked like he'd stepped out of a horse's stall.

Literally. He *so* didn't belong here, and he couldn't wait to get back to the stables.

The second they stepped into the lush green wonderland of the solarium, Julius didn't need to play tour guide. Rose's presence lit up the room like a homing beacon, his demon instincts carrying him right to her.

Her musical laugh hit his ears before he saw her, and when he turned the corner . . .

Sitting on a bench between Olive and a blond woman, her head tossed back in laugher, Rose's beauty made him stumble.

Fuck, she was gorgeous.

Luminescent.

A sharp wave of need ripped through him, both the man and the demon wanting to whisk her away and keep her for themselves. But there was also a *rightness* he'd never felt before.

A strength that made him feel as though with her by his side, he could be anything . . .

A fierce loyalty that for her, he would *do* anything . . .

Feelings of love stirred and welled . . . and then . . .

"D-Damian?" The woman on Rose's left shifted in her seat, her wide eyes trained on him. "Is that really you?"

Damian regretfully pulled his eyes away from a startled Rose, and to the woman who wasn't a stranger after all. In fact, she was the very reason why his growing feelings for Rose couldn't happen . . .

She was the ex who'd hexed him.

24

hEx Me

Rose glanced back and forth between Damian and Callie, unable to hide her confusion as the two of them stared at one another. "You know each other? What are the chances of that?"

Callie's smile flickered tentatively, her cheeks looking a little pale. "Extremely low I would've thought. The Goddess works in mysterious ways. We haven't seen each other in a long time. It's been what? Fifteen years?"

"Eighteen." Damian's tense voice threw Rose off. His eyes flickered from gray to hazel to that golden amber, signaling his inner demon was precariously close to the surface as he glared at the other witch. "Hex so many people that you've lost track of time, Cal? And you used to blame my perpetual lateness on my Hunting."

Rose furrowed her brow, trying to follow. "Can someone shine a little light on the situation here because I've obviously been left standing in the dark."

Eighteen years.

Hexes.

Olive gingerly touched her arm, casting a wary glass at Damian and Callie. Rose digested the scene in front of her, slowly putting two and twelve together.

She turned toward her new friend and potential business-partner/boss with a gasp. "You're the witch who hexed Damian?"

Callie's gaze quickly shifted around the group, everyone now looking at her with varying expressions of anger and outrage. "I can explain. I know it looks bad, but—"

"Looks bad? No, it *is* bad. A *Soul* Hex. For what? Because he didn't get you a corsage?" Rose snapped. She faced the woman whom she had hoped to call a friend, her agitated Magic lifting the hair off her neck as her emotions climbed.

"It's not what it seems . . ."

"Oh, so you *didn't* hex him?"

Callie shifted uncomfortably in her heels. "No, I did . . . but it wasn't supposed to—"

Rose held up a hand. "Save it for someone who likes listening to meager excuses."

"Rose . . ." Damian touched her hand, whipping her attention back to him and the tense flexing of his jaw muscle. "I came here because I need your help. It's Jasper."

"What's wrong?" She wrapped her fingers around his, but he gently pulled them away. She tried not to read into it, too worried about the stallion. "Is he okay?"

"He won't let anyone near him, and if he keeps kicking like he is, he'll bring the whole barn down on top of him. We need you back at the sanctuary."

Callie's own realization sank in. "You're the owner of Mari's Sanctuary?"

Damian threw her another glare. "Didn't think I'd ever make something of myself, did you? Despite all your best attempts to assure I didn't."

"Damian, I—"

"Let's go." Rose stepped between them, as much for their sake as Callie's. "Before Jasper hurts himself, and before I do something Gran will really give me a lecture about."

Damian nodded, and in another blink, they were off, Olive and Julius following closely behind. Rose got behind Damian on his bike—ball gown be damned—and Julius called for his car from the valet. In less than a few minutes, they were all speeding back to Mari's, ignoring things called traffic laws.

While Rose worried about Jasper and what they'd find when they arrived at the sanctuary, she also couldn't take her mind off what had happened back at Guastavino's.

The ex.

The ex who'd hexed Damian.

The very reason why Damian had spent the last eighteen years believing happily ever afters couldn't be in his future.

If not for Jasper, she'd be back at that gala giving that witch a personal lesson about magical responsibility and how it was never in anyone's best interest to hex someone in matters of the heart. And to think she'd almost agreed to become a partner at Sparks of Hope.

It wasn't as if she had any other offers on the table, and a she-demon talon to the torso was pretty damning evidence that maybe Hunting wasn't for her despite the fun she'd had and the asses she'd kicked.

Rose stewed on the back of Damian's motorcycle, furious over Damian's and her stolen futures, until they arrived at the sanctuary. The second she stepped into the barn, all her focus shifted to the frightened horse kicking the crap out of his stall.

Relief washed over Miguel's face as they rushed into the barn. "Thank God. I just pulled out the tranq gun . . . just in case."

"How is he?" Damian worriedly scanned the horse from a distance.

"No better. No worse."

Rose eased closer to the stall. "Hey, boy . . . what's going on, huh?"

Damian snatched her arm before she reached the latch. "Let's make sure he's responding to you before you get too close."

Jasper huffed, blowing out a heavy breath that moved Rose's

hair off her face. It almost looked as if he rolled his eyes, and Rose giggled.

"He's fine." She held out a sugar cube—his favorite. He nervously pranced closer, and after lapping it up, sniffed and continued to lick her fingers before pushing his nose into her palm for rubs. "You're trying to tell us something. Aren't you, boy?"

"Yeah. That he'd like to kick us in the head," Damian muttered.

Jasper huffed again.

"Stay back. All of you." Rose shot everyone a warning look as she reached for the latch. "He'll stay calm as long as he doesn't feel cornered by a crowd."

All eyes were on her as she carefully stepped into the stall. Damian shifted so he stood right on the other side, free to leap over at a moment's notice. She shot him a warning look as he took the tranq gun from Miguel's hand.

"You won't be needing that," she told him.

"And I'm keeping it handy in case we do." He stared her down, silently daring her to disagree.

It was Rose's turn to roll her eyes.

Jasper fidgeted, flinching when she laid a gentle hand on his neck. "It's okay, boy . . . we're going to help you."

He shifted on his feet as she coasted her palms over his rust-colored coat, slowly relaxing as she called on her Magic a small portion at a time so she didn't startle him. Jasper's anxiety—and pain—landed on her chest like an anvil.

"He's hurt . . ." Rose mumbled quietly.

Damian stepped closer to the gate. "Can you pin down where?"

Up his torso and around his flank, she performed her own magical MRI . . . and then she ran her fingers down his back left leg . . .

He whinnied loudly, pawing at the hay-covered floor.

"It's in his back hoof," she announced.

Damian cursed. "An infection. That makes sense. If something had been wrong with the muscles or tendons, he'd show swelling and other signs of discomfort. With a hoof, there's not much to see. Do you think you can keep him calm long enough for me to check it out and treat it?"

"Sure." She rubbed the horse's nose before dropping a kiss onto his white diamond. "You'll be a good boy, won't you? You want someone to help you. You just don't know how to ask."

She snuck Damian a pointed look.

Those exact words could be used on someone other than Jasper, and Damian realized it, too, because with a grunt he said, "Let me grab some supplies," and disappeared into the treatment room.

❖ ❖ ❖

With Jasper's standoffish personality, neither Damian nor Miguel would've found the damn foot abscess until it had spread into his leg, and maybe even his joints. Now with it drained and cleaned, and wrapped up as best as could be managed, Jasper acted like a whole new horse, even playfully swinging his head around to nip the back of Damian's shirt as he secured the last inch of gauze.

He wished he could enjoy the happy mood shift, but the more he tried, the more his mood plummeted. He disappeared into his office to try and get his head on straight after seeing Callie for the first time in years, but instead, the second witch occupying his mind sat on the edge of his desk.

As if remembering the last time they'd been in this same position, Damian's cock twitched in his pants. But neither his cock— nor his growing feelings for Rose—would distract him this time.

And his feelings *were* growing. Exponentially. There was no doubt about it, especially after he saw the way she'd handled Jasper with such calm-headed tenderness.

Damian was falling in love with her, and as if karma had a mean streak and thought he needed reminding that it was a bad idea, it'd put Callie in his path, too.

Fueling what he already knew, his demon pushed uncomfortably close to the surface. His senses shifted, heightening as they did when the bastard was seconds away from making a resurgence. With a low, chesty growl, Damian pushed him back . . . and then stopped.

There was one last thing he needed to do, and although he hated the idea of it, the bastard was the best non-human for the job.

He needed to break things off with Rose.

End their FB arrangement. *Now.* Before they took their relationship an inch further, or he developed even an ounce more feelings and Callie's hex went into full effect.

He knew firsthand what happened in relationships in which he let his beast take the lead. Rose deserved more than he could give her. Literally. Because of the Soul Hex, he'd never be able to give her his whole heart, and if he did, that demon bastard would snatch it *all* away.

Completely.

His humanity. His heart. *Rose.* All of it gone in a blink, and he knew her well enough to know she wouldn't accept it easily. Like him, her stubbornness knew no limits. To make sure she had a chance at happiness, he needed the demon prick to sever the ties.

It was the last thing he wanted to do, but the only thing he *could* do.

To refrain from reaching out and touching her, he shoved his hands into his pockets and turned her way. She frowned, reading his tense body posture. Tension escalated when he devoured the sight of her standing against his messy desk, hay stuck to her gold-flecked gown, her hair loose and hanging down across her bare shoulders.

Her outfit probably cost more than he earned in six months, and yet she hadn't balked a second as she'd stepped into Jasper's dirty stall.

Rose watched him carefully. "We caught the infection early enough that Jasper will be okay, right?"

He cleared his throat. "After a round of antibiotics he'll be good as new. Catching it early was key though. If it had gone unchecked much longer, it wouldn't be as easy a recovery."

"Then what's with the frown? Do you need me to come over there and turn it upside down?" She smirked sexily.

"No." *Shit, that came out a bit too abrupt.*

Rose's smile tightened, and Damian cursed silently, hating her now-guarded expression.

He softened his voice but pushed himself to get this over with. "We need to talk, Rose."

"*Rose?* Not Ro, or little witch?" She kicked up single eyebrow. "Then you mean a *talk,* and not just a talk."

"Our arrangement needs to come to an end." Unable to fully face the hurt in her eyes, he shifted his attention to the stack of files on his desk. "It's not working for me anymore, and since your service hours are almost fulfilled, it seems a natural thing to do. Don't you think?"

She studied him in silence, her face a blank slate. He couldn't read a damn thing. Not a frown or an eye-twitch. He grabbed her time log from the nearby file cabinet, and after scribbling his signature, handed it over.

It took a few thunderous heartbeats for her to accept it, and when she did, her emotionless mask cracked. Anger lightened her eyes with little gold flecks as her fingers clenched the form. "You're releasing me from my community service?"

"I'm not dismissing you. I'm certifying that you've completed them."

"I still have a week."

He pushed himself to keep going, but fuck . . . "You haven't considered all the hours you put into things like the sanctuary cam, and the time you've spent organizing the adoption fair. Speaking of which, if you email me everything you've planned so far, we can use your blueprint to take it from here."

Magic lit up her palms, and at this point, he wouldn't blame her for setting his ass on fire. Hell, he'd do it himself if he could.

"You don't want me working the adoption fair, either?" Hurt softened her voice, and damn if he didn't ache to pull her into his arms.

"Your time could be better spent elsewhere. I'm sure there are other lost causes you could help. It's a big city."

"And that's it . . ."

"That's it." Damian forced the words to fall from his tongue. "And thank you for everything you've done around here."

"Well, you're not welcome." She waited a beat, studying him before turning around and storming to the door. As she reached the threshold, she whirled back around. "Oh, and Damian? Fuck you. I didn't do any of it . . . the cam-feed, the fair . . . none of it for *you*. I did it for the animals. So you can take your gratitude, your fake indifference, and tough-guy exterior, and shove it where the sun doesn't shine."

She stormed away. He casually followed, stopping at the doorway when he heard her murmured conversation with Olive and Julius.

His brother looked directly at him, his mouth turned into a disappointed frown.

Olive said something that Julius agreed to, and then the three of them left. No glares over the shoulder. No second looks. Rose was there one moment and gone the next.

Damian leaned against the wall, his chest aching from the inability to take a deep breath. It felt like a lot more had walked away than his brother, his fuck buddy, and her sister.

It felt like his damn heart had disappeared, too.

25

Supernatural Scooby Squad

Damian's lame attempt to put distance between them had hurt more than Rose anticipated, and the shock of it had—at first—thrown her for a loop. Then as Olive had sat in the passenger seat of Julius's Audi, sending out an SOS to the rest of their group, Rose's shock had slowly turned to anger.

Now on the bottom-level gym of Vi and Linc's brownstone, she took her aggravation out on a small army of sparring dummies, hurling Magic at the stuffed figures, one zap after another until they melted down to the floor.

If only she could deal with a certain half-demon veterinarian the same way.

The front door opened, and Harper's soft curse echoed through the room. "Shit. We should've forgone the boozy ice cream and brought the straight booze." She glared at everyone accusingly. "Why did no one tell me this called for the hard hitters?"

Rose let her hands drop to her sides, the first time in close to an hour. The marathon Magic use had worked her into a good sweat. Who the hell needed Zumba?

"What boozy flavors did you bring?" Rose downed a nearby water bottle in one long series of chugs.

Harper peeked into the bag. "Cherry Champagne. Brownie Whiskey Cake. And Cake Batter Vodka."

"Toss me the vodka . . . and I hope you bought more than one."

"Do you take me for an amateur?" She scoffed and handed her a pint along with a spoon. "I learned from the Great Lincoln Fuck-Up that it's always best to have additional vodka."

"Hey," Linc complained. "I made up for it, didn't I?"

Vi patted his arm affectionately. "Yes, you did, babe."

Rose stuck a heaping spoonful of vodka batter in her mouth, and for good measure, sent a final magical bolt to the only remaining half-melted dummy. It hit with a loud crackle, snapping the poor guy in half. "If only that had been a certain jerk-turd veterinarian . . ."

Olive stole a glance at Harper. "How many of the vodkas did you get?"

"Four. You think we need more?"

Julius looked around curiously. "This may be a stupid question, but why would you need more?"

"Because Rose Maxwell doesn't resort to name-calling unless she's really pissed."

"And I'm really pissed." Rose whirled on Julius, waving her petal-pink plastic spoon under his nose. "What the hell is your brother thinking? Or is he not thinking at all? Huh?"

He lifted his hands in surrender. "I haven't the slightest, love. In case you didn't realize, we're not the heart-to-heart-talk kind of brothers. But my guess is it has something to do with Callie."

"Whoa. Pause and rewind." Vi blinked, confused. "Callie? The woman you met at the winery opening? The one who offered you the job with Sparks of Hope?"

Rose snortled humorlessly and shoveled another spoonful of ice cream into her mouth. "Did I forget to mention that lovely, karma-sucktastic fact? Yeah. That lovely, sweet witch who thought I'd make the perfect partner is the ex."

"The ex what?"

"*The*. Ex. She's the witch who hexed Damian when he was a teenager, dooming him to a life without knowing what it's like to love someone."

Vi's mouth opened and closed, and opened again.

"Exactly." Rose nodded. "I obviously can't take the job now."

"You were thinking about taking the job?" Olive asked.

"I was considering it. Life has made it obvious that I epically suck at everything else, but now that plan went up in a puff of smoke, too. As did all the work at the sanctuary because . . ." She flailed her hands in Julius's direction.

Hell, they swam in the same gene pool. It was close enough.

Julius almost looked guilty. "You don't suck at Hunting."

All heads swiveled his way.

"You *don't*. You probably think I was sweet-talking you to get my way, and yeah, there was a bit of that happening, but you *are* incredible at it, Rose," Julius admitted. "Honestly, I don't know why we haven't brought more witches into the program, but if you want a spot, it's yours."

She tried—and failed—to see any kind of motive behind his words. "Are you forgetting the Times Square debacle with a certain lovelorn she-demon?"

He waved it off. "That was my fault. Hunting isn't something you can just fall into, and if you are serious about giving it a go, I'll make it happen. I already have the perfect trainer in mind . . . and before you ask, it's not my—"

She shot him a warning glare.

"Him," Julius finished, refraining from saying Damian's name.

Sitting next to her, Olive reached for one of the unopened ice creams. "So *why* can't you take the job with Sparks of Hope? I mean, if it's something you really want to do."

Everyone looked at the youngest Maxwell triplet.

"She hexed Damian. I get it. Bad, bad witch. But she didn't hex *you*. Her company has done amazing work all over the world. Imagine what you could accomplish if the two of you put your magical brains together."

"I . . . I couldn't do that."

"But why?" Olive pushed.

From anyone else, Rose would've thought the person emotionally stunted, or cruel and uncaring. Knowing Olive was neither of those things meant her sister had an underlying motive for the line of questioning. She sat patiently, waiting for Rose to figure it out on her own.

And she did.

She couldn't work with the woman who hexed away Damian's happily ever after because Rose wanted to *be* his happily ever after.

Despite not looking for love, love had found her in the unlikeliest of places . . . in a broody, grumpy, ill-tempered half-demon former-Hunter-turned-veterinarian.

Sometimes karma—the snide bitch—had a wicked sense of humor. It made certain that Operation Equine Freedom had ended with a trip to the police station, and that Representative Ramón sentenced Rose to community service hours at the sanctuary where she'd witnessed the heart beneath Damian's tough exterior as he treated the animals in his care.

She'd never had a chance not to fall in love with him.

"I love him." The realization stole her ability to stand, and she dropped onto the floor in a puddle of emotions. "I'm *in* love with him, a man who irritates me so much I don't know whether to rip off his mouth with a tweezers or rip off all his clothes with my teeth."

Harper nodded, as if knowing her predicament. "Personally, I'd choose nakedness, but that's me."

"Do you know what makes this worse? None of it matters. We could be soul mates, and it wouldn't change a thing because of that freaking hex."

Bax leaned against the wall and folded his arms over his chest. "That is a bummer, but look on the bright side. He hasn't lost his soul, which means while it sucks for you—having already done the falling in love part—he's in the clear. No feelings? Soul intact. Everybody wins."

Being glad Damian's soul remained intact didn't make Bax's words hurt any less. In fact, a serrated dagger to the heart would've hurt less than this pain. Although he chose not to use it, Damian *did* still have his heart, which meant her feelings weren't reciprocated.

Bax, about to take his first bite of ice cream, found himself with empty hands as Olive stole his pint. "Hey! You already have one of your own!"

"You don't deserve this." She drilled him with a hard glare.

He immediately backed off, hands in the air. "All yours. Jeez. Just putting a positive spin on the situation."

"Next time, don't. Don't spin. Don't weave. Just . . . don't."

Dropping onto her back, Rose stared at the ceiling. She appreciated everyone's attempts to boost her spirits, but the truth was that there was no way to spin this that didn't suck broomsticks for someone, and that someone was her.

It was as plain as the vodka ice cream now churning like a rock in her stomach.

While she'd fallen head over heels in love with Damian Adams, she'd done the falling alone. Love really is a lonely road.

✦ ✦ ✦

One in the morning had come and gone, and Damian had no plans on hitting the pause button on his massive to-do list anytime soon. Idle time meant time to think.

And dwell.

And question.

And . . . damn it. That ache in the center of his chest flared back to life. It had appeared a few days ago and came and went with no rhyme, reason, or explanation, and each time it returned, it stole more and more of his ability to take a deep breath.

He fought through it, tossing the last feed bag onto the growing stack in the outer barn's storeroom, already having mentally moved on to the next task.

He locked up and turned toward the main building. An engine rumbled in the distance, and headlights, a good fifty yards away, bounced down the gravel lane at a fast clip. Instincts put him on alert for an emergency case, but when the car pulled to a stop, he recognized Julius's shiny Audi and headed straight into the clinic.

"I know you saw me, Damian," Julius hollered. His car door slammed shut, and his footsteps followed.

"Whatever brought you here can take you right back out. I'm busy." He opened his med fridge and inventoried the antibiotics.

"Busy in the middle of the night?"

"I'm busy day and night. Even if I'm sitting and twiddling my damn thumbs, I'm busy. Especially when it comes to anything you say or do. Don't let the barn door hit your ass on the way out."

Julius sighed and did the opposite, walking around the small treatment room, his hands touching everything left out on the counters. "Oh, there will be ass-hitting, but it'll be me kicking yours once you take your head out of it. Wouldn't want to give you a concussion to go along with your stupidity ailment."

Damian slammed the fridge shut and whirled on his brother. "Don't you have someone else to annoy?"

The bastard smirked. "At the present moment? No. Don't you feel lucky?"

"Go find one because I have shit to do and—"

"More mistakes to make? Because honestly, I don't know if you could possibly make one bigger than you did earlier tonight."

Damian pushed past his brother, ignoring another soul-sucking flare of pain. "I'm not talking about Rose, least of all with you."

"Considering the pretty witch and her Supernatural Scooby

Squad would love nothing more than to clip your demon tail and shave off a few scales, I'm your only option."

"You're not an option. You're a thorn in my side. Don't you have Council duties to fulfill, or are you still working the old Julius Kontos way of employment: look busy but let those around you do all the work."

"That was a long time ago, Damian." Julius followed him as he made unnecessary checks on all the animals. "In case you don't remember, we both acted like dumb shits back then."

"You were extra dumb and loads shittier," Damian muttered.

"You're right. I was . . . and I'm sorry about that."

Damian paused, turning around. "Did I stumble through an upside-down world or something? Julius Kontos doesn't do apologies. Isn't that what you've always said?"

Jules shot him a sardonic look. "Turning over a new horn isn't easy, but I'm trying. As I'm sure you know, it's easier falling back on old habits than it is to make new ones."

"You mean like when you baited me into taking your Hunt assignments growing up? Or when you bribed me into dragging Rose into it?"

"Like I said . . . old habits. But you can't fault me for my own when you're obviously still letting yours dictate your life."

Damian reached the stairs to the loft and stopped, making it clear his brother wasn't invited upstairs. "I'm not taking life advice from someone who's made it his own personal goal to dupe everyone around him into thinking he's something he's not. You strut around in your expensive suits and drive your fancy cars, but I know for a fact you prefer vintage heavy metal T-shirts and that rusty-ass pickup you used to throw all your money into."

"Ruby?" A nostalgic glint twinkled in his eyes. "I still have her. She's in the garage with the rest of my collection."

"And when was the last time you took Ruby out for a night drive?"

"Ruby wouldn't pass a basic inspection and would get me arrested for single-handedly evaporating the ozone layer the second her engine turned over. And yeah, you're not entirely wrong. There's always a certain amount of theatrics within Supernatural society. But we're not talking about me here, Dam. We're talking about you and what the hell was going through your head when you sent Rose Maxwell packing. Do you have your eye on the Miserable Man of the Year award?"

Hearing her name fall from his brother's lips was like a scythe to the damn chest all over again. His fingers clenched on the banister, the wood cracking.

Julius continued, "We both know that was a huge fucking mistake."

"I don't know anything of the kind," Damian lied. "As for that award, I'm not a man, remember? At least not all man . . . which is what someone like Rose expects. Hell, it's what she deserves."

"She deserves to be pissed off to the point of melting plastic with her pretty little magical hands? Because that's what I witnessed when I took her over to her sister's place."

Another jab to the chest, this one momentarily stealing his ability to take a breath.

"She's pissed? Good. Then sooner or later, she'll realize it was for the best." Damian headed up the stairs.

"The best for who?" Julius shouted up.

"For both of us!"

"Liar," Julius called as Damian reached his apartment door. "You won't Hunt because it's easier to blame your demon for fucking things up than it is to admit that it's not the demon that's the problem."

"It *is* the problem. If it weren't for that bastard's love of the job, Callie never would've—"

"What? Hexed you? Newsflash, brother, you were a sixteen-year-old shithead whether you embraced your demon side or you didn't. But the key ingredient there is *sixteen-year-old*. You were a damn kid, Damian. Kids screw up. They learn. Except—it seems—for you, because you're standing here making a nearly identical mistake as a thirty-four-year-old."

"I'm not making the same mistake. In fact, breaking things off with Rose is—"

"What most people call a self-fulfilling prophecy of doom," Julius retaliated. "You're blaming your inner hellion for why you can't have a future with her, when in reality it's your human self that's sabotaging it all. Hex be damned."

Damian growled, hating that his brother's words began penetrating their way into his head.

"You deserve to be fucking happy, D. You and Rose both. If you didn't think it was possible, then you wouldn't be using it as an excuse to duck your head in the sand. You wouldn't be fighting so hard to protect that dusty-ass heart and soul."

"If I wasn't fighting against something, I wouldn't know what to do with myself," Damian admitted.

Julius went silent, the first time for as long as Damian knew him. Hell, he didn't know his brother was capable, so he used it to his advantage.

"You didn't have to fight for a damn thing in your life, Jules," he admitted without the least bit of animosity. "You didn't have to constantly prove yourself to Ezeil when we were out in the field. Anything you did was always enough. I—on the other hand—to be worthy of even a second of his time, had to train harder. Be quicker. I needed to *be* the Scourge of the Underworld and literally fight my way through the ranks, and it still wasn't good enough for the old man. I had to fight my way through every damn inch of life."

"And I'm sorry about that, Damian. I am," Julius said truthfully. "But you're not fighting now. As a matter of fact, you're doing the exact opposite. You're giving up the best thing that could happen to anyone. Ever."

Not saying another word, his brother turned and walked out the way he'd come, leaving Damian standing by his apartment door . . . and realizing his words made more sense than not.

Hurting Rose was the last thing Damian wanted to do, but he couldn't see another way. If she was angry at him, she'd keep her distance, and while it sucked right now, time would ease them back to their regularly scheduled lives.

Him being an antisocial grump . . .

Her being a happy social butterfly . . .

And both of them without the other . . .

26

Red Bull Cures All

Rose paced the length of her grandmother's cottage, a stack of magical quiz cards in her hands. As soon as a question flew from her mouth, she began the invisible timer, and when it ran out, she flicked her wrist, an obnoxious buzz filling the room.

"Hey!" Vi shot her a glare from the couch. "I was about to answer that one!"

"So what's the answer?" She shot her sister a daring look and waited. "What's the final ingredient in an Energy Rejuvenation Potion? Thyme? Witch hazel? Or—"

"Red Bull!" Vi grinned wide.

"Lavender, Violet. *Lavender.*"

"I like my answer better. Goddess knows I could go for a Red Bull right about now. How long have we been at this?"

"Barely two hours."

Vi flung herself onto the couch with a dramatic groan. "It feels like a lifetime. I need a break. I need a snack. And I really do need a Red Bull . . . or a Rejuvenation Potion."

"Is that what you'll say when the head of a vampire hive comes knocking and asks for your help in keeping their residents in line? *I'm sorry you're having issues with rogue vamps, but I need to rustle up a Red Bull first.*"

Vi frowned. "Well, when you say it like that . . ."

"Hello! Hello!" Edie's voice chimed as she entered the house, two brown grocery bags in her arms. "I thought you girls would be finished by now."

"There's no such thing as finished when Rose is leading the magical study session. I can't believe I'm actually missing the tweedy librarian's flash cards." Vi perked up. "You didn't happen to grab any Red Bull, did you?"

Vi and Rose took the bags from their grandma.

"Can't say I did, sweetheart. Sorry."

"You know who will have some?" Vi grinned at Rose. "Dad. And I happen to know where he keeps his stash. I'll be back. Study break!"

Rose cried out, "We're not—"

She *poof*'d, leaving her alone with Edie.

"I think I preferred when she couldn't do that. She's getting too damn good," Rose complained, tossing the flash cards on the kitchen table with a sigh.

"She's getting good at a great many things although I'm not so sure your sister sees all her improvement." Edie eyed the flash cards knowingly and began putting the grocery items away. "How are things going with potions? Any progress?"

"She thought Red Bull was the last ingredient of a Rejuvenation Potion, so how do you think?"

Edie chuckled. "Technically, one can substitute it for the ginseng, but it's not common knowledge. Are you sure that's the only reason why you've been at this for hours?"

She plucked a grape from the bowl on the counter. "Why else would I be here on a Saturday night? It's not like I have something else to do or anyplace to be . . . or a person to see."

"No one? Are you sure about that?" Her grandma watched her like a hawk, wearing a knowing look.

Rose growled. "Vi told you, didn't she? That blabbermouth couldn't help flapping her lips about Damian. Did she tell you he signed off on my community service hours so that I never have to darken his doorstep again? Super sweet and thoughtful of him, right?"

"Vi? No. She was suspiciously closed-mouth about everything."

Her mouth dropped. *"Olive? Are you serious?"*

"It was only out of concern for you, I assure you. Maybe also a deflection as I asked about her current living arrangements—which *did* come to me through Violet." Edie focused on Rose from across the counter. "But you should know I won't be distracted in this instance. Talk to me, sweetheart."

"There's not much to say. Damian and I agreed to have a temporary thing." Even being a grown witch and Edie being Edie, she wasn't about to say *fuck buddy* to her grandmother. "It ran its course. We crossed the finish the line. Game over."

With each word she uttered, it became harder to breathe. By the end, her chest ached.

Edie watched her thoughtfully, her lips pursed in thinking mode. "Are you sure it's over?"

"I told you he signed off on my community service, right? That was him telling me to have a good life. Seems pretty finished to me."

"Maybe . . . maybe not."

She smiled wanly, and reaching across the island, took her grandma's hand. "I know you mean well, Gran, but not everyone is as lucky as you and Violet. Not everyone gets to meet their soul mate and live out a fairy-tale happily ever after."

"So you don't have strong feelings for the good-looking vet?"

"It doesn't matter if I'm in love with Damian. He won't risk getting too deeply invested with anyone, and as much as I love him, I love myself more. I won't settle for anything less than someone's whole heart, and he'd never be able to give that to me."

Edie's mouth slid into a proud grin. "How did I become so lucky to have three such intelligent, strong-minded, and independent granddaughters?"

"Because we inherited it from our intelligent, strong-minded, and independent grandmother." She squeezed Edie's hand as realization dawned. "But you're right. I am strong-minded. And independent. And determined. Just because I can't have the man I want doesn't mean I can't have the life I want."

The older woman's eyes twinkled. "That sounds a lot like a plan is brewing . . ."

"It's more than a plan." For the first time in the few days since she'd walked out of the sanctuary and away from Damian, Rose knew exactly what she wanted. "I'm finishing what I started. I'm seeing this adoption fair through to the end, and if Damian Adams doesn't like it, he can suck a flying broomstick. I'm not there for him. I'm doing it for the animals . . . and myself."

"Let your Magic guide you and it'll never steer you wrong." Edie nodded, dishing out her favorite wise words.

"And when that's done, I'm going to see a demon about an internship . . ."

Her gran looked a little confused now, but that was okay. Rose wasn't . . . For the first time in months, she'd begun seeing everything a lot more clearly.

She wrapped her grandmother up in a hug that nearly picked the barely five-foot witch off the ground. "Thank you, Gran."

"For what? All I did is listen, sweetheart. You did the rest."

And with a renewed determination, Rose vowed to do even more. She didn't need to work odd jobs. She didn't need to go on some great search for a tailor-made hobby. And she sure as hell didn't need to work for Callie Sanderson.

She could—and would—damn well work—*and live*—for herself.

❖ ❖ ❖

It had been nonstop since Damian rolled his ass out of bed, exhausted and sleep-deprived, with a horrendous chest pain that made him think he was having a heart attack. Factor in a faulty fire alarm that wouldn't shut up, a sanctuary full of skittish animals that didn't realize it was a false alarm, three emergency drop-ins, the regular sanctuary upkeep, and a constant stream of phone calls all from vendors for the adoption fair with questions he couldn't answer, and it had been the morning from hell.

If one more thing happened, his head would explode, and with the sternal pain that had grown to include a vise around his head, that could be quite literal.

"Damian!" Terrance burst through the office doors, wincing when he released a low warning growl. He dropped his voice. "Sorry, boss, but we've got a problem."

"Is anyone dead?" Damian massaged his temples.

"Uh . . . no."

"Is anyone in the process of dying?"

"Not that I'm aware of . . ."

"Then it can wait a minute."

Terrance shifted on his feet nervously, his gaze skirting around the office. The kid obviously wasn't leaving without talking to him.

He sighed, leaning back in his chair. The phone rang—yet again—and he ignored it, recognizing the number of the taco truck vendor he'd promised to call back with information on the fair. Information he still didn't have. Stuff about permits and setups.

Nope, he wasn't thinking about it right now. One crisis at a damn time.

"What's wrong, Ter?" Damian finally asked, putting the kid out of his misery.

"I took the horses out for their field time, and then I came back for Jasper and thought I'd let him amble around the lower ring a bit . . . slowly get him back on his feet, you know?"

He waited a beat. "This doesn't sound like a problem so far."

Terrance gulped. "He jumped the fence and is now in the field with Butternut and Squash."

That got Damian's attention. He was on his feet, grabbing leads and hustling outside, the teen hot on his heels as they turned toward the front field. Sure enough, three horses stood in the pasture. Except Jasper wasn't being aggressive, which is what they'd been concerned about and why they hadn't yet introduced the horses.

The stallion looked damn near docile as he stood next to Butternut, both their heads bowed to the grass, nibbling on what greenery poked out from the ground. A few feet away, Squash rolled around on the ground in back-scratching bliss.

"I'll be damned . . ." Chuckling, Miguel came to stand next to them at the fence. "I didn't realize you were thinking about socializing them already."

"I wasn't. Evidently Jasper decided to socialize himself," Damian said dryly.

Terrance grinned. "It was freaking amazing. I latched the lower gate, and then when Jasper heard a whinny from up here, his ears perked up and he took off like a bat out of hell. He leaped the fence as if it had been no higher than a fallen toothpick."

"Guess he's feeling better, huh?" Miguel quipped with a smirk.

"We need to make sure he didn't damage anything on his little jumping excursion," Damian pointed out, already doing a distant visual scan of his back leg. "Last thing we need is him backpedaling his recovery."

"Why?" Terrance asked. "I mean, isn't it a good thing he's feeling good enough to do these things?"

"Actually, this is the recovery stage where you have to be even more careful because when they feel better, they can easily overextend themselves without realizing and set themselves back for the long haul. Let him be for now, but within the hour, we need to get him back to his stall so I can do a quick exam."

"Will do. I'll let you know when I get him settled."

With a nod, Damian turned back toward the main house, Miguel walking at his side. The older man was quiet even for him.

Damian sighed. "Out with it already. I know you're gearing up for something. You may as well let it out. You think I was an ass for sending Rose away."

Miguel cocked a bushy white eyebrow. "Now that you mention it . . ."

He had mentioned it, and he'd been thinking about it every minute for the last few days. Not only because he had to field a million phone calls about the adoption fair, which he was convinced was about to be one hot mess because he didn't know what the hell he was doing.

The sanctuary wasn't the same without Rose.

He didn't realize how much she'd ingrained herself into their everyday routine until she suddenly wasn't there. Even Terrance, who always whistled while he worked, did his chores in silence, his jokes reduced to quiet mutters.

She was still the first person Damian looked for in the morning, in the afternoon, and during breaks, and she was definitely the last person he thought about before falling asleep.

He cursed. "Aren't you the same person who basically told me I was playing with fire for getting mixed up with her? I didn't imagine that conversation, right?"

Miguel frowned. "Maybe. But—"

"But what? I finally listened to your advice—something that you claim I don't do enough—and now you're telling me I was a horse's ass?"

"You called yourself an ass. I agreed." The older man's mouth twitched into a small smirk. "And yes, I did tell you to be careful with Rose, but I think I was wrong to warn you off."

"You weren't wrong. You were smart. Definitely smarter than me. I should've kept my distance from day one. Since I didn't, I now have to live with the consequences."

And evidently this new chronic pain in his chest. The office phone could be heard ringing even before he stepped into the office.

Despite looking for Rose around every corner, and hoping she'd magically appear, he told himself that he'd done the right thing by sending her away. That incessant chest ache meant she'd become an integral part of his life, and if they'd traveled that path much longer, it would've spelled disaster for them both.

27

Miss Maxwell

It was go-day, and Rose spared no expense and cashed in every IOU to make the Marisol Animal Sanctuary and Clinic Adoption Fair a success. It was three hours until the public arrived and while all her volunteers seemed to have things organized and running smoothly, there was still a lot to do and a veterinarian to avoid.

In a move that wasn't her finest, she'd coordinated with Miguel to nail down final arrangements—which included getting the bulk of the setup done while Damian was MIA. He'd made it clear he didn't want her to be involved in the fair, but she'd already spent too much time—and put too much heart—into the event to let it fizzle out.

Hence why she snuck glances over her shoulder about every two seconds, half-expecting a surly somebody to come storming toward her. But so far so good.

"Here." A travel mug appeared in front of her, and holding it was an exhausted Olive. "You better take this before I guzzle mine and yours, and if that happens, don't come crying to me later complaining that you're tired."

"Jeez. Aren't we feisty this morning . . ." Rose took it gratefully and inhaled the sweet peppermint aroma. "If I didn't know you were a witch, I'd think you had an angel bloodline. This is exactly what I needed. It physically pained me to get out of bed this morning. Thank you."

"I still haven't gone to bed," Olive muttered. She cursed, realizing her mistake the second Rose shot her a look. "I *know*!"

"What do you know? That you should've accepted Bax's offer weeks ago?"

Olive glared over the rim of her coffee mug.

"Glare at me all you want, but you know I'm right. Bax knows it, too, which is why he keeps hounding you about it."

"I'm going to accept it," Olive muttered grudgingly.

"What was that?" Rose cupped her ear into a funnel. "I don't think I heard you right."

"You heard me fine. I'm telling him yes. *But*," she added quickly, seeing Rose's excitement, "I'll tell him when I'm ready to tell him. And I swear to Goddess, Rose, if he finds out a moment before I'm ready for him to, I will go on a hexing spree starting with you."

She lifted her hands in mock surrender, pantomiming locked lips. "He won't hear it from me, but you're making the right choice."

Olive snorted. "Remind me of that when I'm in bed listening to a celestial sexcapade soundtrack through the wall."

As if talking about the Guardian Angel had conjured him, Bax, Linc, and Adrian stepped out from the old unused storage barn. They'd spent the better part of the morning converting it into a homey place where families could sign themselves up for one-on-one visits with the adoptable animals.

"All finished, boss. What's next on the list?" Bax's gaze flicked to Olive.

The youngest triplet transferred all her attention to the travel mug in her hand, studying it as if it were an ancient magical text in need of deciphering.

"Terrance and Miguel are prepping Butternut and Squash to be moved to the other barn, so maybe we can bring down Bella and the puppies?"

"Ooh! Puppies!" Olive tore her attention away from her coffee and headed toward the front barn. "I volunteer to be on puppy paw-trol."

"I'll help." Bax's announcement earned him a slight huff from the youngest Maxwell, but it didn't deter the angel in the least, Bax grinning wide as he kept pace with her.

"Setup is mostly winding down. All that's left is to help Vi greet the late-arriving vendors and help them set up their stations if they need it. Otherwise, when the public starts showing, we'll need at least two people guiding them into some semblance of a parking lot. Miguel said we can use the field in front of his place for that."

"Greeting and parking. On it." Linc nodded and he and Adrian sauntered off.

Rose stood in the fair's hub and glanced around, a deep sigh rolling from her chest.

All the planning. All the details. And all the untangling of last-minute issues. Everything had finally come together in the end, and still her nerves got the best of her. It happened with every event, and this was no exception. Or maybe it was. Maybe she felt the nerves more acutely because to her, this sanctuary was a lot more than an animal sanctuary.

It had been *her* sanctuary.

She hadn't realized it until she no longer had to wake up each morning and navigate the Belt Parkway to be there at the crack of dawn. But this place, these animals, and definitely the people, had burrowed into her heart.

That included Damian.

Over the last few days, every thought that wasn't about the fair or the sanctuary was about him. She cringed thinking about all the extra time and head space Damian would have when the event was over, and for that reason, she didn't want it to end.

"Rose!" Terrance waved eagerly, a beaming smile on his face as he walked Squash. Next to him, Miguel led Butternut. "This looks awesome!"

"It's definitely coming together."

Movement on Miguel's right caught her attention. The second her gaze locked with Damian's, her heart fluttered. Actually fluttered as if a swarm of butterflies had taken up residence.

Wearing his signature worn blue jeans and a pale blue button-down work shirt, he looked the same as he had any other day she'd spent at the sanctuary, and yet he looked even better. She stood, feet frozen to the ground as the three men and two horses approached.

Miguel broke the silence first, his gaze scanning the rows of food trucks already setting up shop. "This is way more than any of us could've ever dreamed up. I don't know what to say, Rose. You've done an amazing job."

Rose blushed. "I didn't do anything the animals didn't deserve. Olive and Bax are getting Bella and the pups, and the other two rescue organizations are settling their adoptees into the barn as we speak. If I had a crystal ball, it would tell us that a lot of furry critters are finding their forever homes today."

"I'll drink a seltzer to that." Miguel chuckled.

Awkward silence hung heavy in the air as Terrance and Miguel bounced their gazes from Rose to Damian, like a visual Ping-Pong match. No one spoke. Or blinked. Damian stared at her, his face devoid of any emotion.

Miguel cleared his throat and patted Butternut's neck. "Terrance, let's get these two settled in the barn and then see who else needs a hand."

They left her and Damian alone, and the second she got over her brief flare of panic, she fought the urge to summon up an excuse—good or not—to leave. But then she thought about her talk with Edie . . .

Nope.

Done running. Done with excuses. Done hiding.

"I was thinking," Rose said at the same time Damian started, "I can't believe . . ."

"You go ahead." She gestured for him to begin.

"After you."

She paused, waiting for him to go first.

His mouth twitched knowingly. "I can't believe you planned all this . . . and that you showed up. Miguel told you I was floundering, didn't he?"

"He may have mentioned it, but I kept on planning the fair even when you told me to drop it. I wasn't about to let it—"

"Fail?" Damian snorted. "That's exactly what would've happened if it had been left in my hands. I have no idea how you keep everything running smoothly, have all the answers, and deal with . . . people. My head damn nearly exploded a few times."

"I heard." She tried—but failed—to withhold a small grin. She had also gotten earfuls from participants complaining about her *rude* assistant. But it all worked out in the end. "I had it handled. Besides, quitting isn't my style. Once I start something, I see it through to the end."

His grin stiffened. "Was that a not-so-subtle jab at me, little witch?"

Yes.

"Why? Do you feel as if it applies to you, too?"

He sighed, shoving his hands deep into his jeans pockets. "Rose, you have to know I—"

"I want to show everyone Jasper, too," she said, out of the blue. "He deserves to find his place as much as the others. If not more."

Damian was already shaking his head. "No way. Not happening."

His immediate refusal had her crossing her arms in front of her chest as she prepped for battle. "Yes way."

"He's not remotely ready to be adopted. He just about took my head off my shoulders two days ago."

"Name someone who hasn't wanted to do that recently."

"It would be irresponsible of me to hand him off to someone else until his behavior improves."

"Did you ever stop to think that maybe he just doesn't like you?"

He didn't look impressed with her comment, his eyes narrowing. "This isn't a joke, little witch."

"I wasn't joking, *Damian*. And considering we no longer have an FBA, it would be more appropriate if you called me by my name, too. Or if you'd prefer to be more formal, Miss Maxwell."

His eyes twitched with a faint wince. "You want me to call you Miss Maxwell . . ."

"Seems only right, don't you think? We no longer have a familiar relationship, and that's how you address people with whom you're not familiar. I can always call you Dr. Adams."

Damian clenched his jaw, obviously not happy with her words or her sarcasm.

She thought she'd won that round, but he stepped closer, his boots bumping into her Converse. One deep breath and their chests would touch, and damn if she wasn't tempted.

"I won't call you babe, or sweetheart." Damian gently tucked a stray lock of hair behind her ear, the touch tingling more than her skin. "I could probably avoid calling you Ro. But one thing I won't call you—unless your bare ass is bent over my desk, or any other flat surface—is Miss Maxwell."

Lust swept over her body like a caress.

Pretending her panties hadn't gone instantly damp at his words, Rose forced her gaze to hold his. "Then I guess you won't be calling me anything. Now if you'll excuse me, I have a fair to get underway and animals to get adopted. Oh, and for your information, Jasper wouldn't be adopted out *today*. If someone fell in love with him enough to put in the effort to form a slow relationship with him, they could be part of his healing process. But you know better . . . Dr. Adams."

She stalked away, not proud for losing her temper, but damn satisfied she hadn't flung herself into Damian's arms and refused to leave.

✦ ✦ ✦

Damian watched Rose walk away for the second time in less than a week, and it wasn't any easier than it had been the first time. Especially after she'd played starring roles in every one of his dreams each time he closed his eyes.

They didn't even need to be closed.

She invaded every thought. Took over every action. He was equal parts savoring every second of it and cursing himself for taking even that little bit of pleasure. Nothing could change their situation, no matter how much he wished it . . . and he *did* wish it.

More than he'd ever wished for anything ever before.

But he meant what he'd said to Julius. Rose deserved to be loved with a whole heart. An entire soul. And he'd never be able to give that to her.

Bax and Olive headed his way, both with three puppies tucked into their arms, Bella walking briskly at their side. If looks could curse, Olive Maxwell would've drilled him with a second hex as she walked by, but Bax slowed to a stop.

"You okay, man?" The Guardian Angel followed his gaze to where it was latched onto Rose by the lower barn, now talking to Harper and a chuckling Miguel. "Ah. Never mind. I get it."

"You do?" Damian pulled his attention away, barely.

"The Maxwell sisters are a whole new level of stubborn. When they get something stuck in their head, it's practically impossible for it to be removed. Not even with celestial intervention or Magic. If the first worked, I would've used it to get Olive to see reason about this roomie thing. And if the latter worked, I would've found the most powerful witch or warlock around and begged them to do their hocus-pocus. Hell, I would've done anything in my power to make it happen."

"Wouldn't the most powerful witch around be Edie Maxwell?" Damian asked, brow lifted.

"We were talking hypotheticals here, man. Not real-world scenarios."

He would've done anything to make it happen. Celestial intervention. Badass witchery.

Anything.

The Guardian Angel quickly hustled to catch up with Olive, but when Rose's gaze flickered his way, Damian couldn't take his eyes off her. A myriad of emotions moved over her face, and he knew his face reflected the same.

He couldn't pin down any one . . .

Because he suddenly felt *everything,* and everything felt like his heart was about to explode.

28

"In Your Eyes"

Damian sat on his motorcycle and debated his next move to the background sounds of children running up and down the quaint suburban street. He'd left the city behind about an hour ago and now stared at the cozy little two-story house with black shutters. A red SUV sat in the drive, a signal someone was home.

He just needed to be adult enough to knock on the door and be ready to do exactly what Bax had suggested the day of the adoption fair.

Anything.

He'd say his piece, plead his case, and then walk away as if the person he was talking to didn't have the ability to take away one of the best things in his life before he had a chance to truly enjoy it.

Rose.

A *future* with Rose, and all the endless possibilities that came with it. The laughs. The tears. The joys. Celebrations and sadness. Hell, he'd even relish the fights because it would mean watching her eyes glow dewy gold and wielding her power like a badass witchy goddess. And it was impossible not to think about the makeup sex.

Damian wanted it *all*.

He wanted *Rose,* and the first step in achieving that was knocking on the fucking door of his past.

A shooting fireball of pain ripped through his chest as he climbed off his motorcycle and damn near fell on his face. From the moment he'd decided to come, his heartburn from hell had grown tenfold, sometimes distracting him from anything and everything around him.

It slowly ebbed as he took one step toward the quaint wraparound porch. It flared again, making him stumble. Sweat plastered his hair to his forehead and cement filled his limbs by the time he reached the red front door.

He prayed like hell he had the right address. He couldn't picture the girl he remembered, who wore aged leather pants and vintage garage band T-shirts, living in a place that looked straight out of the pages of *Country Home* magazine.

"Here goes nothing." He groaned, lifting his shaking hand to the brass knocker.

The door opened before his arm dropped to his side, and Callie stood on the threshold, her eyes blinking as if checking whether he was a mirage. The only thing more surprising than him being there was the fact she didn't slam the door in his face.

"Cal." Damian nodded, at a loss for any other words.

"I placed a bet against myself on how long it would take for you to come to my door." She flashed him a tentative smile. "You'll be pleased to know I won."

Because of course she knew he'd be there.

He'd never been able to get much past her, even when they'd been dating. With a strong witch lineage that included Seers and psychics, she had premonition skills better than most Supernaturals'.

"Sorry to disappoint you by not turning around, but this couldn't wait." Damn, that ache was back, feeling like a thousand knives jabbing the underside of his sternum.

"That's not what I . . ." She sighed. "Is everything okay?"

He almost laughed at her genuine look of concern. "No, everything is definitely not okay, but you're going to help me make it a hell of a lot better. Because despite the fact that I was a shit boyfriend back in the day, you owe me."

Her eyes narrowed on him, studying him carefully. "Damian . . . ?"

His vision went a little fuzzy. "You need to . . ."

Callie eased a little closer. "I think you should sit down."

"No, I need . . ." He swayed, and a split second before his knees gave out, Edward Scissorhands wrapped his knifelike fingers around his heart and squeezed like it was a fucking stress ball.

Damian toppled onto a startled Callie, her own legs buckling under his weight. "Nisha! I need you! Now!"

A slender, dark-haired woman hovered in Damian's periphery, her mouth opening in a clear sign of shock. "Is that—?"

"Yes! Help me get him into the house and onto the couch!"

Damian groaned. "You need to take it back, Cal. Remove the hex. *Please.*"

Callie's face swam in and out of focus, her green eyes softening as she peered down at him. "Oh, Damian, I wish I could . . ."

The two women worked together to get him to a nearby couch. There, his body pitched sideways, assaulted by another wave of pain that nearly toppled him to the floor. Damian huddled into a ball in an attempt to stop the agony, but he wasn't about to back down now.

Not until he got what he'd come for. "Callie, please. I'll do whatever it takes . . . I . . . I need her, Cal."

"Damian, look at me," Callie ordered gently, her fingers pinching his chin and guiding his head toward her.

He forced his eyes open, deep-breathing through the pain. "Looking . . ."

"I *can't* remove the Soul Hex."

"Cal, I—"

"There's only one person who can dissolve it, and only one way in which to do it . . . and judging by the state you're in right now, I'd say you're halfway through the process. You have to finish it."

"H-how?" he asked, sucking down a groan. "T-tell me."

"It won't be easy . . . and it'll go against what you've always erroneously believed is your nature."

"I don't care. I'll d-do anything . . . anything for a ch-chance with h-her."

A small, fuzzy smile pulled up his ex's lips. "Waiting eighteen years to hear you say those words about another woman wasn't what I had in mind for how this played out, but I guess it's better late than never. You're going to want to tone down the groaning and tune up the hearing because this is a very delicate process."

Damian didn't care if it consisted of twelve million steps and the offering of a vital organ. He'd do whatever it took to break this damn hex, and once it was gone, he'd go even further to show a certain brassy witch that he was done looking for excuses.

They belonged together, and he wasn't about to let something as minor as a Soul Hex prevent that from happening.

✦ ✦ ✦

Rose swirled her strawberry Witch's Brew and listened to the conversations around her, jumping in only when someone dragged her into it. It had been a long time since they'd all gotten together at Potion's Up, and the success of the first soon-to-be-annual Marisol Animal Sanctuary and Clinic Adoption Fair was as good an excuse to celebrate as any.

Every adoptable animal now had a forever home—even Jasper, whose new family ran an equine therapy program farther out on the island that catered to both two- and four-legged patients.

Yet Rose couldn't bask in it. She was five minutes away from calling it a night, climbing into her flannel PJs, and devouring the leftover boozy ice cream in her freezer. She would've dove beneath her weighted blanket an hour ago if Olive hadn't magically sealed her ass to the chair.

A foot kicked her beneath the table, startling her into noticing her rear end was no longer plastered to her spot.

Olive silently mouthed, "Are you okay?"

She shrugged, the noncommittal gesture deepening her sister's worried frown. It was time to make an exit before she infected the rest of the group with her grumpy funk. "I'm calling it a night, guys."

"What? No!" Harper looked aghast, nudging her chin toward Bax and the other guys. "If you'd rather have an FO, G Night, we can get rid of these losers and go back to your place."

"FOG Night?" Olive scrunched her nose, mentally deciphering the Harper lingo like everyone else. "I need a Harper handbook because I have no idea what the hell you're talking about."

"FO, G," Harper said, her tone like *duh.* "Fuck Off, Guys."

"Don't we usually call it a Girls' Night?"

The succubus shrugged. "I'm trying new things and seeing what sticks."

Rose smiled. "That's sweet of you to offer, but I think I need an Alone Night with the leftover pint of Cake Batter Vodka ice cream."

Everyone's attention shifted off Rose.

Another presence—a magical one—stood nearby.

Even though Olive was the sister gifted with their father's shifter sense of smell, Rose knew who it was without looking. Magic sensed Magic, and sensing the other witch, hers flared, stirring wildly through her veins, practically begging to be let loose and wicked-witch some shit up.

Callie stood less than three feet away, her hair pulled up into a half-bun, and, for the first time since they'd met, she wore jeans and a knee-length tube sweater. She cast a wary glance at their table, whose occupants had now gotten to their feet.

"Hi." Callie shifted awkwardly on her feet, stealing a look toward Olive, Vi, and Harper, who'd taken position at her side. "I hate to interrupt your night—"

"Then don't," Harper snapped.

Rose shook her head, and her friend backed down. "What do you want, Callie? I already told you I'm not interested in your proposition."

"I know, and I totally accept that. I was hoping we could talk about . . . the other thing." Callie cleared her throat as if something were stuck. "I don't blame you if you want to tell me to jump in a boiling cauldron, but I hope you'll at least hear me out. Give me the chance to explain."

Rose snorted. Hear out the woman who'd single-handedly destroyed any hope she had at being with the man she loved? Not likely.

After quick hugs with her sisters and Harper, and a wave to the guys, Rose headed for the door, ignoring the witch trailing after her.

"I get it, Rose," Callie cried out.

She whirled around. "You *get* it? What exactly do you get? That it's unethical to mess with a person's heart? With their very soul? That's something every witch learns before they even leave kindergarten, but maybe you were absent that day?"

Rose stepped closer, letting her Magic bounce on her fingertips. "As far as I'm concerned, you're no better than the Gryndors or the Valentin Bissets of the world. The Supernatural Council may not see Soul Hexes as a crime—yet. But I do. It's unethical and immoral, and it's so far beyond inhumane. Everyone deserves to be loved and to fall *in* love, and you took that away from Damian. You took that away from *me*."

"I never intended to hex Damian. Actually, I did, but . . . I'm not explaining things very well."

Rose cocked an eyebrow. "Gee, you think?"

"My family comes from a long line of Seers, but the gift was never very strong with me . . . until I met Damian. The second I laid eyes on him, I knew we were linked *somehow*. We were the same age, and he was my ultimate bad-boy fantasy come to life, so naturally I first thought maybe it was a soul mate connection . . ."

Jealousy flared in Rose's stomach like a raging ulcer.

"It wasn't," Callie added quickly, as if sensing her turmoil. "Not long after meeting Damian, I *Saw*, for the first time, two possible roads for Damian: one extremely dark, filled with pain and strife, and the other filled with hope and possibility. I'll give you one guess which path he was on when we met."

Rose crossed her arms over her chest as if she could hug away the ache in her chest. Damian had already told her he'd once been in a dark place. "And?"

"And my Sight showed me what needed to happen to divert him away from that self-destructive path and lead him to a life of hope, possibilities, and indestructible love."

"A hex?"

"A hex. If it didn't happen, if I didn't conjure it before he reached the point of no return, then that love-filled future would've never had a chance in hell. *Your* future together would've been in jeopardy. I mean, you're in love with him, right?"

"It doesn't matter if I'm in love with Damian. Because of the hex, he'll never be able to return it. So that happy love-filled future you Saw can't happen anyway."

"Eh." Callie wrinkled her nose, her lips twitching with a knowing smile.

"Eh? What does *eh* mean?"

"It means I needed to give him a little time to set up and now that I have," Callie leaned closer and whispered, "you should go outside."

Olive walked to the window and peeked through the blinds, Vi and Harper right behind her. The trio practically yanked the blinds down to get a good look.

Vi chuckled. "You really should go outside, Ro."

"Like, immediately." Harper nodded with a giggle.

Rose glanced to Callie, who wore a cat-that-ate-the-canary grin on her face. "What's going on?"

"Trying to help a guy break a curse," Callie answered cryptically. "And if you're interested in doing the same, you really should get out there before he gets arrested for indecent exposure . . . or *gets* exposure."

Since she obviously wasn't getting any answers from anyone any-time soon, Rose pushed her way out Potion's front door and came to a dead stop.

Standing in the middle of the street, John Cusack style, Damian held an ancient boom box over his head while Sara Bareilles' version of "In Your Eyes" blared from the speakers. But instead of sporting a long trench coat, Damian wore boxers.

Only boxers. Red ones decorated with little cartoon witches and swirls of Magic that said MAGIC MAKES THE WORLD GO 'ROUND.

Horns honked as he blocked traffic, but a few nearby drivers watched with rapt amusement. From the open door of Potion's Up, her own friends cackled and Olive, always the historian, held her phone up to record the show.

"What the hell are you doing?" Rose stepped out onto the side-walk. "Damian, seriously . . . what is happening here?"

"I'm making a grand gesture . . . one endearing enough for you to hear me out." He smiled, lips twitching nervously. "Please tell me it's working."

"This is New York. Doing things like *this* will get you run over."

As if in agreement, a chorus of honking horns went off. Damian didn't budge. He didn't look around him. He didn't take his eyes off *her*.

With a sigh, she dragged him onto the sidewalk. "I can't hear you out if you've been flattened into a pancake."

"So you'll listen to me?"

She chuckled, exasperated. "Do I have a choice?"

"You always have a choice with me, little witch."

When she heard the endearment she'd grown to love, her throat closed.

He set the still-playing boom box at their feet, his hands shaking slightly. "Damn, that thing gets heavy after a while. I thought you'd never come outside."

"Where did you find it? A Smithsonian museum?"

"Julius."

His answer surprised her. "So you've—"

"Been an idiot," Damian interjected. "A raging pile of asshole."

She cocked an eyebrow. "I was about to say you've been getting along better, but if you expect me to disagree with your Mad Libs, you'll be waiting a long time, doc."

He flashed his sexy grin. "You called me *doc*."

"I'll be calling you an ambulance because hypothermia is minutes away from setting in if you don't get to the point of all this."

"I was wrong to send you away," Damian admitted, his voice husky with emotion, and yeah, his hands shook again. "So, so fucking wrong."

She really looked at him, noticing the slightly green, dewy hue to his skin. "Are you okay?"

"I will be once you hear me out." Damian's smile trembled, and for the first time since she'd known him, the man looked unsure. He also looked about to yak. "I was wrong to pretend what we had was nothing more than a convenient arrangement when it was *so* much more. Falling in love with you has been everything I'd ever hoped for and then some."

"Everything, huh? Then why did you . . ." She forgot how to breathe. "What did you just say?"

Damian stepped closer, and as if he'd sucked down a healthy dose of fresh air, his coloring improved. He even stood a little straighter, a gorgeous, nervous smile tilting up the corners of his mouth.

"I love you, Rose Maxwell." His admission made her knees knock together. "I never had a chance to do otherwise because you're *it* for me. My match. My conscience. My beating heart and my next breath. I didn't realize it until you weren't there. When you walked out of that barn, you took my heart with you. Because *you* are my heart."

Tears filled her eyes as she flicked a glance back at Callie. "I don't understand. The hex . . ."

Callie smiled regretfully. "Not even the witch who casts a Soul Hex can break it."

Rose whipped her head back to Damian, frantic. "Then you need to take it back. Now. I won't be responsible for bringing you that kind of unhappiness."

He shook his head, swallowing audibly. "I'll never take it back, and Callie can't break the hex because I was the only person who could do it."

"I don't understand."

"The only thing that can break a Soul Hex is knowingly, and willingly, succumbing to it. Go *all* in. To put *everything* on the line, with no guarantee of a happy ending. To keep my heart, I had to risk my heart."

Callie stage-whispered from the sidewalk, "He had to create a grand gesture."

Tears clouded Rose's vision. "You hate grand gestures. You don't see the point of them, or what's so great about them."

She used his earlier words against him, and judging by his sly smirk, he realized it. "I didn't then, but I do now. I realize so much more than I ever had before, and not only how wrong I was, but how empty my heart was until I met you. No way could I lose my heart and soul to a teenage hex . . . because they're not mine to give away, little witch. They're yours."

Rose lost the war with her welling tears. One fell, and then a second. Fat rivulets dripped down her face, turning her into a soggy, snotty mess. She was not a pretty crier.

Damian's hands cupped her face, thumbs gently rubbing all her fluids away as he dropped his forehead onto hers. "Every *really cold inch of me* is yours, Rose Maxwell. You'll make me the happiest Dr. McGrumpy Pants in this realm and in every other if you say there's even a chance we can have a future together."

"There's not a chance," Rose whispered through her tears. Damian's worried eyes searched hers, and she gifted him a watery smile. "There's only one hundred percent certainty because I love *you*, Damian Adams. I love your grumpiness, and your dry humor. I love the way you care for those who can't care for themselves. I'll gladly own your heart if you accept mine in exchange."

"Now that's a deal I'll happily make."

Their mouths clashed in a kiss Rose felt right down to her soul. Her Magic flared bright, wrapping around them in swirls of pink and covering them like a warm blanket.

But it wasn't the only thing linking them.

Rose chuckled as Damian's gaze landed on the obvious golden link connecting their bodies . . . and their hearts. "Is that what I think it is?"

Rose nibbled her bottom lip nervously. "If you think it's a soul mate link, then yes. Guess you were more right than you thought, doc. We really do hold each other's hearts in our hands."

And it was a gift that not even an ex's hex could take away.

Epilogue

Bella and Cusack—named after the actor who took part in one of Rose's favorite cinematic grand gestures—yipped excitedly as they bolted through the two-bedroom Harlem apartment, the mom-and-son duo chasing each other from room to room.

Rose laughed at their antics and tucked yet another box of Olive's belongings into Bax's spare bedroom—strike that.

Olive's *new* bedroom.

As much as her little sis had delayed it, she hadn't been able to hold Bax at bay for very long. It was finally moving day and everyone had shown up not only to provide physical labor, but to make sure the witch didn't keep driving over the bridge and end up renting some place in Jersey.

"Here's another box of books." Damian tucked his box with all the others in the corner. "That makes like twelve boxes of books and I've yet to see anything else . . . like clothing."

Olive stepped into the room with a medium-sized duffel and dropped it onto the unmade bed. "Here. *Clothing.* You happy?"

Rose and Damian chuckled as they watched her exit the room.

Taking Rose off guard, Damian hauled her into a hot, hard kiss that nearly melted her from the inside out.

She curled into him happily. "Not that I'm complaining, but what did I do to deserve that? I ask so that I can keep doing it again, and again."

"Then keep being you, little witch." Damian grinned mischievously. "Do you think we can sneak in a quickie if we close this door and pretend no one's home? There's a bed right here."

"Like hell you will, Damian Adams!" Olive *poof*'d into appearance right next to them, a horrified look on her face. She glanced at her bed as if to make sure they hadn't already started. "I've already accepted the fact I'll have to listen to sexcapades, but I will not have them occur in my own freaking bedroom."

"Sexcapades?" Bax came in with one of the last boxes. "Who's having sexcapades?"

"You." Olive glared at him. "And Damian and Rose."

Bax shot them all a confused look. "We're having sexcapades? Together, or is this a tag-team thing?"

Olive growled, tossing up her hand, and stormed out.

They all laughed as Bax followed her. "Oh, come on, angel! That was funny!"

Damian chuckled. "How long do you give them until they kill each other?"

She glanced at her watch. "That was the last box, and they promised us pizza so I'd say . . . maybe two hours? Around the time we make it halfway back to the sanctuary. How long do you think it'll take them before figuring out the rest?"

Hearing Olive and Bax banter back and forth from the kitchen, Damian answered, "I give it a month. Tops."

Rose wrinkled her nose. "I'm not so sure. Ollie may be the quietest of us Maxwells, but she's by far the most stubborn. She just hides it better."

"Then I guess we'll have to wait and find out."

Ozzy Osbourne's "Bark at the Moon" played from Rose's vibrating back pocket, the identifiable ringtone already telling her who was on the other end.

Damian chuckled at hearing it, more the longer she let the song play out. "You better answer it. She's not exactly known for her patience."

"Which is why I'm trying to teach her. It's a fair trade. She teaches me the badass Hunting skills, I teach her how to live in civilized society." Instead of waiting for the chorus to repeat again, she answered her trainer's call. "Good early evening, Charlotte Elise. How may I direct your call?"

Charlie's wolfy growl reverberated from the other end of the line. "How many times have I told you to never to call me Charlotte?"

"Probably the same amount I told you that just because we're trolling for intel doesn't mean we have to embrace the hygienics of a troll."

"Your ass is going to embrace my boot if you don't get down to headquarters right now. We picked up a new assignment. Fifteen minutes and not a second later." Rose's Hunting mentor hung up.

Damian tried—and failed—to contain his smirk. "She's softening up to you, I see."

"Julius thinks it's just a matter of time before she rolls over and shows me her belly."

He laughed, cupping her neck and pulling her into a hot, hard, and way too quick kiss. "Be careful out there, little witch."

"Always." From the other room, Olive's annoyed Bax-instigated rant had her grimacing. "Actually, I think I'll be safer with Charlie's backside-embracing promise than you will be here with the new roomies."

Something crashed in the kitchen and Damian cursed. "Fuck. I think you're right."

Supernatural Singles World Glossary

Alpha: The leader of a shifter pack (see *Shifters*). Warning: may growl, bite, or snarl. Bites are usually worse than their bark so make sure you're up to date on your tetanus shots.

Example: Lincoln may be the Alpha of the North American Pack, but all his friends and family know it's really Violet who's the boss.

Angel: Celestial, Warrior, and Guardian; don't wear halos (they clash with their wings); often possess potty mouths . . . and tattoos. Lots and lots of tattoos.

Example: Bax may be a Guardian Angel, but there's nothing angelic about his thoughts regarding a certain Maxwell triplet . . .

Bwitch: Bitch + Witch = bwitch; can be used as a term of endearment between friends, or a term for someone you don't like with proper tonal inflection.

Example: Violet, Rose, and Olive are Harper's bwitches . . . best friends who happen to also be witches.

Demon: Supernatural entity with historical ties to the Underworld; do not always possess tails or horns. Popular "topside" occupations: CrossFit instructors & DMV employees.

Example: Damian's inner demon is a little grumpy, a lot mischievous, and super-mega horny—for Rose.

Demon Portal: Supernatural gateway travel for demons; require demon bloodletting.

Example: A little demon blood + mental image of destination and BAM, Damian can go anywhere his heart desires . . . but not without a price.

Hex: A magical curse; can also be exchanged with four-letter words (i.e., swearing).

Example: "Hex me, Damian Adams is hot as hell," said Rose.

Hunter: Supernatural bounty hunter: less Dog, and more Winchester brothers; often hired by the Supernatural Council (see *Supernatural Council*) to bring in the nasties who don't play nice.

Example: When Damian was a teenage Hunter, he possessed more brood than Dean, had way more grump than Sam, and kicked way more rear ends than a professional soccer player kicks balls.

Hunting: The act performed by a Hunter (see *Hunter*); supernatural ass-kicking.

Example: Said in the voice of Mama Incredible, "Leave Hunting to the men? Rose doesn't think so . . . Rose doesn't think so."

Magical Triad: Witch-born triplets; a set of three siblings born into a magical family.

Example: Violet and Olive may be her sisters, but they were also her womb-mates for eight months.

Mate: A partner with whom a shifter has entered a Mate Bond (see *Mate Bond*); not to be confused with True Mate, or the Australian term for friend.

Example: Rose is happy that her sister Vi found her True Mate, but she's perfectly happy with her own life in the single lane.

Mate Bond: The act of taking a mate (see *Mate*); supernatural marriage involving one or more shifters. Unbreakable marriage. Not an Australian friendship.

Example: Whoever said a diamond is forever never heard of a Mate Bond, the gift that keeps on giving.

Pack: A community of Supernatural beings who have the ability to turn furry, scaly, or hairy at will; group of shifters (see *Shifters*); a pack is led by an Alpha (see *Alpha*).

Example: A pack of shifters is not to be mistaken for the eight-pack abs in Damian's possession. Demon Hunting did his body good . . .

Prima: The Head Witch in Charge; the badass of witches; currently Edie Maxwell, soon to be Violet Maxwell.

Example: The Prima is the Head Witch in Charge. You really don't want to fuck around with her.

Prima Apparent: The Head Witch in Charge's intern; learning the Prima ropes; soon-to-be Prima.

Example: Rose never regretted stepping down as her grandma's Prima Apparent. She only regrets falling on her backside as she did.

Shifters: Supernatural beings with the ability to turn furry, feathery, or scaly; members of a pack (see *Pack*).

Example: While some shifters may be all bark with no bite, there are definitely those that will bite first and ask questions later.

Soul Hex: Magical hex involving one's soul; hard-core Magic; seemingly unbreakable.

Example: Damian's Soul Hex prevents him from falling in love, because if he does, his inner demon will take over and the humanity he's fought so hard to maintain will slip away. Not happening on his watch.

Supernatural Council: Board of Supernatural badasses; Supernatural avengers; protectors of Supernatural law and order; led by the Prima (see *Prima*); also consists of shifter, angel, demon, and vampire representatives.

Example: Rose never thought the Supernatural Council, which she'd nearly led, would be the ones to saddle her with stall-mucking and poop shoveling. And yet . . .

True Mate: A soul mate; one's destined match; the perfect complement to both the human and Supernatural souls.

Example: When someone finds their True Mate, it is a literal interpretation of the Jerry McGuire quote, "*You* complete *me.*"

Vampires: The Undead; those who drink blood as a main source of sustenance; do not combust in sunlight; do not sparkle; may be born vampires or made vampires; prone to tooth decay.

Example: Vampires do not sparkle or burst into flames while in direct sunlight, and while they do require blood as their main food source, they're quite fond of Italian cuisine. The more garlic, the better.

Witch/Warlock: A spell caster; Supernatural being able to wield Magic.

Example: Rose may no longer be in line to be the Head Bwitch in Charge, but that doesn't mean you shouldn't avoid getting on her bad side.

Acknowledgments

For me, second books in a series are always more difficult to write than the first. I think it has something to do with spending so much time with your characters in book one that it's hard to convince yourself that it's okay to move forward. There's quite a list of people who convinced me—and maybe dragged me kicking and screaming—through the process of writing *Not Your Ex's Hexes*.

First off, a huge thank-you to my hubby and kids for embracing eat-out nights and delivery dine-in as well as you did when I was under deadline. I choose to think it was more a show of support and less due to the fact you didn't want me setting off the smoke alarm yet again.

In no particular order, a big shout-out and thank-you to everyone at St. Martin's Press, from marketing to publicity, to the art department (can we say "hey, baby" to the gorgeous cover). Kerry Resnick (designer) and illustrator Carina Lindmeier can do no wrong. For *Not Your Ex's Hexes*, I was blessed to work with two incredible editors, Jennie Conway and the super supportive Tiffany Shelton. Not only did they call me out on my exorbitant amount of em-dashes and ellipses, but they made sure I knew I had support every inch of the way and through every keystroke.

Kristin Dwyer, my publicist . . . lady, you're a rock star. I don't know how you do half of what you do and keep things straight. Hell, I don't know how you can keep ME straight. (If you have a step-by-step process for the latter, my hubby is totally interested in learning your Magic.)

My agent, Sarah E. Younger. This makes our ninth book together, and all I can say is that I'm so glad you're on this journey with me. Here's to nine more, and then nineteen . . . you get the picture.

Tif Marcelo, Annie Rains, Rachel Lacey, and Jeanette Escudero, my Girls Write Night. My cyber witch's coven. I must have done something right in a previous life to have you four incredibly talented women by my side. You're not only my "Honey, no" voices, but you're the ultimate cheerleaders. Not to mention great azz-kickers. You always know how to get my butt in gear.

Thank you to all the readers and reviewers. You all are amazing!!!

About the Author

Amie Otto

April Asher, aka April Hunt, was hooked on romantic stories from the time she first snuck a bodice-ripper romance out of her mom's bedside table. She now lives her own happily ever after with her college-sweetheart husband, their two children, and a cat who thinks she's more dog—and human—than feline. By day, April dons dark-blue nursing scrubs and drinks way too much caffeine. By night, she still consumes too much caffeine, but she does it with a laptop in hand, and from her favorite side of the couch.

From the far left cushion, April Asher pens laugh-out-loud romantic comedies with a paranormal twist, but when she's not putting her characters into embarrassing situations with supernatural entities, she also writes high-octane romantic suspense as April Hunt, her thrill-seeking alter ego.